Staff Sergeant Torin Kerr Returns . . .

"Shouldn't you be at the first level by now?"

"Sir!"

Torin fell into step at the lieutenant's right shoulder as Franks hurried off the concourse and out onto the road that joined the seven levels of Simunthitir into one continuous spiral. Designed for the easy transportation of ore carriers up to the port, it was also a strong defensive position with heavy gates to close each level off from those below; the layout ensured that Sho'quo Company would maintain the high ground as they withdrew to the port. If not for the certain fact that the Others were traveling with heavy artillery—significantly heavier than their own EM223s—and sufficient numbers to climb to the high ground over the piled bodies of their dead, she'd be thinking this was a highly survivable engagement. Ignoring the possibility that the Others' air support would get off a lucky drop.

"Well, Staff, it looks like we've got the keys to the city. It's up to us to hold the gates at all costs."

And provided she could keep Lieutenant Franks from getting them all killed—but *that* was pretty much business as usual.

—From *Not That Kind of a War* by Tanya Huff

WOMEN

OF WAR

EDITED BY

Tanya Huff
and Alexander Potter

DAW BOOKS, INC.
DONALD A. WOLLHEIM, FOUNDER
375 Hudson Street, New York, NY 10014
ELIZABETH R. WOLLHEIM
SHEILA E. GILBERT
PUBLISHERS
www.dawbooks.com

First Printing, July 2005

1 2 3 4 5 6 7 8 9

DAW TRADEMARK REGISTERED
U.S. PAT. OFF. AND FOREIGN COUNTRIES
—MARCA REGISTRADA.
HECHO EN U.S.A.

PRINTED IN THE U.S.A.

ACKNOWLEDGMENTS

CONTENTS

INTRODUCTION

> " . . . the dagger is to defend yourself at great need.
> For you also are not to be in the battle."
> "Why, sir?" said Lucy. "I think—I don't know—
> but I think I could be brave enough."
> "That is not the point," he said. "But battles are
> ugly when women fight."

—C.S. Lewis
The Lion, The Witch and the Wardrobe

I'VE ALWAYS HAD TWO REACTIONS to Lucy's conversation with Father Christmas.

First: of course battles are ugly when women fight. War is ugly when anyone fights. There's no such thing as an unugly war.

Second: of course battles are ugly when women fight. Historically, anthropologically, by the time women get involved in war we've moved past the posturing and the rhetoric and gotten down to the ugly business of survival.

We did wonder, way back in the beginning before the stories started coming in, if the gender of the authors would make a difference in the approach. Fourteen stories is definitely too small a sample for any kind of social commentary but it was interesting to discover that the majority of the writers involved in this anthology—all women—didn't actually include a war. Wars had happened or were about to happen but generally, the stories deal with women warriors. Women who were about to be warriors, women who were warriors, women who had been warriors and the personal costs they paid for taking up arms.

It was just as interesting to find that almost all the men who contributed did include a war. The exception being Steve Miller who wrote, as usual, with Sharon Lee. The only thing I, personally, am willing to conclude from this is that women, as a rule, take war more personally than men.

As for the actual stories, well, there are warriors you know, equally memorable warriors you'll be reading about for the first time, and ways of waging war that will almost seem like art.

Tanya Huff

Historically, war has been defined as largely the province of men. This has always been something of a mystery to me. I was raised in a largely female enclave—five older sisters and a very strong mother. As such, the power of the female has always been obvious to me. I remember being in first grade and finding it patently absurd that anyone anywhere would judge women unfit for combat. Anyone who didn't believe women could and would fight, as well if not better than men, simply hadn't met my family.

From a biological standpoint, testosterone (among other things) has an obvious effect on men, leaving us with a higher tendency toward aggression, physical violence, and territorial behavior. Granted, we are not necessarily dictated by biology, but neither should we discount it and assume it powerless. The biological evidence points up an obvious question. If biology presents us with men who are more likely to gravitate to warlike behaviors and reactions, does it automatically follow that women are more peaceful? Over the years of studying feminist theory and gender differences, I've heard a number of arguments to that effect.

I'm not convinced. I think I've spent too much time surrounded by women to truly believe women are *by nature* more peaceful than men. React differently, fight differently, resolve conflict differently? Definitely. But by nature less inclined to fighting and war? Not only am I not convinced, I'm incredibly drawn to female characters in fiction who explore this topic.

Throughout those years of shifting pacifism and feminist studies, I've remained fascinated by the concept of female warriors and how gender plays out in the human phenomenon of war. This interest is one of the many reasons for my attraction to the fantasy and science fiction genres. Where patriarchal human history defined war as man's territory, and woman as having no place there, fantasy and science fiction broke down those walls. The plethora of strong female characters in traditionally male domains captured me from an early age, and the genre has never failed to deliver.

Women of War grew out of these interests. A collection of stories from all over the fantasy and science fiction continuum, with one driving theme—the main character must be a female warrior. Her circumstances could vary, but she must be at heart a warrior—trained for and suited to battle, however that battle might be defined by the individual author. The results have been everything I could have wanted.

The stories that follow explore women in war from a number of perspectives—from god-touched warriors to enlisted personnel, from officers to new recruits to veterans—and from a number of worlds. What links each to the next is the strength of that central female, as she goes about doing what must be done, however she must do it. Each story offers insight not only into an unforgettable female fighter, but also into how war is experienced by these women, and by their respective societies.

I hope you enjoy as much as I did the intense women who explode off the following pages, and the worlds to which they take you.

Alexander B. Potter

FIGHTING CHANCE

by *Sharon Lee and Steve Miller*

Sharon Lee and Steve Miller are best known for their Liaden Universe novels and their several short stories featuring a bumbling wizard named Kinzel. Steve was the founding curator of the University of Maryland's Kuhn Library Science Fiction Research Collection; Sharon has been executive director of the Science Fiction and Fantasy Writers of America, and has also served as president of that organization. They live in Maine, with lots of books, almost as much music, more computer equipment than two people need, and four muses in the form of cats. As might be expected of full-time writers, Sharon and Steve spend way too much time playing on the Internet, and have a Web site at www.korval.com.

"TRY IT NOW," Miri called, and folded her arms over her eyes.

There was a couple seconds of nothing more than the crunchy sound of shoes against gritty floor, which would be Penn moving over to get at the switch.

"Trying it now," he yelled, which was more warning than his dad was used to giving. There was an ominous sizzle, and a mechanical moan as the fans started in to work—picking up speed until they was humming fit to beat.

Miri lowered her arms carefully and squinted up into the workings. The damn splice was gonna hold this time.

For a while, anyhow.

"Pressure's heading for normal," Penn shouted over the building racket. "Come on outta there, Miri."

"Just gotta close up," she shouted back, and wrestled the hatch up, holding it with a knee while she used both hands to seat the locking pin.

That done, she rolled out. A grubby hand intersected her line of vision. Frowning, she looked up into Penn's wary, spectacled face and relaxed. Penn was okay, she reminded herself, and took the offered assist.

Once on her feet, she dropped his hand, and Penn took a step back, glasses flashing as he looked at the lift-bike.

"Guess that's it 'til the next time," he said.

Miri shrugged. The bike belonged to Jerim Snarth, who'd got it off a guy who worked at the spaceport, who'd got it from—don't ask, don't tell. Miri's guess was that the bike's original owner had gotten fed up with it breaking down every third use and left it on a scrap pile.

On the other hand, Jerim was good for the repair money, most of the time, which meant Penn's dad paid Miri on time, so she supposed she oughta hope for more breakdowns.

"Must've wrapped every wire in that thing two or three times by now," she said to Penn, and walked over to the diagnostics board. Pressure and speed had come up to spec and were standing steady.

"My dad said let it run a quarter-hour and chart the pressures."

Miri nodded, saw that Penn'd already set the timer and turned around.

"What's to do next?" she asked.

Penn shrugged his shoulders. "The bike was everything on the schedule," he said, sounding apologetic. "Me, I'm supposed to get the place swept up."

Miri sighed to herself. "Nothing on tomorrow, either?"

"I don't think so," Penn muttered, feeling bad about it, though it wasn't no doing of his—nor his dad's either. Though some extra pay would've been welcome.

Extra pay was always welcome.

"I'll move on down to Trey's, then," she said, going over to the wall where the heavy wool shirt that served as her coat hung on a nail next to Penn's jacket. "See if there's anything needs done there."

She had to stretch high on her toes to reach her shirt— damn nails were set too high. Or she was set too low, more like it.

Sighing, she pulled the shirt on and did up the buttons. If Trey didn't have anything—and it was likely he wouldn't— then she'd walk over to Dorik's bake shop. Dorik always needed small work done—trouble was, she only ever paid in goods, and it was money Miri was particularly interested in.

She turned around. Penn was already unlimbering the broom, moving stiff. Took a hiding, she guessed. Penn got some grief on the street—for the glasses, and for being so good with his figures and his reading and such—which he had to be, his dad owning a mechanical repair shop and Penn expected to help out with the work, when there was work. Hell, even *her* father could read, and figure, too, though he was more likely to be doing the hiding than taking it.

"Seen your dad lately?" Penn asked, like he'd heard her thinking. He looked over his shoulder, glasses glinting. "My dad's got the port wanting somebody for a cargo crane repair, and your dad's the best there is for that."

If he could be found, if he was sober when found, if he could be sobered up before the customer got impatient and went with second best . . .

Miri shook her head.

"Ain't seen him since last month," she told Penn, and deliberately didn't add anything more.

"Well," he said after a second. "If you see him . . ."

"I'll let him know," she said, and raised a hand. "See you."

"Right." Penn turned back to the broom, and Miri moved toward the hatch that gave out onto the alley.

Outside, the air was pleasantly cool. It had rained recently, so the breeze was grit-free. On the other hand, the alley was slick and treacherous underfoot.

Miri walked briskly, absentmindedly sure-footed, keeping a close eye on the various duck-ins and hiding spots. This close to Kalhoon's Repair, the street was usually okay; Penn's dad paid the local clean-up crew a percentage in order to make sure there wasn't no trouble. Still, sometimes the crew didn't come by, and sometimes they missed, and sometimes trouble herded outta one spot took up in another.

She sighed as she walked, wishing Penn hadn't mentioned her father. He never did come home no more except he was smoked or drunk. Or both. And last time—it'd been bad last time, the worst since the time he broke her arm and her mother—her tiny, sickly, soft-talking mother—had gone at him with a piece of the chair he'd busted to let 'em know he was in.

Beat him right across the apartment and out the door, she had, and after he was in the hall, screamed for all the neighbors to hear, "You're none of mine, Chock Robertson! I deny you!"

That'd been pretty good, that denying business, and for a while it looked like it was even gonna work.

Then Robertson, he'd come back in the middle of the night, drunk, smoked, *and* ugly, and started looking real loud for the rent money.

Miri'd come out of her bed in a hurry and run out in her shirt, legs bare, to find him ripping a cabinet off the wall. He'd dropped it when he seen her.

"Where's my money?" he roared, and took a swing.

She ducked back out of the way, and in that second her mother was there—and this time she had a knife.

"Leave us!" she said, and though she hadn't raised her

voice, the way she said it'd sent a chill right through Miri's chest.

Chock Robertson, though, never'd had no sense.

He swung on her; she ducked and slashed, raising blood on his swinging arm. Roaring, he swung again, and this time he connected.

Her mother went across the room, hit the wall and slid, boneless, to the floor, the knife falling out of her hand.

Her father laughed and stepped forward.

Miri yelled, jumped, hit the floor rolling—and came up with the knife.

She crouched, the way she'd seen the street fighters do, and looked up—a fair ways up—into her father's face.

"You touch her," she hissed, "and I'll kill you."

The wonder of the moment being, she thought as she turned out of Mechanic Street and onto Grover, that she'd meant it.

It must've shown on her face, because her father didn't just keep on coming and beat her 'til all her bones were broke.

"Where's the money?" he asked, sounding almost sober.

"We paid the rent," she snarled, which was a lie, but he took it, for a second wonder, and—just walked away. Out of the apartment, down the hall and into the deepest pit of hell, as Miri had wished every day after.

Her mother . . .

That smack'd broke something, though Braken didn't find no busted ribs. The cough, though, that was worse—and she was spittin' up blood with it.

Her lungs, Braken'd said, and nothin' she could do, except maybe ask one of Torbin's girls for a line on some happyjuice.

The dope eased the cough, though it didn't stop the blood, and Boss Latimer's security wouldn't have her in the kitchen no more, which meant no wages, nor any leftovers from the fatcat's table.

Miri was walking past Grover's Tavern; it was a testament

to how slim pickins had been that the smell of sour beer and hot grease made her mouth water.

She shook her head, tucked her hands in her pockets, and stretched her legs. 'Nother couple blocks to Trey's, and maybe there would be something gone funny in the duct work he was too big to get into, but Miri could slide through just fine.

Even if there wasn't work, there'd be coffeetoot, thick and bitter from havin' been on the stove all day, and Trey was sure to give her a mug of the stuff, it bein' his idea of what was—

A shadow stepped out from behind the tavern's garbage bin. Miri dodged, but her father had already grabbed her arm and twisted it behind her back. Agony screamed through her shoulder, and she bit her tongue, hard. Damned if she'd let him hear her yell. *Damned* if she would.

"Here she is," Robertson shouted over her head. "Gimme the cash!"

Out of the tavern's doorway came another man, tall and fat, his coat embroidered with posies and his beard trimmed and combed. He smiled when he saw her, and gold teeth gleamed.

"Mornin', Miri."

"Torbin," she gasped—and bit her tongue again as her father twisted her arm.

"That's *Mister* Torbin, bitch."

Torbin shook his head. "I pay less for damaged goods," he said.

Robertson grunted. "You want my advice, keep her tied up and hungry. She's bad as her ol' lady for sneaking after a man and doin' him harm."

Torbin frowned. "I know how to train my girls, thanks. Let 'er go."

Miri heard her father snort a laugh.

"Gimme my money first. After she's yours, *you* can chase her through every rat hole on Latimer's turf."

"But she ain't gonna run away, are you, Miri?" Torbin

pulled his hand out of a pocket and showed her a gun. Not a homemade one-shot, neither, but a real gun, like the Boss's security had.

"Because," Torbin was saying, "if you try an' run away, I'll shoot you in the leg. You don't gotta walk good to work for me."

"Don't wanna work for you," she said, which was stupid, and Robertson yanked her arm up to let her know it.

"That's too bad," said Torbin. "Cause your dad here's gone to a lot a trouble an' thought for you, an' found you a steady job. But, hey, soon's you make enough to pay off the loan an' the interest, you can quit. I don't hold no girl 'gainst her wants."

He grinned. "An' you—you're some lucky girl. Got me a man who pays a big bonus for a redhead, another one likes the youngers. You're, what—'leven? Twelve, maybe?"

"Sixteen," Miri snarled. This time the pain caught her unawares, and a squeak got out before she ground her teeth together.

"She's thirteen," Robertson said, and Torbin nodded.

"That'll do. Let 'er go, Chock."

"M'money," her father said again, and her arm was gonna pop right outta the shoulder, if—

"Right." Torbin pulled his other hand out of its pocket, a fan of greasy bills between his fingers. "Twenty cash, like we agreed on."

Her father reached out a shaky hand and crumbled the notes in his fist.

"Good," said Torbin. "Miri, you 'member what I told you. Be a good girl and we'll get on. Let 'er go, Chock."

He pushed her hard and let go her arm. Expected her to fall, prolly, and truth to tell, she expected it herself, but she managed to stay up and keep moving, head down, straight at Torbin.

She rammed her head hard into his crotch, heard a high squeak. Torbin went down to his knees, got one arm around her; she twisted, dodged, was past, felt the grip on her shirt, and had time to yell before she was slammed into the side of the garbage bin. Her sight grayed, and out of the mist she saw a fist coming toward her. She dropped to the mud and rolled, sobbing, heard another shout and a hoarse cough, and above it all a third and unfamiliar voice, yelling—

"Put the gun down and stand where you are or by the gods I'll shoot your balls off, if you got any!"

Miri froze where she was, belly flat to the ground, and turned her face a little to see—

Chock Robertson standing still, hands up at belt level, fingers wide and empty.

Torbin standing kinda half-bent, hands hanging empty, his gun on the ground next to his shoe.

A rangy woman in neat gray shirt and neat gray trousers tucked tight into shiny black boots. She was holding a gun as shiny as the boots easy and businesslike in her right hand. Her hair was brown and her eyes were hard and the expression on her face was of a woman who'd just found rats in the larder.

"Kick that over here," she said to Torbin.

He grunted, but gave the gun a kick that put next it to the woman's foot. She put her shiny boot on it and nodded slightly. "Obliged."

"You all right, girl?" she asked then, but not like it mattered much.

Miri swallowed. Her arm hurt, and her head did, and her back where she'd caught the metal side of the container. Near's she could tell, though, everything that ought to moved. And she was breathing.

"I'm okay," she said.

"Then let's see you stand up and walk over here," the woman said.

She pushed herself up onto her knees, keeping a wary eye on Robertson and Torbin, got her feet under her, and walked up to the woman, making sure she kept outta the stare of her weapon.

The brown eyes flicked to her face, the hard mouth frowning.

"I know you?"

"Don't think so," Miri answered. "Ma'am."

One side of the mouth twisted up a little, then the eyes moved and the gun, too.

"Stay right there until I tell you otherwise," she snapped, and her father sank back flat on his feet, hands held away from his sides.

"Get behind me, girl," the woman said, and Miri ducked around and stood facing that straight, gray-clad back.

She oughta run, she thought; get to one of her hiding places before Torbin and her father figured out that the two of them together could take a single woman, but curiosity and some stupid idea that if it came down to it, she oughta help the person who'd helped her kept her there and watching.

"Now," the woman said briskly. "You gents can take yourselves peaceably off, or I can shoot the pair of you. It really don't matter to me which it is."

"The girl belongs to me!" Torbin said. "Her daddy pledged her for twenty cash."

"Nice of him," the woman with the gun said.

"Girl," she snapped over her shoulder. "If you're keen on going for whore, you go ahead with him. I won't stop you."

"I ain't," Miri said, and was ashamed to hear her voice shake.

"That's settled then." The woman moved her gun in a easy nod at Torbin. "Seems to me you oughta get your money back from her daddy and buy yourself another girl."

"She's mine to see settled!" roared Robertson, leaning forward—and then leaning back as the gun turned its stare on him.

"Girl says she ain't going for whore," the woman said lazily. "Girl's got a say in what she will and won't do to feed herself. Girl!"

Miri's shoulders jerked. "Ma'am?"

"You find yourself some work to do, you make sure your daddy gets his piece, hear?"

"No'm," Miri said, hotly. "When I find work I'll make sure my mother gets *her* piece. She threw him out and denied him. He's no lookout of ours."

There was a small pause, and Miri thought she saw a twitch along one level shoulder.

"That a fact?" the woman murmured, but didn't wait for any answer before rapping out, "You gents got places to be. Go there."

Amazingly, they went, Torbin not even askin' for his gun back.

"You still there, girl?"

Miri blinked at the straight back "Yes'm."

The woman turned and looked down her.

"Now the question is, why?" she said. "You coulda been next turf over by now."

"Thought I might could help," Miri said, feeling stupid now for thinking it. "If things got ugly."

The hard eyes didn't change and the mouth didn't smile. "Ready to wade right in, were you?" she murmured, and just like before didn't wait for an answer.

"What's your name, girl?"

"Miri Robertson."

"Huh. What's your momma's name?"

Miri looked up into the woman's face, but there wasn't no reading it, one way or the other.

"Katy Tayzin," she said.

The face did change then, though Miri couldn't't've said exactly how, and the level shoulders looked to lose a little of their starch.

"You're the spit of her," the woman said, and put her fingers against her neat gray chest. "Name's Lizardi. You call me Liz."

Miri blinked up at her. "You know my mother?"

"Used to," Liz said, sliding her gun away neat into its belt-holder. "Years ago that'd be. How's she fare?"

"She's sick," Miri said, and hesitated, then blurted. "You know anybody's got work—steady work? I can do some mechanical repair, and duct work and chimney clearing and—"

Liz held up a broad hand. Miri stopped, swallowing, and met the brown eyes steady as she could.

"Happens I have work," Liz said slowly. "It's hard and it's dangerous, but I'm proof it can be good to you. If you want to hear more, come on inside and take a sup with me. Grover does a decent stew, still."

Miri hesitated. "I don't—"

Liz shook her head. "Tradition. Recruiting officer always buys."

Whatever that meant, Miri thought, and then thought again about Torbin and her father being on the loose.

"Your momma all right where she is?" Liz asked and Miri nodded.

"Staying with Braken and Kale," she said. "Won't nobody get through Kale."

"Good. You come with me."

"Grew up here," Liz said in her lazy way, while Miri worked through her second bowl of stew. "Boss Peterman's territory it was then. Wasn't much by way of work then, neither. Me, I was little bit older'n you, workin' pick-up and on the side. Your momma, she was baker over—well, it ain't here now, but there used to be a big bake shop over on Light Street. It was that kept us, but we was looking to do better. One day, come Commander Feriola, recruitin', just like I'm doin' now. I signed up for to be a soldier. Your momma . . ." She paused, and took a couple minutes to kinda look around the room. Miri finished her stew and regretfully pushed the bowl away.

"Your momma," Liz said, "she wouldn't go off-world. Her momma had told her there was bad things waitin' for her if she did, and there wasn't nothin' I could say would move her. So I went myself, and learned my trade, and rose up through the rank, and now here I'm back, looking for a few bold ones to fill in my own command."

Miri bit her lip. "What's the pay?"

Liz shook her head. "That was my first question, too. It don't pay enough, some ways. It pays better'n whorin', pays better'n odd jobs. You stand a good chance of gettin' dead from it, but you'll have a fightin' chance. And if you come out on the livin' side of that chance, and you're smart, you'll have some money to retire on and not have to come back to Surebleak never again."

"And my pay," Miri persisted, thinking about the drug Braken thought might be had, over to Boss Abram's turf, that might stop the blood and heal her mother's lungs. "I can send that home?"

Liz's mouth tightened. "You can, if that's what you want. It's your pay, girl. And believe me, you'll earn it."

Braken and Kale, they'd look after her mother while she was gone. Specially if she was to promise them a piece. And it couldn't be no worse off-world than here, she thought—could it?

"I'll do it," she said, sounded maybe too eager, because the woman laughed. Miri frowned.

"No, don't you spit at me," Liz said, raising a hand. "I seen temper."

"I thought—"

"No, you didn't," Liz snapped. "All you saw was the money. Happens I got some questions of my own. I ain't looking to take you off-world and get you killed for sure. If I want to see you dead, I can shoot you right here and now and save us both the fare.

"And that's my first question, a soldier's work being what it is. You think you can kill somebody?"

Miri blinked, remembering the feel of the gun in her hand—and blinked again, pushing the memory back away.

"I can," she said, slow, "because I have."

Liz pursed her lips, like she tasted something sour. "Have, huh? Mind sharing the particulars?"

Miri shrugged. "Bout a year ago. They was kid slavers

an' thought they'd take me. I got hold of one of their guns
and—" she swallowed, remembering the smell and the
woman's voice, not steady: *Easy, kid . . .*

" . . . and I shot both of 'em," she finished up, meeting
Liz's eyes.

"Yeah? You like it?"

Like it? Miri shook her head. "Threw up."

"Huh. Would you do it again?"

"If I had to," Miri said, and meant it.

"Huh," Liz said again. "Your momma know about it?"

"No." She hesitated, then added. "I took their money.
Told her I found the purse out behind the bar."

Liz nodded.

"I heard two different ages out there on the street. You
want to own one of 'em?"

Miri opened her mouth—Liz held up her hand.

"It'd be good if it was your real age. I can see you're
small. Remember I knew your momma. I seen what small
can do."

*Like waling a man half again as tall as her and twice as
heavy across a room and out into the hall . . .*

"Almost fourteen."

"How close an almost?"

"Just shy a Standard Month."

Liz closed her eyes, and Miri froze.

"I can read," she said.

Liz laughed, soft and ghosty. "Can you, now?" she murmured, and opened her eyes, all business again.

"There's a signing bonus of fifty cash. You being on the
light side of what the mercs consider legal age, we'll need
your momma's hand on the papers."

Braken eyed Miri's tall companion, and stepped back
from the door.

"She's in her chair," she said.

Miri nodded and led the way.

Braken's room had a window, and Katy Tayzin's chair was set square in front of it, so she'd get whatever sun could find its way through the grime.

She was sewing—mending a tear in one of Kale's shirts, Miri thought, and looked up slowly, gray eyes black with the juice.

"Ma—" Miri began, but Katy's eyes went past her, and she put her hands and the mending down flat on her lap.

"Angela," she said, and it was nothing like the tone she'd used to deny Robertson, but it gave Miri chills anyway.

"Katy," Liz said, in her lazy way, and stepped forward, till she stood lookin' down into the chair.

"I'm hoping that denial's wore off by now," she said, soft-like.

Katy Tayzin smiled faintly. "I think it has," she murmured. "You look fine, Angela. The soldiering treated you well."

"Just registered my own command with merc headquarters," Liz answered. "I'm recruiting."

"And my daughter brings you here." She moved her languid gaze. "Are you for a soldier, Miri?"

"Yes'm," she said and stood forward, marshaling her arguments: the money she'd send home, the signing cash, the—

"Good," her mother said, and smiled, slowly. "You'll do well."

Liz cleared her throat. "There's a paper you'll need to sign."

"Of course."

There was a pause then. Liz's shoulders rose—and fell.

"Katy. There's medics and drugs and transplants—off-world. For old times—"

"My reasons remain," Katy said, and extended a frail, translucent hand. "Sit with me, Angela. Tell me everything. Miri—Kale needs you to help him in the boiler room."

Miri blinked, then nodded. "Yes'm," she said, and turned to go. She looked back before she got to the door, and saw

Liz sitting on the floor next to her mother's chair, both broad, tan hands cupping one of her mother's thin hands, brown head bent above red.

Miri'd spent half her recruitment bonus on vacked coffee and tea, dry beans and vegetables for her mother, and some quality smokes for Braken and Kale. Half what was left after that went with Milt Boraneti into Boss Abram's territory, with a paper spelling out the name of the drug Braken'd thought would help Katy's lungs.

She'd gone 'round to Kalhoon's Repair, to say good-bye to Penn, and drop him off her hoard of paper and books, but he wasn't there. Using one of the smaller pieces of paper, she wrote him a laborious note, borrowed a piece of twine and left the tied-together package with his dad.

Liz'd told her she'd have a uniform when she got to merc headquarters, the cost to be deducted from her pay. For now, she wore her best clothes, and carried her new-signed papers in a bag over her shoulder. In the bag, too, wrapped up in a clean rag, was a smooth disk—*intarsia work,* her mother had murmured, barely able to hold the thing in her two hands.

It was your grandmother's, she whispered, *and it came from off-world. It doesn't belong here, and neither do you.*

"I'll send money," Miri said, looking into her mother's drugged eyes. "As much as I can."

Katy smiled. "You'll have expenses," she said. "Don't send all your money to me."

Miri bit her lip. "Will you come? Liz says—"

Katy shook her head. "I won't pass the physical at the port," she said, and coughed. She turned her head aside and used a rag to wipe her mouth.

She turned back with a smile, and reached out her thin hand to rest it on Miri's arm. "You, my daughter. You're about to begin the adventure of your life. Be bold, which I know you are. Be as honest as you can. Trust Angela. If you find love, embrace it."

The cough again, hard this time. Miri caught her shoulders and held her until it was done. Katy used the rag, and pushed it down beside her on the chair, but not before Miri saw it was dyed crimson.

Katy turned back with another smile, wider this time, and held out arms out. Miri bent and hugged her, feeling the bones. Her mother's lips brushed her cheek, and her voice whispered, "Go now."

And so she left, out the door and down the hall and into the street where Liz Lizardi was waiting, and the adventure of her life begun.

PAINTED CHILD OF EARTH

by Rosemary Edghill

Rosemary Edghill's first professional sales were to the black & white comics of the late 1970s, so she can truthfully state on her resume that she once killed vampires for a living. She is also the author of over thirty novels and several dozen short stories in genres ranging from Regency romance to space opera, making all local stops in between. She has collaborated with authors such as the late Marion Zimmer Bradley and the late SF Grand Master Andre Norton, and has worked as a science fiction editor for a major New York publisher, as a freelance book designer, and as a professional book reviewer. Her hobbies include sleep, research for forthcoming projects, and her Cavalier King Charles spaniels. Her Web site can be found at http://www.sff.net/people/eluki.

IN A THOUSAND TOWNS her name was legend. Had been, at any rate, once.

But that was a long time ago.

She had been a captain of fifty when Corchado was a power in the land. Then cities farther south had risen up fat and acrimonious on trade, and now Corchado had become the northernmost outpost of the Alarine Empire, and the castle hill from which a duke had reigned had long ago been reduced to flatland lest an enemy army seize it for a stronghold. There was war on the northern border, but then, wasn't there always?

And there was still work for a hero.

Bandits to be rousted out (a drawn-out and thankless task, that, and a new set always came from somewhere), dragons to slay (she had not seen any in years, thank whatever gods you choose), corrupt overlords to oppose (though the Alarine bureaucracy saw to it that no vassal lorder managed to grow too fat on Imperial property), and, always, the little wars between town and town.

But because of the sword she carried, she chose her quarrels carefully. And somehow, when word got around that Ruana Rulane the Twiceborn had come with the god-sword Shadowkiss to settle the matter of who owned fifty hectares of bottom land and the irrigation rights to a stream, the contestants decided to resort to lawyers instead of lances. She could not remember the last time she had drawn her sword in such a dispute.

Once the thought might have irked her. But that was a long time ago.

The years passed, but Ruana Rulane did not change. Such was her nature; Shadowkiss had taken her as its companion, and the sword's companion would live until the end of the world.

Once that would not have been long. A lesser guardian than Ruana would have gone drunk on the magic of holding in his hands a true solid bit of what came before Time; a weapon forged to fight gods' wars for them. And then Shadowkiss would have offered that man glory, or vengeance, or truth, or love, bending him slowly to the delicious work of annihilation. And that sword and that paladin, in merciless inevitable stages, would have slain the world. Such was the nature of the sword the gods forged.

But Ruana Rulane was different. She was a hero, but she was no man. And so the dazzling abstract lures Shadowkiss could offer held less power over her. She would not give the sword its proper employment. She would not turn it to the butcher-work of war.

She asked it—why?

What is the purpose of destruction, when it is neither end nor means? Why is war better than nurture? How does vengeance serve the common good? Why is honor worth more than life? What good is glory?

If not me, who? If not now, when?

And the sword answered. And every answer it gave, she challenged, and mocked, and asked again. Until, slowly, the nature of the answers the sword gave changed.

But so slowly.

Living things learn, she had told a man once. He had said her hellblade lived and so must die. But Shadowkiss could be neither destroyed nor defeated. For the sword to live, it must change.

And so Ruana went about her inglorious work; delivered babies, fed the hungry, irritated the mighty. And bore with her the changeling weapon that was curse, sword, and lover.

Shadowkiss.

She was heading westward, back toward the border town of Corchado, when she first heard about the Monster of Paloe.

She'd stopped for the night at an inn; gave a coin to the ostler to stable her horse and walked into the common room. Shadowkiss was slung across her back; awkward, but needs must when the sword was longer than her leg.

Conversation stopped when she came in. The inn's occupants judged her: not tall enough for a man, beardless as a boy, obviously neither. Conversation started again, subfusc, as the tavernmaster came out from behind his bar.

"And what is it you want here, gelding?"

Ruana smiled without mirth. "Why, goodman, nae more than tha can provide: dinner and bed and stabling for my horse. My name is Rulane Twiceborn."

Years ago—how many now?—that name would have made men pale in terror, but the tavernmaster simply frowned, as if he were trying to remember something he'd learned long ago and since forgotten.

He tried to find something to take offense at, but the stranger with the songsmith name only asked what he was in the business of providing; and the coin she put into his hand was sound, if its stamping was strange. Ruana took her place by the fire and her peggin of beer and settled in to hear the gossip of the road.

But all the inn's inhabitants weren't so incurious as the tapster. There was a conferring and a jostling at the far end of the room where the regulars gathered, and eventually— she watched it all, with a sense of amused inevitability— they sent their delegate to try her.

He was a tall man, and southern-dark. A fairing-ring glistened in one ear, the copper showing through the gold in places. His teeth were sound and white. He dandled a small instrument of a type becoming more common now: the strings of the harp-bow extended beyond it, down a long neck fraught with tuning frets.

"I am Loyt Singerson," he said, "and I think you are a legend."

"An' legends drink beer," Ruana answered, "then there be many a legend here tonight."

Singerson smiled. "So they may say in the North. In the South, they say legend is bound in the strings of the harp. My poor *loyt* is not a harp, but she will serve for a song."

He set a wooden bowl upon the table, and put his foot upon the bench where Ruana sat to steady his instrument, and swept his hand across its strings. All around him, talk quieted as the first notes struck the air.

He sang of kings out of Lostland, of changeling children who found their way home only to find home gone to dust with time. He sang of heroes, of dragonslayers, and a queen who had taken a sword for a lover.

A person with a suspicious mind, Ruana decided, might think that last tale based on herself.

By the time his singing was done, Loyt's wooden bowl was full with copper coin, and no one cared any longer about the stranger with the sword.

Those who drank there were working men, tied to the land and their crafts. They left by ones and twos, and soon only Loyt and Ruana remained, dicing in the corner by the fire. She had luck and the skill of years, and he was very good at cheating. Nevertheless, she had won much of his store of coin from him by the time he chose to speak.

She had known it would come to speaking, soon or late.

"In the hills, a day's ride from here—north, that would be—lies a village much troubled. By what, the villagers of Paloe cannot say, for they do not know. But it screams in the night like a woman in childbed, so they say. And the women there weep for lost children. That they know."

Ruana smiled grimly and drank from her wooden mug. "An' tha knew me to tell me this, why did tha not name me to them? Yon bowl mought have held silver as well as copper."

Loyt smiled, and his white teeth flashed. "They would not thank me to bring them a legend in the flesh, Twiceborn."

He did not ask to see the sword she carried, then or later.

Once upon a time there was a boy called Moonflute. As in Starharp and Moonflute; two great gaudy nonexistent legends that you could throw away your whole life over and at the end of it not know whether you'd gotten anything worth having, or, indeed, anything at all.

He was called Moonflute because he didn't have any other name at all; a child-of-the-mist, as the saying goes, left on the priest's doorstep nine months and a bit after some big feast-day, born to a woman who thought it better to leave town. The gold she left around his neck went for his keep, and the priest was careful to melt it down before he sold it. Some patrimonies aren't worth claiming.

The boy grew, and was apprenticed, and was called an airy handful of things until he was old enough to have opinions and ensure that one name stuck.

Moonflute. The Starharp's shadow, that would make the Starharp show itself so that it could be played; so that playing it would wake the Crownking, who would summon the quarreling gods to order and bring peace to the world. A suitable name for a big-eyed boy who looked too much like the lord of Corchado for anyone's peace and who believed, fiercely, in the singer's tales of nobility and grandeur chanted for a coin in the dooryard of the alehouse where he served.

He grew tall on his father's blood, lean on scraps, and fast on numerous would-be beatings. The likeness didn't disappear with age.

The year that he was twelve, a passing traveler, a bit too well-dressed to be where he was, asked his name. When told it, with defiance, the traveler did not laugh. He spoke, afterward and at length, to Moonflute's master, who spoke in turn to Moonflute. The innkeeper said nothing to the point, but gifted his startled scullion with a generous cut of the roasting mutton joint and a whole heel-end of new bread for his supper.

That night Moonflute broke his indentures. He was nobody's fool. He had no intention of ending his life as someone's gelded prettyboy, and if the stranger who had given him a whole silver coin for serving him had anything else in mind but that, it was probably worse. So he left. He'd meant to do it sooner or later. He wasn't going to be a pot-boy all his life. He was going to be a hero. Moonflute was going to find the Starharp, just like the legends said.

Heading south from Corchado he wandered for a trackless while, then found his luck in the defeat of a nest of bandits where all that was needed was recklessness, a torch, and a borrowed—he meant to return it, truly—horse. Moonflute continued south with a new sword and his own horse and the beginning of a name, drunk on possibilities. Perhaps his fortune lay in Alarra, in the army of the Emperor. But how much better to come to that a hero rich with deeds and exploits. He was young; the world was wide.

He gathered deeds as a miser gathers coins; each one never enough. Years passed without his notice, and each shift and diversion he was led to was only temporary—but he had years to squander. What he did in these scant few would—he thought—leave no mark upon his soul.

He was young, and hungry for more things than food. It was not adulation that he craved, though he did not know it yet. It was a sense of place. Fierce, impatient, idealistic; he held himself as the minimum acceptable standard for humanity and had no compassion for those who were less. And though he was not so very gifted, there were many who were less.

His father's father's father across a score of generations had burned as ardently—but the needs of each priest, beggar, soldier, and clerk in the Gray Duke's duchy had schooled him, if not to compassion, at least to kindness. But Moonflute had no ties to earth; the heavens drew him to fiery cometary progress.

When word came to him of the Monster of Paloe, it was plain to Moonflute he must attempt it. All the pat celebrations of the singer's tales vied for pride of place in Moonflute's imagination. A hero had a place in the world, and this triumph would surely be enough to make him one even in his own eyes. His mind veered among expectations that ranged from anticlimax to fable. Certified monsters were nearly as rare as real wizards; to ride into Alarra with its skin for a saddlecloth would be a splendid thing, and to ride into the village whose fields it terrorized with the great beast dead across his saddlebow would be . . .

Almost enough. Almost.

So with some work he found the village and announced that he had come to end their trouble. The villagers were glad to see Moonflute, with his fine horse and his fine armor and all the gaudy trappings of heroism. The forester who had tried to trap the monster had been eaten, and the monster was not yet enough of an impediment to the collection of Alarra's taxes to warrant the sending of kingsmen. The headman was lavish in his relief, and promised the wanderer liberal reward for fear he should change his mind and leave instead. They feted him richly, and at dawn they sent him forth to the hunt.

His horse was silky black and grain-fed; skittish and neat-footed, with a mane as fine as a woman's hair; splendid and suitable for the hero he would someday be. He had won it at dice.

It died a little after mid-morning.

The forester had died in these hills; the monster's lair must be nearby. As he rode, a shadow blotted out the sun.

Before he could remark on it, before he could look, the creature he had sought landed slipshod on his horse's neck. He had one glimpse of a flat spade-shaped head and eyes that glowed pale silver before he was flung, savaged and dripping, from his frenzied beast. That was not the worst.

Nor was lying at the bottom of the ravine, looking up at his legs as the blood trickled along them and hearing the splintering of bone that followed the horse's dying screams.

No, the worst was knowing that sword and dagger had been lost in the brushwood tangle of his descent, and that at least one leg was useless, vised between the interlocking branches that pinned him. He was trapped, and the monster would come back. He had seen its eyes. It would come back for him. And he might not be dead by then.

He'd been a fool, and he was paying for that luxury now in the only coin that closes such debts.

Ruana Rulane rode through the autumn fields, and on into the woods that framed the deep forest. There would be no heat in the autumn sunlight until the late afternoon; Ruana was glad of her heavy cloak and the warmth of the horse between her knees.

She loosened Shadowkiss in its well-greased sheath, and told over the ashwood shafts of the hunting spears she'd bought from the forester's widow, and wondered what prey she sought.

A monster, the villagers said. That could be anything. But wolves wouldn't take children when sheep could be had. And Worm would blight the land and leave the children and the folk to starve. The forester had spoken to his wife of a cat before he was killed himself, but the tracks were weeks gone and the cats in these woods hunted rabbits, not men.

Somewhere in the back of her mind, a memory stirred.

She came finally into the rocks and the open land, and her horse and the carrion feeders shied at the same moment. She saw the half-eaten horse, still in its gaudy trappings. Its neck had been bitten through, and there were deep claw-marks upon its shoulders and its flanks. The memory came clear, and she remembered.

Tiger. No creature of sorcery, but Death in a gray dappled coat. She'd seen them in the east. Over mountains and rivers, beyond lakes wide enough to fool the eye that there was no other side, at the far side of deserts burnished bright and hard as glass, there was a place where cats with teeth as long as knives hunted men: a land whose forests stretched like feasting-halls from mountain to desert. Men did not rule there.

This was not a land for tiger. Perhaps some tribute-wagon bound for Alarra had disgorged its cargo untimely.

She looked about for a place to tie her horse, and finally wedged its reins beneath a boulder far enough from its dead fellow that it wouldn't, probably, choose to bolt.

The ashwood spears would be useless. They would kill wolf and boar, but not tiger. She left them with the horse. Then she pulled Shadowkiss from its sheath and walked slowly forward, studying the ground for signs. The sword hoarded daylight, giving it back in ocean-colored fire, and the print of the wide clawed pads was blatant in the blood-muddied dust.

Then she heard a low coughing growl.

It had cost him dear, but Moonflute had freed his leg. He could not stand, but he could crawl, and the gilt of his sword-hilt glittered among the fallen leaves.

His sword arm was useless; bruised to aching numbness in the fall and clawed by the monster besides. He did not think about that. Only the sword mattered.

At last he could clasp his fingers about it, and rolled onto his back, panting with exhaustion, drawing his sword awkwardly to him with the hand he could still use.

And stared once more into the eyes of the Monster of Paloe.

It was as if someone had taken the small cats of the forest and somehow made them bigger than stags. Its fur was the ash gray of a dying fire, and upon that ash lay the spots and stripes of a gray darker still. From its upper jaw hung two enormous fangs as long as his hand.

It crouched in the brush a few yards farther down the slope. Only its eyes betrayed it to his sight: pale and inhuman as death, they glittered in the autumn sun. It watched him unmoving. Soon it would rush forward, and his brief life would be over.

No one would know that he had lived, or how he had died.

Slowly, painfully, he pulled his sword upward.

The flash of light on metal caught Ruana's eye.

The dead horse's rider was still alive.

Farther down the slope, she saw the tiger in the brush. In a moment it would charge.

She had seen tiger killed in the east. They had been trapped in pits, or caught with nets. To take them on the ground—as she had seen nobles try for sport—required aliphaunts and archers, packs of dogs in armor, horses trained from foalhood.

But it was intent upon its prey, and that gave her a chance. It would kill the boy, and for a few brief instants it would be distracted. She could make her try for it then. He was only a boy, she thought, with a brief hard life to him. Why should she interfere, when all the years he could expect were a handful to those she had already lived? How could he mind losing such a little thing?

:Let him be,: agreed the sword in her hand. *:He would not want to meet a legend.:*

No! she answered, seeing the long-woven trap at last. How many years since she'd taken her sword—god-sword, hell-sword, lover, and curse—and gone roving? There was always legend for idle hands to weave. But when all those years had worked on her, what was left to speak for humanity against the will of the gods? What was left of what she had been to do battle with the sword?

"Nae this time, ye poxy piece ae glass!" Ruana raised Shadowkiss in her hand and ran down the hill toward the boy and the Paloe Cat.

The boy was down but game, holding his sword in his off hand like a spear while blood rilled down the useless sword hand and pattered on the earth. The cat snarled when it saw Ruana. It would not charge in the face of this new thing.

But neither would it flee.

"Nae this time!" she shouted again, and ran at the crouching spotted shape.

It was large, and savage, and not afraid of Man. It unsheathed talons longer than her fingers and slashed at Ruana, wailing.

But Shadowkiss was there instead of living flesh.

The blade did not bite deep, but the small pain it gave was enough. The beast doubled back on its haunches and sprang.

And then the sword sheathed itself in the creature's belly

and slid out gaudily red behind the shoulder, sliding down through the beast's vitals as it fought to get at her.

And Ruana knew that despite all this it would not die before it killed her—for if she could not age, then she could surely die, if her guts were scattered upon the earth.

There was crushing weight, and heat, and then cold.

And then the dark.

Mind returned, and before she had the sense of her body she groped with numb fingers until she encountered the checked bone hilt of Shadowkiss, laid across her as if for a lorder's funeral.

She was not dead.

She grunted, and rolled to her knees.

She was red with tiger blood, but its terrible hind claws had not done their mortal work, for the god-sword had severed the monster's spine. Its foul weight had crushed the breath from her lungs as it had died atop her. That was all.

And then someone had pulled it off.

The boy—he had a man's growth, perhaps, but he was still a boy to her—knelt in the blood-soaked leaves a few feet away, cradling his useless arm in his lap. His sword lay beside him on the ground. His hand was wet with the tiger's blood.

He looked up and met her eyes.

She knew those eyes. They were a little darker than amber. She had seen them first in a room when Corchado was a power in the land, when the Gray Duke's word was law.

When the Gray Duke had sought to take Shadowkiss for himself, but trusted a hero instead.

How many years, how many lives, between those eyes and these?

"Ah kent tha braw eld granther, hinny," she said, slipping into the tongue she had spoken as a child.

The boy stared at her, his eyes glazed with pain and

shock. Plainly, he had not understood. Well, they all spoke an uncouth tongue in the South.

Carefully, Ruana got to her feet. "Whit ik tha nam?" she asked. She shook her head to clear it. "Thy name? How art tha called?"

"Moonflute," the boy said, a note of reluctant defiance in his voice. "I seek the Starharp."

And Ruana Rulane began to laugh, harshly, like a battle-field crow. For Shadowkiss was the Starharp, and always had been, and he had found what he sought.

She cleaned the glass-green blade and sheathed it, then carried Moonflute up the hill. Along the way, they found his dagger.

She cleaned and bound his wounds with bandages from her packs, and gave him water and wine from his own sup-plies. She found a level place to camp a little farther from the dead horse, where she could tie her own horse securely, and brought him there. She went back to his horse, and brought away all that could be usefully brought.

Then she made a fire, and settled down to cook.

She felt him watching her.

She knew what he thought and what he guessed. Loyt had guessed. And she knew the boy's name. Moonflute. Seeker of the Starharp.

Seeker of Shadowkiss.

He would know its legends. Most of the legends were even true.

More or less.

When the meat was roasted, she cut it into two portions and offered him one. If he knew he was eating his horse, Moonflute didn't mention the fact.

Day waned into evening, then into night. Ruana Rulane rolled herself into her blankets and slept.

All the brief years of his life he'd intended to become a hero, a legend. Now Moonflute was confronted with legend in the flesh: this silent woman who had—so simply!—saved him from death.

And who carried in her hand a thing out of singer's tales, a glass-green blade set with rubies, a blade that had slain ghosts and dragons, the sword that Chayol Rising Star had once carried into battle.

He knew what it was: the god-sword Shadowkiss, ornate legend from the Eastern Kingdoms. His heart's desire and suicide, all in one hawk's wing sweep of shimmering ocean blade.

A blade carried by an immortal queen—Ruana Rulane, the Twiceborn.

She did not look like an immortal queen.

She spoke like a peasant—when she spoke at all. Her leathers were worn and scarred with use, and her boots were shabby. Her cloak was dusty and mended. Her horse was little better than a mountain pony, a beast he'd be ashamed to ride.

It should be mine! Shadowkiss should be mine!

A hurt too deep to name ate at him until sleep pulled him deep.

She woke an hour before dawn, as the fire guttered to embers. Ruana quickly added wood to waken it. They could cook the rest of the meat for breakfast; if she put Moonflute on her horse they would reach Paloe by midday. . . .

Or she could saddle up and ride away now.

He wanted Shadowkiss. She had seen it in his eyes last night. If she left him at Paloe, he would follow her. He would follow her until he died.

Or until the moment he touched the sword.

She sighed, shaking her head sadly. She'd expected to feel amusement from the sword—saving the boy had been futile after all—but instead all she sensed was a faint flicker of—regret?

And a sense that Shadowkiss was gathering its energies in a way that the god-sword had never gathered them before.

If she had saved Moonflute from the tiger, she had also doomed him. One man in ten thousand looked upon what she carried with lust, yet none could claim Shadowkiss while she lived, for the god-sword had chosen her, and their partnership would endure until the end of the world.

:*Let him choose,*: the sword whispered to her. :*Let him choose.*:

Leave now, and he would die here, alone, for his ankle was yet too tender to bear his weight. Take him to Paloe, and he would follow her—and die.

:*He has a choice,*: the sword urged. :*He still has a choice.*:

He's young, Ruana thought, with something close to despair. She thought of years squandered like water poured out upon parched earth, as Moonflute chased a dream that fled forever just out of reach.

Unable to stop.

Unable to choose.

She unsheathed Shadowkiss and struck the blade into the earth.

The smell of roasting meat roused Moonflute to wakefulness. He startled up all at once, the pain of bruised muscles reminding him of where he was.

But he had eyes only for the sword.

Shadowkiss stood quivering in the earth where Ruana Rulane had sheathed it, green-glowing and jeweled red.

Death to touch.

"Take it," Ruana said evenly. "An' tha wilt."

He stared at her, wondering if this were a trick.

"You . . . you're *giving* it to me?" he asked.

"Nay. I canna do that. An' tha take it, that's thy choice to make. Tha kens what will happen an' tha try, Moonflute."

He knew. He knew what she was offering him. And the only choice he had to make was: die or change.

Choose life instead of legend, and carry the memory of the choice with him forever, to taint and twist and moderate every heroic act for the rest of his life.

Or usurp the sword. Its touch would kill him instantly. But every choice he had ever made had led him here, and legends did not turn back.

A morning-bird called, and suddenly life was sweet, and every momentary physical pleasure he had ever tasted came back to him, warm and vivid and repeatable, if only he lived.

Slowly, he levered himself to his feet with his own scab-barded sword. He reached out his hand.

And the sword spoke to him.

:It's a glorious thing to kill yourself to keep from looking silly.:

"I won't!" said Moonflute, stung. And before he knew he had chosen he drew back.

Ruana took up the sword again, sheathed it, and the look she gave Shadowkiss made Moonflute feel he was seeing what he was not meant to see.

"Thy leg is nae hale enough for standing. Sit," she said, squatting again before the fire.

He did as he was told, and when they had finished their breakfasts, she helped him to mount her horse, and they rode toward Paloe.

"Happen it be there's a horse to spare in Paloe for the siller," she said, walking beside him, "an' the villagers will want to see that yon cat is dead. Tha can bring thy saddle along then. 'Tis a fine brave thing, an' tha would not wish to see it lost."

"It's all I own," Moonflute said bleakly. His saddlebags were slung over the pony's withers, and his saddle blanket was lashed behind the saddle. *It's all I am.*

It had never occurred to him to wonder if there might be an end to his story that was not death. He had been offered that ending, pat as a verse in a singer's tale, and refused it. He did not want to be an aside in the Song of the Twiceborn, a joke tossed off across the strings of the *loyt* to make men laugh into their cups.

He still wanted to be a hero.

They reached Paloe at midday, as Ruana had thought they would. She told them the beast was dead.

She left Moonflute behind in the village and took a couple of the villagers and several horses back with her to where the tiger lay. They returned at dusk with the remains of Paloe's monster lashed to two of the horses and Moonflute's saddle upon another.

The villagers spiked the tiger's head on a post at the gateway of the village; in a few weeks there would be nothing left but a clean-picked skull and a story to frighten the children. Perhaps in the spring Loyt would come to hear it, and make another song.

There was feasting that night. Ruana would rather have been upon the road, but it would have been unkind to blight their pleasure, and in feasting, they reassured themselves that there was reason to feast. And in truth, it was late in the day to set out, for one who wandered where the road took her.

When the feast was done and the fire burned low, the villagers asked her, over and over, for the tale of the monster's death, and from this Ruana knew that Moonflute had said nothing to them, though he could have told the tale in her absence and said what he wished.

She could give them safety. She could give them their lives. But she could not give them the words they hungered for.

"Hear me and heed me, villagers of Paloe, and I will tell a tale like no tale you have ever heard, and more: the tale of a true thing. I will tell the tale of how Ruana Rulane, the Twiceborn, came to the village of Paloe and slew the Death that comes in the night—yes, took into her immortal hand the god-sword Shadowkiss, forged before the world was

forged, and slew a monster out of legend." Moonflute
moved closer to the fire and held out his cup to be filled, in
the way that tale-singers did when they began a tale.

He spoke of terror in the night, of a creature with burning
eyes birthed by Darkness Itself, a monster that fed on man-
flesh and would not be slaked.

He spoke of a hero who rode out of the East, a hero who
carried a sword forged by gods, who slew the monster in a
mighty battle, though it screamed and fought and called
upon unholy powers to aid it.

Of himself, he did not speak.

And the eyes of the folk of Paloe grew round with wonder and satisfaction, and their lips moved silently as they
told over the best parts of the tale to themselves.

"And so it was that with one great blow the Twiceborn
clove the monster of Paloe in two, and the light of Evil departed from its eyes, and the shadow of darkness departed
from its heart, and its black blood poured out upon the earth
in a steaming gush, and it lay dead. And Ruana Rulane
leaped to her feet with a great cry of triumph, and bran-
dished the god-sword Shadowkiss above her head, and the
droplets of the monster's blood fell upon the earth like rain,
and she shouted aloud with joy at her victory. And now is
my tale told, the tale which is no tale, but the true account of
the slaying of the monster of Paloe," Moonflute finished.

Now the villagers were satisfied, and the ale-jug went
around one last time. The women gathered sleeping babes
into their aprons, and the husbandmen lifted larger children
onto their shoulders, and all moved slowly toward their
beds.

Ruana lingered before the fire, watching Moonflute stare
into it.

"Art a tale-singer, then, hinny?" she asked, when the silence had stretched long enough.

"No," Moonflute said wearily. "But I was a pot-boy in an
alehouse in Corchado. I heard them often enough. I know
how a tale should go. I told the people what they wanted to

hear. If . . . it wasn't all the truth, I know their lives. They don't have time for more truth than this."

"Aye," Ruana said. "I know them too." Once she had been one of them. A very long time ago.

"I wanted all the tales to be true," Moonflute said. "Not more. Not less. Heroes, and justice, and glory at the sword's point. I wanted . . ." he stopped.

There was only one thing in her gift, and Ruana gave it.

"I knew . . ." Ruana thought hard. "Not thy sire. He'd have left no bye-bairn of his to rot. Nor yet thy gran'ther. But a laird of thy blood, so I reckon. 'Twas he who trusted me to keep the sword."

Moonflute smiled, and his smile was painful to see. "He was a hero, then."

"Aye," Ruana said. It was the truth. "Precious little glory in it, d'ye ken. Glory is for kings and priests and the dead."

There was no more to say, and so she got to her feet, and walked to the headman's house where she would sleep that night.

The birds that called before the dawn woke her. In the darkness, Ruana got to her feet and dressed, picked up her sword and her saddlebags, and headed for the stable.

Moonflute was there waiting for her.

His injured arm was in a sling—it would be many days before the bruised shoulder was well again—but he stood beside a new-bought horse with his saddle upon its back.

Waiting for her.

She saddled her horse in silence. There was nothing to say. She knew what he wanted, and would not ask her for.

Would it indeed be such a bad thing, to have a companion upon the road?

He will tire of it, she thought, and knew he wouldn't.

He will die, she thought, and knew he would.

It will hurt when he dies, Ruana thought with an inward sigh.

But pain was life, was being human—and a moment in

the brush on the side of a hill had shown her the peril that could come of forgetting to be human.

She swung into the saddle and looked down at him.

"Well, come on then, my hinny; an' tha want to be uncomfortable, I'd best show thee the easiest way of it."

"I will," said Moonflute.

SHE'S SUCH A NASTY MORSEL:
A Web Shifters Story

by Julie E. Czerneda

Julie E. Czerneda, a former biologist, has been writing and editing science texts for almost two decades. A regular presenter on issues in science and science in society, she's also an internationally best-selling and award-winning science fiction author and editor, with seven novels published by DAW Books Inc. (including two series: the Trade Pact Universe and the Webshifters) and her latest, Species Imperative. *Her editorial debut for DAW was* Space Inc. *Her short fiction and novels have been nominated for several awards, including as a finalist for the John W. Campbell Award for Best New Writer, the Philip K. Dick Award for Distinguished Science Fiction, and won two Prix Aurora Awards, as well as being on the preliminary Nebula Ballot. She currently serves as science fiction consultant to* Science News.

LIKE MANY YOUNG BEINGS, it came as something of a revelation to me that my elders had been young once themselves. Or at least younger, with all that implied about having made choices—or mistakes.

It was the latter that intrigued me most. Or formed the

single defining aspect of my own life—whichever way you preferred to look at it.

Me? I'm Esen-alit-Quar, Esen for short, Es in a hurry or from a friend. During my first few centuries of life, however, I was almost always "Esen-alit-Quar! Where's that little troublemaker?"

Not that I ever intended to cause trouble. In truth, I went to great lengths to avoid causing anything at all, understanding that anything that attracted the attention of my elders was not going to end well.

Unfortunately, I possess a curiosity equal to any hunger of my flesh. Half answers, hints, suggestions of "you'll know when you're as old as we" only fanned that curiosity, particularly as I found it hard to believe I'd ever be as old as any of my Web. The Web of Ersh. We were six, led by the oldest and thus first among us, Ersh herself. Unimaginably ancient. Different. The center of all things. And the most likely individual to find fault with me at any given moment.

Or the secondmost. For Ersh had younger sisters, daughters of her flesh: Ansky, Lesy, Mixs, and Skalet. It was Skalet who took my occasional missteps as her duty to announce—or even better, cause.

Me? Oh, I sprang from Ansky's flesh, not Ersh's. Worse still, I wasn't a sister/daughter—or whatever one called a relationship in which being given life was more like amputation. I'd been born.

How was this possible? The question would prompt Lesy to giggle. Solitary Skalet would scowl and confer in anxious scents or other means with the like-minded Mixs. Ansky herself would smile and say it took practice.

The subject of my origin was one I knew not to bring up around Ersh.

There was no one left for me to ask, for we six were unique and alone among all other forms of life. Only we were Web beings, able to manipulate matter and energy— more specifically, our matter and our energy—in order to disguise ourselves.

And to hold information. Our Web's noble purpose was to gather and retain the accomplishments of other, ephemeral intelligences within our almost immortal flesh, shared only with Ersh, to be assimilated by her and then passed, in the amount and content she saw fit, to each of us.

The least of that bounty to me. Which didn't help quench my curiosity, leading me very early to seek my own answers. *Why?* was my favorite conversation starter, perhaps because it made my elders flinch.

Now when Ersh deigned to offer the answer to a question, one had no choice but to live with the consequences. But my curiosity was so vast—or, more accurately, my ability at that age to imagine such consequences so limited— that I would continue to push Ersh for answers long after any other of my kin would wisely back away. It didn't help that those answers were most often doled out to me, in typical Ersh fashion, not when I first asked, but rather when she felt knowing them would educate me even more than in their substance.

So it was with war.

War wasn't a new concept to me. I'd assimilated the cultures, histories, and biologies of thousands of intelligent species from Ersh. I was familiar, if never comfortable, with war as a fact of life for some, the inevitable end of life for others.

What was new was the warfare lately shared by Skalet. Even filtered through Ersh, her memories of the Kraal's battle for Arendi Prime and its aftermath were like a stain, affecting my every thought. How had a Web-being, sworn to preserve ephemeral culture, become so very good at waging its wars?

Not that I thought the question through in quite those terms. With what Ersh would doubtless consider a selfish fixation on my own life, I wanted to avoid learning any more than I had to about war and destruction. In particular, I didn't want any more lessons on the subject from Skalet.

Skalet probably felt the same. Certainly she made it abundantly clear our sessions together were a waste of her talents in tactics and strategy. When Ersh wasn't in range, that is. Otherwise, as well argue with the orbit of Picco's Moon as one of Ersh's decisions about my education.

Still, there had to be a way. Rather than grumble to myself, I decided to go to Ansky. However, it is the way of our kind that we literally have no secrets from Ersh. Something which hadn't actually occurred to me when I decided it was safer to approach my birth mother than the center of our six-person universe.

My chance came during Ansky's turn to make supper, a tradition at those times when our odd family gathered in the same place, in this case, Picco's Moon.

Carved, like the rest of Ersh's home, from rock almost as old as she, the kitchen was a sparse, practical room, able to accommodate a variety of cooking skills while safely housing a maturing Web-being prone to explode without notice. When it was just Ersh and I, food came out of the replicator and the counters became cluttered with what had her attention at the time, from greenhouse cuttings to bits of machinery. When Lesy played chef, gleaming porcelain of unusual shapes appeared, and woe betide any who disturbed her delicate—and often unidentifable—concoctions. I was definitely forbidden entrance.

Ansky, being more competent and Esen-tolerant, greeted my arrival with a friendly, if absentminded, wave of welcome.

"I can help," I offered, grabbing the largest knife available and curling lip over fang in mock threat. Assorted vegetables were already cowering on the countertop.

For some reason, Ansky rescued the knife from my paw with a deft slip of an upper tentacle. She liked to cook as a Dokecian, the five-limbed form possessing sufficient coordination to stir the contents of pots, dice vegetables, and carve meat all at once. I watched her wistfully—my own ability with the form still limited to pulling myself around and under furniture, at constant risk of forgetting which handhold to release before tugging at the next. A regrettable incident involving a tableful of crystals and a coat rack had led Ersh to forbid me this form indoors.

"I'd ask you to do the dishes, but . . ." her voice trailed away meanfully.

My current self, my Lanivarian birth-form, abhorred water, something Ansky knew from experience. "I've gloves," I assured her, my tongue slopping free between my half-gaping jaws. I resisted my tail's urge to swing from side to side. Smiling was fine, but Ansky wouldn't approve a lapse of good manners.

We settled in, shoulder to shoulders, working in companionable silence. If my washing technique lacked finesse, at least the clean dishes arrived intact on the counter. I wasn't the only one who measured my growth by such things.

But I hadn't come to Ersh's steamy, fragrant kitchen— which had perfectly functional servos, so the physical effort to produce both steam and fragrance was unnecessary, but no one asked me—to be helpful. I'd come with a problem.

Of course, Ansky knew it as well. "So. What is it this time, Esen?" she asked after a few moments.

I almost lost my grip on one of Ersh's favorite platters. "It?" I repeated, keeping my ears up. All innocence.

My birth-mother wasn't fooled. "Let me guess. Skalet's latest enterprise."

My tail slid between my legs as I scrubbed a nonexistent spot. Confronted by the very subject I'd hoped to discuss, I found myself unable to say another word.

"She's become such a nasty morsel."

I couldn't help but stare up at her. Each of her three eyes were the size of my clenched paws. Two looked down at me, their darkness glistening with emotion. "Did you think this sharing was welcomed by any of us? The taste of her memories, even first assimilated by Ersh, were—unpleasant."

I remembered Ersh-taste exploding in my mouth, the exhilarating flood of new memories filling my body. Remembered too much. Skalet hadn't merely observed the Kraal's latest war—she'd helped orchestrate it.

That conflict and her cleverness would be my next lesson. There would be lists and details beyond what Ersh had filtered for me during assimilation. Worst of all, there would be Skalet's unconcealed pride in her work. *How could she?*

I wouldn't put up with it. I'd hide until she left again. I'd—I'd undoubtably be found, reprimanded, and have my lesson anyway.

To hide the shaking of my gloved paws, I shoved them deep in the suds-filled sink to rescue drowning utensils. "I don't understand her," I said finally, unable to keep a hint of a growl from the words. "She acts as they do. Why?" With great daring, I clarified: "Why does Ersh permit it?"

"You'll have to ask Ersh."

The noise I made wasn't polite, but Ansky refrained from comment. "When she's ready, I'm sure you'll find out." Then she said something strange, something I would come to understand only later. "The forms we take are ourselves, Esen-alit-Quar. We are no more immune to our individual pasts than any civilization is immune to its history. Never fall into the trap of believing yourself other than the flesh you wear, no matter its structure. Skalet—" A tentacle nudged the pot I was holding in the air. "Enough gossip. I need that one next."

Much later, having done Ansky's cooking justice, I was doing my utmost to appear attentive and awake, my posture as impeccably straight as a form evolved from four-on-the-floor could manage. My involuntary yawns, however stifled, likely ruined the effect. "Was there anything else, Ersh?" I asked, before I could yawn again. It had been a longer day than most, given my now-departed Webkin had left disarray and laundry sprawled over their rooms. Being least and latest made any mess my responsibility.

The tall mound of crystal that was Ersh in her preferred

form gave an ominous chime. "Should I not ask you, Youngest?"

One of those "examine your soul for spots" questions. I was suddenly alert, if incapable of figuring out a safe answer.

Before I needed to do so, Ersh continued. "You would know more about Skalet's fascination with war."

How? I didn't quite gnash my teeth. I should have realized Ersh would have shared with each before they left her again. I couldn't blame Ansky. All Ersh had to do was take a nibble and she'd know all we'd done and experienced.

On the bright side, while I couldn't deny my question, she might answer it. "Yes, Ersh," I said hopefully.

Ersh leaned forward and I eased back, careful of my toes should she decide to tumble. A graceful and powerful mode of locomotion, but one I judged safer observed from a distance. "You wonder why I tolerate it?"

This being a far less comfortable question, I did my best to shrink in place without appearing defensive. It was a posture I'd yet to master, but the effort sometimes mollified Ersh. At least it made me feel a smaller target. Then, as usual, my inconvenient curiosity overwhelmed my sense of self-preservation. "You let her do terrible things," I whispered. "Why?"

"I let her be her form's self, Youngest," a correction, but mild. "The consequences are as they are."

"Beings suffer and die."

"Skalet engages in war, Youngest." As if this was an answer.

I tilted my head, wary but wanting more. "What of the Prime Laws? She ends sentience before its time."

"The Kraal are a violent species."

"Their species is Human," I corrected automatically.

Ersh's chime grew a shade testy. "A technicality. The Kraal refuse to mingle their genetic material with others of that heritage. It will not be long—as we measure time—before this is a matter of inability, not social preference. You would be wise to pay attention to this process. It is not uncommon among ephemeral cultures."

The ploy was familiar. Distract the youngest and she'll follow along. "Why—" I said stubbornly, "do you let Skalet participate so fully in this culture?"

Ersh settled herself with a slide of crystal over crystal. Reflected light ran over the floor, walls, and ceiling, making me squint. "You know the beginnings of that answer, Youngest." There was no doubt in her voice. "You were there, when Ansky and I discussed Skalet's first mission with the Kraal. From that, everything else has followed."

I'd been there? Before I could open my mouth to dispute this, however poor a decision that might have been, memory *rearranged* itself. To be more exact, memory reared up and shook me in sickening fashion from head to paw, recollections of that time before I had words of my own to use abruptly gaining coherance. With the perfect memory of my kind, it seemed I had recorded much I knew Skalet herself would have wished to know—

Or not.

Pressure mattered. Little else. Time. I knew the passage of days, marked them by movement conveyed by waves pressing against me.

Me. Me. Me. I knew me, that I existed, if then I had had no language in which to express that knowledge.

But the memory of a Web-being is perfect in every detail. So it was that when Ersh challenged me to consider such things as beginnings, I recalled my own—and by so doing, I applied what I'd learned since to the experiences so precisely recalled. The result was—interesting.

The waves of pressure which so entertained my protoself had been generated by three sources. The inner workings of Ansky's body—the pulse of heart and lungs, the rush of blood through arteries, the gurgling of her digestive tract—all of these transferred through the ammniotic fluid in which I rested as a symphony of pressures against the cells of my exquisitely sensitive skin. I'd hum along.

Then, there was the impact of large muscle movement. Oh, be sure I noticed when Ansky dropped to all fours, or stood on two legs, or bent over, or laughed.

Last, and most intriguing to recall, sound. I'd registered everything I'd heard through the walls and fluid of my living cradle through ears disposed to greater range than most sentient beings possessed.

Especially when those around me were, well, shouting.

I ignored innumerable heated discussions about Ansky's lamentable condition, cuing my memories to one word: Skalet. Sure enough, they'd argued about her as well.

"Skalet? She's incapable! A coward! I tell you I'll be fine. Send me. You know I'm better at learning culture, at blending in with other species. Let our Web-kin skulk somewhere else."

Skalet? Even as I tried to wrap my brain around what Ansky was saying, very loudly and with enough passion to shake my surroundings, Ersh replied, "Thanks to your blending, you can't travel until this latest creation of yours is uncorked and given to its father. I intend to monitor this emerging kind of Human closely. Skalet will go and she will learn them for us." The unspoken "or else" penetrated Ansky's abdomen; either that, or I was influenced by my subsequent wealth of experience with that tone.

My world shifted and jiggled, then a tidal wave hinted that Ansky had moved to another chair and dropped in it without care for me. Parental she wasn't. "It won't be long." This with certainty. Warmth implied a paw pressed over me. I kicked at it. "She's impatient."

Really, I wasn't. Especially in hindsight.

"She?" Ersh's chime was nicely ominous. "Don't become attached."

Perhaps my presence—or her preoccupation with its inconvenience—gave Ansky a little more spine than usual. "Becoming attached is my skill, Ersh. Who else brings back the interpersonal details we need about a sentient species? Who learns what it is to *be* that form? Skalet?" The growl under the word brought an instinctive echo from me, albeit consisting of a pathetic, soundless tensing of a breathing system that had no air in it yet. "Skalet spends her time in other forms—which is as little as possible—hiding in bushes. She uses gadgets to record from a distance, then presumes to tell us she's gathered information firsthand. But she'll have no convenient hiding places at this Kraal outpost. As befits a culture almost constantly in conflict, they're more fanatical than she is about surveillance. Her devices will be useless."

"Yes." Ersh somehow made the word smug.

I blinked free of memory, for an instant finding it odd to have air against my eyes. "You threw Skalet off a cliff," I concluded, doing my best to restrain a likely regrettable amount of triumph at the thought. Ersh had tossed me from her mountain to encourage my first cycle into Web-form. Skalet's plunge had been no less perilous for lack of rock at the bottom. For I knew the Kraal.

Not personally, being too young in Ersh's estimation to leave her Moon, but the assimilated memories of my Web-kin were clear enough. Kraal society had evolved an elaborate structure in which every individual had an allegiance to one or more of the ruling Houses through birth or action. Moreover, those allegiances, called affiliations, were permanently tattooed on each adult Kraal's face. While they allowed no images of themselves until death, to ensure only final affiliations were recorded for posterity, their gates were guarded by those who remembered faces exceedingly well. Only those who had been introduced by a known and trusted individual would be admitted, given that advancement through Kraal nobility typically involved assassination of rivals by as clever a means as possible.

Not a group to overlook a stranger.

"Why?" My favorite question. I stared at Ersh, a mountain of crystal shaped in hardness and edge.

Her voice could be as warm and soft as any flesh. "Why did I put her at risk? Because Skalet resisted being other than herself. The idea of a different form influencing who she was terrified her. She would be crippled by that fear, useless to our Web, unless forced to live it."

"Why the Kraal?" I whispered.

"A act of charity, Youngest." I must have looked confused, because Ersh clicked her digits together with an impatient ring. "Like Skalet, Kraal do not welcome physical contact, unless in practice drills. Like Skalet, they do not welcome personal questions. They share an obsession with intellect and games. And respect authority."

I ignored the last, most likely aimed at me. "What happened?"

As Ersh winked into the blue teardrop of her Web-form, I realized my curiosity was once more taking me where I'd doubtless regret going.

Not that fear could stop instinct. I released my hold on this form, cycling into my true self, and formed a mouth for Ersh's offering of the past.

Gloves froze and stiffened; coat fabric froze and crinkled. The slight *whoof* of air that escaped the face mask with each breath added its moisture to the rim of ice searing both cheeks and chin, that flesh rapidly losing all feeling anyway. Another being might have feared the cold, the darkness, and the howl of a wind that ripped unchallenged across this plain of floating ice from an empty ocean six hundred kilometers away.

Then again, another being wouldn't have preferred chipping frost from the antenna array, a duty that entailed far more than finding and climbing a ladder in the dark, over company and warmth. But Skalet craved these moments of solitude, no matter how punishing to her Humanself.

For the Kraal outpost was as close to a hell as any Human legend remembered by the Web. At the southern pole of an uninhabited world known only by a number, those assigned to it faced two seasons: a summer of sharp blinding ice crystals, in air that struggled up to minus twenty degrees Celsius under an unsetting sun; or a winter of utter darkness, where ceaselessly drifting snow erased the tracks of any who dared move outside at temperatures that solidified oil, let alone flesh.

Not that either season made hiding easier. In the summer, movement could only be concealed within tunnels through the snow, joining each of the domes. In the winter, radiation leaked by suit or building would betray them. For this was an outpost of that deadly kind: a spy set in place for a war that might come their way, at best an expendable asset, at worst, a prized target.

Skalet, to her surprise and growing dismay, fit in too well.

The eighteen stationed at the outpost were, to put it plainly, disposable. The arrival of another such was occasion for no more than a shifting of bunk assignments. Skalet's calm acceptance of a lowermost bed had nothing to do with stoicism, although it impressed the Kraal. Dumping heat was essential for a Web-being forced to hold another form and the temperature at floor level in all the buried domes was close to freezing. A cold bed was thus, as Skalet would say, *convenient*.

But her behavior set a pattern. Ersh's orders and her situation notwithstanding, our reluctant Web-kin wanted as little to do with Kraal as possible. She took the worst shifts. She'd seek out the most dangerous, dirty tasks and do them alone. She'd eat first or last and clean up every trace of her existence. Unfortunately for Skalet, everything she did to avoid the other eighteen at the outpost only served to enhance her reputation. The others admired her fortitude, nicknamed her Icicle, and whispered of rapid promotion. Several went so far as to broach offers of support, gambling, with the single-mindedness of true Kraal, her inevitable rise in rank would similarly increase that of her allies.

Skalet had no idea how to stop any of it, short of disobeying Ersh and fleeing this world.

Case in point, this afternoon's trip out to the antenna array. Skalet would have let someone else take the dangerous duty—and praise—but such excursions were her only escape from the populated tunnels and tiny rooms of the outpost.

And there was, she admitted, a peculiar satisfaction in pushing this form to its limits. There could be no radiation released outside the protection of the walls and snow cover—a snow cover that had to be routinely reduced or they'd be buried permanently. Such radiation would not only risk discovery of what was to be a secret from all Kraal but House Bryll, but would also ruin the observations being made by the sensitive equipment—the reason for being here in the first place.

This meant no light or beacons to guide her from the safety of the outpost to the array. Instead, Skalet reached for and found the guide line leading from the dome entrance to the distant equipment. If she let go, it was a step in any direction to be completely lost. If she was in truth what she seemed, it would be a long while before her frozen body would be recovered.

They'd lost two techs this winter, before her arrival, a distressing tally even for the Kraal.

Skalet knew every step of this journey, the ramplike rise to the surface from the dome entrance, the hit of wind, the emptiness to every side.

But even she kept her glove, stiff and frozen, on the line there and back.

It took as long to peel off the rock-hard layers of frozen cold-weather gear as it had to stagger out to the array, dig free the ladder's base, climb the ladder, dig free the chipping tools, and hammer clear the tracks, wires, and supports. All the while the wind. All the while the knowledge that nothing else stood above ground. Hopefully.

Skalet fought her numb fingers and toes, hanging her

coats by their hoods on the hooks lining the corridor walls. No space was wasted. Her gloves went into mesh hanging from the ceiling, taking advantage of the warmer air to dry. Boot liners joined the gloves. Drops of sweat melted from her hair and she swept the loose strands impatiently beneath their strapping. She'd shave the stuff, but to be inconspicuous among the fashion-obsessed Kraal of this era meant shoulder-length locks confined by annoying leather bands. *Inefficient.*

A similarly-banded head popped out from one of the small round doors. "Good timing, Icicle."

Skalet raised one eyebrow. "How so, Lieutenant?"

Lieutenant Maven-ro, a capable sparring partner when not exhibiting a curiosity the equal of a certain Web-kin's, and as little welcome, flicked her fingers against the bright red tattoo curled on her right cheek. House Bryll held her affiliation, that promise of unquestioned obedience, if not the return vow of unwavering protection. Front line Kraal soldiers understood their worth. Skalet's own cheek bore a twin mark, though applied in paint rather than imbedded ink. "We've guests."

Guests? How had she missed an arriving transport? Alarmed, Skalet reached for the knives in her belt. The energy weapons the Kraal favored were forbidden within the domes. Fire was the enemy; extinguishers hung at intervals on every wall and drills woke them just as regularly. Were these guests a new threat?

"An unexpected visit, but by one who is entitled to do so." Maven-ro's eyes gleamed approval. "Come. A meeting's called. Your presence is commanded, Icicle. If you've sufficiently thawed, that is."

Humor. The Kraal, like other Humans, were prone to its use in stressful situations. Skalet saw no purpose to it.

The thought of some Kraal authority interested in her didn't help her feel any better.

* * *

Meetings were held in the one room large enough to hold everyone, the dining hall. Not by accident, it was the only portion of the outpost to benefit from the Kraal aesthetic— at least to the extent that the wall without kitchen equipment was crusted with gilded metal plaques commemorating the achievements of House Bryll in battle. A small and central spot was reserved for accomplishments from this obscure little outpost. The Kraal were also afflicted with Human optimism.

In Skalet's judgment, the expected future of the place was more accurately seen in the lack of ornamentation anywhere else. The poorest Kraal House indulged in ostentatious display everywhere possible; even warships boasted wood carving and lush upholstery. Here was ice, frost-covered metal, and bags of supplies.

Reluctantly accepting her tiny glass of serpitay, the ceremonial drink no Kraal gathering of import could start without, Skalet eased behind others. She couldn't disappear from view completely; her Humanself was taller than most of the Kraal assigned here. Every set of shoulders was braced, as if ready for anything.

A querulous voice demanded, "This is all?"

"The full complement, Your Eminence." The outpost's commander, Dal-ru, touched the backs of his hands to his tattooed cheeks and bowed, a gesture echoed by everyone in the room. "We await your pleasure."

The pleasure they awaited belonged to the oldest Kraal Skalet had ever seen. Ersh-memory held older, but not by much. In a culture like the Kraal's, such age meant extraordinary value to a House, toughness, or, most likely, both. The female's maze of tattoos warred with wrinkles; her face might have been heartwood, ringed by the passing of countless seasons, a record of survival and success, for they were the same among Kraal.

Impressive.

"What's the status of the fleet?"

"Fleet, Your Eminence?" Skalet was amused by the immediate tensing by everyone in the room. She knew, as well as they there'd been nothing on their scans for months. Which made the obedient Kraal likely to offend this noble no matter what. Dal-ru took the braver course. "We haven't detected any ship movements."

Her Eminence had not come alone, although her entourage was peculiarly small for a noble away from flagship or homeworld. Undoubtably, Skalet thought, others waited outside the domes, perhaps within the connecting tunnels. A courier, for such the noble must be, traveled with sufficient force to affect the actions desired by her House. Here and now, she was flanked by only two black-garbed guards, taller than Skalet, more muscular than the most· fit crew of the outpost, girded with every weapon possible, including several that would be fatal to all if used in this room. Now one stooped to whisper something urgent in the courier's ear. She shooed him away impatiently. "Then that's the status, isn't it?" she snapped. "I trust you have eyes on all scans for when that changes?"

Seven Kraal bowed hurriedly and dashed from the room. Two had been in front of Skalet. Thus exposed, she found herself caught by the curious regard of the old noblewoman's milky eyes. "Who are you?"

Skalet's bow was impeccable, the brush of knuckles to fake tattoo exquisite. Inwardly, she trembled. "S'kal-ru, Your Eminence. Tech Class—"

"Ah. The Dauntless Icicle. Attend me." The noblewoman rose to her feet without assistance, a smooth efficient motion that lifted Skalet's eyebrow in involuntary appreciation. *Admirable.*

I knew Ersh filtered my Web-kin's reactions to their own experiences before sharing them with me, probably viewing most as nonessential to my learning. Oh, I assimilated physical sensations, such as taste, and useful emotions such as fear, but, to this point in my life, the latter came to me so dimmed the memories could have belonged to any of us. This sharing was different. The intensity of Skalet's fascination with the old Kraal came through as clearly as the remembered chill from the outpost. I fluffed out my fur and shivered. "I thought Skalet didn't want to be noticed."

"What have I told you about asking questions before you've finished assimilating?"

"Wasn't a question," I mumbled, hastily dipping back into memory.

Ersh, as usual, was right. I now owned this part of Skalet's past—whether I wanted to or not.

"They tell me you don't feel the cold, S'kal-ru. Is this true?"

Skalet, granted the unthinkable privilege of being allowed to sit in the presence of such high rank, hesitated.

"Come now. I didn't invite you here to be a statue. If you won't converse, let me hear that lovely voice of yours. Your commander didn't exaggerate. Surely you sing."

Banter, from someone like this, was even more unthinkable. Skalet felt her skin warming as her stressed form dumped heat. Luckily, this intimate setting was, as befitted the outpost, barely above freezing. Their breath mingled and twisted in the air like the fumes of forgotten dragons. "I don't sing, Your Eminence," Skalet said with a hidden shudder, then added honestly. "I don't mind the cold."

"You don't let yourself mind it. That is good. Very good. So few learn to control the flesh, to put aside the instincts that would keep us cowering by the fire."

As this didn't seem to require a response, Skalet merely looked attentive. Her Eminence had taken Dal-ru's office, a room hardly used since its location in a poorly insulated storage dome made it impossible to heat properly. Cases of beer lined the wall behind the ancient Kraal. She'd ignored them, more intent on this strange conversation.

"So tell me, Icicle, of the state of affairs among the Houses of Bract, Noitci, and Ordin."

On familiar ground again, Skalet took care to answer as any Kraal here could. "The Bract and Noitci share fourth-, possibly fifth-level historical affiliations; both hold ninth-level affiliation with House Bryll. Ordin is a newer House, also affiliated to House Bryll." She flicked her fingers over her tattoo. "Through us, Ordin gains third-level affiliation with both Bract and Noitci."

The wrinkles and tattoos reshaped into a look of pure satisfaction. "The nexus being ours. The position of strength."

Skalet frowned slightly in thought, but didn't dare speak.

She didn't have to. The Kraal was terrifyingly good at reading faces. "You see some flaw," she guessed softly. "Interesting. Tell me. I grant you leave to criticize your own House."

"As you wish." Challenged, Skalet drew upon memory. "House Arzul, powerful yet inherently unstable, recently lost reputation and ships to Noitci, itself a fairly weak House, but thanks to a high-status alliance, temporarily enjoying a tenth-level affiliation with Bract, one of the strongest and noblest." She found herself warming to her topic. Her own kin had no appreciation for the subtlety of this culture. "Arzul will rally to reclaim those losses. The nobles of Ordin are too impatient for power and lineage to let this opportunity slip by, or worse, be taken by a rival. They will attack Arzul, acquire affiliation with Noitci through blood debt, and thus gain ties to Bract. Unless House Bryll acts, it will be forced from the nexus to the outside of a new, powerful set of alliances, losing a great deal of status. Perhaps more than a House can afford to lose." A disgraced Kraal House was like a fresh corpse to scavengers. Something to dismember.

"Acts how?" softer still. The Kraal noble leaned forward, creased chin on one palm, sunken eyes intent on Skalet. "Go on."

Skalet could see it so clearly, like pieces on a board before a skilled hand swept them aside. "A preemptive move against Bract. Remove its alliance with Noitci by assassinating the First Daughter before her union, then remove the five who remain in the Bract Inner Circle."

The wrinkles mapped nothing worse than curiosity. "You'd sacrifice a powerful ally and two former lovers of mine to what gain, S'kal-ru?"

"The audacity of the strike would enhance our affiliation with Ordin, a House of significant future promise should Bryll help it survive its own impetuousness. At the same time, Arzul would lose its patron, removing it as a threat to Noitci. Noitci, its alliance cut, would in turn be diminished, as would any affiliations outside of House Bryll held by Noitci and Arzul, drawing both closer to Bryll. Finally, and most importantly, existing alliances would mean the Inner Circle of Bryll would dominate that of Bract in the next generation. The closest affiliations between Houses of true power. All Kraal would benefit."

"This presumes success."

Skalet let herself smile, nothing more.

"Few think in generations. They want gains now, in their lifetimes."

"'What are lifetimes but strokes on a canvas?'"

"You quote N'kar-ro. Not easy reading, S'kal-ru. Again, you impress." The noble paused, wrinkles deepening. "How has Bryll overlooked such quality as yours?"

Not a safe question. "I should return to duty, Your Eminence."

"Your duty is to keep me company while we wait."

"Wait for what?" Skalet's own audacity shocked her.

The courier merely nodded, as if she'd expected the question. "For fools, S'kal-ru, who lack your grasp of tactics. Oh, they see the same patterns, but rather than the prick of a pin in the hollow of a neck, the certainty of poison built for one, they prefer the sound of trumpets and mountains of rubble."

"A planetary assault force?" Skalet's eyes widened. All she'd learned of Kraal pointed to a growing control and finesse of conflict, not a return to the devastating attacks that had almost ended this race in its infancy. "Against what target?"

The other woman's mouth twisted and she turned her head to spit decorously over her own shoulder. "Farmland. Factories. The uninvolved. The *sous*."

Sous. Noncombatants. The quiet majority of Kraal, who served their affiliations through a lifetime of peace and accomplishment, fueling the vast economy that afforded the great Houses their wealth—by convention and utter common sense, untouchable.

Until now. "You must stop them!" Skalet blanched at the ring of command in her own voice. "Forgive me, Your Eminence. I meant no disrespect."

"I heard none. Conflict as a challenge to advance a House tempers our society. Strip challenge from conflict and we become no better than Ganthor, squabbling for the day's profit. Yet even that shame can be forgiven, with time." Her fingers formed a gnarled fist, punching down through the air between them. "To attack those who provide for all? That, S'kal-ru, is to court our own extinction. Which is why I need you, Icicle."

Perhaps some part of Skalet remembered the Ersh and the Prime Law. If so, she made a choice to disregard both for the first time in her life.

"What do you want me to do, Your Eminence?"

Circles within circles, folded back on each other until the overall pattern of Kraal society appeared more an orgy of snakes than an organization of Humans—or those whose ancestry traced back to the same trees. Despite the perception of the non-Kraal, war had never been a game to those who created the Great Houses and defended them. They waged their power struggles without losing sight of the future or their desire to make it as they wished. There was much to admire in a culture that took charge of its own evolution.

Until those who believed they had the right chose the

short path, the one that wasted the lives and resources on which the future depended.

Skalet fastened the strap of her goggles around her neck, then methodically checked the laces and zips of her clothing. One opening and this form could suffer frostbite and impairment. She could risk neither tonight.

Her role was deceptively simple, elegant in Kraal terms. The Bryll assault fleet would pass in range of this outpost on its way to attack the Bract homesystem, to take advantage of their scans to detect and warn of any Bract ships in the area. Their fleet would remain unseen until it was too late to mount a defense. Except that Her Eminence, as Courier to Bryll's Inner Circle, specifically those within that Circle in opposition to those mounting the assault, had sent a coded message to the Bract, recommending this system as the ideal place for an ambush.

Bryll would sacrifice her own, Skalet the pin to prick the unsuspecting throat.

Maven-ro, always alert to comings and goings, appeared in her doorway. "Didn't you just come in, Icicle?"

"Hours back." Skalet shrugged her fur-cased shoulders. "Weather's worsening. We can't risk anything impeding reception." She flicked two fingers against her pseudo-tattooed cheek. They'd all been briefed by Dal-ru on the importance of protecting the fleet.

Maven-ro's look wasn't as approving as usual. In fact, she began to frown. "It's bad enough out there even Her Eminence's guard has come inside. There's no indication of ice buildup yet. Stay."

Skalet lifted a brow. "If I wait until there's a problem, it could be too late. You know that."

The Kraal shook her head. "There's attention to duty and there's being a fool, S'kal-ru. The winds have doubled. You won't be able to stay on your feet, let alone hold to the guide line."

Skalet rattled the clip and safety cable around her waist. "I'm prepared."

Maven-ro threw up her hands. "Fine. Go freeze stiff. If we find you this spring, we'll stand you up as a flagpole."

It didn't seem like humor. Puzzled, Skalet watched as the other walked away, slamming a door unnecessarily behind her, then returned to her own preparations.

It was worse. Unimaginably worse. The moment the outer door retracted, the wind howled inside the tunnel, blowing Skalet off her feet, rolling her along the icy floor until she hit the yielding edge of a fuel bag. The rubbery material gave her a grip as she pulled herself to her feet.

At least it was a steady wind, to start. She could force her way against it and did, reaching first the doorframe, then the outer wall, and, after groping in the dark, the guide line. She clipped herself to it, and pressed out into the night.

Lean, drag a foot free, move it up and forward, push it into yielding softness to the knee, to the thigh. Skalet couldn't predict her footing. Drifts were curling and reforming like living things. All she could do was drag the other foot free, up and forward, push it down, and progress in lurches and semi-falls.

She'd run out of choices. There was no living mass except that behind her. Without a source, she could not release her hold on this form and choose another more suited to surviving these conditions. Not and return to the outpost as S'kal-ru. Only living matter could be assimilated into more Web-flesh, and she'd need to replace what she used.

There was escape. She almost considered it as the wind lifted her for an instant, her grip torn from the guide line, one outer glove sailing free and only the cable jerking snug around her waist keeping her in place. She could cycle into a form that flew on this wind, pick one able to hide beneath ice for however many decades it would take for Ersh to notice her absence and send one of her kin to retrieve her. *Disgraced.*

Skalet dropped to the ground as the wind caught its breath, then drove herself to her feet. If she failed for whatever reason, Her Eminence had another option. She could destroy the outpost and all the talented, complicated beings in it, including herself. *Wasteful.*

It was only a question of one step after another. This form would obey her will. It would endure. Skalet pulled her right hand, now clad only in the liner, within the sleeve of her innermost coat, shoving the cuff through her belt as tightly as possible. She would need those fingers able to function once at the ladder.

Her goggles were coated with snow, despite the fur trim around her hood. No matter. What use were eyes without light? She leaned into the wind again, trusting to the cable. One step after another, a movement that grew only more difficult as she lost feeling below her knees. No matter. She could not control time or the movement of starships, but she could control this body. It would succeed.

At some point, the howl dimmed to a whine and the force pushing her back lessened. Skalet smiled, lips cracking, blood burning her chin. She had reached the array.

The clip had frozen shut. Rather than waste energy fighting it, Skalet drew her knife and cut the cable around her waist. She staggered and caught herself with a grip on the ladder as the wind tried to peel her away again. The climb was a nightmare. Not only were the lower rungs half-buried in a rising drift, but she could not longer judge where her feet would land. Three times Skalet neared the top, only to lose her grip and slip back down.

Once on the platform, she didn't bother looking for the ice-breaking tools. Skalet felt her way down the nearest strut to its linkage with the rest, found the fastener. She drew her knife once more, then shook her head. No traces. Even if House Bryll was as devastated as the courier implied, there would be an investigation. Like other Humans, the Kraal were curious, tenacious beings. Unlike other Humans, the Kraal took the assignment of fault to extremes. For the crew of this outpost to outlive their doomed fleet, this had to appear an accident.

Skalet put away her knife and pulled off the outer glove on her left hand, securing it in her belt. Her fingers turned numb almost immediately, but she managed to grip the fastener and twist. It was meant to be mobile to minus seventy degrees Celsius, so the antenna could be replaced at need. It wouldn't budge.

Cursing substandard equipment, Skalet stripped off her liner and the other glove, restraining a cry as the wind seemed to flay her skin. She pressed both palms around the fastener, warming it with her own, slightly greater than Human, heat. The core of her body seemed to chill at the same time, a dangerous theft. Skalet fought to hold form as much as she fought to keep her hands where they had to stay.

Another twist. Nothing. She screamed in fury and drove her fist into the metal, feeling a knuckle break, but something else give as well. *Satisfaction.* Another twist and the fastener came free.

By now, Skalet's hands were shaking so violently she could barely get them back into the gloves. She couldn't feel any difference with the protection on, but knew it was necessary. Form-memory was perfect. If she lost fingers to frostbite, she'd remember herself that way forever. She refused to believe it might be too late.

Meanwhile, the wind, now her ally, was busy at work. The strut creaked and groaned, succumbing to the force hammering it. Skalet touched the support, feeling irregular shudders. Good. It would take only the slightest of bends to make the antenna uncontrollable. As if hearing her thoughts, the strut snapped and the array began to tilt.

The outpost—and the fleet—was blind.

Time to leave. Skalet made her way back down the ladder, groping in the dark with her left hand for the guide line. The right she'd drawn inside her coat completely, cradling it next to her heart, a source of searing pain as the flesh thawed and the abused knuckle complained of ill treatment. *Reassuring.*

She'd anticipated an easier return journey, the wind shoving from behind and her trail already broken through the drifts. Instead, with a perversity she should have expected, the wind was a wall in her face and her footsteps had filled with snow. There was only the guide line and the strength of her grip on it.

Her progress became a series of forward stumbles, never quite on her knees, never quite stopping. At any moment, Skalet expected to collide with a Kraal hurrying from the outpost to see what had gone wrong, to try a futile repair. Ephemeral and fragile, yet they readily risked their fleeting lives. *Exceptional.*

Then the line came alive in her hand, yanking her backward into the snow before becoming limp. Skalet stood and gave a sharp pull in the direction of the outpost. The line came toward her with no more tension than its weight dragging through the snow.

The entire array must have become unstable, the bent antenna a sail catching too much wind. Whether the structure had toppled to the ground or merely leaned didn't matter. It had moved enough to pluck the uncuttable guide line from the outpost dome.

So much for meeting a Kraal.
So much for finding her way back.

I whined and curled in a ball, my tail covering nose and eyes with a plume of fur. Despite this, and despite being perfectly safe and warm, I shook miserably. I'd assimilated nothing like this before. I'd never felt what it was like to truly risk one's formself. My other Web-kin, being far more sensible, would have cycled long before this point. I would have. Skalet's resolve was as horrifying as the Kraal themselves.

If I could have stopped remembering, I would have. But Ersh had given me all of it and I whirled through Skalet's memories as haplessly as a snowflake—or the Kraal fleet.

*   *   *

This form reacted to fear with a rush of blood to the ears, a sickness in the stomach. Skalet ignored biology, intent on her problem. She couldn't see, feel, or hear her way to safety. The broken line in her hand, however, would give her the distance from the array to the outpost. The wind in her face would give her direction. A risk, given that same wind had already swung one hundred and eighty degrees, but an acceptable one. If she reached the end of the guide line and found nothing, she could walk in an arc bounded by the line—if she could move it—and have a fifty percent chance of being right. Or have to abandon this form when it reached its physiological limit.

But not before.

The guide line proved harder to combat than the wind. Though light, its length gave it considerable mass and weight. Exposed portions flailed with every gust, the rest being buried by the snow of a continent. Skalet barely managed to hang on to the piece by her side and keep moving. Her best estimate put her near or within the outer ring of domes, but they were difficult to detect under good conditions, let alone in the dark. Her goal was the ramp down to the central dome.

Her feet started fighting a drift larger and more compact than most she'd encountered. Gasping with effort, Skalet nonetheless felt a thrill of hope. There were always drifts curving around the slight rise of each dome. She began step down the other side and suddenly lost her footing as well as her grip on the line. Before she could recapture it, it was gone.

Skalet sat on the slope of the drift and replayed memory. She knew this area, had walked its winter night a hundred times. Yes. She should be able to see the dome from here.

Skalet pulled her hand from inside her coat, using both to remove her goggles. Instantly the cold hit her eyes and lashes, freezing them shut. She rubbed away the beads of ice to peer into the darkness, flinching at needles of hard, dry snow.

There. Skalet threw herself at that dimmest of glows, re-fusing to believe it was anything but the rim of the door she'd left hours earlier. Seconds later, she was moving down the ramp, waist-deep in new snow but out of the wind at last. The door. Her fingers wouldn't work anymore. Sobbing with fury, tears freezing to her cheeks, Skalet fought this be-trayal as she tried to open the latches.

They opened of their own accord, a figure mummified in fur blocking the light from within. With an incoherent cry, the figure caught Skalet in gloved hands and drew her inside.

The warmth, near the freezing point, was an exquisite agony. Skalet shuddered on the iced floor, gulping air that didn't burn her lungs. The figure pulled off hood and gog-gles, becoming Maven-ro.

She crouched beside Skalet. "So the Icicle can freeze after all," she shook her head. "Give your report then get to medical. Scan's gone down at the worst possible time. I'm off to see what I can do about it."

"No . . . no point," Skalet wasn't vain about her voice as a Human, but even she was shocked by its reed-thin sound. She got to her knees, wheezing: "The array . . . it's col-lapsed . . . the storm. Guide line's ripped loose . . ."

Maven-ro's face paled beneath its tattoo, but her mouth formed a firm line. "It is our privilege to serve. The fleet re-lies on us, S'kal-ru." She stood, replacing her goggles and hood. "I must see what can be done."

With her better hand, Skalet found and held the other's sleeve, used it to pull herself to her feet. What she hoped were feet—she couldn't feel them. She didn't understand why she felt compelled to stop the Kraal; a flaw in this form, perhaps. "There's duty and there's being a fool. You told me that, Maven-ro." She staggered and Maven-ro was forced to steady her. "Dare you think I would give up and return if there was any hope of restoring the array?"

Maven-ro lowered her head. She dragged off her goggles with one hand, keeping the other firm on Skalet's belt. "For-

give me, S'kal-ru. There are none braver—" Her fingers
flattened protectively over the tattoo on her cheek; her eyes,
haunted, lifted to meet Skalet's. "But now I fear the worst."

Hands and feet bandaged with dermal regenerators,
which with typical Kraal sensibility did nothing to relieve
pain, Skalet was in no mood for company. But her visitor
that outpost night wasn't one she could refuse, however
dangerous.

The courier waved the med tech from the tiny clinic.
"Have you heard, S'kal-ru?"

The surprise attack, the ragged desperate signals, and incoming casualty lists had silenced the domes. Kraal walked
in a daze, huddled in anguished groups, worried about their
future, their affiliations. Except this one. "You brought
down your own House," Skalet observed, curious. Under the
blanket, her bandaged fingers gripped a knife.

The courier smiled. Her age-spotted fingers lifted to the
mask of tattoos on her face, selected one. "With you as my
poison, I have cleaned it of those who would have destroyed
it. Bryll will rise to prominence once more."

"I don't doubt it."

"But you doubt your own future."

Skalet smiled thinly. "I'm a realist. With what I know, I
should prepare to disappear." Which, given transport and a
moment unobserved with some living mass, S'kal-ru the
Kraal would do.

The old woman's eyes narrowed to slits. "Let go the
knife. You are of more value than risk to me."

A figure of speech? Then again, a noble who aged in this
society would be no fool at all. Skalet brought her empty
hand above the blanket.

"Good. I have another future for you to consider, S'kal-
ru. I warn you. It means none of the comforts of homeworld
or hearth. No lineages sprung from your flesh."

"I don't seek such things."

"No. No, I believe you don't. Yet you embody all that

Kraal aspires to be, which is why I won't see you wasted."
As Skalet twitched, the tattoos around the other's lips
writhed. A smile, perhaps. "Hear me out."

"I'm at your command, Your Eminence."

"The Noble Houses must communicate, one to the other,
even in times of distrust and blood debt. To this end exist
such as I, individuals of such clear honor we are given extraordinary latitude without hesitation. There are no watches
on our comings and goings. No impediments to our actions;
no constraint beyond affiliation. We are few, but we are cru-
cial to the survival of our civilization, as you have seen. I
would have you train as my successor, S'kal-ru." The old
Kraal moved her hand slowly, carefully, toward Skalet's
cheek. Involuntarily, Skalet reared her head back and away.
Then, for no reason save self-preservation, she froze to permit the touch. Cold, dry fingers traced the fake tattoo once,
lightly. "This might pass muster here, but never on a Kraal
world. If you permit me, I will make it real. A ninth-level affiliation through me to House Bract, today's power. What do
you say, Icicle?"

To be secretive yet a decision-maker, to be needed for her
abilities, not just as another collector of dry facts and genetic
information.

Skalet found a way to bow gracefully, even lying down.

"I take it you finished." Ersh tumbled to where I stood staring out the window. Picco's orange reflection cast shadows the
color of drying blood. I found it singularly appropriate.

"Yes," I said quietly. "It's called seduction, isn't it? When
you are brought to desire something until it's impossible to
refuse it."

"Apt enough." A chime that might have been pleasure. Or
impatience. The tones were regrettably similar. "Skalet
might not have grown so—attached—to this culture, had she
not been taught to thrive in it."

"Thrive?" I growled. "She's responsible for the deaths of
thousands."

"That's what war is, Youngest," Ersh agreed. "A uniquely ephemeral conceit, to settle disputes by ending life."

"Then why? Why do you let Skalet continue? Why not send Ansky or the others?"

"Why tolerate insolence?" I acknowledged the rebuke by lifting my ears, which had plastered themselves to my skull in threat when I wasn't paying attention. Ersh touched a fingertip to the stone sill of the window and the bell-like sound echoed from the corners of the room. *Apology accepted.* "Skalet's mission to the Kraal outpost was her first successful interaction with another species. It has been her only success. She can spy on any species, glean information from a host of cultures, but fails every time to get closer. Except with the Kraal. So you see, Youngling, it is not always simple to decide which of your Web-kin goes where. It matters where they feel they can belong."

I had to assume Ersh was telling me something important, but it made no sense. "Skalet wants to belong to the Kraal?"

Ersh didn't often laugh as a Tumbler. The species was prone to a more taciturn outlook. But now she tinkled like a rush of wind through icicles. "Esen-alit-Quar. You have so much to learn. Skalet may be obsessed with the Kraal and this form, but she is one of us above all else. She would never forge true bonds outside our Web."

I shuddered at the thought, heretical and yet attractive, in the way sharp edges attract fingertips. There was a trap I would avoid at all costs. Along with war.

Like many young beings, I would have to wait for the future to prove me wrong.

THE CHILDREN OF DIARDIN:
TO FIND THE ADVANTAGE

by Fiona Patton

*Fiona Patton was born in Alberta and grew up in the
United States. In 1975 she returned to Canada, and
after a series of unrelated jobs including electrician
and carnival ride operator, moved to rural Ontario
with her partner, one tiny dog, and a series of ever
changing cats. Her Branion series which includes*
The Stone Prince, The Painter Knight, The Granite
Shield, *and* The Golden Sword *has been published by
DAW Books. She has just finished the first book of
a new series tentatively titled* The Silver Lake, *also
for DAW.*

THE LATE SUMMER SUN shone down on the fruit-
laden orchards of Armagh, dappling the flanks of the
hound pack racing through the trees in otherworldly silence;
not hunting but simply running for the sheer joy of laying
paws to earth. In the lead, Fothran and Pepitain, the alpha
male and female hounds of Goll mac Morna, Sub-Captain of
the Fianna of Ulaidh, ran as effortlessly as the wind, their
ruddy pelts flashing in the sun like fire. Behind them, Sarrack, long-legged hound of Cunnaun, ran beside Garra's
huge, tan-pelted Camlan and spotted Droga of the Bard

Daighre—old and gray-muzzled, but still fast and strong. Making up the bulk of the pack behind came the hounds of the Ulaidh Fianna: siblings Farran and Daol always together, black-pelted Derkame and Deealath, golden-flanked Gloss, and tangle-coated Fooam with her whelp of the same name, leading a dozen more of every size, shape; and description. In their midst, the enchanted children of Diardin, members of the Fianna all, white pelts and red-tipped ears betraying their Sidhe blood, ran together with their own mortal hounds close behind.

Keeping pace beside her older siblings Isien and Tierney, Brae Diardin ran as if nothing in the world existed beyond the wind whistling through her ears and the rich scent of sun-warmed earth and flowers mingling with the heady odors of the dog pack all around her. She wanted to bark and howl and jump high in the air with the thrill of it. With a double skip, she suddenly veered sideways, leaping straight over her younger brother Cullen—just fifteen and newly accepted into the Fianna—then put on a burst of speed and danced away as he snapped at her flank. She could have run for days but all too soon Goll's high, piercing whistle called them back to camp. Fothran and Pepitain turned in a wide arc and, behind them, the pack flowed through the trees like so many streams of fur and flashing collars of gold and silver.

They reached the outskirts of the Fianna's summer encampment within minutes, the children of Diardin and their hounds breaking off at the edge of the orchards. One moment four white and four brindle-colored dogs milled about; the next, four long-legged, copper-haired youths sprawled on the ground, laughing and panting with their hounds dancing about beside them. Ever practical Isien immediately made for the place they'd hidden their clothes while Tierney aimed a punch at Cullen. The younger brother avoided it neatly, then tripped over a small hillock and went straight over backward. Laughing, Brae walked a few paces away, enjoying the feel of the wind on her skin and the last of the scents of field and woods that slowly faded from her mortal senses.

She noticed the heavy-set man standing in the nearby copse of ash trees long before he tossed her a tunic with a disapproving snort.

She grinned widely at him. "Thanks, Cunnaun, it's Tierney's." She threw the tunic at her older brother, ignoring the egregious frown of her battalion's Sub-Captain with practiced ease. "Are you looking for Sarrack?"

He glowered at her. "I was looking for you and the rest of your irresponsible kindred," he growled, then grunted as his own hound stuffed her nose into his groin. "Yes, and you too, you fickle little wretch." He fondled the dog's ears before turning a new scowl on the children of Diardin. "And have been for the past hour," he continued. "Put some clothes on, for Anu's sake; I need to talk to you."

Accepting the tunic Isien held out to her, Brae cocked her head to one side. "Is there word from Tara?"

He shook his head. "From Glencolumbkille in Donegal. A vast company of strange, martial creatures were seen rising from the sea two days ago."

"Creatures?" Isien asked.

He nodded as Tierney and Cullen ambled over to join them. "Some were like men but thin and twisted like blighted branches; others were the size of trees and as broad across."

"Giants?"

"Could be. Apparently they had green beards and long, flowing hair, like strands of kelp."

"*Sea* giants."

"Again, could be. The messenger didn't see them herself; she just has the word of a terrified villager from Stranoran. Goll wants a scouting party sent to check it out. One that's fast and silent. Naturally I thought of you." He glanced over at the four youths, noting with a frown that the two brothers were now attacking each other with rolled up tunics. "For the fast, anyway. You're to leave at once and be back by dusk tomorrow at the very latest. I need two minimum," he said, holding up two large, scarred fingers.

"I'll go," Brae offered at once. "We've been here too long already and I'm bored."

"Count me in. I'm bored too," Tierney added, catching Cullen's head in the crook of one arm.

"You're not leaving me behind," his brother warned in a muffled voice.

Cunnaun cast an expectant glance at Isien, who stretched languidly before raising a copper-colored eyebrow at him.

"What?"

"Only three eager volunteers among Diardin's heirs?" he asked in a sarcastic voice.

She glanced over at her siblings, who gave her three equally wide grins, then sighed. "I suppose. I *had* wanted a bath and a nap. And what are you doing?" she demanded as Brae began to pull her tunic off again.

The younger woman blinked at her. "If we go in hound form we can run on four feet the whole way," she answered. "It's faster."

"And spy on the enemy without weapons or clothing," Isien replied caustically. "It's stupider."

Tierney threw one arm over his birth-mate's shoulder. "Ah, c'mon, Sis, you know it's . . . funner."

"Funner?"

"Sure. And this way you won't have to listen to Cullen complaining the entire way, either. That'll be quieter."

"Hey!" Pulling out of his grip, his brother glared resentfully at him.

Isien nodded. "Very good point."

"You put us down in a patch of nettles." Twisting his right forearm to peer at the line of fine stickers in his wrist, Cullen shot an injured look at his older sister.

"*Shh!*" Tierney snapped at him, then turned to stare out at the coast of Donegal. "This is not good," he breathed.

Beside him, Brae and Isien nodded.

They'd run until the sun had set, then taken a few hours sleep—curled up together with their hounds under the lee of an ancient and moss-covered portal grave—then continued to run through the moon-silvered pastureland of Armagh and Donegal until Brae scared up a hare. They broke off to give chase then, after a quick—very small—meal of rabbit meat shared between eight, carried on running. Just after dawn they reached the coast and climbed a high, limestone outcropping overlooking the sea. As they peered through the scant underbrush at the dawn-streaked beach, they saw dozens of huge figures rising from the surf to join those already on land. A heavy trail of broken underbrush and churned sand leading east told them that far too many had already begun the trek inland.

His eyes wide, Tierney nudged Isien in the shoulder.

"How big would you say they were, Sis?"

"Ten, twelve feet tall, maybe?" She squinted. "The smaller ones only look five though."

"They could be goblins," Brae supplied. "Daighre mac Morna says that giants traditionally use goblins as servants. And that Tory Island," she gestured out to sea with her chin, "is the ancient home of the Fomair: giants, goblins, and demons."

"I don't see any demons," Cullen said, his tone almost disappointed.

"Yet. Or maybe they've already landed."

"That's a comforting thought."

Moving his lips silently, Tierney made a swift count of the figures on the beach. "Twenty-odd in sight, likely the same from the look of that trail, maybe five or six times that number still in the waves that I can see." He turned. "We need to get back."

"But we still don't know why they're here!" Cullen protested.

"I think it's pretty obvious," his older brother snapped at him. "They're armed and armored. They're not here to trade, whelp."

"But . . ."

"We'll track those that have already left the beach as far as they've gone and try to estimate some numbers and some intent," Isien decided. "C'mon."

Cullen frowned. "So, we're not going to do anything about the ones on the beach?" he asked.

Tierney rounded on him. "What do you suggest?" he snarled. "Take them all on just the four of us?"

Cullen pulled back behind Brae. "No, it's just . . ."

"Just what?"

"We're just gonna run?" he asked plaintively.

"No," Isien answered. "We're going to track, *then* we're going to run and run fast and hard back to Armagh and report what we've seen *as we were ordered to do.* We're scouts today, Cullen, not fighters." Returning to hound form, she plunged back down the hill with Tierney and Brae and the dogs behind. After one, last, uncertain glance at the beach, Cullen followed.

"Dozens?"

"Many dozens of dozens."

"Giants?"

"And goblins."

"Fomair." Cunnaun spat a disgusted wad of phlegm at the wall of the council tent while his brother Goll fingered the pommel of his sword with a deep frown. Brae and Isien shared a knowing glance while beside them Tierney and Cullen argued over a hunk of salted pork, uninterested in a conclusion the four of them had already reached.

The siblings had arrived in camp by nightfall and been taken immediately to see Sub-Captain Goll mac Morna, the leader of the Armagh Fianna. Now as his brother began to mutter darkly, he fixed them with a penetrating stare.

"Did you see any commanders?" he asked.

As one they shook their heads.

"Weapons?"

"Spears," Brae supplied.

"More like tridents," Tierney amended around a mouthful of meat.

"Armor?"

He frowned. "Maybe leather."

"Maybe?"

"It could have been leather stripping, it could have been plates, it was hard to tell from a distance," Isien answered.

"I wanted to get closer," Cullen said to no one in particular.

"It looked like scales to me," Brae said. "*Green* scales."

Cullen nodded vigorously.

"Could they have been wearing copper armor?"

"Maybe. Or *scales*," she stressed.

"Shields?"

"Greenish, with a wave and dolphin crest embossed in the middle," Isien said.

Cunnaun swore. "King of the Sea."

"I thought he was a myth," Tierney protested.

"So did we all."

"We tracked several dozen around Skelpoonagh Bay toward Ballybofey," Isien continued. "There was a large farmstead on the way. Destroyed. They didn't even bother to butcher the livestock; they just ate it raw and left the bones."

"Farmers?"

"We didn't see any bodies. Hopefully they fled."

"They might have gotten eaten too," Tierney added with unnecessary force. Beside him, Cullen glanced down at his piece of pork, then dropped it with a grimace.

"So what do you mean, no mortal weapon can harm them?"

The four Diardin had been dismissed a few minutes later. They'd taken a loaf of bread and another hunk of salted meat to one of their favorite spots, a small copse of birch trees to the west of the encampment. Isien replied to Cullen's question with a shrug as she handed him a piece of bread. "It's not that they can't harm them, it's that apparently only one in three blows ever strikes true," she explained. "The last

time the Fianna faced the King of the Sea was forty years
ago. His giants killed dozens of our people and nearly over-
ran all of Ulaidh before they were stopped."

Tierney looked up from where he was sitting and
stroking his hound Keenoo's ears. "So how *were* they
stopped?" he asked.

"I'll bet Captain Fionn challenged the King of the Sea to
single combat," Cullen said excitedly.

Isien smiled at him. "In a way, yes. He bargained for the aid
of the Tuatha De Danann. The greatest of their number, Gwyn
ap Nudd, the Lord of Annwn, gave Fionn the sword of Nuada,
from which none could escape, and the Spear of Lugh, which
ensures victory. With them, he challenged the Fomair's greatest champions, one by one, and slew them all. Finally he faced
the king's eldest son Morcail Octia, a warrior as tall as an oak
and as ferocious as a wild boar. They fought for a day and a
night, and when Fionn finally struck Morcail's head off, his
body turned to stone and sank into the earth to become a great
standing stone that's said to have magical healing properties.
With the cream of his army slain, the King of the Sea fled back
to Tory Island, swearing that some day they would return and
enact a terrible vengeance."

"Looks like today's the day," Tierney noted.

"So where are the weapons now?" Brae asked.

"Fionn returned them to the Lord of Annwn." Isien
leaned forward. "If we could get them back, we could defeat
the King of the Sea again; maybe even kill him this time,
once and for all."

Brae cocked her head to one side. "They say Gwyn ap
Nudd is the god of dogs and that his hunting pack, the Cwn
Annwn, number in the hundreds," she mused. "That would
be a lot of help if we could convince him to join us in battle
as well as lending us the weapons."

"Yes, but they also say the entrance to his kingdom is
guarded by a sacred labyrinth that no mortal can traverse,"
Tierney pointed out.

"But we aren't mortal, are we?"

"No, but it's on Ynys-Witrin in southern Logres. That's a long way. Across the sea. The giants would have overrun the entire country by the time we got back."

"Not if we take an otherworldly road," Brae answered, scratching absently at one ear. "I remember Mam telling me stories about her adventures with the Sidhe when I was a whelp. She says all the graves of ancient times are linked by a network of magical passageways where time and distance flow differently."

"Differently how?"

"Sometimes faster, sometimes slower. You could travel for years and years and only be gone a single night, or travel for miles and miles and have it only feel like an afternoon stroll if you knew what paths to take."

"Wish I'd known about that when I was a whelp," Cullen noted, sniffing absently at a blackberry bush.

"You're still a whelp," Tierney retorted.

"Bite me."

"Bring your leg over here and I will."

"So how do you know what paths to take?" Isien asked, glaring at both her brothers to silence them. "We might get back only to find everyone we know is dead and dust. It does happen, you know."

"Mam said that both time and distance smell like water," Brae explained. "When they're flowing along in the now—flowing normally—they smell like water running over rocks on a warm summer's day; flowing quickly they smell like rushing rivers in autumn; and flowing slowly they smell like melting ice dripping from fern fronds in the spring, kind of earthy and cold."

"What about winter?" Cullen asked.

"Time and distance standing still."

"Shouldn't you take that path then?"

"I'm not sure you can," she answered, but Tierney turned a frown on his little brother.

"What do you mean, *you*," he asked.

Cullen blinked. "Well, *I'm* not going."

"What happened to *you're not leaving me behind?*"

"That was a scouting mission. This is taking off on the eve of battle. Our battalion's leaving for Donegal at dawn. I don't want to go traipsing around a bunch of damp, smelly underground passageways looking for some otherworldly lord who may or may not give us some kind of mythic weaponry, then maybe get lost forever in the meantime while everyone else is out killing giants."

"That was a mouthful," Tierney noted.

"Shut up. I'll miss the battle; when Fionn calls for a champion, I'll miss my turn. I have my rock all ready and everything."

"Rock?"

"His rock for the battle cairn," Brae said fondly, bumping Cullen with her shoulder. "So they'll know if he's been killed." When Tierney rolled his eyes, she shrugged. "I carried my first rock around for weeks."

"And so did he," Isien answered, shooting Tierney a warning glance. "But it doesn't matter. If we take the paths that smell like spring we'll be back long before dawn."

"And if we're not back everyone'll think we've run away," Cullen insisted.

Brae nuzzled his hair. "No, they won't, pup."

"It's my first battle, Brae."

"I know, but there's a lot more to battle then just fighting. It's not all sets of champions whacking away at each other, you know."

"Sure, there's *battalions* of champions whacking away at each other."

"And other—just as important—elements. The champions who see them through are just as courageous as the ones who do the whacking."

"Like what?" Cullen's voice sounded so deeply suspicious that Brae laughed.

"Strategy, tactics, supplies," she offered.

"And advantage," Isien added. "You should never fight anyone without it: advantage of ground, of surprise, of superior numbers . . ."

"Of superior weapons . . ." Tierney added.

"And that's what we're going to find: the superior weapons of the Tuatha De Dannan so that the champions of the Fianna, Fionn and Caoilte and Fiachna and Creidne and Cunnaun . . ."

"And me," Cullen added indignantly.

"And you . . . will have the advantage and defeat the enemy decisively with the least number of battle stones left behind. Don't you want to be one of the heroes who turn the tide of battle to our favor?"

"Well, sure, but I wanted to do it with my own sword."

"And you will. We'll be back in plenty of time."

"Promise."

Isien rolled her eyes. "Promise."

"I knew I was going to miss the battle."

"Cullen . . ."

"We've been traveling for days . . ."

"Enough."

Brae glanced back, but on seeing that Tierney was not planning on enforcing the order with anything more than a snarl, carried on down the passageway, the scent of dripping water making her nose twitch. They'd been walking along increasingly dark passageways for several hours—not days, whatever Cullen might think—but she was starting to get as restless as he was. Now, however, she just took a deep whiff of the moisture-rich air, and carried on, the others and their four hounds trailing along behind her.

They'd entered a court grave at Ballymacdermot a mile from the encampment with the intent of leaving their gear and clothing behind, tucked up just inside the first of the court's segmented stone gallery chambers, but had quickly discovered that the passageways streaming out before their otherworldly sight were too many to trust to hound form; it took human brains to choose the most slowly flowing path going the most steadily westward. With the best nose in human form, Brae took the lead; Tierney with the best vision came next; and Isien with the best hearing took up the rear in case anything came up behind them.

"Convenient," Cullen had muttered sulkily. He'd been given the designation of "fastest" and told to walk beside Isien, so if anything went wrong, he could run back and get help.

"I don't like running away," he snarled.

Tierney made to bite him, but Brae moved swiftly between them. Nuzzling her youngest brother's shoulder, she pushed his chin with her head. "You're not running away," she whispered. "You're saving us if we need saving. We're all counting on you, pup."

"So why does he have to act like I'm useless?" he muttered back, casting a dark look in Tierney's direction.

"Cause he doesn't like running away either."

"Oh." Mollified, Cullen carried on, giving his older brother a mingled look of resentment and smugness that made Brae just shake her head.

The smell of dripping grew stronger, the walls became wet and the sound of actual running water grew loud in their ears. Tierney and Isien caught up each other's hands and Cullen began to press against Brae's side as it grew darker and darker. She squeezed his arm comfortingly as they began to descend.

"We must be under the sea," she whispered, as the four hounds began to whine quietly.

He nodded tightly. "I'm *so* happy to hear that," he answered. "Because I always wanted to die by drowning."

"No, you didn't, you wanted to die in battle."

"Oh, right. I forgot."

They continued on in silence, then some time later began to ascend again. It grew brighter and brighter; finally they came out into a wide, smooth-cut cavern with water dripping through holes and cracks above and dim sunlight filtering in through a narrow cleft in the rocks to one side. With a sigh of relief, they squeezed through.

The portal grave they exited was far older than the one they'd entered, its crumbling stones covered in lichen. Rain pattered against its capstone. Brae blinked as she looked out at the vast, reedy marshlands stretching out before them. Far to the north, she could see the two legendary raised lake villages the Logres druids had built for their La Tene learning center, and to the east, a great tor surrounded by a circle of small hills standing like a collection of islands in a gray and misty sea.

"Ynys-Witrin," she said.

Tierney joined her at the entrance. "Is this as close as we can get?"

"Seems like."

"We may have to swim for it."

Peering past his shoulder, Cullen grimaced. "In the now time, right?" he groused.

"Right." Brae glanced up with a sigh. "In the now time . . . in the rain."

Behind them, Isien began to pull food and water from her pack. "Then we'd better eat first," she said, handing her a piece of wrapped honeycomb. "Then change."

A short while later, eight hounds splashed through the Somerset marshlands, raising crowds of midges and indignant waterfowl in their wake. Brae and Cullen quickly forgot the rain and the time and began to dance about playfully, enjoying the feel of the water streaming off their pelts, while Isien and Tierney kept an watchful eye on the tor to the east, nudging the younger two—more or less gently—back in the right direction when they strayed. When they finally climbed onto dry land at the base of Ynys-Witrin, they were covered in weeds and soggy seed casings.

They spent a few moments shaking the water from their coats, then began to climb, following the rising, twisting labyrinth that stretched out before them. Isien took the lead first, nose to ground, ignoring the false turns and jumping over the broken or washed-out areas without breaking stride. When she grew tired of picking out the faint, rocky path, Tierney took over, then Brae, then Cullen. He quickly out-distanced the older three, leaving them growling and snarling in irritation, only to find he and his hound, Chekres, resting on a shelf before a narrow, Y-shaped split in the turn. Resisting the urge to snap at him, they rested a moment, then carried on with Isien in the lead again.

When they finally made the standing stone at the top of the tor, the sun, glowing faintly behind a thick bank of clouds, told them it was nearing noon. The three oldest immediately began to search about for the entrance to the Lord of Annwn's kingdom while Cullen trotted to the edge, peering down at the landscape far below. He changed in one fluid moment to glance back at them.

"Hey Brae, did you know that sheep look like little white rocks from up here?" he asked, scratching at Chekres' flank.

With a shake, she and her own hound, Balo, joined them at the edge. Far away she could just make out a few patches of dry pasture land covered in hundreds of tiny white dots. "How do you know they *aren't* rocks?" she asked, pushing a lock of sopping wet hair from her face.

"Some of them are moving."

"Oh." Her stomach growled and she growled absently back at it. "I could really go for some mutton right about now," she announced.

"Me too." He turned. "So, when is this Lord of Annwn supposed to show up, anyway?" he asked over his shoulder. "I'm getting hungry."

"He doesn't show up," Isien answered. "We have to find him."

"How?"

"By finding the entrance. And if you'd get off your rump and come help us look for it, we might find it some time today."

"So that we don't miss the battle you keep whining about," Tierney added.

"Oh, right." With one, last, wistful glance at the sheep, Cullen returned to the standing stone.

They snuffled about, each one taking an area around the stone until Brae found a crevasse that smelled faintly of subterranean stone. She gave a yip and the others gathered around her excitedly, scratching at the rocks until they'd opened up a space big enough to squirm through.

They found themselves inside a narrow cavern, a dozen shadowy pathways snaking off into the darkness.

Tierney changed and glanced around. "Now what?" he asked.

With a grin, Isien trotted to the entrance of the widest tunnel and began to bark.

In no time, they heard the faint sound of answering baying echoing off the walls and a heartbeat later, the cavern was filled with otherworldly hounds. A huge, white male, sporting a collar of gold, strutted, stiff-legged and suspicious, toward them, and all eight crouched to the ground. Ignoring the mortal hounds, he sniffed at Tierney very hard, then Cullen. The older brother remained absolutely still, suffering the inspection with a stony expression, but the younger rolled over on his back and smacked the alpha male impudently across the muzzle. The alpha male snapped gently back at him, then turned to sniff, then nuzzle, both Isien and Brae. Raising his head he gave a single bark and Gwyn ap Nudd suddenly stood before them.

The Lord of Annwn seemed as tall and slender as a birch tree, with long limbs covered in fine silver cloth. His thick, white hair, cascading across his shoulders, was plaited with red ribbons and ruby beads that sparkled in the shrouded sunlight. He carried a tall hunting bow that shone like gold and he smelled of the hunt. Resisting the urge to paw at his legs, the four siblings changed and Isien quickly spelled out their mission.

The Lord of Annwn pursed his lips when she was finished.

"Long have I been the ally of Fionn mac Cumhail," he said formally, "but longer still since I took up arms against the Fomair. However, my bond with the Sidhe hounds is older still," he said, smiling down at the alpha male, who reared up to lay his huge white paws on his master's chest. "So I will grant the Captain of the Fianna the use of my weaponry once more. For a price."

The four siblings glanced at each other.

"What price?" Tierney asked.

"A new hound for my Cwn Annwn."

When they hesitated, he gave an elegant shrug. "Of course, if you don't really need my weapons to turn the tide of battle to your advantage . . ."

"I'll do it," Cullen answered promptly.

Tierney rounded on him, but the Lord smiled. "Done." He clapped his hands and suddenly Gwyn ap Nudd, hound pack, and Cullen vanished.

The three remaining siblings stood in shocked silence. Tierney stared down at the weapons lying ignobly at his feet as if they were a pair of serpents, then turned to his sisters as Chekres began to whine. "We lost a member of the Fianna," he breathed. "Cunnaun's going to kill us."

Brae shook her head. "Forget about Cunnaun," she countered. "We lost a brother. Mam's going to kill us first."

"I gave him into your keeping, whelp!"

Tierney let out a loud yip as their mother suddenly became a great, white she-hound and nipped his ear sharply, then turned on the others. Isien backed up a step, Brae shoved instinctively behind her, but all the hound did was growl low in her throat before shifting to become a tall, copper-haired woman, with blazingly angry eyes once again.

The three remaining siblings had found the pathway to their mother's home in Anglesey all too easily. Standing at the entrance to the Bodowyr burial chamber in Llanidan, they'd looked across the field at her stone cottage seated at the edge of the forest, then at each other, but finally, had begun to run.

Now, storming into her cottage, Diardin threw open the lid of a large, brass-bound trunk before giving her three children a furious glance. "I specifically gave him into your care when I allowed him to join the Fianna, did I not? Did I not say, Tierney, Isien, look after your little brother, he's a featherhead? Did I say trade him to Gwyn ap Nudd's Cwn Annwn hound pack for a handful of magic beans? No, I did not! Tukre, don't you dare growl at me!"

Tierney gripped the Spear of Nuada's hide-bound haft, but said nothing as his hound cowered behind him. Brae looked relieved that she hadn't mentioned her or Balo.

"We didn't trade him," Isien protested, placing her hand over Tukre's muzzle as their mother began to pull on various pieces of old, worn armor and leather traveling clothes. "He jumped."

"You should have caught him!"

"We tried; he just vanished."

"He wanted to be a hero," Brae said almost apologetically. "He wanted to be the one to give the advantage to the Fianna and that was the lord's price."

"Oh, it was, was it? We'll see about that," Diardin snapped. Throwing a cloak about her shoulders, she fastened it with a silver pin in the shape of a dog, then caught up a bronze sword in a faded leather scabbard and attached it to her belt, before stalking from the cabin. "Jesse, stay," she said over her shoulder to the old hound lying by the hearth. "You lot, come with me."

When they reached the entrance to the Bodowyr burial chamber, she turned. "Take the weapons to the Fianna; I dare say they'll be in dire need of them by now. Follow that passageway," she pointed, "and stay on it. It will lead you directly to a court grave west of Glencolumbkille. *Do not* stray from it for *any* reason, not if the King of the Hill's Shining Beast itself were to cross your path. Understand?"

"Mother . . ." Isien began, but Diardin cut her off with a gesture.

"Later. Right now I have a few things to explain to your brother and," she added with a dangerous growl, "to a certain *Lord of the Otherworld*." Turning on her heel, she headed down a southward bending passageway, the scent of dripping water flowing all around her.

The three remaining siblings watched until she disappeared around a bend, then, after sharing a single worried glance, began the long journey back to Ireland.

On the west coast of Donegal, battle had been joined for two days. Fionn mac Cumhail had led a dozen hastily gathered battalions of Fianna against the Fomair, commanded by the Sea King's eldest son, Dolar Durba, who stood in the ancient one-eyed, one-armed, and one-legged pose of cursing in a small coracle far out to sea, gesturing and screaming out magical invectives over the crash of the surf. Hundreds of giants and goblins had already reached the shore; hundreds more fought their way through the waves to reach shore. Despite their traditional preference of single combat, the Fianna had resorted to a three-on-one attack method just to even the odds. When the children of Diardin appeared as battle was joined on the second day—muddy, exhausted, and worried about Cullen—to almost throw the sword and spear at their legendary Captain, the Formair had already pushed the beleaguered Irish troops off the beach. With a martial cry, Fionn had caught up the sword, tossed the spear to his nephew Caoilte, and plunged into the fray to rally his people. Without pausing for breath, the children of Diardin followed.

Now, as the sun began to set beyond the sea, Isien, Tierney, and Brae fought together with their hounds, hacking at the knees of a giant the size of a yew tree. Because of their otherworldly blood, every second blow struck true, but even so, it had taken all their combined skill even to tire the creature out. But finally one of Isien's slashing attacks cut a hamstring and the giant went down. The three siblings leaped for its jugular. Tierney took a blow to the skull that sent him flying, but that distracted the giant long enough for Brae to leap onto its chest and drive her sword into its throat. The blood that welled up was a deep, dark, greenish black. She leaned on the blade, throwing all her weight behind it as the wound twisted and fought to expel the weapon and close up again. The giant thrashed madly, trying to throw her off, but suddenly Tierney and Isien were up and latched onto his arms, the hounds on its legs. The giant jerked them about like a maddened stag, blood spurting and spewing into Brae's face as she fought to keep her grip on her sword hilt. There was blood in her eyes and blood in her ears, but she hung on the blade and finally the giant grew still. With a tired snarl, she wrenched her sword free and tumbled off the creature's chest.

Tierney and Isien landed beside her, taking the opportunity to breathe for a moment, safe behind the giant's bulk.

Scraping at her face, Brae peeled one eye open. "Champions," she growled, spitting a mouthful of dark blood at the sand, "are overrated."

"Tell Cullen," Isien gasped.

"I would . . . Balo, stop licking me . . ." she said, pushing her hound's face away, "but it looks like he's missed the battle after all."

"The battle's . . . not over."

"When it is," Tierney growled wearily, "and when I get my hands on him . . ."

"If . . ."

"When," he repeated firmly. "I'm gonna bite him from here to Ynys-Witrin and back. Magic beans. He's not worth a handful of magic beans."

"Was he worth a pair of magic weapons?" Brae asked softly.

Tierney sighed. "I'll let you know when the battle *is* over. But I know one thing, I wish we'd kept them ourselves," he added as a goblin face and an arm brandishing a long, bronze sword suddenly loomed over the giant's body. "Diord Fionn!" he shouted as he flung himself toward the creature, the hounds in tow.

"Right, diord whatever," Isien muttered as she dragged herself up to join him. Brae scraped the last of the blood from her eyes with a disgusted grimace before following her.

The fighting continued without abatement all through the next day. Dolar Durba in his coracle got closer and closer to land as his giants began to throw the Fianna back again despite the otherworldly weapons wielded by their leaders. As a dozen giants finally broke through their lines, the Sea King's son gave a great shout of triumph and leaped ashore, but before he could close with the first of his enemies, there came the sudden and eerie call of hunting horns rising up over the battle like the wail of a thousand banshees. Everyone on the beach froze. Otherworldly baying filled the air and, as the hounds of the Fianna took up the call, the capstone from an ancient, half-buried portal grave nearby suddenly exploded into the sky. It sailed a dozen feet to come crashing down before Dolar Durba as a hundred great white hounds with red-tipped ears and blazing eyes poured from the entrance. A legion of Tuatha De Dannan led by Gwyn ap Nudd himself followed. They threw themselves against the Fomair, every slash of teeth and bronze and silver weapons striking true and, with a great cheer, the Fianna rallied behind them.

Brae gave a shout of joy as she recognized the young hound running beside the alpha male. It leaped for Dolar Durba and he aimed a blow at its head, but before it could strike true or wide, a great, white she-hound flung herself upon him, snarling and howling. He toppled over into the surf in surprise. The dog savaged him, striking with lightning speed at his face and hands and throat. Soon the water churned with greenish black blood. He finally managed to throw her off and dove for deeper water, swimming desperately for his coracle. Bristling with fury, the she-hound then turned on the nearest giant with the younger hound at her side.

The fight went out of the Fomair soon after that. With their leader wounded and running for his life, the remaining giants fled into the surf after him. Those that couldn't follow were brought to bay by the Cwn Annwn, who drove them into the waiting blades of their masters. The battalions of Fianna turned to pursue those who'd made their way inland and, by the time the sun touched the waves to the west, the battle was over.

On the beach, Fionn mac Cumhail returned the sword and spear to the Lord of Annwn with much ceremony while his commanders clasped hands with the Tuatha De Danann; the hounds of the Fianna mingled happily with the Cwn Annwn after the alpha male and Fothran had made a bristling circle of each other, and the remaining children of Diardin flung themselves onto their brother—pointedly ignoring a furious scolding from Cunnaun. The white shehound trotted over to the lord's side, and suddenly their mother stood before them. An attendant handed her cloak to Gwyn ap Nudd and he draped it over her shoulders before fixing her children with a reproving stare.

"You should have told me you were Diardin's," he said sternly. "I would never have taken one of her children for my own had I known of it. But," he said with a softer expression, "if she allows it, you may run with my Cwn Annwn any time you wish, especially you, little male," he said fondly. "For you are a fine hunter."

Cullen made to answer, but at a swift look from his mother, closed his mouth again, and just smiled as the lord glanced out at the setting sun before offering Diardin his arm.

"It grows late, My Lady," he said formally. "Shall we take our leave or will you tarry here a while?"

"I'm ready to return home," she replied. Accepting his arm, she fixed her children with a firm stare. "Look after Cullen," she said to the two eldest. "*Properly.* I don't want to have to deal with this sort of nonsense again. And you," she turned a dark gaze on her youngest son, "are too old to have your mother running to your rescue every five minutes. It's time you grew up a little." She kissed him to take the sting from her words. "Come and visit in the autumn."

The two then swept away, the Tuatha and the Cwn Annwn flowing after them. Cullen watched them go with a wistful expression until Brae bumped him with her shoulder.

"So, where's your rock, pup?" she asked.

He gave her a sheepish grin. "With my pack."

"Good thing they didn't need to count it then, isn't it?" Fishing through her belt pouch, she handed him the worn piece of limestone. "Try to pick a smaller one next time, will you? It nearly broke my wrist."

He nodded.

Beside them, Tierney watched the last of the Tuatha De Dannan file through the portal grave, before turning to Cullen. "So how'd Mam get you back, whelp?" he asked.

The younger brother glared at him and he raised his hands with a grin. "Hey, I didn't say why, I said how."

"She just told him to," Cullen answered haughtily.

"That was all?"

"Mm-hm."

"So, how did she get him to commit his army?"

"Again, she just told him to."

"But why would he obey her?"

"Wouldn't you?"

"Well, yeah, but . . ." Tierney rubbed his ear. "Yeah," he allowed.

Giving him a smug look, Cullen turned to stare at the coracle almost out of sight on the distant waves. "So, it looks like it did come down to a set of champions whacking away at each other after all," he said in an accusatory tone. "Mam and the King of the Sea's son. Some advantage to miss an entire battle for."

Beside them, Cunnaun snorted loudly. "It came down to a mother hound defending her whelp," he said, glancing down at Cullen. "Whelp."

"What kind of advantage is that?"

"The oldest advantage there is." He turned away. "Now for Ahu's sake, put some clothes on; we have burials to see to," he said over his shoulder. "And hero or not, you're doing your share."

"I'd still have rather won with my own sword," Cullen growled, glaring resentfully at the man's back.

"And you will," Brae answered. "One day. That's the advantage of winning. You get to win again." Throwing one arm over his shoulder, she drew him back to the beach. Tierney and Isien followed, their hounds in tow, while behind them the sound of fleeing giants faded into the distance.

NOT THAT KIND OF A WAR

by Tanya Huff

Tanya Huff lives and writes in rural Ontario with her partner, four cats, and an unintentional Chihuahua. After sixteen fantasies, she's written two space operas, Valor's Choice *and* The Better Part of Valor, *and is currently working on a series of novels spun off from her Henry Fitzroy vampire series. In her spare time she gardens and complains about the weather.*

WE STILL HAVE ONE HELL of a lot of colonists to get off this rock before we can leave." Captain Rose frowned out at Sho'quo Company's three surviving Second Lieutenants and the senior NCOs. "And every ship going up is going to need an escort to keep it from being blown to hell by the Others, so we're on Captain Allon's timetable. Given the amount of action up there . . ." He paused to allow the distant crack of a vacuum jockey dipping into atmosphere to carry the point. "We may be down here for a while. Bottom line, we have to hold Simunthitir because we have to hold the port."

"The Others have secured the mines," Second Lieutenant di'Pin Arver muttered, her pale orange hair flipping back and forth in agitation. "You'd think they'd be happy to be rid of us."

"*I'd* think so. Unfortunately, they don't seem to." The captain thumbed the display on his slate, and a three dimensional map of Simunthitir rose up out of the holo-pad on the table. "Good news is, we're up against a mountain, so as long as our air support keeps kicking the ass of their air support, they can only come at us from one side. Bad news is, we have absolutely no maneuvering room and we're significantly outnumbered even if they only attack with half of what they've got on the ground."

In Staff Sergeant Torin Kerr's not inconsiderable experience, even the best officers liked to state the obvious. For example: *significantly outnumbered.* Sho'quo Company had been sent off to this mining colony theoretically to make a statement of force to the Other's scouts. They'd since participated in a rout and now were about to make one of those heroic last stands that played so well on the evening news. No one had apparently told the enemy that they were merely doing reconnaissance and they had, as a result, sent two full battalions—or the Other's equivalent—to take the mines.

"Lieutenant Arver, make sure your remaining STAs . . ."

And what fun, they'd already lost two of their six surface to air missiles.

" . . . are positioned to cover the airspace immediately over the launch platform. See if you can move one of them up here."

A red light flared on the targeting grid overlaying the map.

"Yes, sir." The lieutenant keyed the position into her slate.

"Set your mortars up on level four. I want them high enough to have some range but not so high that any return fire they draw may damage the port. You're going to have to take out their artillery or we are, to put it bluntly, well and truly screwed. Staff Sergeant Doctorow . . ."

"Sir."

Doctorow's platoon had lost its Second Lieutenant in the first exchange.

"I want all accesses to the launch platform in our hands ASAP. We don't need a repeat of Beniger."

With the Others beating down the door, the civilians of Beniger had rushed the ships. The first had taken off so overloaded, it had crashed back, and blown the launch pad and half the port. Granted, any enemy in the immediate area had also been fried, but Torin figured the dead of Beniger considered that cold comfort.

"Lieutenant Garly, I want one of your squads on stretcher duty. Get our wounded up into port reception and ready to be loaded once all the civilians are clear. Take position on the second level but mark a second squad in case things get bad."

"Sir."

"Lieutenant Franks . . ."

Torin felt the big man beside her practically quiver in anticipation.

"You'll hold the first level."

"Sir!"

Just on the periphery of her vision, Torin saw Staff Sergeant Amanda Aman's mouth twitch and Torin barely resisted the urge to smack her. Franks, Torin's personal responsibility, while no longer a rookie, still had few shiny expectations that flared up at inconvenient moments. He no longer bought into the romance of war—his first time out had taken care of that—but he continued to buy into the romance of the warrior. Every now and then, she could see the desire to do great things rise in his eyes.

"You want to live on after you die, Staff . . ." He danced *his fingers over his touchpad, drawing out a martial melody.* *"Do something that makes it into a song."*

Torin didn't so much want Lieutenant Franks to live on after he died as to live on for a good long time, so she smacked that desire down every time she saw it and worried about what would happen should it make an appearance when she wasn't around. The enemy smacked down with considerably more force. And their music sucked.

The captain swept a level stare around the gathered

Marines. "Remember that our primary objective is to get the civilians out and then haul ass off this rock. We hold the port long enough to achieve this."

"*Captain.*" First Sergeant Chigma's voice came in on the company channel. "*We've got a reading on the unfriendlies.*"

"On my way." He swept a final gaze over the Marines in the room and nodded. "You've got your orders, people."

Emerging from the briefing room—previously known as the Simunthitir Council Chamber—the noise of terrified civilians hit Torin like a physical blow. While no one out of diapers was actually screaming, everyone seemed to feel the need to express their fear. Loudly. As if maybe Captain Allon would send down more frequent escorts from the orbiting carrier if he could only hear how desperate things had gotten.

Captain Rose stared around at the milling crowds. "Why are these people not at the port, First?"

"Port Authorities are taking their time processing, sir."

"Processing?"

"Rakva."

Although many of the Confederation's Elder Races made bureaucracy a fine art, the Rakva reveled in it. Torin, who after twelve years in the Corps wasn't surprised by much, had once watched a line of the avians patiently filling out forms in triplicate in order to use a species-specific sanitary facility. Apparently the feathers and rudimentary beaks weren't sufficient proof of species identification.

"They're insisting that everyone fill out emergency evacuation forms."

"Oh, for the love of God . . . Deal with it."

Chigma showed teeth—a distinctly threatening gesture from a species that would eat pretty much anything it could fit down its throat and was remarkably adaptable about the latter. "Yes, sir."

"Captain . . ." Lieutenant Franks' golden brows drew in and he frowned after the First Sergeant. "Begging your pardon, sir, but a Krai may not be the most diplomatic . . ."

"Diplomatic?" the captain interrupted. "We've got a few

thousand civilians to get off this rock before a whole crapload of Others climb right up their butts. If they wanted it done diplomatically, they shouldn't have called in the Corps." He paused and shot the lieutenant a frown of his own. "Shouldn't you be at the first level by now?"

"Sir!"

Torin fell into step at his right shoulder as Franks hurried off the concourse and out onto the road that joined the seven levels of Simunthitir into one continuous spiral. Designed for the easy transportation of ore carriers up to the port, it was also a strong defensive position with heavy gates to close each level off from those below; the layout ensured that Sho'quo Company would maintain the high ground as they withdrew to the port. If not for the certain fact that the Others were traveling with heavy artillery—significantly heavier than their own EM223s—and sufficient numbers to climb to the high ground over the piled bodies of their dead, she'd be thinking this was a highly survivable engagement. Ignoring the possibility that the Others' air support would get off a lucky drop.

"Well, Staff, it looks like we've got the keys to the city. It's up to us to hold the gates at all costs."

And provided she could keep Lieutenant Franks from getting them all killed—but *that* was pretty much business as usual.

"Anything happen while I was gone?"

Sergeant Anne Chou shook her head without taking her attention from the scanner. "Not a thing. Looks like they waited until you got back."

Torin peered out over the undulating plain but couldn't see that anything had changed. "What are you getting?"

"Just picked up the leading edge of the unfriendlies, but they're packed too close together to get a clear reading on numbers."

"Professional opinion?"

The other woman looked over at that and grinned. "One fuck of a lot, Staff."

"Great." Torin switched her com to command channel. "Lieutenant, we've got a reading on the perimeter."

"Is their artillery in range?"

"Not yet, sir." Torin glanced up into a sky empty of all but the distant flashes of the battle going on up above the atmosphere where the vacuum jockeys from both sides kept the other side from controlling the ultimate high ground. "I imagine they'll let us know."

"Keep me informed."

"Yes, sir."

"You think he's up to this?" Anne asked when Torin tongued off her microphone.

"Since the entire plan is that we shoot and back up, shoot and back up, rinse and repeat, I think we'll be fine." The lieutenant had to be watched more closely moving forward.

Anne nodded, well aware of the subtext. "Glad to hear it."

The outer walls of Simunthitir's lowest level of buildings presented a curved stone face to the world about seven meters high, broken by a single gate. Running along the top of those buildings was a continuous line of battlement fronted by a stone balustrade about a meter and a half high.

Battlements and balustrades, Torin thought as she made her way to the gate. *Nothing like getting back to the basics.* "Trey, how's it going?"

The di'Taykan Sergeant glanced up, her hair a brilliant cerulean corona around her head. "She's packed tight, Staff. We're just about to fuse the plug."

They'd stuffed the gate full of the hovercraft used to move people and goods inside the city. Individually, each cart weighed about two hundred kilos, hardly enough to stop even a lackluster assault, but crammed into the gateway— wrestled into position by the heavy gunners and their exoskeletons—and then fused into one solid mass by a few well placed demo charges, the gate would disappear and the city would present a solid face to the enemy.

As Trey moved the heavies away, Lance Corporal Sluun moved forward keying the final parameters into his slate.

"First in Go and Blow, eh?" Lieuentant Franks said quietly by Torin's left shoulder.

"Yes, sir." Sluun had kicked ass at his TS3 demolition course.

A trio of planes screamed by, closely followed by three Marine 774s keeping up a steady stream of fire. Two of the enemy managed to drop their loads—both missed the city— while the third peeled off in an attempt to engage their pursuers. The entire tableau shrieked out of sight in less than minute.

"I only mention it," the lieutenant continued when they could hear themselves think again, "because there's always the chance we could blow not only the gate but a section of the wall as well."

"Trust in the training, sir. Apparently Sluun paid attention in class."

"Firing in five . . ."

"We might want to step back, sir."

" . . . *four* . . ."

"Trust in the training, Staff?"

". . . *three* . . ."

"Yes, sir. But there's no harm in hedging our bets."

". . . *two* . . ."

They stopped four meters back.

" . . . *one. Fire in the hole!*"

The stones vibrated gently under their feet.

And a moment later . . . *"We've got a good solid plug, Lieutenant."* Trey's voice came over the group channel. *"They'll need the really big guns to get through it."*

Right on cue: the distinctive whine of incoming artillery. This time, the vibrations underfoot were less than gentle. Four, five, six impacts . . . and a pause.

"Damage?"

"Got a hole into one of the warehouses, Staff." Corporal

Dave Hayman's voice came over the com. *"Demo team's filling in the hole now."*

"Good." She tongued off the microphone. "Everything else hit higher up, sir. I imagine we've got civilian casualties."

Franks' lips thinned. "Why the hell isn't Arver pulsing their targeting computers?" he demanded grimly.

Shots seven, eight, and nine missed the port entirely.

"I think it took them a moment to get the frequency, sir."

Ten, eleven, and twelve blew in the air.

Confident that the specialists were doing their jobs, the Marines on the wall ignored the barrage. They all knew there'd be plenty to get excited about later. Electronics were easy for both sides to block, which was why the weapon of choice in the Corps was a KC-7, a chemically operated projectile weapon. Nothing disrupted it but hands-on physical force, and the weighted stock made a handy club in a pinch. Torin appreciated a philosophy that expected to get pinched.

Eventually, it would come down to flesh versus flesh. It always did.

As another four planes screamed by, Torin took a look over the front parapet and then turned to look back in over the gate. "Trey, you got any more of those carts down there?"

"Plenty of them, Staff."

"All right, let's run as many as will fit up here to the top of the wall and send those that don't fit up a level."

"Planning on dropping them on the enemy?" Lieutenant Franks grinned.

"Yes, sir."

"Oh." Somewhat taken aback, he frowned and one of those remaining shiny patches flared up. "Isn't dropping scrap on the enemy, I don't know . . ."

Torin waited patiently as, still frowning, he searched for the right word.

"UnMarine-like?"

Or perhaps he'd needed the time to make up a new word. "Look at it this way, sir, if you were them and you thought there was a chance of having two hundred kilos dropped on your head, wouldn't you be a little hesitant in approaching the wall?"

"I guess I would . . ."

He guessed. Torin, on the other hand, knew full well that were the situations reversed, Lieutenant Franks would be dying to gallantly charge the port screaming *Once more into the breach!* And since her place was beside him and dying would be the operative word, she had further reason to be happy they were on this side of the wall. If people were going to sing about her, she'd just as soon they sang about a long career and a productive retirement.

The Others came over the ridge in a solid line of soldiers and machines, the sound of their approach all but drowning out the scream of the first civilian transport lifting off. Marine flyers escorted it as far as the edge of the atmosphere, where the navy took over and the Marines raced back to face the bomber the Others had sent to the port. One of Lieutenant Arver's sammies took it out before it had a change to drop its load. The pilot arced around the falling plume of wreckage and laid a contrail off toward the mountains, chased away from the massed enemy by two ships from *their* air support.

According to Torin's scanner, these particular soldiers fighting for the coalition the Confederation referred to as the Others were mammals; two, maybe three, species of them given the variant body temperatures. It was entirely possible she had more in common physically with the enemy than she did with at least half of the people she was expected to protect—the Rakva were avian, the Niln reptilian, and both were disproportionately represented among the civilian population of Simunthitir.

The odds were even better that she'd have an easier time making conversation with any one of the approaching enemy than she would with any civilian regardless of species. Find her a senior noncom, and she'd guarantee it. Soldiering was a fairly simple profession after all. Achieve the objective. Get your people out alive.

Granted, the objectives usually differed.

Behind her in the city, in direct counterpoint to her thoughts, someone screamed a protest at having to leave behind their various bits of accumulated crap as the remaining civilians on the first level were herded toward the port. It never failed to amaze her how people hung on to the damnedest things when running for their lives. The Others *would* break into the first level. It was only a question of when.

She frowned at an unlikely reading.

"What is it, Staff Sergeant?"

"I'm not sure . . ." There were six, no seven, huge inert pieces of something advancing with the enemy. They weren't living, and with no power signature, they couldn't be machinery.

The first of Lieutenant Arver's mortars fired, locked on to the enemy's artillery. The others followed in quick succession, hoping to get in a hit before their targeting scanners were scrambled in turn. A few Marines cheered as something in the advancing horde blew. From the size of the explosion, at least one of the big guns had been taken out—along with the surrounding soldiers.

"They're just marching into an entrenched position," Franks muttered. "This won't be battle, this will be slaughter."

"I doubt they'll just keep marching, sir." Almost before she finished speaking, a dozen points flared on her scanner and she switched her com to group. "It's about to get noisy people!" She dropped behind one of the carts. Lieutenant Franks waited until the absolute last moment before joining her. She suspected he was being an inspiration to the platoon. Personally, she always felt it was more inspiring to have your lieutenant in one piece, but hey, that was her.

The artillery barrage before the battle—any battle—had one objective. Do as much damage to the enemy as possible.

Their side. The other side. All a soldier could do was wait it out and hope they didn't get buried in debris.

"Keep them from sneaking forward, people!" It wasn't technically necessary to yell; the helmet coms were intelligent enough to pick up her voice and block the sound of the explosions in the air, the upper city, and out on the plains, but there was a certain satisfaction in yelling that she had no intention of giving up. She pointed her KC-7 over the edge of the wall. "Don't worry about the artillery—they're aiming at each other, not at you!"

"Dubious comfort, Staff!"

Torin grinned at the Marine who'd spoken. "It's the only kind I offer, Haysole!"

Ears and turquoise hair clamped tight against his head, the di'Taykan returned her grin. "You're breaking my heart!"

"I'll break something else if you don't put your damned helmet on!"

The di'Taykans were believed to be the most enthusiastically nondiscriminating sexual adventurers in known space, and Private Haysole di'Stenjic seemed to want to enthusiastically prove he was more di'Taykan than most. While allowances were made within both branches of the military for species-specific behavior, Haysole delighted in stepping over the line—although in his defense he often didn't seem to know just where the line was. He'd made corporal twice and was likely never going to get there again unless casualties in the Corps got much, much worse. Given that he was the stereotypical good-humored, well-liked bad boy of the platoon, Torin was always amazed when he came out of an engagement in one piece.

"*Staff.*" Corporal Hollice's voice sounded in her helmet. His fireteam anchored the far end of the wall. "*Picking up unfriendlies approaching our sector.*"

Torin glanced over at the lieutenant who was obviously—obvious to her anyway—fighting the urge to charge over to that sector and face the unfriendlies himself, mano a mano. "Mark your targets, people; the official number seems to be one fuck of a lot and we're not carrying unlimited ammo."

"Looks like some of them are running four on the floor. Fuck, they can really motor!"

"What?"

"Uh, sorry Staff, old human saying. One group has four legs and they're running really fast."

"Thank you. I'm guessing they're also climbers or they wouldn't be first . . ." And then she was shouting in the sudden silence. "At the wall," she finished a little more quietly. "Stay sharp."

"Artillery seems to have finished smashing things up," Franks murmured as he cautiously stood and took a look around.

The two lower levels were still more or less intact, the upper levels not so much. The question was if the port had survived. And the answer seemed to be yes as a Marine escort screamed in and another civilian carrier lifted off.

The distinct sound of a KC-7 turned Torin's attention back to the plains.

"Our turn," Franks murmured. "Our turn to stand fast and say you shall not pass."

Had that rhymed? "Sir?"

His cheeks darkened slightly. "Nothing."

"Yes, sir."

All Marines qualified on the KC-7. Some of them were better shots than others but every single one of them knew how to make those shots count. The problem was, for every one of the enemy shot, another three raced forward to take their place.

"I hate this kind of thing." Franks aimed and fired. "There's no honor in it. They charge at us, we shoot them. It's . . ."

"Better than the other way around?" Torin suggested.

He shrugged. Aimed. Fired. "I guess so."

Torin knew so.

The enemy wore what looked like a desert camouflage that made them difficult to see against the dead brown grasses on the plains. Sho'quo Company was in urban camouflage—black and gray and a dirty white—that hopefully made them difficult to see against the walls of Simunthitir. Most of the enemy were on foot but there was a scattering of small vehicles in the line. Some the heavy gunners took out—the remains of these were used as cover at varying distances from the wall. Some kept coming.

Torin pulled the tab on a demo charge, counted to four, leaned over the wall, and dropped it. The enemy vehicle blew big, the concussion rattling teeth on the wall and windows behind them in the port.

"I suspect they were going to set a sapper charge."

"Odds are good, sir."

"Why didn't you drop a cart on them?"

"Thought we'd best leave that to the end, sir. Get a few carts stacked up down there and they'll be able to use them to get up the . . . Damn!"

The quadrupeds were climbers and they were, indeed, fast. One moment there were only Marines on the wall, the next there was a large soldier with four heavily clawed legs and two arms holding a weapon gripping the edge of the parapet. One of the heavies went down but before the quad could fire again, Lieutenant Franks charged forward, swung his weapon so that the stock slammed in hard between the front legs, and then shot it twice in the air as it fell backward off the wall.

He flushed slightly as Marines cheered and almost looked as though he was about to throw himself off the wall after it to finish the job. "I was closest," he explained, returning to Torin's side.

He wasn't. She hid a smile. Aimed. Fired. Hid a second smile as the lieutenant sighed and did the same. He wanted deeds of daring and he got target practice instead. Life was rough. Better than the alternative though, no matter how little the lieutenant might think so. *Do or die* might have more of a ring to it but she much preferred *do and live* and did her damnedest to ensure that was what happened for the Marines under her care.

Another civilian carrier lifted off. So far they were three for three.

"Artillery seems to have neutralized each other," Franks murmured, sweeping his scanner over the plain. "That's some nice shooting by Arver's . . . What the hell?"

With the approaching ground troops dug in or pulling back, Torin slaved her scanner to the lieutenant's. The inert masses she'd spotted earlier were being moved forward— no, *pushed* forward, their bulk shielding the pushers from Marine fire.

"Know what they are, Staff?"

"No idea, sir."

He glanced over at her with exaggerated disbelief, as he activated his com. "Anyone?"

"I think they're catapults, sir."

"*Cat*–apults, Corporal Hollice?"

"Yes sir, it's a pre-tech weapon."

"And they're going to what? Throw cats at us?"

"No, sir. Probably rocks."

Franks glanced at Torin again. She shrugged. This was new to her.

"They're going to throw rocks at us?"

"Yes, sir."

"I'm not reading a power source, Hollice."

"They use, uh, kind of a, uh, spring thing. Sir."

"You have no idea, do you, Corporal?"

"Not really, sir. But I've read about them."

Franks took another look through the scanner. "How do the mortars target something with no energy read?"

"Aim and fire, sir. They're not that far away."

"Not so easy with an emmy, Staff." Franks mimed manually aiming one of the mortars and Torin grinned.

Then she stopped grinning as the first of the catapult things fired and watched in disbelief as a massive hunk of ore-laced

rock arced overhead and slammed into level five. The wall
shattered under the impact, flinging debris far and wide.

"Cover!"

Then BAM! BAM! BAM! BAM! Not as deafening as artillery but considerably more primal.

Most of the rock screamed over their heads, aimed at the
remaining emmies now beginning to return fire from level
four.

Most.

One of the rocks grew larger, and larger, and . . .

The wall bucked underfoot, flexed and kicked like a living thing trying to throw them off. A gust of wind blew the
rock dust clear, and Torin saw that a crescent shaped bite
had been taken out of the top of the wall. "Chou?"

"Two dead, three injured, Staff. I'm on it."

What if they gave a war and nobody died . . . Never
going to happen. "Listen up, people, next time you see a
great hunk of rock sailing toward you, get the fuck out of the
way! These things are moving a lot slower than what we're
used to!"

Only one emmy spat back an answer, blowing one of the
incoming rocks out of the sky.

"Oh for . . . COVER!" A piece of debris bounced off
Torin's helmet with enough force to rattle her teeth and a
second slammed into her upper back, fortunately moving
fast enough that her vest absorbed most of the impact.

"Arver!" Spitting out a mouthful of blood from a split lip,
Franks screamed the artillery lieutenant's name into his
com. "You want to watch where you're dropping that shit!"

*"You want to come up here and try and aim this thing
manually?"*

"I don't think you're going to have time for that, sir."
Torin nodded out over the wall. Under cover of the rocks,
which were probably intended to be as much of a distraction
as a danger, the Others had started a second charge, the
faster quadrupeds out front once again and everyone else
close behind.

The odds of deliberately hitting a randomly moving object were slim. The Marines switched to full automatic and sprayed rounds into the advancing enemy. Bodies started hitting the dirt. The enemy kept coming.

"As soon as you can take out multiple targets, start dropping the carts!"

Out of the corner of one eye, Torin saw Juan Checya, one of the heavy gunners, sling his weapon, flick on a hovercraft, and, as it lifted on its cushion of air, grab the rear rail with both augmented hands and push it to the back of the wall. As soon as he had the maximum wind-up available, he braced himself and whipped around, releasing the cart at the front of the arc. It traveled an impressive distance before gravity negated the forward momentum.

The quadrupeds closest to the casualties keened at the loss of their companions and seemed to double their speed. Torin found it encouraging, in a slightly soul-deadening way, that they grieved so obviously. Grief was distracting. Unfortunately, not only distracting for the enemy. "Sir . . ."

Franks rubbed a grimy hand over his face, rock dust mixing with sweat and drawing vertical gray streaks "I'm okay, Staff."

"Never doubted it, sir."

Above and behind them, a fourth civilian carrier rose toward safety.

"One carrier remaining." Captain Rose's voice on the command channel. Torin almost thought she could hear screaming in the background. She'd rather face a well-armed enemy than civilians any day. *"Lieutenant Franks, move your platoon back to level three and take over stretcher duty from Lieutenant Garly who will hold level two!"*

"Captain!" Lieutenant Franks slid two steps sideways and blew a biped off the wall. Although it might be a new species, Torin missed any other distinguishing features—after a while, the only thing that registered was the uniform. "Unfriendlies have broken the perimeter!"

"That's why we're moving the perimeter, Franks. Fall back!"

"Yes, sir! Staff . . ."

"Sir! Fall back by numbers, people! You know the drill! Keep low so the second level has as clear a shot as possible! And Amanda, I want that covering fire thick enough to keep out rain!"

"You got it, Torin!"

The word retreat was not in the corps vocabulary. Marines fell back and regrouped. In this particular instance it wasn't so much back as down. The heavies leaped off the wall into the city and then joined in providing covering fire so that those without exoskeletons to take up the impact could come off the wall a little more slowly. And then it was a fast run up the lowest level of the spiraling street, squads leapfrogging each other as Lieutenant Garly's platoon swept the first level wall, keeping the enemy too occupied to shoot down into the city.

Given the fire from the second level, a number of the enemy decided that the safest thing to do was to follow the Marines down to the street.

Also, without Marines on the outside wall to keep the sappers away . . .

The explosion smelled like scorched iron and filled the street with smoke and dust. Swearing for the sake of swearing, Torin ducked yet another rain of debris.

"They're in!"

Squad one made it through the second level gate. Torin and the lieutenant crouched behind a rough barricade as squad two followed. As a clump of the enemy rounded the curve of a building, a hovercraft sailed off level two, plummeted downward, and squashed half of them flat.

"I think that's our cue, Staff."

"Works for me, sir."

They moved back with the squad, Torin keeping herself between the lieutenant and the enemy. The largest part of her job was, after all, keeping him alive.

They were no more than four meters from the gate when a pair of the quadrupeds charged over the wreckage of the hovercraft, keening and firing wildly as they ran. Their weapon was, like the KC, a chemically powered projectile. The rounds whined through the air in such numbers that it almost seemed as though they were being attacked by a swarm of angry wasps. No choice but to dive for dirt and hope the distinctly inadequate cover would be enough.

Shots from the second level took the quads out just before they reached the squad.

Torin scrambled to her feet. "Let's go before more show up."

No one expected the quads to have riders: smaller bipeds who launched themselves from the bodies. One of them died in the air; the other wrapped itself around Haysole and drew its sidearm. Haysole spun sideways, his helmet flying off to bounce down the street, and got enough of an elbow free to deflect the first shot. Between the frenzied movement, and the certainty that taking out the enemy would also take out Haysole, no one dared shoot. Torin felt rather than saw Franks charge forward. He was a big man—because he was a second lieutenant she sometimes forgot that. Large hands wrapped around the enemy's head and twisted. Sentient evolution was somewhat unimaginative. With very few exceptions, a broken neck meant the brain was separated from the body.

Turned out, this was not one of the exceptions.

"You okay?" Franks asked as he let the body drop.

"Yes, sir."

"Then let's go . . ."

They stepped over the body, which was when pretty much everyone left on the street noticed that the harness strapped to the outside of the uniform was festooned with multiple small packets and what was obviously a detonation device.

Rough guess, Torin figured there were enough explosives to take out the gate to the second level. The high ground didn't mean much if you couldn't keep the enemy off it.

Franks gave Haysole a push that sent him stumbling into Torin. "Move!" Then he grabbed the body by the feet and stood, heaving it up and into the air. The explosion was messy. Loud and messy.

It wasn't until Franks slumped onto her shoulder as she wrestled him through the gate that she realized not all the blood soaking his uniform had rained down out of the sky.

He'd been hit in the neck with a piece of debris.

As the last squad through got the heavy metal gate closed and locked, he slid down her body, onto his knees, and then toppled slowly to the ground.

Torin grabbed a pressure seal from her vest, but it was too late.

The lower side of his neck was missing. Veins and arteries both had been severed. He'd bled out fast and was probably dead before he hit the ground. There were a lot of things the medics up in orbit could repair; this wasn't one of them.

"Damn, the lieutenant really saved our asses." Sergeant Chou turned from the gate, ignoring the multiple impacts against the other side. "If they'd blown this sucker we'd have been in a running fight to the next level. Is he okay?"

Torin leaned away from the body.

"Fuck." Haysole. The di'Taykan had a way with words.

Chou touched her shoulder. "Do you . . . ?"

"I've got it."

A carrier roared up from the port, its escort screaming in from both sides.

"That's it Marines, we're out of here!"

"Staff . . ."

"Go on, I'm right behind you."

They still had to make it up to the port but, holding the high ground as they did, it shouldn't be a problem. She spread the body bag over Second Lieutenant Franks and sealed the edges as Lieutenant Garly's platoon started spending their heavy ordnance. From the smell of things, they'd dropped something big and flammable onto the street behind the gate.

This wasn't the kind of war people made songs about. The Confederation fought only because the Others fought and no one knew why the Others kept coming. Diplomacy resulted in dead diplomats. Backing away only encouraged them.

But perhaps a war without one single defining ideology was exactly the kind of war that needed an infinite number of smaller defining moments.

Torin smoothed out the bag with one bloody hand then sat back and keyed the charge.

Maybe, she thought as she slid the tiny metal canister that now held Lieutenant Franks into an inner pocket on her combat vest, maybe it was time they had a few songs . . .

THE BLACK OSPREYS

by Michelle West

Michelle West is the author of several novels, including The Sacred Hunter *duology and* The Broken Crown, *both published by DAW Books. She reviews books for the online column* First Contacts *and for* The Magazine of Fantasy & Science Fiction. *Her short fiction has appeared in dozens of anthologies, including* Black Cats and Broken Mirrors, Alien Abductions, Little Red Riding Hood in the Big Bad City, *and* Faerie Tales.

THE AVERDAN VALLEY at night: moon low and red, stars bright. Light enough to see by, no torches required, although they were lit and carried. The earth was broken, the scent of newly turned dirt almost overwhelming.

Commander Kalakar stood at the side of one of her oldest friends, Commander Allen, called the Eagle, and with reason. His eyes were bright in the darkness; bright and keen—but they were dark as well. He touched her shoulder, just that; no words necessary, and therefore none offered. Standing side by side in companionable silence, they could count the dead.

Not accurately, of course; that would come in the morning, and the days that followed. And she would be there, for all of it. Looking for her own House colors among the fallen, looking beyond the crest of sword and rod that signified loyalty to the kings, and the kings' army.

"Ellora."

She nodded quietly.

"The master bard has offered his services, if you require them."

She wanted to say no; the dead couldn't hear his song, after all. But she bit back the word, held it, transformed it into motion. A nod. Some things best left unsaid could be, for now. The living would remember that a master bard of Senniel College had been present upon the field. And the living—most of them—would care.

She didn't give a damn.

Verrus Korama AKalakar joined her as Commander Allen took his leave. He was injured, but not incapacitated, and he carried pen, ink, the slate across which paper would be laid. For the names. For the names, most of which she wouldn't remember, to her shame.

"We won," he said softly. To remind her.

"We always do," she replied. Heavy words. She let pride seep through them and fall away. "Where is Duarte?"

Korama closed his eyes.

In the South, over a dozen years past, they had come for war. The Empire in whose army Ellora AKalakar served hadn't started it, but they responded to its call. She had crossed the stretch of water that knew no natural divide, in the large, long boats of the Empire of Essalieyan. At the head of the armies were three Commanders: Devran ABerrilya, Ellora AKalakar, and Bruce Allen. They were known as the Flight, three great birds of prey, Northern birds: Eagle, Hawk, and Falcon. She flexed those wings now, as if she could stretch pinions and return to the safety of perch and hood after a long hunt.

But she had unleashed the fourth: Ospreys, the Black

Ospreys. It was to the captain of that disbanded unit that she
now strode, stepping carefully over the remains of fallen
horses, men, broken weapons—the detritus of success. The
stench didn't bother her; her nose had gone numb with exposure. The living had already been culled from these fields,
this broken terrible place that was the aftermath of magic.
Some would return, but in dignity.

Some, never.

So many Annagarians here. Once they had been her enemies, or the sons of her enemies. It made no difference now;
they looked at her, numb, and the fact that she was a woman
upon their fields, in the depths of their valleys, failed—at
last—to register. Some men drank, and some sang; Northern
words blended with Southern until she couldn't separate
them. Nor did she try.

She was an officer, after all. She had accepted that duty
almost the day she had accepted the service of men; gods
only knew what those men held sacred. She knew what she
did. She had learned to cultivate tunnel vision with care.

Tonight, the tunnel was long and dark.

Primus Duarte AKalakar was alone. And not alone. Hovering there, at the edge of his grief, and enmeshed in their
own, stood the men and women who had once served the
Kings—served *her*—as Black Ospreys. They paid their re-
spects, in as much as they knew how, to their fallen. Duarte,
holding the body of Sentrus Alexis AKalakar, knelt in their
center.

She had crossed this valley before to reach him. It had almost been easier then. The twelve years that separated that
passage from this one were at once insurmountable and
flimsy.

Duarte AKalakar looked up. Looked past Cook, past
Fiara, past the listing banner of the Tyr upon the field. His
grip tightened briefly. He did not want to let go. Could not,
he realized, hold on. He had been called Primus for more
years than he cared to count, and it all came to this, this mo-

ment. Loss. His fingers brushed hair from the face of a dead woman. His lips touched her forehead. Hard to believe she could be at peace now; she had never been at peace before.

"Duarte."

He rose, carrying Alexis. Listing, like the banner, under her weight. He would miss her anger. It was the first thing she had offered him, when they had met in the South. He had been AKalakar. She had been Alexis.

Cook, seeing the Kalakar, offered his arms, and Duarte hesitated. He wanted to carry Alexis home.

But home, he realized bitterly, had *always* been in Averda. In the Dominion of Annagar, the land of their enemies, when the creation of the unit had first been sanctioned. He handed Alexis, with care, to Cook; Cook had always been the largest of the Ospreys, and against his broad and bloody chest, she looked small. Diminutive. She had always seemed that way to him when she slept—and only then. He paused. Put her long blade in slack hands. Cook shifted her body so that it lay against her chest.

Primus Duarte AKalakar stepped through the small barrier of the living, and went to meet the woman whose House Name he bore.

Duarte had not been born AKalakar. Nobody was. He had been offered the name when he had arrived in the office of Ellora AKalakar. She was not, then, the ruler of House Kalakar, but it was acknowledged that she was damn close. Her hair was a pale, thin gold, shorn so it rested in a wave above blue eyes; her face was round, her bones wide, her lips slightly pursed in annoyance.

She was surrounded by paper. If there was any order to the piles that littered the huge surface of her desk, it was an entirely intuitive order; he didn't doubt that she could find what she wanted, but he *did* wonder if there was anything of value to be found there.

It was clear that she wondered the same thing.

"Duarte Sorrelson?"

He nodded. He was dressed in the robes of a different order, and from the tightening of her expression, it was not an order she favored. Then again, the magi did little to make themselves popular with anyone outside of the Order of Knowledge. He had made certain to wear the symbol of the mage-born across his chest; it hung there, quartered moon, each quarter graced by the iconic symbol of one of the four elements.

"AKalakar," he replied. As she did not tell him to sit, he ignored the fine, empty chairs that girded the visitor side of that desk, biding time, as if it were a test.

She pulled one piece of paper from the wreckage, glanced at it, and let it fall. "You've come seeking employment."

He nodded.

"You are a member in good standing of the Order of Knowledge."

He hesitated for just a moment, and then said, with the barest hint of a frustrated smile, "The words good standing would probably be contested."

To his surprise, she looked at him, really looked, as if he had said the first thing that made him worth looking *at*. "You don't look like a mage," she said at last.

He shrugged. "Lack of gravitas?"

"Lack of slouching. Lack of beard. Lack of hubris." She stood then. "Understand that I am *not* looking for a House mage. We have enough of those."

As it was not yet clear what she *was* looking for, Duarte chose to be respectful; he said nothing.

"You are aware that House Kalakar maintains a large House Guard?"

He nodded. It wasn't exactly a secret.

"Do you have problems with the concept of military authority and military discipline?"

"Not the concept, no."

She raised a pale brow. "Sit."

He sat.

"You were trained with the warrior magi?"

He raised a brow. "The Order of Knowledge does not commonly discuss its constituent parts with those who are not members."

She shrugged. Waiting for a different answer.

After a moment, he shrugged as well. "Yes."

"You are not, I see, considered powerful for one mage-born."

It was almost an insult. "No, I'm not."

"And you were considered somewhat unorthodox in your approach to your studies within the Order."

He nodded again. Assessing her, being assessed.

"The Kalakar House Guard is need of a mage."

"I believe it has two."

"It had two."

"And now?"

"Now it is in need of at least one." There was no humor at all in her smile. There was, however, a challenge. "How good is your Torra?"

"Almost flawless."

"Good. That would be useful; mine is lacking." She paused, and then added, "A number of my soldiers speak the language well enough for the type of diplomacy they'll be involved in."

"How long?"

Her smile stilled. "How long?"

"How long until the war is joined?"

She said, "You're bright, for a mage."

He waited.

"Two months."

He nodded. "You have other applicants, no doubt. I'm interested in the post."

"I have five applicants," she replied. "I can second several, if necessary. You understand that you will be a part of the Kalakar House Guard, should you accept this post?"

He nodded.

"Familiarize yourself with our rules," she told him. "There will be paperwork to sign. I will have it delivered to your domicile." She paused, and then added, "Members of the Kalakar House Guard are offered—and expected to take—the House name."

So, he thought, that was true. He tried not to look eager. It fooled neither of them.

Commander Kalakar met him in silence on the field. She did not ask about Alexis; she could see the answer in every shift of exposed muscle. His face. His hands.

But she offered him this much. "She was mine."

He nodded bleakly, saying nothing. The sky was bright, and the possibilities of the future were, as they always were for the living, endless. The dead walked a different road, and short of following Alexis, it was a road closed to them both.

He was not yet tired of living.

But he understood the honor she obliquely offered Alexis AKalakar, and he hesitated. Once, there would have been none.

The border skirmishes that characterized diplomacy between the Southern Dominion and the Northern Empire had done little to prepare the armies of the Twin Kings for the savagery of the battle itself.

Months, months spent at sea and on dry land, hoarding food and guarding supply lines, had brought them to Averda, for it was in Averda, at last, that there was any purchase upon the heart of the Dominion's gathered forces.

Whole units of enemy Annagarians had been destroyed to the last man, for they failed to understand an offered surrender. Whole armies had been offered up as carrion, and among the fallen, many of the Imperial officers and soldiers who had worn the kings' colors with such early pride.

This was expected; war was war.

But the actions of the enemy within *this* war were almost beyond comprehension. Whole Imperial villages had been razed, their occupants destroyed, their bodies left in smoking ruins: men, women, and children all. The South em-

ployed slaves in almost all levels of life; they had not seen
fit to take slaves from these villages. They had left death,
and the death was ugly.

Not beyond imagining, for a mage.

But for the soldiers? The laws that prevented like deaths
chaffed and strangled, and in the end, many of the Kings'
own were offered to the gallows for their actions of reprisal.

It was to the gallows that Duarte looked, as they were
erected. But it was to the woman he owed his allegiance that
he at last went.

"Give them to me," he asked Commander AKalakar quietly. He forced deference into the words, and it was not entirely feigned. Having seen Ellora AKalakar at the head of
the House Guards that were her pride, he had discovered
that she could lead men anywhere, and they would follow.
Because she was *almost* one of them.

She was writing. On the field, there were few things that
were so necessary that they needed to be signed by a Commander. Among these were writs of execution. Each Commander was responsible for signing the warrants of those
men whom, in the opinion of the military police, deserved
death. It was considered a formality.

Duarte meant to test this supposition.

Exposure to Southern sun had darkened Ellora AKalakar's
skin and her complexion; exposure to Southern warfare had
darkened other things. She looked up from this task, Verrus
Korama a shadow by her side, as he always was.

"What do you mean?" She asked him, half bitter. "Will
you serve as official executioner here?"

"Yes," he said, stark word offered in the darkness of
shadowed tent. There were stockades being built, but it
would be days before they were finished, and the hewing of
wood, the lifting, the fitting, would occupy the army for
some time.

"Why?" She set the papers aside, staring at him.

"I've listened to the Annagarian prisoners," he told her quietly. "You all have."

She nodded.

"They are convinced that the Northern armies are too weak to wage war," he continued softly. "The presence of women upon the field only strengthens this belief. We will slaughter the whole of the Dominion without shaking that certainty if we continue to fight on the terms that we have."

"We are the kings' army," she told him firmly. But she lifted a hand, and after a moment, Verrus Korama chose to retreat.

"And how many of our own—how many of our civilians—will we sacrifice in the name of those kings? The kings are *not here*. But we are."

"Tread carefully."

"I am. But you are signing writs of execution for two women and one man, and I think, AKalakar," he added, using the House name, and not the military title, "that I can make better use of them."

She said, softly, "What use? If I grant you this request, there will be some difficulty for me; Commander Devran ABerrilya is not noted for his tolerance of poor discipline."

"A better use than gallows fodder, although it'll end—for them—in the same way." He was silent for some time. "We need a different way to wage war."

"What different way?"

"Their way. We need to speak their language." He did not flinch; he did not move. He did not fail to meet her eyes. "You cannot ask this of your regular units."

"Ask what?"

A game. But he was adept with words. "That they become your personal monsters."

Her pale brow rose. "I accept no monsters in my service, Duarte AKalakar. I accept men and women who accept *my* command."

"They will," he replied. Games, all games, these words. He knew what he had to do. Had come far enough in this

war, and with this woman, that he was willing to do it. To be
her sacrifice. "But they have already proven that they have
the strength—or the lack of moral fiber—to do what I think
must be done."

"And that?"

"Change the face of the conversation." As if war were
just that, no more.

Verrus Korama returned when Duarte AKalakar left the
tent. He stood in the same spot that he always occupied; to
the left of her back, his hand upon his sword. His expression
was smooth and neutral; he was her calm. She had none. The
hand that was raised above the inkwell shook. She understood the anger that had driven these soldiers to their acts of
desperation and rage; to rape, to disembowelment, to dese-
cration of the not quite dead. To execute them, however, was
the order of the kings. Distant kings.

"Well?" She asked, without turning. Without signing the
documents.

"You know what Commander ABerrilya will say," he
said quietly.

"I don't give a rat's ass about Devran."

She could feel the Verrus' smile; it would be brief.

"Castration of prisoners of war is considered a capital
offense."

She said nothing, waiting.

"But I believe that Commander Allen might listen if you
choose to make your request. These executions will not be
popular with the men."

"Will we win this war?" She asked him. Because she
could. Doubt, in the silence of her own space, was her own
business.

"Not without loss. Perhaps not without the loss that
Duarte AKalakar envisions."

"You must know what he intends." Because she did.
And she had never been a woman who ascribed to the theory that the ends justified the means. Pragmatism warred

with something else, and she knew that it might win. That it would be costly. How costly? Ah, that was the question. "If we lose," she said, to herself, exposing all, "then all we will be are—"

"Monsters." She knew a moment of anger, then. But she had always been a pragmatic woman. An intuitive one. She understood everything that Duarte AKalakar offered her, and she had never expected that offer to come—if it came at all—from a mage.

"Call the Duarte AKalakar back to my tent," she told him quietly.

Primus Duarte AKalakar faced the Kalakar, arms shorn of the weight of the dead in a way that he would never be. "This was her home," he said at last. His words were bitter, but his voice was soft.

After a moment, she nodded. "Yes. This was. She was never at home in the peace of Averalaan. Not after the war."

Because this was honest, because they were two officers alone, Duarte relented slightly. "Not before the war, either. She came looking for death. She didn't much care whether it was her own."

"Only the first time," the older woman whispered.

Because this, too, was true, he said nothing.

"I made you a promise."

He nodded, remembering it.

Alexis Barton. The first name on the list of three. Fiara Glenn. Auralis, no family name given. It was to Alexis that he had gone first, and perhaps, had he chosen a different person, things would have unfolded in a different way.

But he hadn't.

He had crossed the grounds trampled to mud by the boots of Imperial soldiers. Had listened to their whispers, their curses, their Weston phrases of anger. Even their songs, delivered in anger like a prayer to the god of war. Which god, which war, no longer seemed to matter. This, he expected.

But Alexis? He could never have expected *her.*

She was knife thin; the ocean passage had been unkind. Her skin was dark and red; it appeared that the sun had been unkind as well. But her face, like the face of a bird of prey, was bright-eyed, unhooded, and she met his gaze with contempt and defiance. She knew that the gallows were being built, alongside the stockade; could see the wooden beams, some too new in his opinion, as they were raised by ropes and battered into standing shape. She could even see the graves that they'd be granted: traitors' graves, in foreign soil.

Her hair was dark and lanky. What food she had been afforded remained, rotting in the sun; she had taken the water, no more. She had been stripped of rank—private, he thought—and the colors of the unit that she had come with. He knew the unit, or rather, could look it up; it was written beside her name.

As was her crime.

"Alexis Barton," he said, as if he were calling roll. Her eyes narrowed. She'd been stripped of regulation weapons as well: short sword, daggers. He doubted she had the strength to pull a bow. But even without these, she was dangerous.

"That's my name," she said, when it became clear he was waiting for an answer.

"You stand accused of breaking the edicts of the kings."

She shrugged. "The Annies don't read enough Weston to know the edicts."

"No. You understand that the civil treatment of prisoners is one of the things that differentiates us from the enemy?"

She spit. "Not the only thing." Her back was to the pen; she faced him, her knees beginning to bend.

He lifted a hand, and fire flared in a bright ring around her feet. It was a warning. It was the only warning she would get. But her brows rose, and she chuckled. "They sent a mage?" She whistled. Low whistle.

"You are not a member of the Kalakar House Guards," he told her grimly. "But you *are* a member of the army under her command. Your behavior here reflects upon her. Do you understand this?"

Her reply made clear that she did, and that it didn't matter. He almost smiled. But the humor would be lost on this Alexis.

"You served the kings," he replied calmly.

"Look where it got me."

"Could you do it again?"

She stilled. She always stilled when she heard something worth listening to. "Any time."

"Your sentence will be held in abeyance, should you choose to serve," he told her quietly.

She looked at him as if he'd either sprouted another head or had started talking in Torra, the Annie tongue. "Abeyance? Big word."

"But not one with which you are unfamiliar."

She shrugged. "I'm familiar with a lot of words."

"I am Primus Duarte AKalakar," he told her quietly. "And if you choose to accept my offer, you will be a private in my company. You will wear *my* colors, and the only law you will serve is *my* law."

"And what law is that?"

"War's law," he replied grimly. "And the Kalakar's."

"What about the kings?"

"They're not here."

"Then who do you serve?"

"Commander AKalakar," he replied. "Choose."

She shrugged. It was her way of saying yes. He knew it, and would come to know it better, in time. "If you do not prove useful, the gallows will still be your home."

She reached out and grabbed his hand. He almost burned her, but something held him back. "This isn't our war," she said, voice low. "It's *theirs*. They called it. They made the rules."

"Yes," he replied, tightening his hand; replying to her unexpected grip.

* * *

Fiara Glenn had been more difficult. Her rage was harder to contain, and he had endured fifteen minutes of it before he cut her short. The offer he made was curt; he was under no illusion. Those that made their way to the gallows could not *all* be of use. Some, the gallows would claim. He could not be certain that she wouldn't be one of them, and he chose—carefully—not to care.

But when she found out that Alexis was his first private, she folded suddenly, the fire swallowed as she tried to re-member basic discipline. He knew, then, that they were ei-ther friends or co-conspirators. Wasn't certain if this was a good sign or not.

And that left only Auralis. The man who would one day be known as the Bronze Osprey, with his bitter anger, his dark past, his desire for death. Duarte had seen men like him before; men who weren't truly aware that the death they wanted was their own.

Auralis had almost found it, and if he wasn't at peace with it—and he wasn't—he was almost unprepared to have it snatched away. He hadn't spoken a word. Confronted by, confounded by, Duarte AKalakar, he had simply nodded, as if he had expected no less.

"Where is Auralis?" the Kalakar asked, as Duarte sifted his way through memory, walking slowly.

"I don't know. With Kiriel."

The Kalakar said nothing. The memory through which he walked, she now walked, and it was just as tortuous a passage.

By the end of the week, he had ten men and women in his service. They came from different units, and they were wary, ugly, angry. Only Cook was peaceful, although he had not yet earned that name; he was Jules from the Free Town of Morgan, and if he had a family name, he wasn't sharing.

Of the men, Cook had taken most easily to army life. His place upon the gallows had been secured by a berserk and terrible rage, one that took him in fits, and left him shaking, almost unaware of his surroundings. Shorn of this rage—as he so often was—he became an odd peace-broker. His size guaranteed his safety, but only barely. His fists did most of his talking otherwise, but without the rage to drive him, he never hit first. He almost always hit last. Cook was unique. He was humble in his acceptance of the offer of service over death.

The rest?

Given that they walked on the edge of certain death, and at that, at the hands of their own, it was hard to instill in them the respect due the kings' army. Duarte didn't bother to try; that respect would render them useless for his purposes.

The Kalakar had come to visit.

Duarte had not expected her, and was genuinely surprised when she interrupted his training run by the simple action of observing it. He was barely aware of her presence, but Auralis and Alexis stopped almost instantly, as if disturbed by the shadow she didn't cast; the sun was high.

He could still see her clearly as she was that day.

"I know why you're here," she told them, taking up a sitting position on a large, round rock and crossing her arms. It would have been easy to mistake that comment, and many of his ten did. But Duarte looked at her carefully.

"And I've come to tell you this: You serve me. I am Ellora AKalakar, Commander of the third army. You are the walking dead." She had their attention. Held it. "You have committed crimes for which the kings' military police would see you executed. Fair enough.

"I believe you're worth more than that. You are not a part of the kings' army, upon this field. You are part of the Kalakar House Guard."

Duarte's attention was riveted on her. When he had approached her, he had chosen caution; he had couched each phrase with care, so that she might have the opportunity, in the end, to disavow his small company.

But it was not just his attention. The words *Kalakar*

House Guard had a power, both within and outside of its ranks, that had not yet become myth. It was a near thing, though. Because it was known that Commander AKalakar's House Guard *was* her family. The whole of it; she had no children, and had disavowed all ties of kin when she had chosen to take the House name. And she had done it gladly.

"What you will be asked to do in the name of this war, only the gods know," she continued. "But you will be asked it, and more, in *my* name. You will *be* AKalakar, and you will be counted as AKalakar."

Duarte closed his eyes.

She rose. "There are three birds of prey upon this field. The Eagle, the Hawk and the Falcon. I offer you the unenviable position of becoming the fourth, fleet and small." She gestured, and Verrus Korama came to stand beside her. He held a standard, which he unfurled before their eyes.

It was not well made; there were few enough who could be spared for such endeavor. But it didn't matter. Upon the field of kings' Gray, wings stretched, claws extended, flew a black bird. Black Osprey.

A whisper went up among his men, his women, these handful of criminals that had yet to become a working unit, if it ever would.

"Your crimes are your own," she told them. "And I will not ask you to detail them; they are your past. It is your present—and your future—that will define you. If you came to the Ospreys by the paths of the gallows, you have come, unknowing, to House Kalakar. If this war is to be won, we must alter its face; we must build our own legends, our own nightmares. Build as you must, and *only* as you must.

"I demand service," she added. "And loyalty. They are the only things I will ask of you; they are *not* the only things that will be asked of you. But serve me loyally from this point on, and that is all that will grace your service record at the end of this war.

"You are *mine*," she told them. "And if you have success in this war, you will *be* mine. I will not disavow you, and I

will not desert you; all roads that lead to the gallows start—
and end—with me."

She left the standard pole planted in the ground, and
shored up by rock. She left without another word. But words
followed in her wake.

"House Guard? You take a risk," Korama told her, when
they were well away.

"I have to," she replied. She stared at her mailed hands;
the sun was bright and unrelenting. "And if we take the
risk, we take it openly. Duarte is no fool; what he needs
from me, I can't yet say. But I can give him what I can." She
paused, and then smiled grimly. "We need to let them hunt,"
she said, seeing clear sky. "We need to learn to speak a different language."

War's language. Death's language.

"You never did care about keeping your hands clean."

"Not much, no, but then again, I don't have to. Some
other poor bastard will be cleaning off the blood."

Not all of the men seconded to the unit were part of the
third army, and this caused strife almost instantly. Devran
ABerrilya surrendered none of his dead, but Commander
Allen chose to trust the instincts of Commander AKalakar,
and in the weeks that followed, more men and women, execution papers unsigned, were taken from the shadows of the
gallows.

Some of the men, Duarte almost rejected out of hand. He
read their records, and he understood that he could make no
easy use of them. But one use did suggest itself, and in the
end, with reservations, he accepted them.

The raids upon the supply lines had been ferocious, and
worse, the Annies were burning their own stockades as they
anticipated lost ground. Food, always an issue with an army
of any size, was in scant supply, and the heat of the Southern summer, drier than the season that graced Averalaan,
made men mad.

The colors of the Black Ospreys were stitched upon sur-coats that had been grudgingly surrendered by quartermasters across the encampment in ones and twos. Armor was returned to the Ospreys, and with it, weapons. Their attitude hovered between surprise and arrogance. He expected no less.

It was his duty to train them; his training was difficult. He had learned enough magery in the Order of Knowledge to test their reflexes; to test their ability to move silently and without detection. He was not a kind taskmaster, but he didn't have to be; popularity was not his concern.

Fear was. Fear could either make a man very smart or very stupid.

Alexis AKalakar was not a man. And she was not afraid. Not of Duarte, and not of the commander. She offered him the respect due his rank—but it was an ungainly, imperfect respect. The Ospreys had not been chosen for their ability to dress well.

When they numbered fifty-five, he began to teach them the shorthand that would become their silent language; it was almost the language of thieves. It was certainly the language of assassins. They took to it as well as the uneducated could be expected to: very.

"This is a lot of training for not a lot of work."

He looked up from the paper he was examining. They were, as always, writs of execution. Without replying, he handed them to Alexis. He couldn't have said why, had she asked. But she was Alexis. She didn't. Instead, she took them. Leafed through them, her dark eyes focused, flicking over the sparse lines that described crimes, names, units.

"AKalakars?" She asked him, when she had finished. It hadn't taken her all that long. He wondered, for the first time, what she had been in her life before the army. When she had joined. Although the army had always been open to women, few indeed were those who picked up sword and stood in recruiting lines.

"AKalakar," He replied. "And Commander Allen's. Commander ABerrilya will send us nothing."

She shrugged. "Given his reputation, it's probably just as well."

It surprised him. "Why are you here, private?"

"To pass along a bit of friendly advice." Her expression was at odds with the word friendly. Her voice was thin edge.

He nodded slowly.

"Keep an eye on Kreegar."

He nodded again.

She set aside five of the writs. "These," she told him quietly.

"You know them?"

"One of them. But I'd take a risk on the rest."

"The others?"

"Fiara will kill at least two of them."

"If she does, she's dead."

Alexis smiled grimly. It was the only way she smiled, but it changed the landscape of her face. "I know." She turned from the tent, stopped, bent slightly, in its flaps. "But Fiara, you can trust."

He almost laughed. "Not a single one of you could follow the orders you were given, not even when it meant your death otherwise."

"Maybe we didn't like the orders." She shrugged. "Take 'em if you want. Fiara can look out for herself."

He stared at the papers for a long time, musing. In the end, he kept five.

Where food was scant, alcohol was less so. It was a mystery to Duarte, who seldom drank; a mystery and a great annoyance. The first time, he chose to overlook it. Two men were sent to the infirmary with wounds that would render them useless for at least two weeks. The second time?

He shed his forced nonchalance. Drinking *after* battle was a time-honored tradition. Drinking right *before* it, time-honored as well. But this?

He found the men—and woman—who were drinking, and he set the alcohol alight. There were cries of surprise and pain as bottles dropped and cracked, some shattering where they hit the sparse rock along the plateau. Alcohol made men brave.

And stupid. Terribly stupid.

One, scarred, ugly in ways that had nothing at all to do with appearance, took exception to his loss. He recognized the man: Kreegar. Alexis' gift. His dagger glinted in the dying blue fire as he rose swiftly, his Weston a smattering of words that would make street thieves proud.

Duarte, dressed in the finery of a Primus of the Kalakar House Guards, lifted a brow. "Put it down," he said quietly. It was clearly not a request.

Kreegar swore. He wasn't drunk enough to stumble; he certainly wasn't drunk enough to slur his words. Just enough to be foolish.

He lunged at Duarte, who didn't bother to move.

In all, the Kalakar Primus was underimpressed. They had trained *with* him. They should be aware of what he could do, by now. Of course, they hadn't seen it all. He was their Captain, Primus Duarte of the Kalakar House Guards. He was also their last jailer.

He used fire that would have been almost pathetic among the Warrior mages of the Order of Knowledge, seconded to the kings. And while the fire burned, and Kreegar screamed, he stepped in with his sword. It was not his favored weapon. Favored or no, it did its work. It passed through Kreegar's chest with unerring accuracy.

And Kreegar? Passed on to the Halls of Mandaros, where judgment awaited him.

All sound died; the wind seemed to hold its breath as he watched the twenty Ospreys who now lingered around him in a circle. If they chose to attack him, it was over.

He could see indecision at play across many faces, some more familiar than others. If the gallows hadn't held them back, death wouldn't.

The silence strengthened, thinned, grew oppressive.

It was broken by Alexis, who turned to her companion. "Pay up," she said, holding out a flat palm.

Her companion was Auralis. "Pay up?"

"You said six days. I said three."

"It was four. The way I see it, there are no winners."

"Then open your damn eyes. I was closer. You owe me."

Fiara laughed. "Don't mess with him, 'Lexis."

"The hells. Pay up," she added, sliding her dagger out of its sheath.

"Sentrus," Duarte said coldly.

Everyone stared at him. He stared at Alexis. Her expression shifted instantly into a clean anger, but she jammed her dagger back into its sheath. She was fond of it; she didn't want to lose it.

Or have it embedded in her chest.

"The rest of you, back to your tents."

Fiara whistled; she made a fist and pumped it once. "Sentrus," she said, managing both syllables without a sneer.

Alexis still faced Duarte. After a moment, she said, "Do I get a raise?"

"My tent," he said, still cold. "Now."

All studied casualness was gone the minute the witnesses were. Alexis faced him across his pathetic excuse for a desk. Field desks were terrible, unless you were a commander. It was a rank he would never attain. And he thanked the gods daily for that fact.

"You've been here three weeks," he told her quietly. He did not refer to her promotion. "I've had Dunbar confined three times; I've broken up eight fights. I've killed three men, including Kreegar."

She lifted a hand. "Permission to speak freely?" she said, with a trace of humor.

His raised brow told her how much he appreciated the attempt. "Granted."

"Nine fights."

He thought, for a moment, that had he actually been a commander, the army would be a *lot* smaller. "Nine, then. Your point?"

"Give us something else to fight. Soon."

"Sentrus—"

"Alexis will do."

"I decide that."

She shrugged. "Whatever. You can add a stripe or a quarter circle to the arm. Or the armpit. It won't make a damn bit of difference. No one trusts you. No one trusts each other. You have no idea if we ever will."

He nodded quietly.

"But with people like us, there's only one way to test it. We're not theoreticians. We're not even army. We're just . . . your cadets." She said the word with a grimace. Lifted her hands, signaling, of all things, retreat. "We only learn one way, Primus. We don't know what you want. We can guess. Some of us are pissed off about it; some don't give a damn."

"What do you 'guess' we want?"

"You want us to fight like the Annies fight. We're ready to do that." She paused, and then added, "But we're not ready to sit, to wait, to be picked off because we're stupid. Give us a fight."

He nodded quietly. "Sixty-seven men and women. You're one sentrus. Who will the others be?"

Her brows rose and then lowered, as if they were wings.

"Not Fiara," she said at last. "And if you repeat that, I'll kill you."

"You'll try."

"Even odds. I've seen you fight. But unlike Kreegar and half of the rest, I paid attention."

He nodded grimly. "Continue."

"Auralis, maybe. You'll have to bust him down, but he'll do."

"That's two. I need at least five."

"Margie. She's grim, but she's got enough discipline to keep things in line unless all hell breaks loose. Stepson."

"Stepson? He's a—"

"Psychotic, yes. But fear works. He knows you'll kill him if he blinks the wrong way; you've been itching to do it. That's what, four of us? Put Cook up as well."

"Cook is—"

"Bloody big."

Duarte hesitated for just a moment, and then he nodded again. "Don't let the tent hit you on the way out."

She muttered something rude under her breath. It was a start.

Ellora AKalakar liked maps.

Which was good; she had to look at a lot of them, and some were of questionable accuracy. She made marks on them, pinned flags to them, removed flags from them, watched as whole river boundaries were redrawn. Birds were the scouts of choice for the Northern army, but a bird's-eye view was not always accurate, and very, very few people could get information from conversations with birds. She found some amusement in watching them try.

Then again, she found mages more or less amusing in general. They were obdurate, arrogant, overweening in their vanity; they fretted about things that she hadn't worried about since the vagaries of youth had been shaken off with a vengeance. With the exception of the warrior magi, they were all considered elderly, although she privately thought much of that age was like carefully applied make-up; age and wisdom, or age and power, were often conflated among mages.

That, and she liked their beards.

Had she hated the magi, she would have found them amusing anyway, because Devran ABerrilya could not abide their presence for more than an hour at a time. He was not a man given to outburst; instead, he used silence like a blunt instrument. He was positively glacial on this particular day.

It was the first time she had pinned a black flag to the map. She thought he might reach out to sweep it away, and apparently, so did Bruce Allen; the Eagle hovered between them, his shadow like outstretched pinions, while the mages talked among themselves.

At length, however, they finished, and they turned their attention to the maps that held them all. The Terrean of Averda and the Terrean of Mancorvo were the most detailed portions of the map; there were only two passages into the Dominion, one through each. But Mancorvo's pass went through the mountains; Averda's did not.

It was therefore in Averda that most of the battle was likely to be fought.

"What will your Ospreys do?" Commander Allen asked quietly.

"What they have to."

"And that?"

She shrugged. "Change the face of the Northern army."

Devran's face grew slightly pinched. "The face of the kings' army does not require changing."

"We've had this argument," Commander Allen said. He looked at Ellora, his gaze keen. "You're sending them into the heart of the Annagarian front."

She nodded. "They're few enough."

"They won't make it," Devran replied.

Her turn to shrug. She did; it was artless. "They were carrion anyway. What do you care?"

"They broke the kings' laws."

"The Annies don't care about the kings' laws, and we're not in the Empire."

"I *said* we've had this argument."

Devran rose. "Will you let her play these games?"

"They're not games," she replied evenly.

He ignored her. He often did. "Her men are barely part of the army; they serve *her*. I do not want our command structure to devolve into a personality contest."

"You command your army," she told him. "I'll command mine."

"You will answer to the kings."

No, she thought, but she didn't bother to say it. She looked at the markers and pins. *I'll answer to their wives, their children, their parents. If they have any who give a damn.*

Sixty-six men and women were not a small force, unless held against the balance of the Imperial army. Primus Duarte AKalakar watched them warily. Truth? He didn't like them. They didn't like him. He was counting on the fact that they hated the Annies more. He had tested this hatred a handful of times, culling their numbers; choosing, with deliberate care, the men who could best serve as examples by dying. He was not a torturer; he generally killed quickly. He did not kill officially.

That would require paperwork and time, neither of which he had in abundance.

No, he thought, as Alexis lifted two fingers in the silence of the occasional snapped branch. It would require *distance*. It would make him just another servant, albeit one with rank. This way, he was master, or no one was.

It was close.

With the Black Ospreys, it would always *be* close.

By killing swiftly, and without any compunction, without any sign of hesitation or remorse, he made the game deadly. More, he made it clear that they were *his*.

He waited a moment. Alexis lifted her left hand, and flattened her palm. He lifted his own, then, as if he were a conductor, and brought them together. She nodded, left her men, her fingers dancing wordless in the air.

She had learned quickly. And she moved.

He was almost captivated by the speed and silence of that graceful motion. His eyes were still on her when she reached his side, and she noticed; she noticed everything. Her brows rose in amusement, but her eyes were steady and unblinking when they came to rest upon the village. The valley contained it. Here, between the perch of too many trees, they could see the planted fields, and beyond them, the huts that were home to the Dominion's slaves. Beyond those huts, a stone manor, the only such dwelling, and behind it, the tall structures that were, in theory, their target. Granaries. They were guarded; he could see horses moving in the distance. They were more easily counted then men. In fact, in Averda, they were counted and prized more highly than men.

He did not look at his hands.

Alexis did. And she smiled. They had traversed the forests with care, avoiding the mounted patrols and guardposts that the Annies relied on. The Imperial army was a theory, now; the Ospreys were surrounded, in all directions, by the forces of the Tyr'agnate of Averda. Callesta.

Learn to speak a different language, he thought.

He glanced back once. Just once.

The night would be filled with sounds of terror: laughter, screaming, the cries of the dying. Some of them would be his; most would not. Twisted fate, then, that the ones that would linger longest, in memory and nightmare, would be those that were not.

But they were parchment, paper; they were the things upon which the first of the Northern messages would be left. Over the corpses of the dead—the many, and the helpless—the banner of the Ospreys would be the only moving thing by night's end, and it would move by the grace of the Southern wind.

Wind was the only thing the Southerners seemed to fear, and the wind carried the Black Ospreys.

Ellora AKalakar looked up as Verrus Korama entered her quarters. He was quiet, which was not unusual; like Devran, his silences were often more telling than his speeches.

He handed her a tube; she touched it. Beneath her hands, it warmed, waiting. She spoke a phrase, placed her thumb against the edge of tube that would either open or explode, and waited.

This was Duarte's work.

Korama waited while the tubing fell away; waited while she uncurled the missive it contained. He even waited while she read it, his posture pitch-perfect, as if it were the only grace-note in a particularly grim second act.

"Kallos has fallen," she whispered. The paper fluttered to her desk. She did not touch it again.

"There was resistance," he said, when it became clear she wouldn't.

She understood what he offered, and refused to accept it. "There would be," she replied, black humor edging all of the syllables. "Any bets?"

He frowned. "Don't," he told her quietly.

"Don't?"

"Don't think like an Osprey. They have that luxury, AKalakar. You don't."

Luxury. "Did anyone survive?"

"In the village? Possibly. At night, it would be hard to be certain."

She didn't ask about prisoners.

She didn't ask about anything. She had come to war, and with her, had brought the certain callousness that any officer must. She balanced on its edge.

"Kalakar."

She had not looked away from Duarte.

"The Ospreys were born here," she said quietly.

"And they were laid to rest in the North," he replied, equally quiet. "We surrendered the colors there. We thought it wouldn't matter." His shrug was dismissive. "We were never a peacetime unit."

She looked at him, gave him that much. The darkness hid many scars.

"This was a different war."

"A cleaner war."

"Duarte—"

"Alexis will stay in the South."

And you?

*   *   *

By the time they were sent to the third village, word had spread. The Northern armies were known, in the South, by the visage of the Osprey, and its wings were black.

The prisoners that the rest of the army gathered—and admittedly, they were few enough—spoke of the Ospreys in bitter, implacable Torra. They spoke of little else, and the words were both curse and promise.

You could have painted targets on their backs, Duarte thought, gazing at his unit. But they would have been small targets, and at that, in constant motion.

The Annies thought they numbered in the hundreds. In the thousands. They thought the wind carried them. They thought the Lord of Night blessed them. Duarte was willing to admit that if there *was* a Lord of Night, they worked in his shadow.

He thought about clipping their wings.

But it was only thought. And if he didn't join them in savagery, if he didn't join them in murder, he gave them the opportunity to vent their rage, to plant the seeds of a different rage in their enemies. Anger made fools of all men.

Even Duarte AKalakar.

The villages around the granaries became focal points for the Tyr's cavalry units. The valleys were not kind to horses; the Ospreys, who used them seldom, less so.

They added *horsekiller* to the long list of epithets they wore as badges. They took their greatest losses in that enterprise. And they suffered the bitterest of their divisions there. Men, women, and children? They were seen as mirrors. Their deaths were markers, the oldest variant of an eye for an eye.

But the horses were harder. Not for Duarte, and not for many of the Ospreys. Fiara, however, was livid. As if the horses were helpless, and the children were not.

Alexis reined her in; it was close.

Duarte felt the first hint of unease, then; he was prepared

to kill Fiara—but he didn't *want* to kill her. Wanted, in fact, the opposite. It was unexpected. Unaffordable.

The Ospreys had lost and gained men; the gallows were empty, their shadows paler and more peaceful than the shadows the Ospreys cast. But each new Osprey that survived Duarte, that survived the insane and suicidal missions that Duarte himself chose, became AKalakar. The name meant something to them.

But not, in the end, as much as the Black Osprey did.

He hadn't expected that.

He didn't expect, truth be told, that *any* of them would survive this enterprise, this terrible act of madness that their war had become. There were even moments—all of them silent—when he welcomed the thought.

War made killers of men and women.

His embraced them. They were his.

Commander AKalakar waited.

She watched the Primus as he crossed the plateau; watched the silence that enfolded him. He did not seem to be aware of it; he was aware of his armor, his steps, the path that led to her and from her.

By his side, in the ragged surcoats that now meant almost everything to the Annies, the Ospreys walked across the camp as if they owned it. She could almost understand why Devran hated them; they were feared. They knew it.

Primus Duarte gave a curt order to the woman who stood closest, and she, in turn, transmitted that order. Hard to imagine that men who could swagger in such a ragged line could also come to so abrupt a halt. But they did, and they watched Duarte recede as she watched him approach.

She said, "You don't look so much the mage."

His smile was slightly lopsided. His eyes were ringed dark, his hair flat against forehead and skull. Like the rest of the mages upon the field, he decried helms, and he never wore them.

She couldn't argue with success. "Primus."

He snapped a brisk salute. He was probably the only Black Osprey who *could.* "Commander."

"Report."

He did. She forced herself to listen. It wasn't as hard as it might have been; there was fascination in his words, and because of it, they were fascinating. She could trace the spiral path of his flight, and it made her uneasy.

He waited, and when the silence stretched, she realized he had finished speaking. And would never finish. The man who had come to House Kalakar seeking employment was almost entirely absent.

"Duarte," she said, without thought.

He waited.

"The Ospreys have been noted by the Tyr'agnati of both Mancorvo and Averda. The Tyr'agar himself has, for the first time in the course of this war, put a bounty on your heads."

He allowed himself to nod.

"The Tyr'agar is in control of the field." She paused, and then added, "He is not the equal of his generals." She wanted to tell him that he could stop. Wanted to, and knew that it was a lie. He had what they wanted: the attention of the Tyr'agar. Now? They had to focus it, hone it, keep it.

"Your men are the face of the army," she whispered.

And saw his reaction, clearly. Turned away.

"You're drinking."

Duarte looked up from the lip of the canteen. Alexis stood in the lee of what could charitably be called a tent. The months that had worn away at his reserve, draining what could equally charitably be called youth, had not touched or tarnished her. She moved like a cat. A hunting cat.

When she moved. It was clear that tonight she didn't mean to.

He shrugged. Stared at the canteen. Something as civilized as a glass had long since been rendered useless. "It's a habit I've picked up," he told her.

She shrugged, stepped into the tent. He could not remember the day; could barely remember the month. But he would remember her, always. "I've got nothing against drinking," she told him, taking the canteen from hands that had gone nerveless, "but they say you shouldn't drink alone."

"They don't say anything to me," he replied, smile hollow but present, as if his face were a mask.

"They do," she said. All humor had left her slender face. It took him a moment to realize that she was replacing the canteen's stopper. "I think you've had enough."

"For what?"

"For now." She set it aside. Or rather, tossed it aside. Her eyes were dark, keen. She took a seat beside him. He really had had enough; he didn't speak.

She surprised him—she always would. Caught his hand between hers. Her arm was dressed, her shoulder dressed; she had almost been killed by the crescent blade of a Southern horseman. Almost didn't count for much.

Cook was a bit of a medic.

He certainly wasn't much of a cook.

"What have you done this time?"

She laughed, and the sound was startling; it was clear and high. Most of her laughter was guttural, visceral.

"I won a bet or two. I busted Auralis down a rank," she added.

"You can't."

"I can't. You can. And did."

"Funny. I wasn't there."

"It was. Funny," she added. "He missed."

With Alexis, it was hard to tell how much of her humor was based in fact. He didn't ask.

"What did *he* do?"

"He pinched Margie's backside."

Duarte laughed. It, too, startled him. Enough that he fell silent, staring at her hands. They moved across his skin, fingers drumming, silent language. A question. The wrong question.

"Yes," he said, shaking her off. "I'm fine."

"Did you hear that we're wanted men?"

"From Commander AKalakar. Where did you hear it?"

"From just about everyone. The Tyr'agar was enraged when we left the horses—"

"Enough, Sentrus."

She stopped instantly. Because there was death in the tone. Even for her.

When she spoke, she was cautious. The way people who stepped on the mage-fields were. Each word was deliberate and slow. "It's not easy, is it?"

His expression didn't change.

"You were a city boy. You were always a city boy. Look at you now. You had money," she added bitterly. "You must have. Maybe even a family." She shook herself free of the bitterness; it was a touch too close to dangerous.

"Now you're surrounded by murderers, thieves, rapists. Every day, and every night. You almost have to be one, just to get by." She paused. "But you're still there, on the thin side of the edge, behind an officer's rank."

"I don't keep my hands clean."

"No. You don't. But outside of the fighting—when there is much—the only people you've killed have been Ospreys."

"And what would you have me do, *Sentrus*?"

"If you were any other man, I'd tell you to join us," she whispered. She looked at the canteen; he caught the bent profile of a nose that had been broken at least once, and was lovely because of it.

It wasn't what he'd expected. Alexis never was.

"And as I'm not, as you so quaintly put it, any other man?"

"Don't." She stood. "I didn't understand you, the first day we met. And after the first village, I thought I might. But by the third?" She shrugged. "I wouldn't bet money on anything you might do. So I've been watching you."

"I've been watching you."

Her smile was a brief, sly flash of teeth. It was a miracle that she still had them.

"Not in the same way. Or maybe not only in the same way."

Dangerous ground, here. But he rose as well. "What have you seen?"

"You've come as far as you *can*. The rest of us? We can go farther, Primus. Some of us—Cook, Amberton—can pretend it's in the name of duty. Most of us don't bother. But most of us aren't thinking either. Most of us haven't figured out that we're here because of you. Oh, we know we'd be feeding the vultures." She paused, watching him. He let her worry.

But worry had its own rhythm. "Most of us think you need us because we're killers. Most of us think you don't need anything else from us."

"They're right."

"But most of us don't understand that we need you because you're *not*." Her hand touched the canvas beside the tent flap, and she winced. "You've let us fly," she told him, looking away. "But that's only half the hunt. Some of us are finally ready to land, Primus."

She looked, for a moment, weary. But only a moment. "Hood and jesses," she said softly, as if the words could actually mean something to her. "Rein us in."

"There's only one way to rein in the Ospreys."

She shrugged. "I know." She started to leave.

"Sentrus." Pause. "Alexis."

And turned back. "We know what we *are*," she said quietly. "Make us something *more*."

"If it weren't for what you are—"

"Duarte, we can go on like this until the army slaughters us all—doesn't much matter which army. But *you* can't. I'm not asking you to do this for our sake—hells, I don't even know what 'our' means. I'm not even asking you to do this for my sake, because I can keep going with the rest. I made my choice, the first time. You gave me a different choice, and I made that one, too. I thought it would help."

He had never asked her why she had done what she had done. Didn't want to ask now. "And did it?" This was as close as he would come.

She shrugged, looking bored. Bored Alexis was at her most restless, her most dangerous. "We fear you."

"With reason."

"But it's more than just fear."

"Maybe for you."

She shook her head. "Not just for me, Duarte. Take the risk, now. Now is the right time."

And he did. He reached out for her wrist, caught it, held it. She almost pulled away. But she didn't. He drew her back, into the tent. And she stayed.

She was the first of the Ospreys that he loved. The first that he trusted. Of the latter, he would find a handful more, over the swift passage of days. The former? He could take another lover if he wanted to part with his balls. Alexis never made a verbal threat, but it was clear, by the end of the following three days, that she was his.

Or, more accurately, that he was hers.

This did not come as a surprise to the Ospreys, much to his chagrin. Fiara was smug enough to let slip that she'd won a betting pool, and Alexis' icy stare was enough to let him know what the betting pool had been about. It should have angered him. It amused him instead, and short of contemplating the rage of the man who had forced them all to war, there was little that did.

He took what he could get.

And found that in the taking, his position had changed. It was a subtle change, for Duarte himself remained much at a distance, ready to kill when judicious pruning was required, but he was trained by the Order of Knowledge; he noticed it.

Alexis had not precisely made him one of them; no more had he made her stand apart. But the line that had separated them blurred, and he realized that she had become the dark face of a den mother, daggers in hand, death waiting her displeasure. And by association? He could not think of himself as father. But she spoke for him, and he allowed it.

He was busy thinking of other things that she'd said. How to rein in the Ospreys without clipping their wings and diminishing their shadow?

Now, he thought, was the time to take risks. But they were Alexis' words.

"We're Kalakar House Guards."

He was prepared for the stares he received, but not prepared to listen to argument; since his expression made this clear, no one offered any.

"We're Black Ospreys, first and foremost, but Commander AKalakar has always made it clear that we're part of her personal force." He paused. Let the words sink in as far as they could; given the Ospreys, he was lucky if they scratched the surface.

"The House Guards won't argue with her. But they won't accept us as soldiers. Or hers."

"We don't need 'em."

Flame shot out in a thin stream; it was met by a curse that did not quite elevate into a scream. Warning shot. He didn't usually give them.

"We're baby killers," he said. "Looters. Rapists. They don't think we know how to wield swords. They don't think we know how to fight a war."

"We're fighting an Annie war."

He held his hand.

"We've been fighting an Annie war on Annie terms," he told them. "And on their terms, we've done some damage. But we've done damage to slaves, buildings, a couple of horses."

"And their riders."

He shrugged. "Three men. Four. Against sixty."

They were the Ospreys' favored odds.

"We've proven that we can go where the House Guard

can't." He paused. Gazed out at the Ospreys who lounged against trees, flat rocks, open ground. For just a moment, he regretted the absence of Commander Berrilya. Because this *was* the Osprey idea of discipline, and it was a pity to waste it.

"We wanted fear. We have it. The fear of every slave girl and child in the Dominion."

This, this was not what they wanted to hear. Too bad.

"But because we've proven that we *can* survive, it's time to up the ante."

"To what?"

"We want," he replied, "the fear of the men who count."

"The Tyr'agar has a price on our heads."

"Yes. For property damage." One or two grim chuckles. Better than he'd hoped for.

"But now we start in earnest. Are you ready for that? You, Sorren? Fiara?" The latter nodded. The former looked suspicious. He wondered which of the two was the smarter. "Are you ready to actually fight? Can you watch each other's backs when the people are running toward you, rather than away? Can you kill men who have a good chance of stopping you?"

Auralis AKalakar laughed. "I can kill pretty much anything that moves. Do they scream?"

"I don't know."

"Why don't we find out?"

Verrus Korama came, as he often did, when the sun was fading and the sky was changing hue. But there was something in his posture this eve that made Ellora take notice. She frowned. It was an open invitation to discussion.

Instead, he handed her a report. It wasn't sealed; it wasn't magically keyed. Not Primus Duarte's, then. She took it, and held it before the glow of burning oil. "What is this?" She said, when her eyes stopped halfway down the page.

"I believe," he replied quietly, "that your Ospreys are stretching their wings."

"Has the primus lost his *mind?*"

"There are those who would argue that that happened months ago."

Her frown was deeper than his; light made it more severe. "He took on their cavalry scouts in broad daylight."

"Apparently."

"With pit traps."

"Apparently."

"How the hells did he dig them without being seen?"

Korama shrugged. "He's mage-born."

She snorted. She'd had enough of mages long before she'd set foot on dry land. Her eyes caught the thread of Weston that she'd abandoned, and she read, her pale brows rising and falling as her eyes crested the words. In the end, she laughed.

"The main body of the three armies were nowhere near the scouting party; the scouts were returning from the front. It's unlikely that they expected this level of aggression within their own territory. The Ospreys took casualties," Korama added.

"I can see that. How accurate are these numbers?"

"Ask the birds."

She'd sooner ask the birds than the mages who flew them. She flipped the paper over. Turned it down and read on. The last page was written in a bold hand, thick, dark strokes of ink above the plain signature of Commander ABerrilya.

"Yes," Korama said, before she could speak. "The commander wishes to know why you chose to deviate from your plan."

"Tell him to get stuffed."

At that, Korama's brow rose. Predictably and comfortably. "I will tell him," he said stiffly, "that he was busy on the front, and you did not have time to confer with him about your change of plans." He turned to leave, and spoke without looking back. "Primus Duarte has changed the dialogue of the war; I believe it is his intent to change the face of the Black Ospreys."

Ellora said nothing. A lot of it. But some tightness of chest had relaxed, and she could allow herself to admit how worried she had become. Not for the war; that was its own burden. For Duarte. For the House Guard.

"Verrus?"

"Commander."

"Tell the quartermaster the Ospreys have lost their standard again. Tell him we need a dozen." It was their calling card, after all.

Auralis was swearing. In and of itself, that was not unusual. He was, however, swearing *at* the Ospreys under his nominal command. His swift action in the attack upon the scouting party had regained him the rank of sentrus, and he seemed determined to make the most of it while he had it. Gods knew, with Alexis' temper and Auralis' open lack of respect, it probably wouldn't be long.

But the tenor of the swearing was unusual. And because it was, Duarte listened. That he used magic to do so annoyed Alexis.

"Would you prefer I go in person?"

"Yes."

She was in a mood. He could squelch it with a curt, cold word, but chose instead not to make his night miserable. He gestured, cutting the magical ties that girded the small encampment, and rose. Alexis followed, like fate. Or fury.

" . . . your armor is practically moving on its own!"

Duarte's brow rose. He glanced at Alexis. She smiled, but it was brief.

"We've done *three times* what the rest of the damn Kalakar House Guard couldn't do once. Shale, you lazy bastard, where the hell is your kit?"

There were no latrines to be dug; the Ospreys, as always, were on the move. But three of Auralis' men were on kitchen duty by the end of the tirade. Only one attempted to argue with the sentrus; he was in Cook's tent. A reminder, as Auralis made clear, that there was a step lower than private.

"This is your work?" Duarte asked Alexis, as they watched the men begin their practice.

"Not mine."

"Why did he mention the House Guard?"

"Because we're part of the House Guard," she said, with a thin smile, "and he's a competitive sonofabitch."

"There's something you're not telling me."

"Love, there's *always* something I'm not telling you." But she caught his hand and squeezed it before letting it drop. Alexis' idea of a public display of affection usually involved bruises.

"Cook's men?"

"Medic tent."

"We don't have a medic tent."

"We do now."

"Alexis—"

She said, voice low, "Cook is willing. He's knocked six heads together, he's broken two ribs, blackened three eyes. The men," she added. "He doesn't usually try to hit the rest of us."

"Alexis—"

"You told them what they had to do. You killed two men. They listened." She looked at his face without touching it. "I want the rest of your cache," she added.

"My what?"

"You're not drinking so much."

"Alexis—"

"It's worth money."

He shrugged. She laughed. One or two of the Ospreys looked up at the sound.

"You're enjoying this."

"Yes," she told him, smile creasing her lips. "You aren't?"

"I'm the primus," he replied, with what dignity he could salvage.

"You are. But you take your chances with the rest of us. It's enough, Duarte."

The Ospreys lost no battles. They were chosen with care, with the subtle magery that had been, in the end, unsuitable for the warrior magi with whom he had chosen to study. They struck quickly, moved quickly, burned forests when they needed an easy way to retreat. They carried food enough for lightning strikes, and lost days to foraging, but the days they lost were also days in which those who would walk again could take the time to find their feet.

But they always traveled back to the army; Duarte always made his report. Commander Ellora AKalakar spent more time with him in the presence of the House Guard, and he, in turn, more time in the company of the House Guard. It was not always easy.

But the last time they returned, their numbers winnowed, new members waiting, the Kalakar took him aside in full view of the House Guard, and asked him the most significant question she had yet asked where others could hear her speak.

"Where are the fallen?"

The question made as much sense as any officer's questions did; Primus Duarte stared at her for a moment, as if trying to translate the words into a language he better understood.

"You've spent little time in the ranks of my House Guard," she said, pitching her voice so that it carried. The wind helped. "So I'll make myself clear. Bring the fallen home."

"It will cost us time," he said at last, as the full import of her words made themselves clear.

"Bring them home," she said again, "or tell us where you left them."

"Beneath the banner of the Black Ospreys," he told her.

She nodded. Turned to Korama.

*   *   *

Aside from the growing outrage of the quartermaster, El-lora heard few complaints. And she listened for them when she walked among her own. The House Guard spoke quietly of the Black Ospreys, but every now and then, they let the unit's colors blend with their own.

The black bird of prey was scattered across the front. The Ospreys chose to leave it when they left the scene of battle. It was their signature. And it was hers.

Devran ABerrilya was in a sour mood. Although she knew it was petty, she was satisfied. Commander Allen was diffident and calm. The map spoke for them.

"He's shaken the confidence of the Tyr'agar," the com-mander said. "The Tyr has moved two of his armies onto the plateau, and one into the valley."

"Valley's no good for cavalry," she said with a frown. "Better for magic."

"There isn't a surfeit of magery from within the enemy's rank." He circled a large area of the map. "We can approach the army on two sides."

"When?"

"Three days. Maybe four."

She nodded.

"Commander AKalakar?"

"Commander Allen."

"Good work."

"The dead don't give a shit," Auralis said, with a grunt. Fiara's complaint was more succinct.

"The commander does."

"Tell her to carry them."

Duarte's expression was about as soft as stone. "She does," he said. And surprised himself by believing it. No one else offered any argument, and this surprised him as well. The Ospreys had taken the time to bury their dead, when they had it. They no longer left the wounded to fend for themselves. Once or twice, Duarte himself had stepped in to cloak the retreat of those who dragged the fallen behind them; he could not hide the blood trail left for long, but it was always long enough.

It took them an extra two days—two days' worth of food—to reach the army base.

The Kalakar was waiting for them.

The House Guard, in full dress, was behind her.

She ordered the House Guards forward, and they obeyed in silence, joining the Ospreys; the difference between the field and the camp evident in the state of their surcoats, the length of their stubble, the overall *smell* of a road that was carved by feet alone.

The House Guards took the dead. They handled them with care, with a solemnity that even the Ospreys couldn't have managed. Or so Duarte would have bet—which was probably why he didn't.

The dead served as a reminder to the living. They were accorded the full honors of the fallen, and if the medals that decorated them briefly meant nothing at all to their corpses, if they should have meant nothing to their comrades, they did.

"We need the Ospreys," Ellora said quietly.

"Where?"

"With the House Guards."

"With the army?"

She nodded. He waited.

"We need the colors," she said, surrendering. "But you built them, Duarte. I would never have said they would become what they've become. I would have been willing to bet," that word again, "that they'd give up the flag to the House Guard."

"They might."

She raised a pale brow. Her eyes were a shade of gray-blue, clear, far-seeing. "Ask them," she said. "But ask carefully. Don't be surprised at their answer." She paused. "And don't kill them for it, either."

*   *   *

"She wants *what?*"

Duarte faced Alexis across about five feet of space. No desk to hide behind, no chair to sit in, no bed to lie on. The sun was high above them, and around them, in the loose, languid circle Commander ABerrilya so despised, the Ospreys waited.

"The Tyr'agar has moved his armies into position," Duarte said, speaking, as Ellora AKalakar had commanded, with caution. "This could be it."

"What could be what?"

"The Annies aren't well-organized. The Tyr's armies are, but they're not the only men on the field. We'll have armies across the plateau and in the valleys, and the commanders think the Tyr'agnate, at least, will be present in the valley."

"And the Tyr'agar?"

He shrugged. "Less clear. We're not a large unit. We aren't accustomed to working within the main body of *any* army. We're not used to battlefield orders. The commander recognizes this.

"But she wants our colors to fly on the field. I think," he added, taking a risk, "that if it were up to her, it would be *only* our colors."

"And she'd take the colors without the *unit?*"

"Yes."

"Sounds good to me," Auralis said, stretching. Duarte considered busting him to private before Alexis could. It had become a bit of a contest—one of many. "But then again, I wouldn't mind mooning Commander ABerrilya."

The mention of his name always had an effect on the Ospreys. Usually it wasn't useful. Today, it might be.

"Realistically," Duarte continued, "it's the Osprey that bears weight. There probably isn't a man in the Annie armies that won't recognize it. And there probably isn't a man in the armies that won't make straight for it, either. Not a good bet."

"You'd let her do this?"

He met Alexis cold, cold glare. "She isn't standing the unit down," he said at last.

"But the House Guard *aren't* Ospreys. We are."

"We're sixty, give or take a few. They number in the hundreds, and within the third army, even that's insignificant. But the Black Osprey isn't."

"No."

"One sentrus." He turned to face the others.

Auralis shrugged. "I'm in, if you are."

Two. Cook nodded. Fiara spit. Margie smiled.

"They're ours," Alexis said, meaning it. "Whatever that bird means, we made it. Where are you going, Primus?"

"The commander is waiting," he said, with gravity. "I'll tender her our response."

Twelve years later, Duarte stood beside the woman who had taken her House, becoming the Kalakar in the process. Across the long, dark stretch of broken valley, trees riven and fallen over bodies that it would take days to recover, he could see the standard of the Tyr'agnate of Callesta. Ramiro kai di'Callesta stood beneath it.

"Do you hate him?" Ellora asked. It wasn't really a question.

Enemies became allies, and allies, enemies, with the turn of time and circumstance. "No. What we did, we felt we had to do. And what he did showed his mettle, even then."

"He was younger. He lost his father in early fighting."

"He was no fool. Not then. Not now."

"No," she said softly. Remembering. "He knew what the colors would mean to the Tyr'agar, and the armies of the South." She was careful not to use the derogatory term Annie. But for the moment, it was difficult.

Sixty men. Three standards. It was overkill. It was, in retrospect, an early target. It was also the only target worth striking in the South. Black Osprey. Northern Osprey.

Northern army.

They were to be positioned in the valley in two days' time. Two days was a *long* time, for the Ospreys. Too long to listen to the military patrols. Too long to pretend that they had a hope of maintaining Imperial discipline. Duarte had them on training runs through the valleys' height—the valleys that the Imperial army had claimed as their own. Beneath the heights, the fields lay, and behind them, the blackened ruins of villages that had been destroyed by either side. No food there; nothing of value.

He reined them in; they let him. They really were birds of prey. His, he thought. But he thought, as well, of the Kalakar.

She wanted the standard; he'd given her the unit. He wondered if she would surrender the latter to battle. The Black Ospreys had done what no unit had honorably done in the history of the Empire. What better way to lose it? To the Annies. To the real war.

She could say a eulogy as she laid the colors to rest.

Alexis touched his shoulder, and he turned, catching her hand. Thinking of death, of her death. It hurt him in ways that he had never thought to express. Wordless, she kissed the side of his face. "Do you trust her?" she asked, her lips beside his ear. The reason, he realized, for her open display of affection.

"She left the choice to us," he replied. It wasn't much of an answer.

"She'd be rid of us," Alexis continued.

He put a finger over her moving lips. "Don't go there," he told her.

"I'm not allowed to go where you go?"

He realized that she might hit him, but took the risk anyway; he caught her and held her tightly, her chain shirt making marks across his chest.

But they didn't have time to reach the field before that battle started. Hubris, on their part, really. If they could go where the enemy was, the enemy could approach them in a like fashion.

They had warning, but not much; they were in the place where the valley narrowed, and the trees along its twisting paths made poor haven for cavalry. The sound of horses were few, the snapping of branches, the sounds of any unit's movement.

But the banner that appeared from between trees that had grown apart, as if they were an open palm, was no Imperial banner. It was red, and across it, the sun in gold shone, eight distinct rays catching and scattering light. The standard of a Tyr'agnate.

And the Tyr'agnate, much like the Ospreys, did not suffer his standard to be raised when he was not upon the field.

Poor field, narrow field. And through it now, the war horses of Averda came, great, armed destriers. Crescent blades had been drawn in silence; Duarte had just enough time to wonder how long they had waited.

He lifted his voice in a cry that had nothing to do with training; it was primal, but unmistakable: his own. He had magic; he used it, sent a flare straight up, where it burst in a gout of traveling flame, like a blossoming flower.

The army was close; he knew it was close.

But not so close as the Tyran of Averda's ruling lord. Against men such as these, the Ospreys had only triumphed by planning, by stealth, by ambush.

And the canny man who ruled these lands—who had lost so much to the Ospreys—had at last learned to speak their tongue. There was a precious irony in that. And death.

Auralis drew both swords, roaring as he did. The dignity of rank deserted him, as did the months of training, discipline, the months of odd leadership that he had been forced to surrender and return to, like a child's bouncing ball. Around him, the men and women who had started to panic froze; they knew what this meant, and the familiarity of it provided what Auralis himself no longer could: command. Authority.

He had no fear.

Instead, he laughed, wild and reckless, and he used the cover of trees to advantage against the horsed men who came with their swords. Had they polearms, it might have gone differently.

But even without, Duarte could count, could add, and could certainly subtract. He turned to Alexis, an instinctive movement that had nothing—and everything—to do with the ambush. She was already gone. He wanted to grab her, to hold her, to hide them both. But it was wrong, and had she remained, she would have failed the Ospreys.

She knew it, damn her.

He used fire where fire could be used; he used the ability to hide where it could be used. Both strategic. This was not unlike an exercise, except in one regard: death was certain rather than a danger.

He welcomed it, as Auralis had done, but for different reason. There were no slaves here, no women, no children, no old men. There were killers. Northern killers, Southern killers, with almost nothing to separate them.

The Ospreys began their plummet.

Ellora AKalakar saw the flare as it erupted in the sky. So did the rest of the army. As a body, the army moved slowly. Not so the commander. Verrus Korama was by her side in an instant.

She pushed past him, but he caught her arm.

Held her gaze.

So many things, in it. Too many. She knew what he offered, and she hated herself for just a moment, because she saw, clearly, that after the war the Ospreys would be a liability. Had always known it.

"I told them," she said, tearing herself free. "They're *mine*. Call up the House Guards—get them moving. *Now*."

His smile was its own reward; he was gone almost before she'd finished speaking. But not before she'd drawn her sword.

Hold on, Duarte. Hold on.

He didn't count the fallen.

He could barely count the living. Mages were seldom required to stand in the middle of the battle; they had other uses. Fiara was wounded, but the man who had wounded her was dead; she could not bring herself to kill the horse that she had injured.

He could, and did.

He sent fire skyward again; it was the last time he could afford to spend power in such a display. He had never bothered with horns; none of the Ospreys had. Theirs had been a language that was best used in silence. Now? Screaming. Death. Slaughter.

"Alexis!"

She was there. Gone. He drew his sword, and followed her, forcing himself to think. To use the talents that had been too meager for the warrior magi, in a different life. He called the Ospreys to him, pitching his voice in Weston. Aware that in so doing, he was also calling the enemy.

But the Ospreys arrived first, and he saw that Cook carried both the standard and Margie. Only the standard would remain; he could see death clearly where Cook wouldn't.

There were trees on all sides; they were a narrow formation that would make the horses impossible to utilize. Men would have to dismount, to fight here.

And they did.

Minutes might have passed; he couldn't say. He cursed the commander in silence, but only in silence; he saw that the Ospreys had planted their standard—*his* standard—in the damp, thick ground of the forest shade. They surrounded it as if it were the only thing that mattered.

To the Annies, it was.

They began to carve their way toward it. They didn't have time to be vicious; where they could spare movement or motion, they were, but they were focused. On the standard. On the Ospreys who, twenty now, protected it with their lives.

It had always been something worth killing for. When had it become something worth dying for?

She hadn't used the sword in years. Not this way. But she used it now, and by her side, her House Guard, silent and grim, used theirs. She had not waited to gather them all; she had taken only those who were already prepared to fight.

They were prepared. The moment they glimpsed the standard of the Tyr'agnate, the moment realization dawned, they were hers, an extension of her rage and her anger. An extension of her pride. She lost them as she fought; the living stepped over the injured and the dead, moving inexorably down the flank of the eastern valley toward its center.

Bowmen would come; they would come late.

She paused for just a moment, and lifted her horn to her lips.

Duarte heard it.

He thought that loss of blood and loss of power must have addled his wits; that hope must have crazed them. The Annies didn't like to fight women, but they had long since stopped thinking of Ospreys *as* women. Fiara stood bleeding and Alexis stood beside her; they were back to back, holding short swords. They might have fallen had Auralis not intervened; Duarte couldn't.

He had been left to guide them, his words reaching them over the din of clashing sword, the rush of sound. It was almost too much; his hand gripped the standard pole for balance, and the Black Osprey fluttered against his forehead.

Three men fell; he could clearly count the Tyran that approached. They, too, were injured; their armor was rent, their swords notched and bloody. They hardly seemed like men at all.

But neither had the Ospreys, in their early evening

flights. Fire flared at their eye level, glinting off helms as they fell back. One more, he thought grimly. Just one, and he would be finished.

But it didn't come.

Instead, seeping through the encroaching ranks of the Callestan Tyran, came surcoats and colors he recognized. Men, he thought. And a woman.

Although she was yards away, a hundred yards, maybe, he could see her face. She was not a mage; she wore a helm. But her skin was pale, and her movements certain; her eyes were blue and clear. She was a commander; it was almost impossible that she could be here, and the forefront of her House Guards, face bleeding where Annies had tried to slow her down.

But she kept coming, and as she did, he heard the Ospreys raise voice, saw them find a strength that had almost abandoned them. They called out her name, as if it were a battle cry and not a prayer.

She had come for them; they were hers.

And Duarte AKalakar surrendered them with a tired grace.

Two thirds of the Ospreys were dead when the Callestans called their retreat. Scattered among them, dying, were Kalakar House Guards. Cook, bent among them, treated them all as if they were his. He looked once to see the standard, and he offered it the grim salute of a nod, no more.

The commander of the third army made her way to Duarte AKalakar, and only when she reached him did she doff helm. Her face was a mess. It would heal, and given her medics and her resources, it would heal well—but he memorized the new wounds that cut across familiar silver scars; these had been taken, and given, for the Ospreys.

She said, "You didn't think I'd come."

It was a gentle accusation. As gentle an accusation as she was capable of making.

He bowed head. She raised it, bending to lift his chin.

"AKalakar," she said. It was the title of all men—and women—present. "Take your standard. Take the men who can walk beside it. The third army is waiting for us." She grimaced. "And probably not with a lot of patience."

He stared at her for a long moment. "I would have spared you this," he said at last.

She said, "I know. But I'm Ellora AKalakar." She lifted her head, and added, "If I'm not mistaken, that's Sentrus Alexis AKalakar, and she's waiting for you."

He turned, in pain, and pain was good.

Alexis caused more.

He stared at the Kalakar now. Helmless, in the dark, she might have been the same woman. The same woman under whom the remains of the Black Ospreys had served; the same woman who had taken them, broken, into the House Guards when war had at last come to its close. She had not left them to die within the valleys; she had not abandoned them before the military tribunal.

But in the darkness at the close of this second war, she surrendered at last to the inevitable. "You served me," she told him.

Past tense. He heard it clearly; it was deliberate.

"Yes."

"Who will you serve, now?"

"I don't know." He bowed to her. "But Alexis belonged in the South, Kalakar. This was her home, and I brought her back to it."

"She changed."

It hurt him. "So did the war."

"Duarte—"

"I don't want to leave her here," he added. "Not alone. She was the heart of the Ospreys."

"So were you."

He shrugged. He had to take his leave of the Kalakar, and it was a parting that he had foreseen twelve years past.

When it had failed to happen, he had sworn he would serve her forever.

So much for oaths.

"Alexis is waiting," she told him gently.

He nodded.

"And the House Guard is waiting as well."

And nodded again. "Let me carry her," he said.

She hesitated for just a moment, and then she gestured. Verrus Korama came to stand by her side, as he often did. He carried something in his hands, and she took it from him, dismissing him as wordlessly as she had summoned him.

Turning to Duarte AKalakar, she gave him what she carried. The flag of the Black Ospreys.

THE ART OF WAR

by Bruce Holland Rogers

Bruce Holland Rogers lives and writes in Eugene, Oregon. His fiction is all over the literary map. Some of it is SF, some is fantasy, some is literary. He has written mysteries, experimental fiction, and work that's hard to label. He also writes a column about the spiritual and psychological challenges of full-time fiction writing for Speculations *magazine. Many of those columns have been collected in his book* Word Work: Surviving and Thriving as a Writer *(an alternate selection of the Writers Digest Book Club). He is a motivational speaker and trains workers and managers in creativity and practical problem solving.*

DEFENSE CHIEF LARA CHUEN was far away, in both light-years and time, watching a battle that she had already seen a hundred times, when a call came through on her priority channel. Lara was floating in space between the human ships and the Scorcher fleet. Not a shot had been fired yet. The alien ships had gathered into a densely packed spherical formation. The whole formation spun like a planet on its axis, and then expanded, contracted, and expanded again. Tactically, the move made absolutely no sense. If human weapons were strong enough to disable the Scorcher ships, the humans could have attacked when the sphere was at its densest. Most of the Scorcher fleet would have been screened by their own ships, unable to return fire.

This had been the first encounter with Scorchers. The human ships stood by in a defensive formation, streaming data at the aliens in the known languages and maths, trying to initiate a peaceful encounter. Meanwhile, the Scorcher ships broadcast a rhythmic hissing and moaning on analog channels. Lara listened to it as she watched. Human computers searched for a data structure in the signal, but on the small scale where dense meaning could have been embedded, there was only the chaotic variation of natural noise. The only coherent signal structure was on the macro scale. It sounded like music. Later, after the humans in this encounter were dead, that assessment would be refined. Martial music.

In Lara's head, the comm signal interrupted. *Ping.*

The Scorcher's spherical formation flattened out. The ships formed a spinning disk. Lara shifted her perspective to watch them from another angle.

Ping-ping, went the comm. Then, more insistently, *Ping-ping-ping-ping.*

"Answer," Lara sub-vocalized. Then she said, "Yes?"

"Stand by for the president," came the secretary's voice over the groaning and thumping of the Scorcher music. Lara sub-vocalized, "Stop playback."

Instantly she was back in her office in the palace. She checked the time—51:58, nearly true midnight. In her head, the president's voice said, "The marines are here."

"In system?" Lara should have gotten the news before the president. Any ship making a jump would return to ordinary space with a relativistic flash that no sensors could miss. Even if a ship came in behind the shadow of an outer planet, the flash should have been detected. Military intelligence had standing orders to report to her immediately, even before the president.

"*Here*, here," said the president. "Their battle group is in orbit, and their commander and his aide are waiting in my anteroom."

"What?" Lara felt her jaw muscles tighten.

"They snuck in. They have some sort of new stealth."

Lara let that sink in. If the marines had new tactical technology, they would want to try it out. "Damn."

"My thoughts exactly," said the president. "They're practically in my office, hell, my bedroom, before we know they are in-system."

"How long are you going to make them wait?"

"I'm not," said the president. At the same time, written words formed in Lara's visual field. *If they have new tech this good, they may also be able to eavesdrop from the anteroom. I don't even know if this channel is secure.* "Get down here." *I want you to come make your case to them immediately.*

"Yes sir. On my way." *It won't be easy.*

The answering message said, *It wasn't ever going to be easy.*

The marines were both women. Colonel Hodges was compact, fit, and seemed young for such a senior rank. Her aide, Shield Lieutenant Rogan, was dark-skinned, much taller than her superior, with an erect posture that made her taller still. Introductions were exchanged. The marines' handshakes were firm.

"In the interest of efficiency," said the president, taking a seat behind his desk, "I'd like you please to imagine that I kept you waiting in the anteroom for twelve hours, then sent you to your quarters without meeting with you or providing a firm time for our meeting. Imagine that we're meeting tomorrow at hour forty-nine after I've kept you waiting again all day."

The colonel smiled and narrowed her eyes appreciatively. "I do admire efficiency." She sat. Her aide remained standing, so Lara stayed on her feet, too.

"Even so, I don't want you getting the impression that you're more welcome than you are," said the president.

"In fact," said Lara, "we're hoping to convince you to leave."

The colonel looked from the president to Lara and back again. "They're coming," she said. She pointed to a spot in the ceiling that was probably a pretty close approximation to the area along the ecliptic that glowed a brighter red every night. "You know what they do."

"We know," Lara said. "We're ready for them."

Shield Lieutenant Rogan smirked.

"Your aide seems to find us amusing," said the president.

The lieutenant's face went neutral. "Apologies if I offended, sir," she said.

Lara addressed the colonel. "I gather neither of you thinks much of our defensive abilities. But we're not proposing to outgun the Scorchers. We've had a colony here for only a few generations, and heavy industry on only two continents. We're poor. Our fleet is small and weak. We know that. But our plan doesn't call for matching the Scorcher weaponry. In fact, our analysis—"

"Your analysis," said the colonel, "has been considered and rejected by the Primaries. Even if you're right, even if the Scorchers can be appeased by flying your ships in funny formations, we can't afford to have an intelligent species out there that knows it can kick us around whenever it wants to."

"Why not?" Lara said. "What does it matter what they can do, provided that they no longer want to do it?"

"They could change their minds."

The implications unfolded. Lara said, "So you're committed to engaging them no matter what?"

"Until we have achieved and demonstrated military parity or superiority," said the colonel. "Yes."

"Why?"

"There's an old military doctrine that says you don't appease aggressors."

Lara shook her head. "If they are aggressors. But we think the issue is more complicated than that."

The lieutenant spoke up. "If I may. There is a political doctrine that says that the wind breaks the oak tree because it resists, but the reeds bend down and survive. Is that what you mean, Madam Chief?"

"No," Lara said. "Not at all."

Rogan looked irritated, as if she'd been expecting the answer to be *Yes*, as if she had prepared a parable to counter the oak and the reeds.

"What I mean is that sometimes the graceful sword beats the strong one. Did you read our report to the Primaries?"

"In summary."

In summary? Lara messaged to the president. *They read it in summary?*

The president did not message a reply. He stood up. "Colonel, did you also read our report *in summary?* You are risking the citizens and resources of this planet just to fulfill a macho doctrine, and you don't even understand the details of our position?"

"I have my orders, sir."

"You have your doctrine and traditions to fulfill. I, on the other hand, have a responsibility to protect my people."

"Your responsibility is limited to this planet," said the colonel. "I'm sworn to service of the entire human race. And your authority—"

"I can't order you," said the president, waving his hand. "I'm just asking you, for the sake of our citizens to at least hold off your engagement. Let our ships encounter the Scorchers without interference. Let us *try*."

The colonel stood up, but said nothing, which Lara took for polite refusal. Either that, or she was busy messaging her aide and wasn't good at doing two things at once.

"Do you know Baeli sword?" Lara asked. "Either of you?"

The colonel still held her peace.

"I have studied kendo," said the shield lieutenant. "It's similar."

Lara smiled. "Hardly."

The first sword master, Abood Chuen, was easy enough to summon. He was a pilot for the defense fleet. The others that Lara had summoned, though, were all civilians. Like many martial arts, Baeli sword was an antique warrior tradition that few modern warriors practiced. It was nearly two in the true morning by the time three masters had been awakened and gathered in the palace gym. Lara overrode the lighting program for the gym and brought the lights to full day.

"So bright!" said Shield Lieutenant Rogan.

"That comes with living on a planet with such long days," Lara said. "We're good at making light and shutting light out." She made the introductions. The sword masters wore quilted robes tied with a sash, a uniform that would have been familiar to the ancients. Besides Abood, there were Michael Chuen and Ghadir Chuen. "And, yes," Lara said, "we are all Fulan Buddhists. No, we are not related."

"Don't insult our guests," said Ghadir. She nodded to the marines. "I'm sure they didn't come all this way without learning something about our culture."

"With all due respect," said the colonel, "is this going to take much longer?"

"A quick demonstration," said Lara stepping to the center of the floor. To Abood, she said, "Lend me your sword?"

Abood opened the case and removed the sheathed sword. Holding it with both hands, he bowed. Lara took it, unsheathed the long blade, and laid the sheath on a mat. She gripped the handle in both hands, assumed a fighting stance, and told the sword to turn on.

Ready, it said.

Lara improvised a fighting form. She began with some sword moves that would be familiar to the lieutenant or any student of kendo. A forward lunge and overhead strike. An upward parry. A slash.

Then she thought a new shape for the sword as she parried again. The blade bent along its edge. If she had been fighting a kendo opponent, his blade would have been caught by hers at the same time that the end of her bent blade struck his shoulder or cut off his ear.

"See, Shield Lieutenant? Not so much like kendo." Lara willed the blade limp, and it hung from the hilt like a silvery whip. She curled and uncurled it like a spring. "But I'm a beginner."

The masters laughed. Lara wouldn't have said, "I'm a beginner" to another Fulan. It was a sort of boast, as if she were saying, "I have a pure mind."

"Abood? Michael?" Lara returned Abood's sword to him.

The two masters bowed, raised their swords, and took their stances. The blades, which had been silvery, took on a bronze color for sparring mode. They would not cut, and they would soften if they met a surface other than the opponent's blade.

"Begin!"

Abood struck. Michael parried. Metal rang, then went silent as the two swords twined together like entangled vines.

Michael tugged, but Abood kept his balance as his blade went limp, then reformed.

Michael's blade thinned and lengthened, curling on the floor until Michael cast it like a fishing line with a nasty hook on the end. The hook and line flew high and wide of Abood, harmless so far. But now Michael had metal behind his opponent.

The advantage evaporated. Abood charged. Michael had to reform a more ordinary blade to parry.

"Stop!" Lara commanded. The fighters bowed to one another and to their audience. "Shield Lieutenant, you have some experience with a blade. Who would you say won?"

"They seemed evenly matched to me."

"Colonel?"

The colonel did not answer at once, as if she were

distracted. "They . . . yes. I would say they were evenly matched. A draw so far."

"Quite so. Michael, with Ghadir this time."

Abood stepped aside. Ghadir unsheathed her sword and came to face Michael. They bowed, took their stances. Michael towered over his opponent this time. Even Ghadir's sword, as big as Michael's, made her look small.

"Begin!"

For a few seconds, neither fighter moved. Each watched the other's eyes. When Michael brought his sword down, Ghadir stepped away from the blow. Her blade swept back, rippled into a flowing shape that might have been Arabic calligraphy, and came forward in time to block Michael's side stroke. Again, metal rang on metal.

Ghadir's blade gripped Michael's. Michael's sword softened, and he stepped back. Ghadir's blade rippled with more calligraphy as Ghadir stepped to one side, then swept her blade in low. Michael's sword caught hers. The end of his blade snaked out, seeking a way past the block. Ghadir's blade seemed to knot around his near the hilt. The tip of her blade snaked toward the tip of his.

The sword tips were like the heads of two cobras, each seeking a way past the other. Ghadir's sword moved more elaborately, but the extra movement only added flourishes. Neither sword could get past the other.

Ghadir pulled her sword away, reformed it. Michael attacked. She parried. Attack. Parry. The blades rang, each time with a higher note. Ghadir's size disadvantage seemed to keep her on the defensive more and more. Michael advanced.

Lara called out, "Stop!"

The fighters bowed.

"Lieutenant? Who is the better fighter here? Who wins?"

"As before, they seem closely matched. But the man has the advantage in size and strength. He's wearing the woman down. To this point, it has been a draw. But if I had to pick a winner, I'd say he's the better."

"No," said the colonel. "This is Baeli Sword. She has defeated him."

"You've been reading," Lara said. That was why the colonel had seemed distracted.

"Yes. I've just read your report to the Primaries. The summary doesn't do it justice." To her aide, she said, "Baeli Sword is far removed from its ancestral arts. If a fighter is struck, of course he loses the match. But anything short of that is a draw. Unless one fighter is . . . more beautiful."

Lara nodded. "All those flowing lines of Ghadir's sword, the sounding of her blade . . . She moves her body and her weapon with grace and supreme artistry." Lara turned to the fighters. "She kicked your ass, Michael."

"She always does," he said.

"Size and strength aren't unimportant," Lara said. "But when a martial art is more a matter of developing the warrior than fighting the war, other aspects matter more. When I'm seeking pilots and crew for my battle fleet, I don't look for the biggest and the strongest. The ships are all the same size and strength. What I look for in the crew is some kind of mental mastery. In Sword, that mastery takes the form of beauty."

"And you think that this is the way that the Scorchers think," said Colonel Hodges.

"Something *like* this," Lara said. "Their weapons are advanced, but perhaps their aesthetics are as well. A big difference with the Scorchers, though, is that they present their beauty first, before they use weapons. Our idea——"

"Is that they would stop at that, if we matched their beauty with our own," the colonel finished for her. "And you think that they scorch human planets because they are shaming us."

"For being bad artists," said Lara. "They don't kill the whole planet. The parts they kill with UV radiation make surface patterns. It's as if the planet is being branded. For all we know, they're writing graffiti that says, 'You suck.' We think that if we answer their aesthetic with our own, that may be the extent of the fight. They may not scorch our surface."

"*May* not," the colonel said. "I'd still rather teach them a lesson on our own terms."

"Let us try it our way. Stand down until you've seen how we have done."

The colonel looked at her aide, who only raised her eyebrows. Colonel Hodges faced Lara again and said only, "We'll see."

We'll see. The words meant what Lara thought they meant. The marines rejoined their fleet. Lara went back to studying recorded Scorcher interactions and to rehearsal simulations with her pilots and crewmen, who were all still on the surface. Lara's own fleet of ships waited in low orbit, empty except for maintenance workers. And two days after the Sword demonstration, Fleet Intelligence pinged her. "Scorcher fleet emerging from the Hawking radiation," the officer said. "They have formed up at 19 AU, but they aren't moving. We've scrambled your crews."

Lara sub-vocalized the commands that would take her into the sensor net. Black silhouettes of Scorcher ships stood out against the Hawking glow. She said, "The marines?"

"Gone," said the officer.

"On their way to intercept?" Damn. She sensed for them. Where were they?

"Gone, I don't know where," the man reported. "They were in high orbit, and then they weren't anywhere. We don't sense them, but they must still be in system. It's only been a couple minutes. No red flash."

"They may not make one, with their stealth," Lara said, though she doubted that the marines had gone more than a few AU from the sun. "Civil defense has been alerted?"

"The alarm is going out. Citizens are taking shelter."

Except for the ones who aren't, Lara thought. But most people would obey the order to go inside and opaque their windows, or even get underground if they could. "I'm on my way to the flagship."

She called the president, told him what she knew so far. He said he'd be watching.

Fleet Commander Nikkono Chuen was waiting for her on the shuttle pad.

"Everything on schedule?" she asked him.

"Crews are on their way. We'll be the last ones up."

During the noisy, vibrating climb into orbit, Lara called Fleet Communications. "I want to broadcast a message to the marines," she said.

"Yes, ma'am. Uh, Madam Chief, we don't know where the marines are."

"I know. So if I can't squirt to them, I'll broadcast. Squirt my message to the sensors and let them broadcast it as radio."

A pause. "Ma'am, if you don't mind my saying so, won't that tell the Scorchers where all of our sensors are?"

"I'd be very surprised if the Scorchers wanted to hit our sensors."

Dim letters formed in the middle of Lara's visual field. *Don't bother.*

The comm officer couldn't be accessing Lara's text channel, and the president hadn't pinged her . . .

Who the hell? she messaged.

Colonel Hodges, here. No need to broadcast from your sensor net. What can I do for you, Defense Chief?

"Belay that," Lara said. She disconnected from comm. *Where?* She was sure the marines were headed toward the Scorchers. That would preclude lightspeed communications. *Where are you?*

Can't say.

How can I be squirting you, unless I know your location?

We have all the best gear, Madam Chief. It would knock your socks off. Wait until you see our other toys.

Stand down. Are you going to stand down? Give us a chance!

Let's say your plan works, Madam Chief. We'll never know if we've finally matched the Scorchers. Relative strength is important information for either side, the weak or the strong.

Colonel, if you attack them, they may consider the interaction completed. If the battle doesn't go your way, we may not get a chance to . . . perform.

I hope to hell that it does go my way. But if not, I wish you luck. Sorry I won't be around, in that case, to see your show.

Fleet Commander Chuen said, "Sensors are getting an analog broadcast from the Scorchers."

"Let's hear it."

The Scorcher music thumped and grated. Lara started to tap the dominant beat on her leg.

Ugh, messaged the colonel. *Can't dance to that.*

We can.

The colonel's text said, *Ha. Bet you can. We're not that different, you and I . . . That's a compliment, if you're not sure.*

Lara laughed.

"What?" said the fleet commander.

"Nothing."

The colonel's last words were, *Tally ho!* Then an end-of-transmission sigil appeared.

"All right, then," Lara said under her breath. "Give them hell."

The Scorchers started to move sunward just as Lara and the commander transferred from their shuttle to their flagship, the *Alpha*. Lara called up the sensor data. She could still feel the gentle tug of her seat restraints as the crew took the ship out of their planetary orbit and into a solar one. She still smelled the ship's interior, the air that was always a little stale in spite of the scrubbers. But what she saw was space. Blackness. Stars burned bright and steady. And far away, still at the distance of the gas giants, the Scorchers continued sunward. Data squirts from the sensors were letting her see all of this in real time. It would be more than two hours before ordinary light and radio signals made it this far sunward from the Scorcher location. Much of the crew saw some version of these images.

"Chief," said Fleet Commander Chuen, "with the marines out there, do we stick to the script?"

He didn't have to defer to Lara, now that they were launched. She was, technically, a political office holder along for the ride. But the plan was Lara's, and she was glad that the commander wanted her advice.

The Scorcher ships formed an undulating line, a wave form that moved in time with a rising and falling whistle in their music.

"It's going to take a while to close with them," Lara said. "The marines have a head start, maybe a big one. I doubt we'll cramp their style at our speed."

"Form up all ships," ordered the commander. "Helm, take us out."

"Lights!" said a crewmember.

The Scorcher ships were flashing lights in time with their music.

"That's something we haven't seen them do before."

"No surprise," Lara said. "They like variety." Every interaction, every Scorcher attack, had been different.

Lara sub-vocalized for the spectral data. The Scorcher lights flashing on and off were intense, but their radiation fell mostly between infrared and UV. This was not a weapon.

Scorcher ships reformed into a square array, nine ships by nine. They flashed lights again, creating geometric patterns on the nine-by-nine grid.

"Think that means anything?" asked a crew member.

No one answered. Who could say?

"Ship's artificial intelligence just mapped two of those patterns to the planetary scorch marks left in earlier encounters," said someone else. The data officer, probably.

If the Scorchers had indeed written "You suck" in UV scorch marks on the surface of human worlds, they had just repeated the insult. If. So much was still guesswork.

The Scorcher ships contracted into a sphere, one of their favorite moves. Lara held her breath. This would be a good time for the marines to attack, if they were close enough.

The sphere expanded, flattened. The Scorcher ships moved in a way that reminded Lara of flocks of blackbirds, all ships changing direction and velocity at once, as if they had been printed on a turning page.

Then it was over. The analog broadcast stopped.

Still no attack. Either the marines had been out of range, or they had waited until the Scorcher ships had issued their challenge by playing their music and dancing their dance. For half a second, Lara thought that perhaps the marines would continue to hold back, would let Lara's fleet close with the aliens.

Space erupted with white light.

"Lord of lords!" someone said.

"What in all the vastness . . ."

The intense brilliance gave way to blackness. Not ordinary blackness. Black blindness. The web of sensors closest to the Scorchers had been fried. There was a hole in the data stream.

"What was that?" Lara said. "Ours or theirs?" She still saw only blackness. No stars, even. Then more distant sensors began to stream their data. The visual resolution was poor, because they were so far away, but Lara saw that there were still Scorcher ships out there. There was hard radiation, too. "Atomics?"

"Analyzing," said a crew member. "The radiation signature is similar to a traditional nuke, but not spot on. Extra particles in the soup. It went off right in the midst of the Scorchers, so I'm guessing it's not one of theirs."

"Play," Lara said. "Commander, give the order to the musicians. It might forestall retaliation. Something just hit the Scorchers, and we're the only thing they can see."

The fleet commander gave the order. Aboard other ships of the fleet, musicians at soundboards began to play. Lara heard the analog broadcast of her fleet's own music. It had a beat like the Scorcher music, but more melody. She had guessed that the Scorchers would want some originality, but written according to what Lara's composers had been able to understand about Scorcher music theory.

There was another flash like the first. Then another.

There was no blackout this time as the light faded. The sensors closest to the event had already been taken out. Lara's visual resolution improved as more sensors redirected toward the empty area and contributed their output. In the dimming glow, Lara counted the Scorcher ships. Still eighty-one.

A beam of white light connected a Scorcher vessel to an empty spot in space. Lara couldn't tell which way the energy was flowing. Was this a marine weapon hitting the Scorchers? Had the marines duplicated the Scorcher particle weapons?

Then a marine ship appeared at the end of the light, its stealth apparently disabled.

More rays of light connected Scorcher ships with invisible fighters.

"That marine ship is hot," someone reported. "Cabin's flooding with gamma."

Get out, Lara thought to the marines in the dying fighter. Escape pods started to launch haphazardly from the hot ship. Beams of Scorcher particle weapons met them. The escape pods had even less shielding. They erupted and bled their atmospheres into space. Six escape pods. Six dead marines.

"Fish in a barrel," someone muttered.

"Shut up," said the commander.

That's how it continued. The Scorchers killed the marine ships, then picked off the escaping crew pods one by one. In minutes, it was over.

"May all sentient beings attain enlightenment," Lara whispered.

"Ladies and gentlemen of the fleet," said Fleet Commander Chuen, "it's show time. Hold positions. Close to one half AU. Throw some improvisation into that music. Let's entertain these bastards."

"And let's hope that the marines didn't screw up our opening night," Lara said.

The Scorchers accelerated sunward much faster than the fleet traveled to meet them. Beyond the orbit of the system's dead binary planet, the two fleets closed on one another.

"Point five AU," reported the helm.

"Cue intro music," said the commander. "A one and a two . . ."

The music started up. *Thump thadada thump. Wheeze.*

Just like Scorchers liked it, Lara hoped.

"Flag undulation," the commander said.

Lara refocused her sensor image to watch her own fleet. The human ships formed a plane that approached the Scorchers edge on. Then Lara felt the acceleration push into her seat, then shove her against her restraints. The planar formation began to undulate like a flag in the wind.

"Tempo," Lara said to herself. "Let's stay on the beat." Actually, the pilots were doing a good job so far. But the hardest maneuvers were still ahead.

"Pinwheel coming up," said the commander. "A one and a . . ."

The human ships formed a spinning spiral. They elongated into a cone. Still spinning, they rotated the cone through all planes, like some geometry demonstration.

"Coaster," the commander said, and again counted out the time as the formation changed. The ships lined up and followed one another as if they were the cars on a roller coaster track. The human fleet traced impressive three-dimensional outlines, then followed the same "track" again. And again. And again, throwing the crews left and right in their restraints. Up and down.

"Flock," the commander said. In a move that looked a lot like the one the Scorchers had just performed, the ships turned in unison, swirled, and barely missed colliding. After that, some basic geometric shapes.

The performance went fast. The ships contracted into the rotating spherical formation that Scorchers seemed so fond of. The music stopped.

No one aboard the *Alpha* spoke. The two fleets had been converging all this while. They were only light seconds apart.

A particle beam sliced from one of the Scorcher ships and through a ship of the fleet, the *Trillium*.

"Damn!" the commander said. "All ships, acquire targets!"

"Wait," Lara said. "Hold fire."

Another beam hit *Trillium*.

"Commander, damage assessment?"

A pause. "Hull breaches. The ship is sealing itself."

Lara said, "As we just saw with the marines, the Scorchers will hit the reactor when they want to kill."

Another beam sliced through the *Trillium*.

"If they keep that up," said the commander, "they'll put more holes in the ship than she can seal. Or they'll punch a hole through a crewman. What the hell are they doing?"

"Giving us a bad review?" Lara said. "Testing us . . ."

"Signal *Trillium*," said the commander. "Abandon ship."

Lara thought of the marine escape pods tumbling free of their ships, taking fire. Dying.

"Commander, keep that crew in place. We've got to do this right, or they're dead. If you trust me, give me a direct channel to the ship's captains and musicians."

"Channel open, Madam Chuen."

Lara superimposed a 3-D grid over her sensor visuals. "This is Defense Chief Lara Chuen," she said. "Attend my visuals, please. Pending approval of your commander, this is how I propose we evacuate the crew of the *Trillium*." She highlighted the damaged ship's position on her grid. "We'll need up tempo music for the transit . . ." She drew a line from the *Trillium*. "That's the x axis." She drew a perpendicular line intersecting it. "There's the *y*. Recovery ships park at either end of *y*. Let's make the positions of the *Trillium* and the two recovery ships the points of equilateral triangles."

"*Trillium* is hit again," said an *Alpha* crew member.

"Crew of the *Trillium*, your escape pods travel this line, one at a time. Park at the intersection of *x* and *y*."

"They don't have fine propulsion control," said the commander. "Not in the pods."

"So they do the best they can. Next pod starts down the *x* axis. The pod in front doesn't leave the intersection until the pod behind is almost there. Fire and cut off your engines to the beat of the music."

"There's another hit."

"She's bleeding atmosphere."

Lara said, "First pod goes left. Next one goes right. Third one left. Alternate recovery ships until everyone's safe."

The commander broke in. "Those are my orders. Where's the music? *Crescent* and *Rigel*, you're the recovery ships. Don't just take your positions. Dance your ships to them. Let's go! *Trillium,* abandon ship."

Another particle beam sliced the *Trillium*'s hull.

An unfamiliar voice broke in. "Uh, Commander, the drummer is aboard the *Trillium*."

"Improvise!" Lara said.

Pss-sst psaaaaaa, hissed one of the sound boards. *Pss-sst psaaaaaa, pss-sst psaaaaaa.* One by one, the other musical voices added their own hiss or moan. Jazz with a Scorcher flavor.

The Scorchers kept punching holes in the *Trillium*, but they did not fire on the escape pods. One by one, the pods moved according to Lara's choreography. One pod didn't move out of the intersection fast enough, and collided with the decelerating pod behind it. Travel along the axes was approximate, not the eight mirror-image flights that would have been . . . beautiful.

It wasn't a beautiful evacuation. But Lara didn't think it was half bad.

As the last pod was recovered, the music stopped.

"They're holding their position relative to us," said the commander.

An analog signal sounded. A tone. Two tones, actually— a note and a dominant overtone. Another, similar tone sounded. And another. They harmonized.

The Scorcher fleet receded.

"They're accelerating back toward the Hawking radiation," said the *Alpha* helmsman.

Lara tuned her sensorium to home, to the blue and white globe of her world. There would be no scorching of its surface. No alien graffiti.

She shut down her visuals. The bright interior of the ship made her blink.

The harmonizing tones kept multiplying. The resulting sound was richer and richer, more and more beautiful.

Fleet Commander Chuen said, "I wonder what that is."

Lara smiled a weary smile. "Do you mean to tell me," she said, "that you don't recognize applause?"

GEIKO

by Kerrie Hughes

Kerrie Hughes has recently learned that being a war-
rior is a challenge in daily life. She recommends
chocolate to help take the edge off of ordinary life in
a cubicle and a healthy dose of sci-fi and fantasy
every evening. She is currently working on a novel
cowritten by her husband, a fellow warrior, where
Geikos will appear again.

REE-LIN watched as her young charge Jerio wandered
from booth to booth at the festival of lights. At thirteen
years of age, the girl enjoyed the rare freedom of an evening
out with only her Geiko, or bodyguard, as escort. Today
Ree-Lin wore the standard violet short robe and black pants
of her profession. The sleeves of her robe were just wide
enough to conceal a personal dagger on her left arm but
short enough to show her dagger cuff on the right arm. Normally she would also wear high leather boots to protect her
shins and knees and to carry her throwing blades, as well as
a fitted leather vest holding a number of deadly secrets; but
today was not a day for this warrior to be outfitted in fighting leathers.

Ree-Lin attracted admiring glances from both men and

women. She had large brown eyes that missed little and high cheekbones that were the envy of most. Her shoulder length mahogany hair was pulled up and back in a high knotted ponytail and secured with an ivory hair pin that served as a fastener and as a weapon, if need arose. She also carried the trademark black staff of a bodyguard during peace time.

Nearly her opposite in looks, Jerio's yellow hair came down to her waist in three long braids, and her bright blue eyes turned up slightly at the corners. Her mouth was small and her nose just a bit long, but the effect was stunning on one as healthy and well-cared-for as she. Today she wore knee length robes embroidered with willow leaves and berries, with bell-shaped sleeves that were long enough to cover half her palms.

She had been looking at a selection of fruits offered by a tired-looking old woman and was about to turn away when she noticed a small boy reach up to the table next to her. He took an apple as another child, a girl perhaps a year older, asked the old woman about the availability of strawberries. Both children were thin and dressed in the homespun garments of the working poor. The old woman politely told the girl that strawberries would not be available until the wind moon, and the girl replied with thanks and walked away. Jerio pretended not to see the boy take a second piece of fruit, presumably for his sister, and instead gave the old woman a senvi to pay for both apples. Ree-Lin saw the old woman look toward the direction the children had gone, and then give a humble bow to Jerio that she returned in kind.

She has a good heart, Ree-Lin thought with pride as she walked over to join her honorary little sister.

The Geiko sighed and chided herself for her maternal ponderings, but she was prone to introspection, and couldn't help but wonder at Jerio's future. *She is so young to the ways of the world. How do I prepare her for the realities of life without scaring her from living it? The world is changing and this last war was a sure sign that more will come.*

Ree-Lin's thoughts were interrupted by the appearance of

a young man approaching Jerio as she walked on to the next booth. The Geiko scrutinized him. *Dressed as a foot vendor, basket of flowers, clean and well-groomed as required by city permits. No trace of weapons.*

Ree-Lin kept one eye on her charge and one eye on the young man as she closed the remaining distance of three paces. He offered Jerio the purchase of a flower and the girl respectfully declined. The vendor bowed slightly with polite acknowledgment and then looked up to see Ree-Lin stopped next to him. He blanched for a second when he realized she was focusing her professional attention on him, then recovered by giving her the traditional greeting of respect, his main and second fingers held together pointing up with his other two fingers touching the thumb as he touched them to his sternum and bowed a full quarter. The gesture was of one who owed respect to the other for reasons known to all; in this case it was because the Geiko had played an important part in ending the war that the festival of lights was organized to celebrate.

Not a threat, she thought as she bowed back to acknowledge his greeting.

A few people passing by at the busy festival noticed the display and also gave her the greeting. Ree-Lin noticed Jerio beaming every time she received the sign. She, however, felt differently about the attention. *They need to let me do my job. I have greeted at least three score, and I am in danger of losing my focus.* She bowed again and returned to her duty as bodyguard.

Jerio stopped at a pastry booth, staring at the display of fragrant orange rolls and cinnamon crisps. With anticipation in her eyes she turned back to see that Ree-Lin had caught up with her. Ree-Lin was older than her companion by nine years, and looked more like a student than the warrior bodyguard of house Zai. She smiled at the unasked question and nodded her approval.

"Would you like me to buy you a pastry as well?" Jerio asked.

"No, I would prefer to wait for a more nutritious snack of felfey with sweet leaf, thank you," she answered. Ree-Lin referred to the traditional grilled lamb with spice, wrapped in a bread pocket and garnished with the green sea vegetable. The savory smell filled the air and mixed with the orange and lemon pastry scents as well as several other delicious treats from other booths around the festival ground.

Jerio considered her answer and replied, "You are correct, that would be the best place to start. We will have orange rolls afterward."

Ree-Lin laughed and they walked over to the nearby felfey booth together.

The festival celebrated the victory of the Liona province over the Swadin province. Yellow and red lights representing their homeland intermingled with the blue lights of humility to the emperor and the violet ones of victory over an honorable enemy.

Ree-Lin had fought as the surrogate for the eldest daughter of a wealthy textile merchant. Her patron, the family Zai, had a standing member on the guild masters' council that represented the lesser families in the textile guild. The eldest daughter, Salthi, was being trained to take over her mother's place on the council when the Elder Zai retired. It spoke well of the family that they could afford the adoption of a Geiko from one of the sanctioned orphanages, where children were trained in fighting arts and scholarship. Ree-Lin had come to the family when she was ten years old, and had spent holidays and school breaks with them until she was finished with her training. Then she came to live with the family as bodyguard, tutor, and substitute for the first daughter in the event of war.

Jerio's face glowed beneath the reflection of the multicolored lanterns and her unreserved smile warmed Ree-Lin's heart. *Such genuine expression; she is a welcome sight after seeing so many young faces dead on the battlefield.* She shook her head. *No, I need to forget that right now; she will say I am brooding and it will spoil her joy this evening.* Her thoughts suddenly brought home just how much she missed her junior sister while she served as assistant to the Tardan in the recent battles. The war, started over a water dispute on the shared river border, was less than ten moons long, but bloody all the same.

After Jerio purchased their meal, the two sat at a bench to eat, shoulder to shoulder. Ree-Lin faced east on the bench and Jerio faced west. In this manner they would not be surprised by attack, yet still faced one another as they talked.

"Ree-Lin," Jerio spoke between bites. "How does it feel to be in battle? I mean . . . what is it like?"

She considered the questions until she had finished her own mouthful of food. "It is like nothing on earth, and everything we fear from man."

Ree-Lin saw Jerio's left eyebrow rise in unspoken inquiry, so she continued. "Think of the comforts of home and family, now think of what you would feel if nothing you knew was there anymore. Think of the fear of knowing that when you lay down to sleep the enemy plots to kill you, and that the next time you eat or drink might be the last."

"That does not sound very romantic or heroic," Jerio said.

Ree-Lin knew that the girl meant no disrespect by her words, so she did not admonish or humor her. "It is not romantic or heroic . . . that domain is for the storytellers and politicians."

Jerio hesitated but asked further, "What is killing like? Is it . . . horrible?"

"It is."

"But what—"

Ree-Lin interrupted, "My little sister, imagine for a moment that a stranger . . . anyone here for instance—" she gestured around her, "is an enemy, and you knew that by killing that person you could either end a war or escalate one, but you won't know what the outcome will be. Now imagine you are asked to kill that person, up close or far away, and live with the uncertainty of the outcome and the knowledge that you killed someone."

Jerio stopped eating for a moment and looked around. She saw a mother carrying a baby and walking next to a man that might have been her husband, two older children laughing at a third who was juggling badly, and several clusters of older men and women conversing with one another and buying food. "Yes, it would definitely be horrible." She looked down at her felfey and did not seem interested in finishing it. "I'm sorry, Ree-Lin, I do not want to make you think about such things when you should be enjoying yourself and relaxing."

Ree-Lin finished her food and smiled at Jerio, then placed a hand on her shoulder. "You are trying to find out where you want to be in the world. If I cannot answer the nosy questions of my little sister, who will?"

Jerio laughed and resumed eating.

I could never find offense in any of her inquiries, Ree-Lin thought as she studied the girl. *She is a thoughtful person with natural ambitions and a desire to do what's right by those she loves. How can anyone be offended by that?*

Jerio rose after she finished her felfey, wiping her mouth on the paper it had been wrapped in. "Where should we get a dagger cuff for Salthi?" she asked while looking around for a trash container.

"That depends upon whether it will be ceremonial or functional," Ree-Lin answered as she rose to walk beside Jerio. The Geiko's tone teased because she knew Jerio would buy a purely ornamental dagger cuff, given Salthi's position as an attaché for the textile guild. As the eldest child of the House Zai, it was the sister's duty to represent not only her honored family, but also the honor of the lesser families working under her family's banner. Salthi was barely trained in dagger fighting, but was expected to wear one as a symbol of the first child's duty to defend the province and if necessary, the emperor. Ree-Lin, as was the custom, would fight in her place.

Ree-Lin's own dagger cuff was functional and forged of heavy striling. Its only decoration was a gelden engraving of the Phoenix of Liona holding the textile banner of the House Zai. Just above the cuff a long red gash from the last battle marred her arm, healing well, but not quickly enough for Ree-Lin. She resisted the urge to scratch it and pointed instead to a booth selling fine ceremonial daggers and cuffs.

This cut needs to heal faster; I am sick of its throb and itch. The Geiko sighed at her thoughts. *I sound like a novice whining at her first real wound. I was lucky that assassin didn't cut my arm clean off. He never should have been allowed to get as close as he did.*

Ree-Lin had earned more than the traditional honor when she took the wound to her wrist during a dagger fight while defending her Tordan in an ambush. Her defeat of the would-be assassin from Swadin had raised the status of her host family to Defender of the Province. House Zai could now be called Zai-Prin. The family was more than grateful to their Geiko for the honor bestowed upon them.

The pair looked at every cuff on the vendor's table. The impressive selection of metal cuffs of all types winked and flashed in the fading sunlight, decorated with everything from etchings to jeweled inlays. Jerio asked intelligent questions of the vendor while Ree-Lin observed. *She is an excellent negotiator and clearly knows the value of what she is looking at; I will offer no assistance with her choice,* she thought with pride.

A merchant's daughter was expected to know matters of business, but Jerio took to negotiating with a rare grace and charm. As the second daughter of a noble house with four children, she was free to choose her place in society. Jerio was trying to decide between studying to be a bodyguard, like Ree-Lin, or to become a trade attaché, and follow in her true sister's footsteps.

Ree-Lin watched the crowd as the girl questioned the vendor and scanned every person who approached and walked by. *Assassins could be lurking anywhere and disguising themselves as anyone. A festival is one of the worst places to guard someone. We should probably spend no more time here than necessary, especially as it gets darker.* She chided herself at the morbid thoughts. *Even safe in our own province I cannot help suspecting danger at every turn.*

A man wrapped in the green robes of a traveling messenger slowly approached. A badge on his robe identified him as a courier from Swift Dark, a service that prided itself on traveling quickly and at night. His presence at a festival after dark, when he should be on the road, raised suspicion.

Perhaps it is his day off, Ree-Lin thought. The Geiko studied his movements and looked for weapons. His eyes met hers for a moment before he approached the neighboring vendor. He did not seem to recognize her position of honor, but that meant little if he were indeed an assassin; a good one feigned indifference until the moment they struck. She kept her hand ready on her staff and continued to watch. The merchant of that booth seemed to be expecting him and handed him an envelope and a few coins of payment after greeting him.

No threat, she concluded.

Another patron, a man of considerable age, approached the booth where Jerio negotiated her purchase. He was nicely dressed and leaned slightly on a walking cane. When he noticed Ree-Lin he bowed a bit, but did not give the usual greeting.

He does not appear to be a threat, she thought as she bowed her greeting in return. *His age is genuine, and he has clouded eyes that probably impair his vision. The only way he could be an assassin is if he were a poisoner. Although . . .*

A woman of matron age that Ree-Lin recognized from town walked up to the old man behind her. "Greetings, Elder Min-lo . . ."

Not a threat, she thought, keeping her eyes on Jerio and an ear on the conversation going on near her.

After a respectable amount of haggling, Jerio chose a gelden cuff with an overlay of striling lined with rare cherly copra, a decorative metal that changed color according to the available light, and was highly prized as a testament to an artist's skill in design work. A ruby-eyed winged serpent design wrapped its tail around the entire band.

"Good choice, little sister," Ree-Lin said, one eye still on the man in the hood and messenger's badge. Jerio smiled at the praise and paid the merchant, then bowed to him and turned back to Ree-Lin.

"You are suspicious of the messenger?" she asked as they moved away from the booth and allowed the next customer proper room to negotiate.

She does not miss much; this is good, thought the body-guard. "I am glad you noticed. Tell me why you think he caught my attention."

Jerio smiled, obviously pleased at Ree-Lin's encourage-ment. "He was dressed as a Swift Dark, but he is here after nightfall . . . and he did not greet you when he saw you."

"Good observation; can you tell me if he was armed?"

"He should be carrying a dagger or short sword for self defense. I did not see the end of a sword, so I would guess he had only the dagger," Jerio replied.

"What else could he have had?"

The girl thought for a moment. "He could have had a gar-rote, throwing stars or spikes, batons in his sleeves . . . he could be an assassin, for all we know."

"True."

"Do you think he was?" she asked with a hint of teenage excitement.

The Geiko smiled and put her arm around Jerio's shoul-der, "What have I taught you?"

Jerio smiled back and squeezed the hand Ree-Lin had on the girl's arm. "That when an assassin is good you won't know until they make their move, and when they are bad they still might get lucky."

"And if they do get lucky?"

"Fight like it might be your last moment on earth."

"Better to keep them from getting lucky, I think."

"You will turn me into a paranoid old woman yet," Jerio said.

"Better than a young dead one," Ree-Lin replied.

Ree-Lin was tiring of the festival, the constant barrage of greetings, and her throbbing wound.

Jerio noticed her rubbing the fresh scar gently in an attempt to stop the itching without disturbing the stitches. "Would you like to head home?" she asked.

Ree-Lin sighed slightly. "I do not wish to spoil your evening, but, yes . . . I think that . . ."

She was interrupted by a small girl, who approached the pair and greeted them with a deep bow. "Would you like to—to—get your fortunes done by m–my m–mistress, the Lady Alima?"

The child was young, perhaps six years of age, and dressed in bright colors worthy of a fore-tellers' assistant. However, the garishness of her baggy, ill-fitting fuchsia and yellow robe overwhelmed her pale yellow hair and fair skin.

Poor child, she must be inexperienced, thought Ree-Lin before saying to Jerio, "I do not wish my fortune told, but perhaps you would?"

Jerio nodded, and another smile lit up her face. "Could we? You know I would like guidance on which profession I should choose, and it should not take very long," Jerio said to Ree-Lin.

Ree-Lin smiled at her sister's excitement. She hoped that the girl would choose diplomatic attaché, as she possessed a natural friendliness and the excellent manners and tact important to diplomatic postings. It also required an intelligent mind and firm convictions, both qualities that Ree-Lin felt Jerio exhibited.

It would certainly be safer . . . well, safer than bodyguard.

If she chose that career, bodyguards would still need to be assigned to Salthi and to Jerio. Ree-Lin knew she could only be an effective bodyguard for one of the girls but not both; the dilemma was compounded if Jerio chose to be a Geiko as well. Then her training would be handled by Ree-Lin, and another would need to be employed for Salthi. Normally this would be a simple matter, but Ree-Lin trusted very few people to protect her adopted sisters, and had yet to agree to any of the applicants who petitioned. *Sometimes I wish I were two people instead of one.*

Ree-Lin realized that the child still waited for a reply, "Yes, we will visit your mistress," she said with a nod.

"Thank you. P–please come with m–me," she said before leading the pair away through the crowd.

They followed the child, who led them to an indigo-colored tent with bright gray streamers and wind crystals decorating the entrance. The child lifted the tent flap to one side and waited for the pair to enter. Ree-Lin took two gelden coins out of her own side pocket to pay the teller's assistant, as was the custom. Children could not buy a fortune without an escort, and in any case the fee was never paid directly to the teller. It was considered bad luck for one so young to ask too many questions about matters that perhaps shouldn't be revealed until the right time. Thus a young person had to be accompanied inside by an elder who could correctly judge the questions asked as worthy of answer.

As they entered, Ree-Lin took one last look around for anyone suspicious. Seeing no one of notice, she touched the largest crystal at the entrance, a symbol of respect to the powers that granted foresight, and escorted Jerio, who also touched the crystal, into the outer entrance of the tent. Once inside, Ree-Lin glanced about to see the child who led them standing at the doorway to the inner room, holding the curtain there as well. She noticed a large bruise on the girl's right wrist.

She seems underfed and somehow out of place. I would swear this little one is afraid, but the signs of long-term abuse are not in her eyes, only the telltale markings of subservience and stern discipline.

The child bowed and stammered out a request, "I w–will n–need to take your staff . . . I mean, no weapons are . . . the fore-teller does n–not allow . . ."

Ree-Lin could see the child lacked the confidence to ask her to disarm before going into the main room. She knew guests were expected to leave their weapons behind before entering a fore-teller's tent, but she was loath to give up everything.

"Of course you may have my staff, as long as you promise to hold it for me and to give it back to me on the way out; I would not want to forget it," she said with warmth.

The girl beamed a shy smile, and with visible relief she took the staff.

Jerio clamped the new empty dagger cuff she was holding to her left arm, the arm not used to hold a weapon, as befitted one who wore it for ornamental purposes. This left both hands free to place on the table for the fore-teller to touch.

The girl stared at the cuff and said, "That is beautiful. Is . . . is it made of gelden?"

Jerio replied that it was indeed gelden and also showed her the cherly copra design.

At this, Ree-Lin stepped forward and placed the gelden coins into the child's hand and nodded. The child thanked Ree-Lin and excused herself to go into the inner tent to see if the fore-teller was ready. As soon as the girl disappeared, Jerio looked at Ree-Lin with a puzzled expression and whispered. "The girl seems frightened."

Ree-Lin nodded and made to reply when the child came back and drew aside the heavy curtain to the main entrance. "You m–may come in."

The pair entered as the child remained outside, dropping the curtain down behind them. Two taipa lights lit the inner tent with a warm yellow glow. They cast the twenty-foot by twenty-foot room in what normally would have been a comforting hazy glow, but to Ree-Lin it provided insufficient light to assess danger.

A low table, curved in the shape of a crescent moon, sat in the middle of the room. A cloth brightly decorated with spirals of gold on a multicolor pattern lay across the length of the table but did not extend over the sides. Two cushion seats were placed in front of the table; the fore-teller sat on another cushion on the opposite side. She had long blonde hair in a single braid and a veil of mesh and pearls that covered the lower half of her face. Bright blue eyes, heavily lined in kohl, twinkled as she regarded them. Around her right ear was an intricate lobe coil of striling that gripped the flesh in three places. It was undoubtedly crafted by a skilled artisan, and seemed to be almost a part of her ear itself. She also wore a light gray body garment and robes of light blue with a white spiral pattern. This seemed odd to the Geiko; all the fore-tellers she had known in the past wore dark clothing and did not cover their faces. Ree-Lin looked at the foreteller more closely.

"Is something wrong?" The teller asked with a raised eyebrow.

Still . . . just because I have seen a few fore-tellers doesn't mean I have seen them all; they are respected and required to be pacifists. Perhaps I should relax. Ree-Lin thought before answering. "No, nothing is wrong, honorable lady."

"Then I bid you both to please sit down," she answered while gesturing to the cushions in front of her.

Jerio and Ree-Lin did as they were bid. The fore-teller placed a medium-sized wooden bowl in front of Jerio. She poured fine sea salt from a glass pitcher into it, then added sand from a slate pitcher as well. With a wooden pestle she stirred the two elements together until a swirl was defined on the surface of the mixture. Then she pulled out a small velvet bag, opened it, and asked Jerio to pull out two stones. Jerio placed her right hand in the bag and did so.

"Now place one stone in each hand and put your hands

on each side of the bowl with your palms up," the veiled woman commanded.

Jerio did as asked, and the fore-teller reached her own hands out to place them over her open palms. The teller was about to touch Jerio but stopped and made a small gasp. Ree-Lin had been watching the fore-teller's eyes and saw that she was alarmed at the cuff on Jerio's arm.

Jerio seemed puzzled, "What is the matter?"

"You have on a cuff of metal, a symbol of defensiveness and a desire to not be open to the fates. It is not permitted."

Jerio looked at Ree-Lin for guidance, and the Geiko said, "I will hold it for you."

Jerio began to take it off while saying, "I apologize, I did not know."

The fore-teller answered, "It is forgivable; you are young and do not know the ways of the spirit world. My girl should have informed you." With that she clapped her hands together and called out, "Misa! Come here!"

The little girl came in quickly and stood just far enough away from the fore-teller to be out of reach. "Yes, mistress?"

"Did you inform my guests that they are not to bring metal to the divining table?"

The child began to tremble. "I, I f–f–forgot, mistress," she replied, on the verge of tears.

The scene unfolding displeased Ree-Lin. She noticed that Jerio was blushing and thought that the girl would most likely be punished. "Lady fore-teller, it is my fault that the child did not take our metal. I insisted, as the bodyguard of this young lady, that I be allowed to keep my weapons and cuffs. I also insisted that Jerio be allowed to wear her own cuff. I know that weapons are not allowed on one who is having their fortune told, but I was unaware that metal itself was banned. I humbly apologize," she said with a small bow of her head. Ree-Lin hoped that she conveyed to the fore-teller that while she was accepting blame for something that clearly did not take place, she was also implying that she would not tolerate the punishment of the child, nor the taking of her own weapons, only the removal of Jerio's cuff.

The fore-teller frowned as if considering what Ree-Lin had said, then looked again at the small child. "You may return to your post," she nearly hissed.

The child turned and left the tent, glancing at Ree-Lin with a frown of bewilderment on the way.

The fore-teller then waited for Jerio to give her cuff to Ree-Lin. The girl was in the middle of unfastening it when she glanced up at the fore-teller and froze.

No longer distracted by the little girl, Ree-Lin noticed Jerio's reaction, and followed her little sister's gaze, at first seeing nothing that would cause such alarm. However, as she regarded the fore-teller, she saw that the woman's right ear was now bare.

Odd, did I miss when she took it off? Was she also delinquent in bringing metal to the divining table? She seems new to the business and is younger than the average fore-teller. Her assistant is definitely not experienced. All of the anomalies prickled at the back of Ree-Lin's mind, telling her that something was wrong.

Jerio seemed to forget about taking off her cuff and began to rise from her seat, "I have changed my mind, please excu—" she began to say.

The fore-teller reached forward with one hand and grabbed Jerio's wrist while reaching into her robe with the other. Ree-Lin started to rise to her feet while pulling her dagger out of her own robe. Jerio froze for a second, her eyes mesmerized by a streak—no, a line of something just under the surface of her skin that snaked down her neck and disappeared under the neckline of her robe.

"Mitalsa!" she said.

The Society of Mitalsa! the Geiko thought as she leaped to her feet.

The select group of well-paid assassins known as the Society of Mitalsa had a unique metallurgical talent: absorbing metal through their skin without harming themselves and placing it into their victims, poisoning the victim's bloodstream. An experienced member of the Society could touch the target and be gone by the time the poison began to act.

The assassin pulled Jerio across the table to her and placed her hand at the girl's throat. Jerio strained against the grip from her awkward position, face down over the bowl. The Geiko spotted a tendril of gleaming metal creeping along the back of the woman's hand. She did not know very much about Mitalsans, few people did, but she did know that the poison could only be delivered through the palm of the hand and that the assassin could not keep the poison inside them for long without harming themselves.

Ree-Lin tensed to dive at the woman to break her hold on Jerio before the striling went into her sister's skin and killed her.

"Stop right there, Geiko, I am here for you, not this girl."

Ree-Lin did as she was told, keeping her eyes on the hand with the poison.

"Why do you want me?"

"You are the one that killed my fellow assassin when he was assigned to eliminate Tardan Ven-shar."

Ree-Lin spoke quietly, "The girl has no part in this, then. Let her leave and we will settle this . . . honorably."

Lady Alima laughed. "Take off all your weapons and metal, and then I will let her go."

With the woman's eyes off her, Jerio punched her right hand into the assassin's side and slipped out of her grasp. The fake fore-teller wheezed from the blow and tried to grab the escaping girl.

Ree-Lin dove across the table and grabbed the Mitalsa's hair as she toppled over from the impact of the Geiko. The action tore off the fore-teller's veil as she scrambled backward to get away from Ree-Lin. The Geiko held her dagger as she came up from the floor and moved to stab the woman. The assassin countered by leaping forward past the knife, but Ree-Lin spun around and grabbed the woman by her braid again. She yelped at the pull and whirled back, grabbing the arm that was holding her hair. Ree-Lin let go of the hair when she felt a warm tingle from the poison on the woman's hand. She immediately retreated and used her blade to scrape the area that was now glistening with metal. It bled quickly and Ree-Lin wiped it on her robe and then spun back as the assassin came at her again. She nearly made contact with her dagger but the woman dodged the knife and grabbed for her arm again.

I cannot let her touch me again!

Ree-Lin delivered a sound punch to the woman's side with her free hand and forced her to let go of the momentary contact. The assassin retreated in an instant and stood for a moment facing the Geiko as she caught her breath. Ree-Lin could see the metal tendrils across her bare face and the trail that led to her hands, ready to deliver a fatal touch.

How long can she hold the poison?

Ree-Lin could feel a tingle where the assassin had touched her and then, much to her horror, felt her knees buckle. She crumpled to the floor and fought to rise again. She could also feel the old wound on her other arm throb from the combat and she lost the grip on her dagger.

I could be dead already! Blessed mother of mercy, this is not how I want to die!

The assassin cursed the Geiko angrily. "Stay still and die or I place your entire house and this whelp under the contract!" she hissed with a gesture toward Jerio.

The threat was real. This woman was sent to kill the one who killed a fellow assassin before their job was finished. In the code of the assassin's guild, if a member was killed after the contract was finished, no retribution was needed, but if an assassin of the guild died before completing a job, the guild was honorbound to send out another assassin to finish the job. They were further obliged to kill the one who prevented the first job from being finished. It was a perverted sense of honor, and the threat of placing an entire house under the contract was serious; entire families could be wiped out.

The Geiko felt her anger rise to a dangerous level. *Jerio is my charge and this assassin will die!*

She grabbed a nearby cushion and threw it at the woman, and then drew her bone hairpin and sent that at the woman with a silent curse of warrior outrage. The weapon hit the assassin in the shoulder as she tried to dodge sideways to avoid the cushion. Ree-Lin struggled up and prepared to throw herself onto the assassin, sacrificing herself to save Jerio.

The woman grimaced at the pain of the sharp hairpin but clenched her teeth and pulled it out. Ree-Lin picked up her knife and tried to scramble away to recover a better position to fight from.

She could see Jerio standing frozen with fear, beads of sweat pouring down her face.

Ree-Lin tried to tell her to run but she found she could not utter a word. The Mitalsan smiled an evil smile and advanced on the Geiko.

At this moment the child Misa entered and gasped. Ree-Lin saw Misa run to where Jerio stood and fall to her knees.

What? she thought just before she felt an acrid touch on her cheek.

The assassin had successfully touched her on the face and the poison took immediate effect. Ree-Lin fought for her life. With great effort, she controlled her arm and the Mitalsan screamed as the Geiko stabbed her in the stomach. Ree-Lin let go of the knife when the assassin grabbed her by the wrist.

Alima's breath became labored and she let go of her attacker to pull the knife out as she stumbled backward. The woman stood up and pulled the knife hilt from her belly. The blade appeared to have disappeared inside her. She took a deep breath and exhaled slowly with her hands over the wound in her stomach. Metal from the dagger began to spill out and enter her hands. She laughed and showed the delirious Geiko her now completely striling-covered hands.

"Fool, you have no idea of the weapon you have given me," she said with ice in her voice.

The Mitalsan laughed and threw the metal from her hands at Ree-Lin, who was horrified to find she was seeing a dozen drops of striling hurtling toward her. Horror turned to desperation as she felt several of the droplets burn her skin and sink into her flesh. Her vision began to cloud, but she could see Jerio behind the assassin and the child Misa coming at her from one side. The child threw the bowl of sand and salt into the assassin's eyes. The fake fore-teller screamed with pain. Jerio took the cuff she purchased for her sister and clamped it onto the exposed ankle of the assassin.

No! No! She can use the metal!

The assassin was frantic to defend herself against her new assailants and to get the cuff off of her leg. She went down to the ground and crashed into the table. Jerio threw one of the tapestries from the wall over the desperate woman and sat on her as she wailed and fought.

Ree-Lin felt her strength give away and knew she would not survive the poisoning, but felt relief that Jerio was killing the assailant by smothering her. She could hear the muffled screams grow fainter and then felt the cool hands of Misa on her own face as she lost consciousness.

The Geiko was surprised to find herself waking in the care room of a healers' home. It was dark outside and she could see a soft light flickering against the ceiling.

Where is Jerio? she thought, and then spoke the question when she realized she had not asked the question out loud.

A healer in tan robes leaned over her and spoke quietly, "She is here and safe; I will get her for you."

The healer left her view and Ree-Lin felt a moment of re-lief before her curiosity overwhelmed her.

What happened? I feel odd, weak but whole. How did I get here? She clenched her hands and feet to confirm and then tried to get up. Tiredness flowed through her and she abandoned the attempt. Jerio then came into her view.

"You look terrible," she said as she held her Geiko's hand.

Ree-Lin smiled, "You look great."

Jerio leaned forward to hug her in a burst of emotion. "Oh Ree-Lin, I was so worried, you have been asleep for three days and Misa was never sure she got all the poison out . . ."

Ree-Lin interrupted her. "Misa? The child in the tent?"

"Yes . . . yes, she told me that her mistress, Alima, was vulnerable to gelden. She wanted no metal at the table because when a Mitalsan is actively absorbing metals she cannot control which metals might be melded into an item."

The Geiko was confused; this was not something she had heard before.

Jerio continued, "Misa is skilled in the same metal transforming qualities; she was an apprentice to Alima."

"She is a Mitalsan?"

"She was an apprentice. Alima purchased her from a slaver a few months ago when the child's skill was discovered. Misa hated Alima, but knows her talents would earn her a death sentence if she ran away."

Ree-Lin knew this was true; an apprentice to an assassin would be bound by the code of the assassin's guild. "Where is she now?"

"I have her safely under guard at home. I am hoping you will take her on as an apprentice Geiko; her skills in metallurgy include the art to pull the poison out of a victim. She will be very useful if anyone is poisoned in the future."

"She took the poison out of me?"

"Yes, and she told me how Salthi's cuff would poison Alima. I put it on her and it sank through her skin like the striling earlobe decoration she wore for poison," she replied with a noticeable tremor in her voice.

"Jerio, are you okay?" Ree-Lin asked as she squeezed her hand weakly.

"I will be. Her death must have been extremely painful and I . . . I have never killed anyone before," she replied as tears began to stream down her face.

The Geiko pulled her little sister closer, "The first time is the hardest; I will not lie to you. It doesn't get better, but it never feels as bad as the first time."

Jerio cried a minute longer and then pulled back. She took a handkerchief out of her sleeve and dabbed away the tears. It took her a minute to compose herself.

She will be fine, but the innocence will never return. I will have to be sure I am available for all the questions she will ask, Ree-Lin thought.

"Ree-Lin, I have decided to pursue the arts of the bodyguard."

This took the Geiko by surprise, "Are you sure, little sister, perhaps you are—"

Jerio interrupted, "I am sure. The contract on your life will not be over, and now Misa and I will be affected by it too. I want this guild of assassins eliminated," she said as she straightened up.

How different she sounds.

Jerio continued, "I will not allow my family . . . or my province to be terrorized by a society that cares only about profit and a misguided sense of honor. And no one is going to change my mind. I won't let them harm you . . . or my family . . . or me . . . I won't let them harm anyone."

Ree-Lin considered this for a moment. "I believe you."

Jerio sobbed once more, but gained hold of her emotions and then leaned into Ree-Lin with a hearty hug. She sat on the edge of her bed and held her hand then said, "When can we get started?"

"Whenever you are ready, little sister."

"I am ready." Jerio replied with solemn dignity.

Yes, you definitely are, the Geiko thought with pride.

SHIN-GI-TAI

by Robin Wayne Bailey

Robin Wayne Bailey is the author of Talisman, Dragon-
kin, Night's Angel, *and* Shadowdance. *His short fic-
tion has appeared most recently in* 2001: The Best
Science Fiction of the Year, Future Wars, Thieves'
World: Turning Points, *and* Revisions. *He's also
edited* Architects of Dreams: The SFWA Author
Emeritus Anthology *and* Through My Glasses
Darkly: Five Stories by Frank M. Robinson. *He's the
current chairman of the Science Fiction and Fantasy
Hall of Fame, an avid book collector, and student of
Ryobu-kai karate. He lives in North Kansas City,
Missouri.*

SHAARA ITOSU sipped from her glass of bourbon,
growing more impatient by the minute as she studied the
constant stream of officers and civilian contractors making
their way through the entrance of Café Mas Mundos. Out-
wardly calm, she ran one hand over her shaved scalp, and
then folding her hands on the table before her, she closed her
eyes and took a deep breath.

A delay of a minute or two, even unintentionally, was
poor manners. To be five minutes late was extremely rude,

yet even that could be forgiven if the offered apology were sufficiently abject. But to keep someone waiting for an hour, especially someone of her rank and status, could only be considered a dire and deliberate insult.

Itosu felt a presence near her shoulder, smelled the mixtures of beer and liquor and sweat mingled with breath mints, heard the gentle clink as a fresh bourbon was placed on the table before her. "Sobre la casa, Commander."

Itosu didn't open her eyes. She knew the proprietor's scents as well as she knew his voice and recognized the easy tread of his squeaky shoes over the noisy din. "Thank you, Pablo," she answered. "You'll go broke the way you supply me with drinks."

"Drinks I can afford," he said in a low whisper. "Remodeling is expensive."

Itosu allowed a brief smile as she listened to Pablo's retreat. His comment bordered on impoliteness, and yet the subtle brazenness of it amused her.

A heavier, booted tread drew her attention. The conflicting odors of starch, cologne, anti-perspirants, and breath fresheners assaulted her senses. The chair opposite hers scraped on the floor as someone sat down. Her table lurched. The bourbon splashed over the rim of her glass.

"You are Itosu?"

Two insults. It was bad enough to be so late, but to neglect her rank as well required a response. Itosu opened her eyes, betraying no emotion as she studied the Tindaran officer who addressed her. He was tall, powerfully muscled beneath his crisp gray uniform. He might once have been handsome, but his face seemed frozen in a permanent sneer. He leaned forward on the table, sloshing her drink again, as he interlaced his fingers.

"I've heard much about you," he continued. "You're something of a legend. . . ."

Rising from her seat, Itosu drew her sword, and in one smooth, lightning-swift motion she severed the newcomer's hands from his wrists. With a modest flourish, she flicked the droplets of blood from her steel, resheathed the blade, and sat back down.

Pablo appeared at the tableside. With a towel he swept the hands onto a tray and made a curt bow. "Qué es su gusto, Caballero?" he said to the Tindaran with practiced aplomb.

The Tindaran stared gape-mouthed at the stumps of flesh sticking out of his sleeves. A red pool spread over the table-top, smeared somewhat by Pablo's towel. Yet already the flow of blood was stopping, and the wounds were beginning to seal. With a controlled sigh, he looked up at the proprietor. "Brandy," he ordered. "With a straw, please."

Pablo rolled his eyes as he shouldered the tray and walked back to his bar. *"Please,"* he muttered with barely concealed exasperation. "Now el hombre remembers his manners."

The Tindaran lifted his arms to study his wounds. "My compliments, Commander," he said. "A very clean cut. Swift, too. I didn't even see the stroke."

Itosu rose without a word, repositioned her sheathed sword on her hip, and left the table. She felt the wary gazes of the bar's patrons on her as she lifted her head and strode out of Café Mas Mundos and into the corridor beyond.

The corridors of Station Ymanja were bare steel polished just brightly enough to cast back distorted reflections of the constant shuffle of people moving through the passages. Most passed by with downcast eyes, unwilling to risk offense with a direct gaze. No one spoke.

Always alert, Itosu watched their hands, noting the weapons that every officer, technician, and civilian carried. An armed society was a polite society, but it was a suspicious and dangerous one, too, especially in times of war.

And especially on a diplomatic station like Ymanja where Humans and Tindarans mixed and mingled and struggled to sort out their differences.

The thin carpet muffled her footsteps as she stepped into

an officers' lift and ascended to level seven, which was reserved for diplomats and upper ranks. As commander of the dreadnought *Katana*, she rated. Itosu brushed her hand over the bio-recognition lock. The door slid open and then closed behind her as she entered.

Her quarters were spartan. That was the way she preferred them. No chairs. Only a thin futon upon which to sleep. A small, delicately carved table held an artful floral arrangement.

The centerpiece of the room was a low teakwood altar. A golden Buddha sat in the center, and before it a shallow bowl of sand with a few polished pebbles. Some sticks of unlit incense stood on either side of the altar. Other quarters on Ymanja provided more amenities and were more lavish, but these suited her and offered a sometimes-welcome change from her quarters aboard the *Katana*.

Placing her sword upon her altar, Itosu slipped out of her uniform, folded it neatly, and set it aside. Naked, she knelt down before the Buddha and exhaled a soft breath. She clapped her hands once, and the incense sticks began to smoke. Then she closed her eyes.

Mokuso. A period of meditation. A time to order one's thoughts, to consider patterns of behavior, and to calm the heart. Each morning, Itosu began her day before her altar, and each evening she ended her day the same way.

Yet tonight the still mind eluded her. Drawing a deeper breath she strove to set aside her doubts, her many concerns. Her *fears*. There was a word she didn't use often. Shaara Itosu feared almost nothing.

Almost.

Opening her eyes briefly, she met the placid gaze of the Buddha. *Guide me,* she prayed. *Help me to see the rightness of my path*. The incense rose, filling her quarters with the scent of jasmine. Turning her palms up, she studied her hands, the fine criss-crossing lines, the strong fingers. Then, taking another breath, she closed her eyes again.

In her unstill mind, she saw more hands. A tray full of hands. Tindaran hands.

A soft chime sounded, alerting her that someone stood outside her door. Itosu's lips drew into a taut line, and her brows pinched together as she rose. Disappearing into a side room, she emerged again in a short kimono of red silk. Retrieving her sheathed blade, she went to the door.

She spoke in a quiet voice to the flat surface. "Reveal."

The door emitted a faint glow, and a holographic image appeared before her. The Tindaran with a pair of bodyguards. "Open," she said. The hologram vanished, and the door slid back.

Crossing his wrists, the Tindaran bowed deeply. Already his hands had begun to grow back. Thin tendrils of flesh would soon become fingers. Straightening, he glanced at Itosu's sword, then brazenly into her eyes.

He grinned. "I hope, Commander, that I've paid my pound of flesh?"

Her response was icy. "I didn't weigh them to be sure."

"Commander, I politely request an audience," he said with a slight incline of his head. "I feel that our previous meeting was . . ." He hesitated, and then his eyes lit up with a twinkle. "Cut short."

Itosu struggled to control the emotions that surged inside her. Her hand trembled on her sword, and she fought the urge to lick her dry lips. His bodyguards watched her, one with an expression of distrust, the other with open animosity. Both kept their hands too close to their holstered laser guns.

"You may come in," she answered. "But your *beautiful boys* may not."

The bodyguards bristled at the insult. It surprised her a little that they recognized it. Beautiful boys. *Yaoi*. Effeminates. Fingers curled around a laser pistol butt. Her sword slid one inch from its sheath.

The Tindaran snapped a command. "Return to the ship,"

he ordered his escort. "Can't you see the altar? I'll permit no violence here."

The bodyguards glared with barely concealed contempt before they spun about and marched away. The Tindaran waited beyond the threshold until they were gone and then stepped inside. Itosu set aside her sword as the door closed behind him.

"You take too many chances," he said.

She stopped his words with her mouth. Wrapping her arms around him, she drew him close, pressed her lips to his, and kissed him with a shivering need.

"This entire venture is one huge chance," she answered when she finally broke the kiss. "One massive gamble." She caught his wrists and lifted them up to study the reforming lumps of flesh. Her eyes misted as she kissed each one. "I'm so sorry, Michael," she whispered. "So sorry! That was the hardest thing I've ever done in my life!"

Michael shook his head. "You played your part exactly as we planned," he answered. "In a few days, I'll have new hands." He smiled down at her. "Although it'll take a little longer before I regain my old dexterity."

Michael put his hands inside her kimono. His regenerating flesh felt hot against her breasts. "I'll help you with your motor control," she promised, as she led him to the futon.

When the door chimed again, they were dressed in their uniforms, he in his gray and she in jet black, and sitting formally on bent knees at either end of her altar. The wall behind the altar was now a viewscreen that revealed a blazing vista of stars and the thinnest edge of planet Oxala, around which Station Ymanja orbited.

Neither of them moved at once.

"We have so little time left," Michael said in a soft voice. "I love you, Shaara."

Itosu bent forward slightly at the waist. "I love you, Michael Cade." Her lip trembled as she ran a hand over the length of the sword she now held balanced on her lap. The lacquered sheath felt cold and unfamiliar, as though she'd lost her bond with the weapon. "I don't know if I can go through with this."

He held up his hands. The fingers were already beginning to take form. "It's too late for doubts, Little Storm." That was his nickname for her. She winced as he spoke it, but she also smiled. "We can end the Endless War, you and I. Save millions of lives." His eyes sparkled as he regarded her across the swirls of incense.

Itosu saw the Buddha in his gaze. "I am Star Samurai," she answered finally, shamed to have shown weakness in the presence of his strength. "Though it's hard, I know my part."

"You're half-Irish, too," he said with a low chuckle. "That makes you a little bit daft." He winked at her. "I'm not sure which part makes you more dangerous."

The door chimed again. Shaara Itosu looked across the altar at Michael Cade, and then closed her eyes briefly, locking the immediate image of him deep in her heart and in her memory. Then, opening her eyes again, she called to the door. "Reveal."

Michael's two bodyguards had returned. A third Tindaran officer stood between them. His head swiveled back and forth as if he was surveying the corridor. Finally he stared straight at the door. His expression was angry and impatient, and the hallway light gleamed on the star clusters pinned to his stiff, gray collar.

"Admiral Brin," Michael informed her. Not that it was necessary. Itosu had studied the files of every known Tindaran of officer rank, and she recognized the man on her threshold.

"Open," she said. The hologram faded as the door slid back. Brin didn't wait for an invitation. With a scowl, he stepped inside with the guards close behind him.

Itosu rose with slow grace, exposing three inches of her sword without drawing it completely. "Mannerless pig," she said in a cold voice. "You enter my quarters without waiting to be invited, and worse, you bring your lapdogs along to sully my floor!"

Brin glared. "Don't threaten me, Commander." His voice was as cold as hers. "Your sword is no match for our pistols."

Michael Cade remained on his knees with his gaze fixed on the Buddha. "There's a saying among the commander's people," he said calmly. *"It's not the weapon—it's the warrior."* He turned his head to regard his superior officer and held up his regenerating hands. "Trust me, Admiral. The commander is quite capable of killing all of us before our fingers find our triggers."

Admiral Brin's scowl deepened as he looked Shaara Itosu up and down. Then he licked his lips and seemed to relax somewhat. "I know your reputation, Commander," he said. "The only human woman in Earth's fleet to command a dreadnought." His gaze lingered on the sword she held as he continued. "The *Katana,* no less. Named specifically for you. I hear its armament is unmatched, state-of-the-art."

Itosu pushed her blade back into the sheath. "As Captain Cade has told you," she replied. "It's not the weapon—it's the warrior." Returning to her former place at the altar, she knelt and sat. Then, with a motion of her hand, she indicated a place for Admiral Brin. *"Irasshai!* Welcome to my quarters, Admiral," she said with a slight bow and in a polite tone. She placed her sword on the teakwood before the Buddha. "If you're nervous, your men may sit by the door."

Admiral Brin scowled again. The subtle insult was not lost on him, yet he made no further point of it and ordered the guards into the corridor. When only the three of them remained in the room, he looked around in consternation. "Have you no chairs?" he demanded. Michael and Itosu both stared at their hands and said nothing. At last, the admiral folded his legs and sat clumsily down in cross-legged fashion. Frowning, he waved a hand at a wisp of jasmine smoke that swirled past his nose.

Brin turned a harsh look on Michael. "I grew concerned

when you failed to return to the *Surtur* with your guards, Captain." He studied the buds of flesh that soon would be Michael's hands and fingers. "I see I had reason to be concerned."

Michael tilted his head. "The fault was mine, Admiral," he explained. "I violated courtesy by keeping the commander waiting for over an hour."

The admiral chewed a corner of his lower lip as he glowered at Itosu. "And you dared to cut off my officer's hands?" His stern look melted as he gave a chuckle and slammed his fist on the teakwood. The incense sticks wavered like grain in a wind. "By the stars, I have new respect for you, Commander!"

Itosu was not amused. "This isn't a coffee table, Admiral, nor a bar. It's a place for meditation and reflection."

Michael leaned toward the admiral. "That's her way of saying don't do that again, or she'll cut off your hand, too."

Admiral Brin reddened as he put his hands in his lap. "You Humans!" he said to Itosu. "You prize manners and politeness so highly that it's made you soft. That's why Tindar is winning the war and why our forces are practically parked on mankind's doorstep!"

Itosu raised one eyebrow as she regarded the admiral. Tindarans had been Human once, and Tindar had been an offshoot colony on the farthest reaches of Humanity's push to the stars. But a trick of science, an experiment gone horribly wrong, had changed them, mutated them into—something different.

Tindarans no longer thought of themselves as Human. They thought of themselves as Humanity's successors, its heirs. And they wanted everything Humanity had.

Shaara Itosu was prepared to give it to them.

Reaching across the altar, she smiled softly at Michael, and he placed his regenerating hand in hers. Her heart shivered again as she felt the warmth of his touch. At the same time, she felt Admiral Brin's gaze upon them. He was study-ing her, studying them both, wondering whether or not to trust her.

Releasing her lover's hand, Itosu rose and turned to the viewscreen. The entire wall was one grand stellar panorama, so real and so three-dimensional that it seemed as if there was no wall at all and she could walk off the edge of the floor and drift away forever. Indeed, the idea had a sudden powerful appeal, and with Michael at her side she might even be willing to take such a step.

But she sighed. She was a Star Samurai, a follower of *bushido,* and the way of the warrior was never the easy way.

"Show the *Katana,*" she said to the viewscreen.

The stellar vista dissolved, and a new scene took its place. The gray, cratered world of Oxala floated with grim majesty against a new backdrop of stars. It filled the view-screen with its lifelessness, rotating at a sad and weary pace, pockmarked and jagged, yet beautiful in a harsh, cold way.

Then, around its nightside edge came the *Katana.* The warship was immense, awe-inspiring even with its star-drives turned off. Its lines were clean, powerful, and its metal skin gleamed as it orbited into the light of Oxala's sun.

"Twenty-five decks and a crew of one thousand," Itosu said. "Two hundred Seimer energy canons, one hundred and twenty Piper volt torpedo launch stations, and a full com-plement of DeWolfe Shatterworld lasers. That's just the of-fensive weaponry."

Admiral Brin got to his feet. He chewed his lip again—it seemed to be a habit of his. As he stared at the screen his ex-pression hardened. "This is the ship that destroyed the *Ger-manicus,*" he said through clenched teeth.

"And the *Oberon* and the *Grendel,*" Michael added as he rose to stand beside his superior officer. "All in the same battle. Three against one, and the *Katana* was unscathed."

Admiral Brin put a hand on the butt of his pistol as he

glared at Itosu. "You wiped out both our bases on the Viper Moon." Venom filled his voice. "I lost a sister and a nephew there!"

Itosu turned her back to the admiral and watched the *Katana* as it orbited out of view again. "Then we're even," she answered without emotion. "Tindarans killed my mother and father in the sneak attack on Catullus twenty years ago. They weren't even military. Just a pair of teachers on a university world."

"Then why do you want to join us?" Brin demanded. Though he kept his voice calm, tension and anger showed on his face. He pinched his brows together; a muscle showed at the edge of his clenched jaw; the veins in his neck stood out against his tight collar. "Why do you want to betray your own kind?"

Itosu sighed, and her breasts swelled against the black fabric of her uniform. With ritual care, she picked up her sword and cradled it in the crook of her right arm. Her gaze fell upon the Buddha as she bent down, and for a brief moment, its eyes seemed to follow her movements.

"This war has to end," she said flatly. "Tindar has the upper hand and the best chance of winning. Earth's military resources are stretched too thin, and morale is at a nadir. They're tired of fighting, and the colonies are exhausted, too. They're vulnerable."

Admiral Brin sneered. "Captain Cade has nothing to do with it?"

Itosu and Michael exchanged glances and then moved to each other's sides. "He has everything to do with it," Itosu answered. "It may not make sense to you, but I love him. I couldn't turn him to my side. So I've turned to his."

Brin sneered again. "You love him—so you cut off his hands?"

Michael spoke before Itosu could. "Until we finish what we've started we have to keep up certain appearances," he explained. He held up his budding hands. "This is no worse than many of us experience at our cutting parties, and that's just for entertainment. After our performance in Café Mas Mundos nobody will suspect there's anything between us, except animosity."

"If anyone thought otherwise, I might lose my command," Itosu said. "I might lose the *Katana*."

Brin rubbed his chin and looked suspicious. "Your crew will follow you to our side?"

Itosu lifted her head a bit higher. "My crew will obey me," she snapped. "In three days' time, the bulk of our fleet will gather at Epsilon Eridani. Earth's president will be there, too, for a conference with his admirals and advisors. A contingent of Star Samurai will serve as honor guard. I'll give you the code frequencies so you can verify everything I'm saying."

"I assume the *Katana* will be at this gathering?" Brin said as he began to pace near the altar. The suspicion faded from his face as he began to consider the possibilities.

She touched the small gold insignia on her collar, crossed sai, the emblem of the Star Samurai. "We leave for the rendezvous point day after tomorrow."

Admiral Brin ceased his pacing and stared toward the viewscreen, at Oxala floating serenely in slow rotation against the field of stars. Itosu watched him, noting his movements, the minute changes in his expression. Brin was an important leader among the Tindarans and, despite his outward bluster, a warrior worthy of respect.

"Then tonight you will join us on the *Surtur* as my guest," Brin said as he folded his arms over his broad chest. "Consider it a diplomatic dinner with a party to follow."

"I'll have to clear it with Fleet Command," Itosu answered. "My assignment here at Ymanja is diplomatic, but we are still at war."

Michael moved closer to Itosu as he nodded to his superior. "She's right," he said. "We don't want to do anything to arouse suspicion."

Rubbing his chin as he continued to watch Oxala, Brin nodded. "Tell your Fleet Command that ambassadors from seven other colony worlds will be attending, and that I will be making a proposal regarding the Kwan Yin insurrection."

Kwan Yin was one of Humanity's most distant outposts, a world once shared by Humans and Tindarans. For the last fifty years, however, the two factions had been at each other's throats, and the planet's ecology had paid the price. Kwan Yin was a microcosm for the greater conflict.

"I'll inform them," Itosu replied, "and I'm sure you may expect me."

"Excellent," Brin said, turning once more to face Itosu. His dark-eyed gaze raked over her again as if he were trying to peel away her layers and see what lay beneath. "Then Captain Cade and I will return to the *Surtur*. We have preparations to make—and menus to plan." He forced a smile. It was a strange thing to see on his hard face. Beckoning to Michael, he turned and strode to the door. Then, he turned once again.

Looking straight at Itosu, he executed a deep, formal bow. *"Shitzurei shimasu, Itosu-san,"* he said in flawless Japanese. He turned to face the door once more and waited.

Michael kissed her lips and brushed her cheek with a newly forming finger. His fresh skin felt hot enough to leave a brand on her face, and yet she leaned into his touch, wishing it wouldn't end. But Michael stepped away to follow his admiral.

"Open," Itosu said. The door reacted only to her voice. As soon as the two Tindarans were gone it closed again, leaving her alone.

Setting her sword upon the altar, she knelt down and contemplated the Buddha. A soft sigh escaped her lips, and she chewed the upper one, unconsciously imitating Admiral Brin's habit.

It had surprised her when he'd spoken her ancestral language. *Shitzurei shimasu.* Good-bye. It was a common enough expression, one of several ways to say good-bye. But this particular expression also had a more literal meaning. *I'm sorry for what I am about to do.*

So am I, she thought to herself.

Itosu took a few moments to reflect on the entire conversation, considering every word, every nuance. An oppressive sadness descended upon her as she considered the path she had chosen for herself. But then a half-hearted smile turned up the corners of her mouth as she remembered Michael's kiss, his touch upon her cheek, the futon where they had made love earlier.

She touched the insignia on her collar, the small crossed sai. Shaara Itosu didn't know where her path led, to honor or to shame, but she knew this: for Michael Cade she would lie and betray, even kill. For him, she would destroy stars.

On the viewscreen, the *Katana* swung around in its orbit. Her ship. Her weapon. As much a part of her as the sword on the altar. She wondered what life would be like when there was no more war, but then she put the thought aside. That was the future. A Samurai lived only in the present.

Rising, she went into another room, showered, and dressed in a fresh uniform. She had much to do and preparations to make. Fleet Command must be contacted about the dinner, and new orders must be sent to her crew. It wouldn't hurt, either, to take a few moments to brush up on the Kwan Yin situation just in case Brin had been serious about that.

Picking up her sword and strapping it over her back, Itosu glanced at the viewscreen once more. "Show me the *Surtur*," she said.

The planet Oxala faded and was replaced by a view of several ships at anchor off Station Ymanja. The *Surtur* was the nearest of them. It was a large, powerful battlewagon, the best in Tindar's fleet, and yet she found it unremarkable, utilitarian, even ugly. Like much of Tindar itself.

*   *   *

The *Surtur*'s stateroom sparkled with polished steel bulk-heads and high intensity lighting, and the noise of music and celebration swept from the room into the corridors, but as Itosu entered on the arm of Michael Cade, everyone fell silent.

The *Surtur*'s captain led the commander of the *Katana* to a place at the head table and pulled back her chair. As Itosu removed her sword and took her seat, he bent close and kissed the top of her shaved head, a gesture that surprised and pleased her.

She found herself between her lover and Admiral Brin. Scattered around the table were other ambassadors and dignitaries, minor functionaries, and officers. She exchanged a few polite words with those nearest and nodded to others. On the far side of the stateroom, a group of musicians resumed their playing.

"It's a beautiful piece of workmanship." Brin gazed at her sword, which she had leaned against the table near her right side. "Is it old?"

"Over five hundred years," she answered.

"Perhaps more," Michael said, leaning forward to address the admiral. "But she can document its history that far."

Brin nodded with appreciation and might have said more, but servers interrupted them, pouring wine and bringing plates with exotic salads, plump fruits, and colorful steamed vegetables with a variety of off-world honey for dipping. Protein cakes followed, melting on the tongue and exploding with flavor, then herb-spiced tofu and gelatins and selections of nuts.

Wine and stronger liqueurs flowed freely among the guests, but Itosu tasted little of it. Neither, she noticed, did Michael or Brin. Quietly, she slid her hand across the table and touched Michael's hand. His fingers were almost fully formed again, with pale and translucent nails. She turned his palm up, noting the soft sponginess of it, the lack of lines. No life line. No heart line or head line.

"You'd be a palm-reader's nightmare," she said conversationally.

"I can't quite bend it yet," he said, trying to make a fist. The fingers only twitched, refusing to obey. "I need some more help with my motor control."

She kicked him under the table.

The servers cleared away the dinner dishes and brought desserts, elaborate confections of cake and cream, with selections of truffles and dark chocolates on the side with steaming hot coffee to chase it down.

"You set an elaborate table. . . ." Itosu said to the admiral.

"For a Tindaran, you mean?" He grinned at her. "We're such barbarians. Most Humans think we chew raw meat and wash it down with blood." Careful not to touch her sword, he pushed back his chair. "If you're finished, Commander, why don't we take a short walk and stretch our legs. The party can do without us for a few minutes."

Intrigued, Itosu grasped her sword and stood up. So did Michael. A few eyes followed them as they departed the stateroom, but most of the guests were too deep in the wine and desserts to notice.

It was only a short distance from the stateroom to the *Surtur*'s bridge. Neither Brin nor Michael spoke until they reached it. The working lights were a softer blue, more in keeping with the sunlight conditions on Tindar. The men and women at the workstations barely glanced up at the three newcomers.

"Tindarans aren't much on formality," Michael explained, noting her expression. "We don't salute. The crew shows respect by doing its job."

Admiral Brin moved across the bridge to the command console. "If you'll step over here, Commander," he said to Itosu, "I have something to show you." He thumbed a control as Itosu moved to his side, and a small viewscreen on the panel flared to life.

Blue and beautiful as a jewel, with soft white clouds swirling in its atmosphere, Kwan Yin floated in space. Itosu recognized it immediately and hid her surprise. Throughout the long dinner, the *Surtur* must have traveled at top speed, risking its engines to cross the light-years.

As she watched the screen, two more Tindaran warships appeared and moved into a lower orbit above the planet. "The *Titania* and the *Sif*," Michael informed her. His voice was stiff, almost flat, and the hard set of his jaw suggested that he was as surprised as she. More, that he was angry. The admiral had commandeered his ship.

"Is this your solution to the Kwan Yin situation?" Itosu asked. She didn't bother hiding her annoyance. "Blow everything to hell?" She looked back at the screen again as the *Sif* fired a barrage of missiles at a communications satellite. The three Tindaran vessels possessed enough firepower to devastate the planet.

"Not everything," Brin said coolly. "For the moment, I'm not interested in the civilian population. However, in a few moments, as Kwan Yin rotates toward us, the only Human military base will appear in our gun sites. Our batteries are already locked on the coordinates."

Itosu nodded understanding. The Tindaran ships must have dropped out of trans-light on the planet's blind side, and the *Sif* had quickly destroyed the satellite to prevent the Humans from noting their arrival. They would figure it out anyway, once they realized the satellite was gone, but that would be too late. Timing really was everything.

Brin turned a key and lifted a cover on the panel to expose a red button. "As our new ally," he continued, "I want you to have the honor of pulling the trigger."

Itosu turned a steel-eyed gaze on the admiral. The bridge had become silent. She didn't need to glance around to sense the tension, or to note the hands resting on the butts of pistols or the hard glares that watched her.

The old bastard wanted a test before he trusted her. A simple thing, really. All she had to do to win his confidence was kill a couple thousand people.

A countdown display appeared in the upper corner of the

screen. It ticked down the seconds until the target was properly positioned and listed the status of the *Surtur*'s weapons systems. As Brin had said, all batteries were locked, the full array of missiles, cannons, and lasers, all waiting to be fired by her single touch.

She looked at Michael and wondered how a face could be both red and pale at the same time. Still, he said nothing, and he kept his stony gaze on Kwan Yin. Yet, by his posture, by the way he stood apart from her, or perhaps in the smell of his sweat, or in the way his newly forming hands seemed to tremble, she realized suddenly that her lover had known the admiral's plan from the beginning.

Itosu reached into a pocket of her uniform and extracted a breath mint. She offered another to the admiral and shrugged when he declined. But their gazes met and locked as surely as the *Surtur*'s were locked on the target below.

A chime trilled across the bridge as the countdown reached zero. Time was up for the Human base. Without taking her eyes from Admiral Brin, Itosu leaned on the firing button.

Nothing happened.

The admiral broke the eye contact and flipped a switch on the console. "Retreat," he said. "Rendezvous at Station Ymanja." The *Titania* and the *Sif* turned away and vanished from the viewscreen.

"It was only a test," Michael said over her shoulder.

Brin flicked off the screen. "I had to know if you were sincere," he said. "And under other circumstances I would have let you destroy the base. But why risk a major diplomatic incident that might interrupt the event you've told us about? It's enough that you were willing to press the trigger." He made a short bow. "Welcome to the winning side, Commander."

Itosu said nothing as they exited the bridge, but inside she seethed with anger. She didn't like games, and she didn't like being played with, and particularly she didn't like

Admiral Brin. She was angry, also, that Michael hadn't contrived some way to warn her.

Back in the stateroom, the dishes had been cleared away. A wilder music filled the air, and conversation and laughter rose in volume as the guests circulated. A server appeared with a tray and glasses of ruby wine. Itosu declined, but both Brin and Michael took a glass, Michael cupping his carefully between his two palms.

A gathering on the farther side of the room caught Itosu's attention. A pair of junior officers had opened their uniforms to expose their chests, and another officer stood close by with his jacket off and his sleeves rolled up. A circle of functionaries stood in a semicircle around them with rapt expressions.

Itosu moved closer as one of the junior officers slashed the other with a knife, drawing a thin red line across pale flesh. So perfect was his stroke that, for a moment, he appeared to have missed, but then, the cut opened, and blood flowed down a well-developed pectoral and into the wounded man's waistband.

But the cut closed again swiftly and everyone laughed. Two blades flashed at the same time as the other two officers cut each other deeply, and as they bled they pressed their lips together in a passionate kiss that ended when their wounds began to close, and they laughed.

"A cutting party," Michael explained as he sipped from his glass.

Steepling her fingers beneath her chin, Itosu watched as one of the higher-ranking ambassadors accepted an offered knife. Giggling nervously and more than a little drunk, he swiped at one of the officers, scoring him across the abdominals. Everyone laughed. Then, the ambassador's eyes shot wide and he tried to recoil as the bleeding officer grasped his face and kissed him deeply.

"Doing your part for interstellar relations," Itosu noted as the ambassador sputtered in the stronger Tindaran's grip.

"For a few, there's a certain sexual element to it," Admiral Brin admitted as he resumed his seat beside her. "But we heal very quickly and feel little pain." He looked at her over the rim of his wineglass. "That's why we are superior to Humans. With the right treatments we can make you one of us."

"Superior?" Itosu raised an eyebrow as she watched the cutting party. Another pair of Tindarans had joined the circle, stripped to the waist and brandishing their knives. Pushing back her chair, she rose.

"What are you doing, Shaara?" Michael asked. In a clumsy attempt to clutch at her hand, he knocked over his wineglass. A red stain spread across the fine white tablecloth.

Fully aware of Brin's gaze upon her, she shook Michael off and walked around the table to join the cutting party. The five Tindarans noticed her at once, and the diplomats and other guests, observing their changed expressions, also took note and fell back.

Itosu loosened the collar of her uniform and turned to one of the Tindaran officers. She glanced at his knife. "Cut me," she instructed. The officer hesitated and glanced toward his captain and the admiral. Then, when Brin nodded, he lunged.

With a subtle movement, Itosu turned her shoulders and leaned aside, letting the blade slip harmlessly past. Placidly, she looked at the startled officer. "Cut me," she urged. Again he lunged, but as he stepped forward, Itosu made a small, unnoticed move and swept his leading foot. Barely aware of what had happened, he fell at her feet.

"Cut me!" Itosu said, turning to the other officers. "This is a party, isn't it?"

Confusion flickered over their faces, but one of them slashed at her with his knife. She moved with lithe grace, avoiding the stroke. When another Tindaran struck at her, she did the same. When a third man swung his knife, she caught his wrist, turned away, and twisted his hand backward, sending him pinwheeling through the air to land in front of the admiral.

Red-faced and embarrassed, two Tindarans attacked her together. Again, she moved aside and lightly shoved one into the other, sending them toppling.

Backed to the corners of the stateroom, the guests began to applaud. They were in a mood for entertainment, and they were getting it. Itosu ignored them as she ignored Brin, who was on his feet, and Michael, who sat breathless and watchful.

A knife flashed at her face. Again, she caught the wrist, turned, and dropped her attacker with a four-corner throw. *Shioi-nage.* His knife clattered on the floor, and with the edge of her toe she kicked it back to him.

A rush of footsteps warned her of the next attack, but at the same instant, an image flickered through her mind of the Buddha on her altar, its eyes calm, its expression meditative and vast. The image was like cool rain on her face.

Anger had brought her to this moment, anger and ego. She turned toward Brin, knowing that she had revealed more of herself than she should have.

She heard the footsteps again—two attackers charging in unison, their breaths harsh and ragged as the cheers and applause of the guests made distant thunder. Itosu spun about. Catching one man's chin with the edge of her hand, she bent his head back and guided him gently to the floor.

The second man lunged at her back. Without rising or looking around, Itosu reached over her shoulder. Her sword hissed from the lacquer sheath on her back, whirled under her arm, and angled upward.

The Tindaran officer gave a cry and, checking his charge, stared downward to where the point of her blade rested against his groin.

"Enough," Itosu said. Rising, she sheathed her sword and extended her hand to each of the five Tindaran officers.

When they had each shaken her hand, she backed a step and made a formal bow, which they returned.

"An impressive demonstration," Admiral Brin said as she returned to her seat. "You didn't take a single cut."

Itosu didn't look at him. The guests were gathering around the Tindarans again, and the cutting party was resuming as if nothing had happened. "The power of your bodies is remarkable," she answered. "But for a warrior there has to be more."

"She's explained this to me before," Michael told the admiral as he put his arm on the back of his lover's chair. "*Shin-Gi-Tai*. Mind, body, and spirit working as one. Shaara didn't take a cut because none of them could cut her."

Itosu touched Michael's arm and brushed her fingertips over the back of one forming hand. The new skin felt so soft, yet so hot, almost feverish. She could sense the sinew and muscle regenerating as she interlaced her fingers with his. They were still stiff, but more flexible than before.

In this one crystal moment, she almost hated herself for what she had done to him.

He seemed to sense her thoughts. "Remember our love," he said, whispering in her ear. She nodded and tried to smile.

Shin-Gi-Tai. Mind, body, spirit.

They all belonged to Michael.

She had known him for as long as she could remember and loved him almost as long. They'd been children on Catullus, and both had lost their families there. As orphans they'd grown even closer, and in time he began to love her back the way she loved him.

But her path was not his path.

Shaara Itosu fought to clear her mind as she stood at the *Katana*'s command console and stared at the viewscreen. Her fingers played idly with the crossed sai on her collar. All her bridge crew wore the same insignia—Star Samurai, every one, handpicked by her and completely loyal. Yet, at the moment she could barely remember their names.

Michael's face filled her thoughts, a younger face and different, yet much the same. Her heart hammered in her chest as she remembered the first time he said he loved her, the first time they embraced, the day she went to Fleet Command, and the day he took ship for Tindar.

She rubbed her eyes. All her tears had dried up long ago—years ago—on the day they'd made this plan together and set betrayal in motion. Where would her path lead now? To honor or to shame?

She knew where Michael's path led.

Epsilon Eridani shone with a red-orange light in the upper corner of her screen, and the dust and ice rings that surrounded it glimmered with an awesome beauty. Nearby, its only planet, a Jupiter-class gas giant, floated at a distance of three-point-three astronomical units.

The rest of the screen was filled with ships: scarred dreadnoughts, warships, cruisers and carriers, transports, and cargo craft. Nearly half of them were docked together in a geodesic formation, creating a diplomatic station not unlike Station Ymanja. The other ships lay at anchor close by.

The gathering represented nearly half of Humanity's Command Fleet. One solid blow at its heart would end the Endless War between Humans and Tindarans. For nearly five hundred years it had raged, fracturing mankind, halting expansion and exploration. War had a way of devouring resources.

A way of eating the soul.

"Commander?" Her executive officer called from his workstation. His voice was deep and professional. "We're informed that the conference is underway. President Duvallier has just brought down the opening gavel."

She nodded. "Thank you, Ghandi," she answered. "Take us out in a slow spiral to the edge of the dust rings." She flipped a switch on her console and touched the plug in her right ear. A chatter of voices followed, and she listened with faint interest to the proceedings.

Numbers danced on her viewscreen readout. With an

eleven-day rotation cycle, Epsilon Eridani generated a strong magnetic field with occasional surges. Nothing to worry about.

Ghandi spoke again, and this time, his usually calm voice betrayed the tension he felt. "Vessels dropping out of trans-light at stellar one-twenty by forty-five degrees!" He shot a glance at Itosu, then looked back at his screen. "Merciful God!" he whispered. "We're really going to do it!"

Her bridge crew—twenty trusted and battle-tested officers—scrambled at their stations. Itosu leaned over her console and fingered the *Katana*'s address system. On her viewscreen, more Tindaran ships dropped out of trans-light and charged across space.

"This is the meeting ground of the universe," she said to her crew. "This is the mother of Tomorrow. How do I know this is so? Because I feel it in my heart, because I see it in the eyes of each of you. We've all been the slaves of history, but today we set the future free. Stand by your weapons; remember the plan; fear nothing."

Wave after wave of Tindaran ships popped into view on her screen. Hungry for glory, tasting his victory, Admiral Brin led the attack from the bridge of the *Surtur*, with Michael in command. She wondered if he was making some noble speech to his crew, if his words echoed her own.

Lasers stabbed across the star-flecked darkness. Torpedoes and missiles streaked through the vast deep like bolts of lightning. Fleet Command's outermost ships exploded in violent fireballs, each so bright they rivaled the glow of Epsilon Eridani. A Tindaran fighter wing strafed the geodesic structure of docked vessels.

Itosu watched the annihilation. There was a terrifying, almost hypnotic beauty to it as ship after ship erupted, as energy coruscated, as vessels burned and shattered on the shoals of the immense red star. Tearing her gaze away, she glanced at her crew. At each of their consoles, viewscreens flickered and flashed, filling the bridge with a wild chiaroscuro of light and shadow and lending their rapt faces a surreal, funhouse madness.

The image on her own viewscreen jumped. Admiral Brin's face appeared. Michael stood behind him. "Itosu!" the admiral shouted. "They aren't fighting back! What the hell is this?"

"Armageddon, Admiral," Itosu answered with icy calm. "But not for Humanity. Welcome to Hell." She pointed a finger across the bridge at Ghandi, who sprang into action at his station.

Behind Brin, Michael Cade drew his laser pistol and burned a hole through the admiral's chest. At the same instant, every weapon on the *Katana* locked onto a Tindaran ship and fired.

On the viewscreen, Michael slammed the butt of his pistol on a button, activating a pre-planned sequence of computer commands. In response, the *Surtur*'s weapons also locked onto Tindaran ships.

Through the plug in her ear, Itosu listened for one more moment as the stream of chatter from the presidential conference continued. Taped broadcasts sent over supposedly secure channels—excellent bait to trick the Tindarans.

As were the ships of Fleet Command. Derelicts, retired and outmoded fighters, battle-damaged carriers, every worn-out craft that could limp or be towed into formation. All to sucker the enemy.

The real Fleet Command, hidden until now behind the gas giant planet, charged into the engagement. The ruby energies of Seimer cannons sliced through the steel of Tindaran bulkheads. Volt torpedoes blossomed with a fury made all the more frightening by their silence. Missiles ripped through metal hulls.

Breathless and sweating, Michael appeared on Itosu's viewscreen again. "We've done it, Shaara," he said. "Years of planning, and we've done it! Tindar will never recover from this!"

Itosu nodded. Years of planning while she'd risen

through the ranks of Fleet Command and he'd worked his way through the Tindaran navy. On their families' graves they'd made a pledge and taken the first steps on the paths that had brought them to this moment.

Michael's voice dropped. "I love you, Shaara," he told her. "Never forget that. Now do what you promised. I can't hold this bridge forever."

Shaara Itosu trembled. "Michael . . ."

His face turned hard. "Just do it!" he said. "I'm already dying! You are my *kaishaku!*"

The assistant, the one who administered the killing coup-de-grace at a ritual suicide. That's what she was. Michael wasn't a true Tindaran. His healing abilities were only the result of the insane science that had originally mutated Tin-daran genes. Now it was burning out his metabolism, con-suming him from the inside out.

This was the path he had chosen for himself, not merely to avenge his family, but to bring an end to the Endless War. This was the vow they had made to each other.

"Tell me one more time," she said, forcing a smile as she did her best to keep her voice from wavering. "What's the sound of one hand clapping?"

Michael matched her smile, and his eyes sparkled. Itosu's heart threatened to break as she saw the fear in those eyes, but she also saw exultation. He answered with gentle laugh-ter. "It's the same sound my hand makes every time I smack your butt!"

Itosu looked over her shoulder to Ghandi. "We're locked on," he informed her with quiet respect. "Firing control is on your voice command." Ghandi was also Star Samurai, and he knew what was happening. Even in the midst of battle, he bowed his head.

Michael spoke from the viewscreen, encouraging her. "Make me shine like a sun!"

"Michael . . ." There was no more to say. She placed her hand on her console's viewscreen as if she might somehow reach through it and touch him one more time. Sad, she thought, that this moment of great triumph would also be a moment of great loss. When she spoke again, the word was little more than a whisper, but it was enough. "Fire."

Michael's image vanished in a burst of white static.

Itosu switched off the screen. Remembering the feverish heat of her lover's final touch upon her cheek, she felt a chill pass through her and shivered, knowing that she would never be warm again.

> *Snow on the mountain*
> *Body, mind, and spirit weep*
> *Silent, a leaf falls*

It was as good an epitaph as any. In a few days when she returned to Station Ymanja she would have it engraved upon her sword.

THE LAST HAND OF WAR

by Jana Paniccia

After studying in Ottawa, Vancouver, Australia, and Japan, Jana is now living in downtown Toronto, where she works at Queen's Park, script reads for a local movie studio, and tries to take advantage of all the conventions, readings, and other fantasy and science fiction resources the city offers. "The Last Hand of War" is Jana's second published short story. Her first appeared in the young adult fantasy anthology Summoned to Destiny, *edited by Julie E. Czerneda.*

SAURILAANA First Castelon of the elite Castelon guard, crouched low in the grass, peering intently through the mist shrouding the edge of the Escraen River. Smoky fog curled through the marshy growth clogging the waterway half-circling her vantage point and climbed through the hills to lay siege against the immense granite cliffs of the Kambarna. Cliffs lined with the rare silver used in the Kambarna soul-binding ceremony—the rite that fused a past spirit to the soul of a living partner.

The First Castelon's gaze fixed on a patch of gray at the base of the towering obelisk marking the domain's

southwestern border. Ignoring the rain now slackening after
an earlier drizzle, she crept closer.

::You're sure he's here?:: Her bonded partner, Laana-
Kendrisha, a former First Castelon of the Kambarna, whispered in Sauri's mind.

::I trained him here—where else would he go?:: Her
own mind voice trembled.

Fingering the silver medallion embedded in the sensitive
skin above her breast that marked her link with Laana-
Kendrisha, Sauri agonized over the need to murder the
young protégé she had taught and cared for: Idrian, now
Idrian*Kasash,* whose binding had linked him with a traitor,
forcing him to flee from the death blow aimed at his newly
bonded spirit.

*::Kasash sent twenty thousand into madness and you
doubt the need?::*

*::But the Spirit War happened two hundred years ago—
Idrian was innocent until he was soul-bound to Kasash-*
Danitai!*::*

::Kasash would begin it all again!:: The former First
Castelon drove images through Sauri's head. Men and women
curled up in deathless anguish, rigid in shock with naught
but a single, coin-sized wound on their chests. Youngsters
screaming in agonizing sickness as soul-bindings went hor-
ridly wrong and spirits hurried into death cast their panic-
stricken memories into innocent minds.

Even in the warm, humid heat of midspring a shiver jan-
gled Sauri's nerves at the vision. Her bow hand quivered.

Before Kasash*Danitai*'s time, the soul-bond had been a
blessing, all young people in the Kambarna undergoing the
sacred rite linking them with spirits of those who had lived
before. For hundreds of years, the soul-bond had acted as a
circle, allowing those of the Kambarna to live two lives: one
as a living member linked to a spirit, and one as a spirit tied
to a living partner. The soul-bond had offered a deep con-
nection with those who could mentor and guide the domain
into continued prosperity.

Until the Spirit War, when Kasash had killed thousands of Kambarna by tearing the soul-silver medallions from their skin. The complete loss of their medallions had brought instant, gut wrenching death to Kasash*Danitai*'s victims. Now, the spirits of those killed during the war had returned, casting a shattering insanity on their living partners that threatened the very future of the Kambarna. For none could live bound to an insane spirit, and twenty thousand such spirits had begun making their return. The only promise the youths of the Kambarna had was the guarantee that should their bindings fail, they would be granted death through the cleansing rites, rites able to separate and heal the spirit of a living person before it was released to await the second life. Kasash*Danitai*'s original victims were granted their only mercy—a swift final end.

The current First Castelon shifted her bow to one hand, wiping the other across her eyes to clear away the wetness that was more than mist and rain. For twenty years she had served the Kambarna, reveling in her bonding and taking her place in the Castelons with pure enjoyment. Sauri exemplified the skills of the elite guard: she enjoyed the tests of endurance and arms, and had made her mark in tests of combat and strategy. Her skill with the ash bow, trademark of the Castelons, was legendary throughout the domain. For almost fifteen years, the security of the Kambarna had been in her charge, and never had she faltered.

::*I can't kill Idrian!*:: She told Laana*Kendrisha*, the spirit who shared her every thought and desire. ::*I hunted these woods with him. I taught him the skills of passage and quietude. I can't do it!*:: Sauri managed two steps through the muddy sludge of the marsh before the voice in her head immobilized her.

::*You are First among the Castelons, as I was. This task is ours.*:: Her bonded partner replayed the ghastly images of death, and Sauri fell to her knees in the mud, reeling with shock.

::*Should all generations bear this suffering?*:: Laana-

Kendrisha demanded. ::*Let Idrian*Kasash *live and the Kambarna will never be healed.*::

"But he's just a boy!" Sauri shouted as she attempted to rise, stumbling under the weight of her gear. "He's—"

::*His death has been preordained for two hundred years. The murderer cannot live to begin a second Spirit War—it is for the good of the Kambarna! You must kill this boy— this Idrian*Kasash. *As First Castelon it is your duty!*::

What life for those without the binding? Sauri tried to imagine losing Laana*Kendrisha* but such emptiness and despair were too terrifying to envision. Leveraging herself up with the stave of her bow, Sauri regained her balance. Her turbulent thoughts centred on the tragedy of Idrian's soul-bound partner.

Once, Kasash*Danitai* had been a Castelon—assigned to protect the outermost cliffs of the Kambarna. He had been part of the force that had kept the enemy Zarristas off the southwestern cliffs, saving the domain's soul-silver mines. A talented warrior, Kasash*Danitai* had been destined for greatness. Only the misdirected fall of a knife cut had shredded his mind by denting, not cracking, his medallion. Yet his wounding had severed him from the spirit of his bound partner, casting Danitai*Emryn* into final death, and setting in motion a war more devastating than any the Zarristas could contemplate—a war whose prime actions now acquired the terrible ability to poison the present.

Was the rampage of death then Kasash's fault? The shattering of mind that led him to cross over to the enemy Zarristas to teach them the devastating weakness of his birth-born people?

No. Kasash*Danitai* had led a tragic life, not one of evil tyranny.

At the last, Kasash*Danitai*'s body had been given a quick first passage: a silver tipped arrow through the heart at the hands of his own First Castelon, Laana*Kendrisha*. Now, Sauri's bonded demanded the second death—the permanent death of Kasash's spirit. But Sauri*Laana*'s former First

Castelon partner's historic quarry had not returned to take root in a killer, a deceitful child, or a liar. Instead, Kasash now lived again as the soul-bound spirit of her own young protégé.

A swishing rustle across the marsh reclaimed Sauri's attention. Returning her gaze to the granite monolith, she pulled a silver-tipped arrow from the quiver laced to her back. Soul-silver: the one substance that could guarantee a quick death, one without causing the dashing of spirit sudden death often wrought. Sometimes it was necessary; the Kambarna had its share of evildoers and soul sick. Better to kill the body without causing madness when the spirit returned. With a lucid host, often the second death came quickly, during the first moments of struggle between spirit and living soul. A host driven mad during the binding could not be controlled.

Nocking the arrow, she edged back toward the willow, using its cascade of waving branches as a shield from her prey. Laana's prey. At least by dying on her arrow, Idrian would be sheltered from the madness violent death caused. His spirit would return to the world fresh, while Kasash's spirit would die its final death.

Mud slicked boots came into view first; the tall leather boots of a Castelon but in the unadorned black of a non-sworn member. Her own by contrast were imprinted with the circle seal of the unit and threaded with silver etched lacing. The boots' wearer crept through the marshland with the faultless steps of a specter, leaving his trail undisturbed as she had taught him.

Has it really been less than a week since I ran him through tracking drills here?

Seven days. A week in which Idrian of the Kambarna had turned sixteen years of age and made his momentous journey deep into the heart of the domain to receive the rite of soul-binding.

Why him? Sauri cried silently, even as the rest of her protégé came into her sight.

His best clothing, a knee-length jerkin and pants of sun-bleached wool with an undertunic of gray, was mired in dirt—dyed muddied brown from three days as a fugitive. An oversized leather harness wrapped his waist, holding two sheaths: short sword and dagger. His amber brown hair had been tied back, yet lanky wisps had escaped to edge his face—a face no longer the innocent youth's she remembered. Lines of tiredness ribbed his eyes in tracks that aged him several years, and a haunted, fuzzed look glazed his brilliant lapis lazuli-flecked eyes. A bruise wound its way down his right cheekbone—the result of a desperate attempt to halt his escape.

Following his soul-binding, Idrian had opened dazed yet lucid eyes and finished the ritual automatically, speaking his new name: Idrian*Kasash*. Years without his bonded had allowed Kasash to evade the insanity of his victims, thus allowing for the successful bonding. While all in the Kambarna had expected the one bound to Kasash*Danitai* to wake in incoherent, screaming panic, allowing for the safe completion of the cleansing rites, reaction had been swift. Kasash-*Danitai*'s spirit could not live. Sauri was still amazed at Idrian's ability to win free of the Castelons guarding the bonding chambers. The loss of his raw talent tore her heartstrings.

Wavering on the edge of pity, Laana*Kendrisha*'s voice prickled Sauri's thoughts into kill fever. ::End it!:: The spirit demanded, her fury blasting Sauri's nerves.

Instinctively, Sauri*Laana* drew the arrow fully, bow creaking with tension.

::Now!::

Sauri released, tensing against the distinctive crunch of arrow through flesh, when sharpened silver would tear a blaze through Idrian*Kasash*'s body, annealing it in death.

The spark of metal on rock met her ears as the arrow shattered against the granite, sending shards of wood flying. Idrian*Kasash* yelped as slivers dug through his skin, slamming him into a panicked run.

::You missed!:: A shamed relief filled Sauri at the cursing of her bonded partner. *::Get him. Now! He can't get away!::*

"Wait!" Sauri commanded aloud, grounding the silent threats and curses of Laana*Kendrisha* in a feat of motionless self-control.

Idrian*Kasash* halted a dozen feet from Sauri's position. "First Castelon?" With a finely trained awareness that knotted the First Castelon's stomach, Idrian turned toward her hiding place. "Why did it have to be you?"

::He must die. He'd murder the world!:: Laana's arguments continued unceasingly, and Sauri's hand tightened on the hilt of her short sword before she paused. She peeled her hand away from the grip, finger by finger.

"Who else? Laana*Kendrisha* would force me to the deed." With a harsh drawn breath against internal attack, the First Castelon took a step toward her protégé. "I see you haven't lost your ability to go unmarked."

The First Castelon recognized the moment when Idrian's eyes hazed over with gray, the indelible sign of one speaking with his bonded spirit. Her protégé's head jerked back and forth as if he were fighting an inner demon. *Which he is,* Sauri realized. Never had she seen such potent denial in someone with a new soul-binding. Her own breath held in her chest as she willed him to succeed.

::He's better off dead.:: This time Laana*Kendrisha*'s barbs aimed to persuade—to touch on sympathies to bring about the death of her bitter renegade.

::Not yet.:: Sauri noticed how Idrian's hands tightened at his sides, knuckles tense and white. She had taught him well. Maybe he could overcome the binding of Kasash*Danitai*'s spirit.

"You still found me." Idrian managed a weak smile, and Sauri choked off her cry. It was hard to imagine Idrian bonded with the one who had started the Spirit War. Yet even his posture was different. His back was rigid, poised for an ambush. Every few seconds his eyes clouded while he conversed with the one who shared his soul.

"I knew where to look." This time Sauri managed the words easily, Laana's contentment flooding her veins as she took a few steps closer to their prey.

"He says you'd kill me." Idrian glanced toward the bent remains of the arrowhead, recognizing the soul-silver; he had seen her make the arrows himself.

::He knows I am here:: her bonded sent. Worse, the spirit of Kasash knew all Idrian knew. If he gained control, or turned Idrian to his purposes, he could easily begin a second purging. *::He has to die!::*

::Idrian can fight him off—hold Kasash from doing harm. I must give him a chance!:: Sauri argued.

::Would you trust the lives of our people to him? To a green youth? Kasash is not evil—worse, he struggles for what he believes is right. How can anyone defend against righteousness? Kill the boy, at least then his spirit will be untainted for the next passing.::

"I can't!" Sauri's vocal denial addressed both bonded partner and fugitive.

::You must!:: The ties binding her to Laana*Kendrisha* tightened. Sauri's hand closed on her sword hilt. Idrian's eyes hazed gray at her movement, his stolen blade in his hand before she could gasp.

Without thought, born instincts and years of training had the sharp-edged steel out of Sauri's sheath and headed in crosswise slant to match Idrian*Kasash*'s oncoming thrust. She barely managed to block his cut, caught short by the innocent face of her protégé now taut with fury. Instead of pulling back, Idrian leaned forward putting his entire weight against her raised blade. Sauri's arm shook as he pressed her back.

"Idrian!" She shouted, desperate for the boy to throw off the mantle of Kasash's domination. *::Please!::*

For a moment, the cloud shrouding his eyes lessened and the pressure on her arm withdrew. Sauri blinked her relief and made to withdraw.

Gray returned to his eyes in a whirlwind. Idrian*Kasash*

knocked the sword from her relaxed grasp, then twisted around to throw her hard against the granite outcropping. Breath was pushed from Sauri's lungs.

::Kill him before we die!:: Laana's voice bit through the dizziness shaking Sauri's skull. The First Castelon twisted to reach her dagger. Before her hand got there, Idrian's came down on her own, his other reversing his dagger's grip. The hilt came down hard on her nape, sending a flash of stars across her vision. Sauri tried to move but Idrian*Kasash* tightened his grip, tugged her around. Still blinking her eyes clear, Sauri missed the dagger's hilt come slamming toward her chest.

Shattering pain mushroomed out from her chest and reached through every nerve, kindling them to finely honed agony. Convulsions wracked her body, bringing her down hard on the wet, jagged rock. Someone shrieked unceasingly, unintelligibly, as pain, confusion, and bereavement echoed into vast emptiness. Utter despair reached out with chill fingers and carried her off into silence.

Ravaging absence shocked Sauri to waking. Something missing. Someone. Missing.

"Laana?" Bleak emptiness jarred where once calm presence had been. "Laana!" This time Sauri screamed, her bonded's name reverberating off the walls with jarring force. Her head ached with devastation. Even the thought of opening her eyes brought wracking contractions of fearful reality.

Footsteps on wood flooring caught her attention. Hands came down on her head. Cool hands. A hot liquid rushed down her throat, bringing ease to the headache, but not to the internal wounds. No, nothing would ease *that* pain.

"First Castelon? Can you speak?" Soft words sounded under the din of internal confusion.

The Kambarna. Even through the wrenching disorientation, Sauri recognised the soft cotton sheets of the Castelons' infirmary, and the bitter scents of alcohol and asprea tea.

Scrunching her eyes tight, she managed, "Who?"

"Tathroi*Ambars.*"

Sauri blinked her eyes open, bile choking her throat. The round face of the Castelons' chief physician came into focus, his fingers pressing his spectacles higher on his nose. When he noticed her open eyes, he withdrew his hands and came to rigid attention. "The midday patrol found you—you were unconscious, but they found no sign of injury. Even your weapons were left." His eyebrows rose in silent question, hoping for but not demanding an explanation from his commander.

Ignoring him, Sauri*Laana* saw she still wore her undershirt, though her other clothes had been removed. Tathroi didn't know, then? Shivering, she wondered that he couldn't see the ever-evolving cacophony of pain reverberating through her body. She shuddered with heart-wrenching loss, barely able to see for the darkness threatening to overwhelm her with the knotting contractions of a soul torn to pieces. Surely Tathroi*Ambars,* the head physician, should be able to tell.

"First Castelon? Are you all right? You had a mild case of hypothermia—a warm bath should halt the shaking."

::Laana!!!!:: Still focused internally, Sauri cried her bonded's name. With the deafening lack of response, she knew she would never be all right.

"First Castelon? The Second is anxiously waiting for word on your health—" the physician prompted.

As soon as the Second heard of her loss, he would be honor-bound to accompany her to the binding chambers in the heart of the Kambarna. His would be the hand to end her life— before the loss twisted her as it once had Kasash*Danitai.*

No. I must bring him down first. A deep hatred twisted in her gut as the face of her tormentor rose in her mind. "I am fine," she said in a voice that brooked no question. "A bath, then sleep—I will be good as new in the morning."

Tathroi*Ambars* nodded grimly, not pleased at her response. "Very well, First Castelon. But let me help you to your rooms."

Rather than argue, Sauri let him haul her up and wrap her in a lambswool robe. Her body quivered as her balance wavered under the strain of Laana's absence. She gritted her teeth and staggered out of the infirmary, refusing Tathroi's offer of help.

Up through the Castelon headquarters, they tread slowly. Castelon barracks were built into the sides of the mountainous Kambarna domain, adjacent to the most compromising locations. Here, at the mouth of the Escraen, the Castelon headquarters stood watch over the area most beleaguered by Zarrista attacks. The southern people yearned for the mystical soul-silver only found in the Kambarna, and rarely a year went by without a major assault.

*This is where Kasash*Danitai *held off the raiders before he went mad*. Even thinking about Laana's enemy made real her own grievous injury. Instead, Sauri kept her eyes firmly fixed on the spartan corridor walls of a compound grimly built for war. Every twenty feet, arrow slits cut through the rock, bracketed by glowing oil-filled lamps, which over centuries had added a dank sooty odor to the barracks. Only the elite Castelons could live poised for war at all times without breaking under the need for constant vigilance. They passed startled Castelons in the halls, both patrols and those off duty. Sauri ignored their surprised glances with the aloofness her position allowed.

The First Castelon's apartment crowned the highest section of the Kambarna's southwestern cliffs. Deep in despair, the climb up the rough-hewn staircases lasted lifetimes, an infinite number of moments to remember she was alone.

Alone.

Tathroi paused at her doorway, waiting. Lost in depression, it took a touch on her shoulder and a whispered, "First Castelon," before Sauri remembered where she was. She rolled her eyes. Most thought her rooms booby-trapped, and obviously the physician gave credence to the rumors. With an annoyed grimace, she pulled open the unlocked door.

No light met them. Keeping the lamps lit had been Idrian's job. A stab of recollection knifed her soul wound, wrenching the sickness deeper. Shuddering, she braced a hand against the doorframe.

"Will you be all right? Should I send someone?"

"I'll be fine." Sauri managed.

Tathroi*Ambars'* eyes shaded with gray mist as he spoke with his bonded. As she noted the interaction, a blistering hatred rose in the remnants of her soul. How could he not see how it made her feel—what it did? How could he not realize Laana was gone? Gone.

"Go!" She grasped his arm and pushing him back toward the entry.

"But First . . ."

"Go. I'll be fine—I'm going to bed. Out."

The physician was shoved, protesting, from her chamber. Sauri slammed the door, and pressed her back to the oak panel as if she could barricade away the outside world. Finally alone, the First Castelon yanked off the borrowed robe and pulled her undertunic over her head. Her spirit medallion lay seamless within her breast, offering the unspoken but torturous truth. A light indentation marred its once perfect silver. A ripple. How could such a tiny mark have torn her soul apart—ripped her to such shattered pieces?

::Laana. Laana. Laana.:: Sauri's wrenching call sparked agonizing pain through her broken soul-bond. Crumpling to the floor, she lost all sense of time as she pleaded senselessly for a response.

As the new day dawned, tears gave way to stunned realization. *If only I had listened to you,* Sauri offered to the memory of Laana*Kendrisha,* stomach knotted with horror. *I should never have trusted him.*

Gripping fingers tight into fists, relishing the sharp tingle of nails digging into her palms, the First Castelon knew she should accept death. She should tell her Second, allow him to escort her to the spirit chambers, take the offered respite, and hope for a clean return. But Kasash still lived. Still offered threat to those she had sworn to protect.

In a way, the possibility prodded her sympathies. She relived the moment of intense hatred for the physician who had not noted her sickness, the chilling depression as he used the tie rent from her. Surely for not recognizing her pain, he deserved treatment in kind. She imagined slashing a medallion from Tathroi*Ambars*' skin—lingered on the desire to strike an indent off a pure medallion, as hers no longer was. The shocking picture captivated thought and imagination, offering heady visions of revenge and retaliation.

No. I will not be the catalyst of a second Spirit War. As she once argued against Laana*Kendrisha*, Sauri now argued as strongly against the insanity the torn binding cast upon her—the bitterness, violence, and hopelessness.

Only one face did she allow the seeds of hatred to cast as an enemy. Only one name did she allow on her lips as a curse. Idrian*Kasash*.

When a page came knocking at her door, she drafted a quick note to her Second, delegating him to assign the patrols for the day and to draw up a plan for capturing Idrian*Kasash*. Anything to keep them out of her way—Idrian*Kasash* was hers. As Sauri stood at her room's one vice, a large window overlooking the cloud covered marshlands, a bitter coldness swept through her.

*I will find you, Idrian*Kasash. *I'll scour the marshes and drag your screaming carcass through the mud. You think you can ruin me? I'll break you so far you'll be begging me to stop before I put you out of your misery.*

Determined steps and movements saw her dressed. She pulled on her linen undergarments, her black leggings, and her black Castelon boots. A light gray shirt went on before dress tunic, embossed with the silver circles of the Kambarna. Dressed, she laced her leather bracers onto her forearms, fastened on sword and dagger, and grasped her

Castelon bow from its stand. Idrian*Kasash* might have the innate strength and stronger build, but she had speed and agility. Even without Laana*Kendrisha*, Sauri was First Castelon.

I will take you down, she swore.

And if she died in the attempt, so be it. Her death was foreordained now. It hovered before her: a darkness on the edge of sight, torn threads of her broken bond pulling her out into a dark and empty void of peacefulness.

But first, the Spirit War had to end. Two hundred years had not seen its conclusion—only a pause as combatants moved to a new frontier of battle. Victims of the war grew in number as soul-bindings linked innocents with once tortured spirits. Madness. Insanity. Death. The obstruction of lives. The breaking of a nation. It had to end.

Mine will be the last hand of war—none else will suffer this! Sauri promised recklessly.

Slipping unseen from Castelon headquarters would have taken a miraculous feat. Instead, Sauri swept down through the barracks as if she were whole. She saluted the guards standing patrol at the foot of the officers' quarters, then paused to inspect a crew of gray-garbed cadets filling the oil lamps in the stairwell.

One young cadet's eyes misted upon greeting, getting the proper form of salute from her bonded spirit. Sauri's fury rose at the girl's cavalier attitude. "How dare you waste your soul-bond to cover your lack of practice. See the Second for punishment detail."

With wide eyes, the blonde girl offered a hand to heart, fingers drawn into a circle that was the proper greeting to a superior. "Sorry, First Castelon—I mean, yes, First Castelon."

At the cadet's surprised words, Sauri recognized her error: using the bond for such things was common. *How dare they take advantage of what they have?* No wonder Kasash had aimed to destroy the bond, with it used in such slipshod manner. Shocked by her anger, the First Castelon

bit out a feeble apology. "Never mind, cadet. Carry on."
Continuing onward, Sauri shut out the murmurs of confusion and questioning she left behind.

Damn, I have to stay calm or someone will guess.

But if any suspected her broken soul-bond, none questioned. No one asked. The First Castelon made it to the iron-garbed outer door without further pause. With a quick nod to the pair of guards stationed there, she exited the barracks. Outside, a practiced glance revealed the half-dozen sentries scattered through the trees and in the grasses nearby.

A brawny man she recognised as Lieutenant Damor-*Avaran* dropped down from a concealed niche in the granite cliff and hurried over, offering a practiced salute.

"First Castelon? Is all well?" he asked.

Sauri nodded curtly. "Fine. I am going after Idrian-*Kasash*."

"A patrol left earlier. Should I call for some guards to accompany you?" He quirked an eyebrow.

Sauri grimaced. "No. I'll meet up with the patrol already out."

"But . . ." Was he questioning her authority now? Sauri stared at him coldly until he stepped back, discomfited. Lips closed tightly on a curse, Sauri headed into the marsh. *He'll get others and follow. I must find Idrian*Kasash *first!*

She slipped past the trees and through grasses no Castelon worth his pay would upset. Boots squelched in the mud. Finding her way back to where she had first found Idrian-*Kasash* did not take long. The granite monolith stood at a right angle to the old river way, and when giving Idrian lessons it had often served as their meeting point—the most recognizable location on this side of the mountains.

Today though, the ground was littered with the prints of others hunting for Idrian. Broken branches and upset leaves marked a rushed search over a careful foray. Hunting the area for signs of movement, Sauri grew frustrated as the trails turned back on each other, adding to the confusion.

Her vision spun as she chased each track down, still battling the numbing dizziness threatening to overwhelm her sanity.

*::Where would Idrian*Kasash *be?::* She thought wildly, mind locked into a path of internal thinking, accustomed to getting responses back. Dead silence answered. Her aching loss throbbed harshly. She gripped her bow tighter, transmuting horror into physical action.

Idrian*Kasash* had struck intentionally, knowing full well the effect his blow would have. He had laid her out for others to find—left her weapons. Which meant he knew she would be coming for him.

::You think you can turn me! Make me a plaything for your new war. I may be broken, but I will not be used.:: Her internal dialogue continued uncontrolled. Unheard.

Idrian*Kasash* wanted her to find him, so where would he go? Nowhere of Idrian's memory drew her. It had to be Kasash's choice.

But where? All the Castelons knew the marshes. In his time, Kasash*Danitai* would have led patrols all over the southwest border. He had helped press the enemy Zarristas back across the Escraen. He knew the land—would know hundreds of hiding holes.

The most significant, then, Sauri reckoned. Two hundred years ago, Kasash and a group of hunters had come against a raiding party in a cavern uphill from the closest bend of the Escraen. It was there his medallion had been crushed, his link with Danitai severed. That day madness took him and in a frenzy of sheer horror he had cut out his first medallion—striking the first blow of the Spirit War. Where else would he go to begin it all again?

Sauri crept through the marshes, bow at ready, keeping her footfalls as quiet as the devastating stillness eating her whole. At one point, she caught the specterlike movement of a Castelon party, likely searching for the same fugitive. As someone bent to examine the area she had just passed, Sauri crouched low in the tall sand-shaded grass. *Not now!* Sauri begged. She nocked an arrow, prepared to win free of restraint, but the party moved onward, tracing her route backward. When all sound of their passing faded, she resumed her hunt.

Tracking silently along the edges of the cliff face, the First Castelon came upon the suspected cave. It bit into the skyward-reaching cliffs of the Kambarna like shards of glass, jagged with loose rock shading its inward passage. Close to her quarry, the ache of desire reared up and prompted her forward.

A dozen steps inside the cave, she found a body spread out on the damp ground. A Castelon. Sauri recognized the girl's face, but could not recall her name. Good with a bow, but better with throwing daggers. Dull, dead eyes were frozen in agony—mouth wrenched open in fear. *What?* Then Sauri saw the torn shirt. With bated breath, she rested her bow on the cavern floor and reached out to open the young Castelon's shirt. She gasped at the mutilation.

He's done it again.

At the edge of retching, Sauri offered a quick prayer for the young Castelon's spirit. Much as that would do. When she came back, surely her binding would cause agony in one more innocent victim.

"You enjoy seeing it—don't you?" Lost in reflection, she startled as a voice echoed through the cave.

Gasping, Sauri turned. A living shadow illuminated the cavern entrance.

"Now that you know how I feel, you must understand my desires." Idrian*Kasash* drew nearer, shining eyes darkened to spirit gray.

"No!" she denied, even as she relived her earlier desire to strike down a cadet. The Castelon at her feet was only a few years older.

Idrian*Kasash* smiled knowingly. "So you don't feel the writhing agony of endless solitude? The pull of starless night on ropes leading out into the beyond?"

Sauri shuddered. His descriptions were too accurate—too perfect an understanding of her pain. Her agony.

"Why should anyone live to suffer this madness—this broken devastation of souls at such soft a blow? The binding is our weakness—not our salvation! Help me end it!"

Sauri's eyes teared in painful recognition. A shock to the skin and her very soul had been torn asunder. Her life shredded with her bonded in an instant blow that otherwise would have caused only momentary pain. Surely it was craziness to allow such a thing—to allow such weakness. Better not to have the soul-binding at all.

Yet, what life for those without the binding?

Laana*Kendrisha*'s steadfast encouragement had helped Sauri through life. The former First Castelon had given Sauri access to her memories—her own joys, her own loves. While the skills were Sauri's own, many a time it had been Laana's memories helping to solve a problem. Without her knowledge, the Kambarna would have suffered—a number of Castelons would have died.

"And your binding with Idrian? Do you detest that too? Should I divest him of your spirit as you divested me of mine?" As she spoke the words, Sauri saw herself striking him down, using her sword to slice Kasash from Idrian's soul. She clenched sword hilt.

"First Castelon . . ." the words were soft, drawn out with grief and regret. For a moment, she saw the bright clarity of lapis lazuli. For an instant, Sauri recognized the young man she loved and admired as a son peek through the shadows of Kasash's madness.

"Trust." His voice was fierce, eyes darkly shaded with gray. Demanding. *Do what must be done.* She could almost hear Idrian's spirit call out for her aid.

Can I trust him? A dagger lay sheathed at his side, his hand twisting its hilt tensely.

No. Idrian had not been strong enough to live up to her trust. His promise. Idrian*Kasash* had torn Laana from her soul because she had thought him able to resist the insanity. Never again. Fury at her own heart-wrenching betrayal waved through her. Poised for revenge, Sauri lunged forward.

"Please—don't let him succeed!" Her enemy's cry struck chords of sadness in her heart, drawing her up short. Idrian's eyes, free of shadows, begged not for his own life, but for her own salvation.

Idrian*Kasash*'s strike at her soul-bond had been an act of vengeance, not of salvation. It was what the Castelons stood against on the embattled borders of the Kambarna. Everything she stood against. By killing Idrian in the same evil way, she would be denying all Laana had desired. All they had lived for. "No," she whispered.

Looking down at the bow lying at her feet, Sauri estimated the seconds it would take to pick up and draw a silver arrow. She could not trust the sword in her hand not to strike a glancing blow. She'd never make it in time. Her hand pulled at her sword, cringing at the knowledge she could be damning all in the Kambarna if she failed.

"No. War." Gray wrapped Idrian's pupils, threatening to overshadow her protégé at any moment. Agony lined his muscles to tension, twisting her heart. His hands clenched into fists at his side. Eyes firmly locked to hers, Idrian stepped forward.

What if it's a trick? Kasash allowing her to see her protégé—lulling her into a false sense of security? He had torn Laana*Kendrisha* from her soul!

If not him, whom can I trust? The Spirit War must end. Here. If she attacked, it could be she who started the second Spirit War—her bringing about the end of her race.

No. Only one could stop it, and it was not she. *Trust.*

With a fluid motion, the First Castelon released her sword hilt and bent to grasp her bow from the cave floor. Reaching back for an arrow, ignoring the terror of failure and betrayal threatening to overwhelm, Sauri watched the hazy grayness of Kasash fight Idrian for survival. Drawing the silver arrow, her eyes met Idrian's.

Her protégé remained steady. Locked in offering. Pleading for one last chance to prove himself. *Trust.*

Sauri relaxed her hand, releasing death. Watched it fly a

dozen feet and take Idrian*Kasash* through the chest. Dropping the bow, she crossed the cavern fast enough to catch his crumpling body and carry him softly to the ground.

Breath wheezed in Idrian*Kasash*'s lungs as she held him close. "No!" A mere whisper of denial. "Better they die—"

"No, better they live," She said, even as the gray faded from her protégé's dying eyes. "The Kambarna will thrive and you will live again. You've saved the Kambarna—not only from Kasash, but from me." A bitter acknowledgment of her own temptation.

"Safe." The words were less than a sigh.

Tears tumbled down her cheeks, dripping down on his hair and face—a face returned once more to innocence in the safe security of death. "Yours was the last hand, Castelon." Sauri said softly, offering him the Castelon's salute—fingers curled in a circle over her heart. "Peaceful rest, until your spirit's life."

Lapis lazuli eyes brimmed with light and hope. A soft smile curled his lips. Then the darkness of the in-between took him gently into its embrace.

The binding chamber had been dug out of ancient rock in the heart of the Kambarna domain, where veins of untouched soul-silver shrouded those within its influence under a mantle of security and protection. Here, generations of the Kambarna had undertaken the soul-binding ceremony, linking them into the past and future of the domain. Here, hundreds of hapless youths bound to Kasash*Danitai*'s victims had undergone the cleansing rites and been granted the promise of the untainted return of their spirits.

Here I will die, Sauri*Laana* thought.

A gray-garbed priest of the Kambarna waited a few steps away, back toward her, granting Sauri a few moments of final reflection. Her Second stood behind the priest, his face pale with shock and uncertainty, hands maintaining a fierce grip on the Castelon bow she had granted him upon her return with Idrian's body. Tears still tracking down her cheeks,

Sauri had laid Idrian's body on the soft grass outside of the entry to their cliff home, then turned to face half of her Castelons, brought outside by a sentry's warning.

"Idrian*Kasash* is dead," Sauri had told her Second, who had stood at the head of the waiting company. "And my soul seeks a safe return."

His eyes had widened in shock at her ritualistic words, words announcing her intention to complete the cleansing rites. But none knew duty like a Castelon, and her Second had offered the proper response. "Should you will it, I would guard your passage."

After the priest gave Sauri the potion that would free her soul into the chamber's safekeeping, as once it had been freed to undergo the bonding with Laana*Kendrisha,* her Second would carry out his duty to her one last time—bringing an end to the first life of Sauri*Laana.* In the moment of first death, Sauri's spirit would pass through the silver lining of the bonding chamber and be healed of the grievous injury her shattered soul-bond had inflicted. Cleansed, she would be given the opportunity to complete the circle representing the Kambarna, returning to offer counsel to a future generation.

But her final thoughts did not tarry on death or what might come after. Instead, Sauri reveled in the memories of her moments of freedom at the edge of the Kambarna domain, sharing in the companionship of a bonded spirit she missed most dearly and a young man wanting desperately to learn the honor of the Castelons. And he had. Oh, he had.

::*The Spirit War is ended*:: Sauri*Laana*, First Castelon of the Kambarna, whispered in a voice only spirit could hear.

WAR GAMES

by Lisanne Norman

*Born in Glasgow, Scotland, Lisanne Norman started
writing at the age of eight in order to find more of the
books she liked to read. In 1980, two years after joining The Vikings!, the largest British reenactment society in Britain, she moved to Norfolk, England. There
she ran her own specialist archery display team. Now
living in America and a full-time author, in her Sholan
Alliance Series she has created worlds where warriors, magic. and science coexist. Her latest novel in
the series is* Shades of Gray, *available from DAW.*

Hope City Hall, parking lot

The scream echoed through her helmet's comm-set, grat-
ing inside the bones of her head. She wished whoever it was
would stop and let her think. Then the blast hit her square in
the chest and plucked her from her feet, flinging her across
the parking lot. She caromed off the pillar and came to a
sudden stop against the wall. The screaming stopped.

She lay staring blankly up at the roof of the parking lot,
her world contracted to the burning pain in her chest and leg.

"Captain down!" Tyler must have picked her tell-tale up
on his HUD feed.

Columbia City Military Museum

"Slade, you're late." Reichart's disapproving tone pulled her from her reverie.

She blinked, images of the parking lot dissipating before the innocuous brass plaque on the Mars memorial. The memories lingered.

"I said, you're late. The first group has already arrived. Your team is waiting."

"Far too late. We all were." She touched the plaque.

"Is she all right?" demanded Reichart.

"Captain's fine," she heard Jones say as a powered glove closed on her unarmored forearm. "Aren't you, Captain?"

Mentally she shook herself.

"I believe you said the first group had already arrived, Reichart," she said crisply. "We've work to do, even if you don't. Jones, let's move it."

"Just see you play your part, Slade," Reichart called out. "Otherwise I'll be reporting you to Commander Sandler!"

"Play my part," she snarled under her breath as she increased her pace.

"Captain," said Jones, trying to catch up. "Captain, wait!"

As she reached for the doorknob, Jones' armored forearm barred her entrance.

"Don't go in there yet, Captain." He met her angry glare with his patient one. "He was trying to rile you. Give yourself a moment. He won't report us. It would mean a full inquiry and put the military in an even worse light."

She let her arm fall, breathing deeply. "He succeeded." She pushed Jones' now relaxed arm aside. "Let's get this over with."

Hope City Hall

"Teams Red, Blue, Green, and Amber, target your designated force field generators and take them out. When the field is down, the main assault, units Alpha, Beta, Gamma, and Delta, will be dropped at your locations. Teams, regroup with your assigned unit, and surround the Government Center. The four teams, under Captain Rice of Red, will then retake the building, without endangering the hostage, leaving the main forces for support and mop-up."

Commander Sandler looked round the group crowded in the briefing room. "I want the leader alive, gentlemen. No one takes President Channing's daughter hostage with impunity. We need a very public trial to show these rebel colonists who's in charge."

"You heard the man," said the lieutenant. "Move out!"

"Looks like you're not wanted, Slade," sneered Harris, standing in front of her as she got up. "He said 'gentlemen'; nothing about the likes of you!"

"Rules you out, then," said Jones, pushing him aside. "No one could mistake you for a gentleman!"

"Yeah? At least I got what it takes to be a specialist, Jonesy."

"What's that, then, Harris?" asked Tyler jovially. He sniffed audibly and pulled a face. "B.O.? Man, don't you *ever* shower?"

"Stow it, all of you." She gestured to her men to follow. "We've got a job to do."

"Aye, Captain," said Jones and Tyler crisply, falling in behind her. Catching sight of the latter's parting gesture to Harris, she chose to ignore it.

When they were in the corridor leading to the ready room, she slowed, letting the other three members of her team pass them.

"You encourage men like Harris by trying to protect me from them. Ignore him. I do."

"We look out for our own, ma'am, and you're one of us," said Jones.

She brushed short auburn curls out of her eyes impatiently. "I can look after myself. I earned my rank; I didn't screw a four-star general to get it like the rumors say!"

"I stopped those rumors," muttered Tyler, his gray eyes hooded. "No one repeats them now."

"I know." Her voice softened as she touched his shoulder. "And I'm grateful, but I have to fight my own battles."

"We're a team, Captain. Just because we're the only one with a woman leader doesn't mean the others can keep taking the . . ."

"Stow it, Jones," interrupted Tyler. "Captain knows the score. Get down to the ready room."

A tiny cold knot formed in her stomach as Jones left them at a trot.

"So it's not just me you're having to defend. I had no idea . . ."

Tyler glanced around then grasped her arm, propelling her down the corridor in Jones' wake.

"Jonesy is speaking crap, Captain," he said, keeping his voice low. "We're all proud to have you as our team leader. We've fought alongside you; you've nothing to prove to any of us." He released her, letting her own momentum carry her onward beside him.

"It's only assholes like Harris who don't know your worth. You do your job, Captain, leave the rest to us. It's our problem, not yours."

The intensity in his eyes right now was too much for her and she had to break eye contact. She couldn't give in to the attraction she felt between them—not here, not now—not ever. The lives of all her team depended on them forming bonds of a very different nature.

"Touch me again like that, mister, and you'll be . . ." she began angrily.

"Yes, ma'am," he interrupted. "Sorry for interfering. Won't happen again, ma'am."

His tone was stiff, angry—and hurt. Dammit! Alienating the few men on her side wasn't what she wanted to do.

"I appreciate the sentiment, sergeant," she began awkwardly, catching sight of Harris and the rest of Green Team closing on them.

"I understand, ma'am. Permission to go ahead and get tooled up?"

"Granted," she snarled as Kirby came level with her.

"Problem, Slade?"

"Nothing I can't handle," she said, striding after Tyler.

Columbia City Museum

She blinked, realizing she was no longer on the *Real Opportunity*, but in the exhibition hall, in the holograph version of the ship, standing in front of her combat armor locker. Jones was finishing his introductory spiel to the group of forty children on the other side of the tinted glass screen. Like that day a lifetime ago, he'd be the one to help her into her suit, not Tyler.

Hope City Hall

The tension was palpable as she strode past Tyler's locker to her own.

"Shall I help you suit up, ma'am?" Jones, already armored apart from his helmet, asked hesitantly.

No one got armored up on their own, and it was accepted specialist practice that the team sergeant always helped the captain—except for today.

"Please," she said, trying to dispel her own anger and hurt. Damn Tyler! Why'd he have to get so protective today of all days? Angrily she opened her locker doors.

Turning round, she backed into the small space, wriggling until she felt her armor snug against her shoulders, round her waist, and between her legs.

Jones bent down. "Your legs, Captain. You need to back in more."

Columbia City Museum

"Captain, your legs," repeated Jones, touching her right knee.

With a start, she looked down, suddenly aware once more

of the museum narrator droning on about the battle armor used by Special Forces in the Mars Rebellion.

"You've not backed up enough, Captain."

She shuffled her legs back until they fetched up against the armor.

Quickly and efficiently Jones swung the hinged front pieces over her calves and thighs and latched them into place over the heavy boots, then stood.

She pushed her hands into the gloves, then shrugged her shoulders and rotated her head until she felt the back of the collar clasp her neck, and her shoulders site themselves into the appropriate joints.

Again, Jones pulled the limb pieces into place, fixing them there, then reached up for the torso section. Eyes level with hers, he glanced quizzically at her.

"Ready," she confirmed, trying to dispel the sense of déjà vu as she tucked her chin against her chest.

Hinged at the shoulders, the torso section came down, just missing her head, until Jones clicked it shut at her groin.

"Comfortable?"

"I'm fine," she replied shortly, lifting her head as he snapped the fastenings closed. She waited impatiently for him to finish. She hated this point, that in-between stage before she hooked into the suit where she always felt like she was being entombed, mummified, inside its bulk.

"Good job they don't have to wear this stuff anymore, eh, Captain?" Jones murmured with the ghost of a smile as he reached behind her neck for the suit's umbilical. "Still, the kids get a kick out of seeing us putting the armor on."

"Yeah," she said, tilting her head to the side to allow him to reach the implant socket just behind her ear. So many changes in so short a time . . . changes that their mission had been responsible for.

Hope City Hall

A slight push, then the jack was home and Jones latched the throat piece.

"Commencing power-up," she said, pulling her suited arms free of their bays.

The armor weighed some fifty pounds even for a suit tailored to her slight frame, and it took much of her natural strength to prevent her arms falling to her sides. She reached her right arm across to her left forearm, flicked back the protective cover, and pressed the power toggle.

Instantly the suit contracted around her body, cushioning against her form-fitting coveralls. A slight tingle behind her ear and a hiss of hydraulics as it hermetically sealed itself round her neck, and suddenly the battle armor weighed as little as she did. On the small forearm view screen, figures began to scroll slowly, giving her readouts on suit pressure, external gravity, and internal temperature as well as her vital signs.

"All in the green," she said, stepping away from her locker.

As she reached for the helmet nestling in the locker door, a pair of armor clad arms snaked past her, snagging it up.

"I've got it," said Tyler over his shoulder to Jones, passing it to her as she whirled to face him. "I'll help the captain check on the others."

"Aye, Sergeant," said Jones.

She felt the mood of her team lighten as conversations broke out—the usual light pre-mission banter that had been missing.

"Sorry, Captain. I was out of line," Tyler said as he handed her the helmet.

"So was I," she murmured, accepting it. "I hadn't realized . . ."

"Forget it." An embarrassed half grin lit his face. "Each to their own. You look after us, we cover your back, ma'am."

As she lifted the helmet, she studied his face, then hastily lowered it over her head as she saw his eyes darken with an emotion neither of them should feel. Momentarily cut off from him and the rest of the ship behind the tinted visor, she took her time locking it in place, delaying the moment of activating the comm system.

The suit commenced the last of its power-up routine. To her left, on the inside of her visor, she could see the same diagnostic list, still all in green, recognizing that the gravity and air around her was standard Earth normal and there was no need for the gravity compensators or her personal air supply to be triggered. Instead, external vents opened and filters began to automatically scrub the air.

She lightened her visor, seeing Tyler fitting on his own helmet. Hologram tell-tales lit up on her right, giving her the exact position of the five members of her team, and showing a locator for the other team captains. In her left ear, the constant feed from their handler, Raines, had already begun.

"Blue One checking in," she said.

"Acknowledged, Blue One," said Raines.

"Blue Two checking in," said Tyler.

"Acknowledged," she said crisply, reaching into her locker door for her pulse rifle and pistol. A movement of her chin to the left and she was checking her suit's level of stored ammo: full. She thumbed open the holster panel in her left forearm and stowed the pistol.

"Blue Three checking in," said Lydecker.

"Blue Four." That was Hutton, their medic.

The rest signed in in quick succession.

"Move out," she ordered in response to Raines' order over the command battle channel.

Columbia City Museum

"Blue Two checking in," the voice in her helmet repeated loudly.

Jones, not Tyler.

"Acknowledged." She left the visor opaqued for now. She didn't want Jones knowing just how sharp the memories were today.

"Blue Three signing in," said the voice of one of the

student reenactors the museum employed to bulk out the display.

"Once more for posterity, eh, Captain?" Jones' voice on their private comm link was full of forced cheeriness.

"Posterity be damned," she snapped. They all thought she'd gotten off light because of the publicity the whole shambles had attracted, but she hadn't. Every day she was forced to reenact the Relief of Hope Colony, the authorized version of course, at this damned military museum. Sandler and his cronies at the Oval Residence had suppressed the truth, called it her *errors of judgment,* made sure only their version had been released publicly.

"Starting battle simulation on my mark in three, two, one. Mark." The voice of the museum tech came over their battle channel loud and clear, sounding as remote as Raines' always had.

Abruptly the setting around them changed, morphing into the streets surrounding Hope City Hall.

Hope City Hall

"Blue One to Base. City Hall perimeter reached," she said from her position crouched behind a low wall surrounding a deserted street café. From behind she could hear bursts of sporadic gunfire. "Holding position."

"Acknowledged, Blue One. Green Team will rendezvous with you in three minutes."

"Incoming, one o'clock high!" yelled Lydecker.   ·

Jumping up, she dove over the wall, rolling and coming up in a crouch, rifle trained on the tall building opposite. The sidewalk exploded as a burst of energy hit it. Globs of molten pavement flew into the air, filling the dense smoke with sparks of fire. A low thrumming told her the suit's air filters were working overtime.

"Where is he?" she demanded. "Dammit, Raines, Beta Unit declared this area cleared!"

"I can't see through the smoke, Captain," said Raines.

Another explosion, closer this time, taking out part of the wall just ahead of them.

"Brolin, find him! We're sitting ducks! Rest, back up ten feet," she ordered. Brolin's low cursing about handlers safe on ships sounded through their private comm channel, making her smile. He was the best gunner around, she could ignore his odd lapse of discipline. Angling her head inside the helmet, she hit the targeting grid control with her chin.

A flash of light caught her eye. Instantly she gave it her full attention, blinking twice rapidly to trigger her auto-tracker.

"Got him! Grid ref . . ."

"On it," Brolin sang out as he launched his missile.

Instinct made her duck as it roared over her head. She tracked it, catching sight of another flash from the distant window with peripheral vision.

"Incoming!" Tyler's hand closed on her arm, jerking her to her feet and hauling her backward.

The blast lifted them off their feet, sending them flying through the air to land in a nearby flowerbed in a tangle of armored limbs.

Her first thoughts for her team, she checked the tell-tales—all present and green, no one hurt. A rapid tattoo of cooling stone fragments rained down on her suit. Movement beneath her drew her attention and she focused on the view outside her helmet.

Tyler grinned up at her. "Gonna have to stop meetin' like this, Cap'n. People gonna start talkin'."

A loud explosion from behind and above boomed out, counterpointed by Brolin's understated, "He's gone now."

"Thanks," she muttered to Tyler, pushing herself off him and getting to her feet. She reached a hand down to help him up as he flicked small chunks of rubble off his suit with his gloved hand. "That was too close."

"It was," he agreed, accepting her help.

"Blue Two, I have a red light on your suit integrity," said

Raines. "Please initiate internal diagnostics and external visual scans immediately."

"Acknowledged, Base," Tyler responded, flipping open his forearm control panel. He scanned it, then pressed a couple of keypads. "Suit's fine, false warning. No need to evac me."

"Let me check," she demanded.

"It's fine, Captain. Raines, you copy? All is green."

"Copy, Blue Two. Warning light extinguished."

"Tyler, tell me you haven't overridden the security checks," she said, switching off the battle channel.

"Green Team approaching on our Six, Captain," interrupted Lydecker.

"Acknowledged," she responded as Tyler raised his eyebrows at her.

"It was a malfunction, Captain. No time for a visual check. There's a hostage waiting for us."

"It better be! I've never lost a man, and I don't intend to start now!"

"Green Team," he said succinctly.

Annoyed, she turned the battle channel back on.

"Nice shooting, Brolin," said Kirby, as he strode over. "Slade, I'm taking over. Fall in behind my men. Now the sniper's been dealt with, we're moving into the building."

"Aye, Captain," she gestured the rest of Blue Team to follow.

"Don't remember anyone putting him in charge," muttered Brolin on their private channel.

"Old man's a glory hound," said Lydecker. "This being a high-profile mission, it's to be expected."

Still concerned over Tyler's suit, she'd ignored their comments.

Columbia City Museum

She blinked the tears back. Why had she taken his word about his suit integrity? She should have insisted on checking it over, found the fractured air line . . . Had she done so, she could have . . .

"Done nothing, Captain."

Jones' voice cut through her reflections. Like Tyler, Jones had an uncanny knack of following her thoughts.

"It wasn't just one incident, Captain, it was the accumulation of several."

"I wish I believed that," she whispered, hand tightening on her rifle as they moved through the garden simulation of Hope City Hall.

Hope City Hall

"Heat signs in two locations," said Raines. "Four people breaking off. Possibly heading toward the level four elevator."

"Possibly, Raines?" snapped Kirby, halting both teams behind a waist-high ornamental wall. "I need accurate information!"

There was a short silence. "Green Team, head for the east side entrance. Take up defensive positions in the underground parking lot. Prevent them from leaving."

"Acknowledged, Base," Kirby replied.

The whole area was too quiet, she thought, following Green Team through the eastern lobby.

"Don't like this, Captain," muttered Lydecker, rifle raised as he checked the ceiling high above them for niches or balconies. There was one, straight ahead above the staircase. "Too many chances for an ambush."

"Stow it, mister," snapped Kirby. "*Opportunity*'s got the place under constant surveillance. Our handlers know exactly where the rebels and hostage are."

A snigger of laughter, then, "You got us leadin' now, Lydecker. No need to worry. None of those dirt farmers can hide from our scanners!"

She triggered their private channel. "Ignore him, guys. Ship scans aren't foolproof. Stay alert and check everything."

A low chorus of acknowledgments sounded. All went quiet as they split forces, each team heading in opposite directions around the curve of the lobby toward the short staircase at the rear.

Her glance flicked up to the small balcony ahead as they hugged close to the wall. Something just didn't feel right. It was too easy. Not even their heavy boots made a sound on the marble floor, as if every sound was swallowed . . .

She stopped, raising her arm to signal her team.

"Sound shields on. Jones, get up here."

"Slade, what the hell are you doing?" demanded Kirby on the command channel. "I gave no such order!"

"Place is too quiet," she hissed. "Might be a sonic device. You got that scanner of yours, Jones?"

"Belay that order! The rebels are civilians, Captain," said Kirby angrily. "Where would they get hold of such devices?"

Jones looked at her. "Never without it, Captain."

"Not our job to know, Captain Kirby." She turned her body slightly so her hand gestures were hidden and signaled Jones to start scanning. "They got hold of other illegal weapons, like that pulse rifle they were shooting at us."

"Move out, mister, and follow my orders!" Kirby's voice almost deafened her.

Jones pulled a small scanning device from his belt then pointed it at the balcony. She watched the display panel as he scanned.

Harris gave a raucous laugh. "Trust a woman to get spooked by silence!"

A loud oath drew her attention briefly from Jones as Harris jostled the man ahead of him and knocked over an ornamental floor vase.

From the corner of her eye she saw the scanner light up like a Christmas tree as the vase hit the floor and shattered.

All hell let loose as wave upon wave of sound emanated from the device concealed on the balcony, shattering all the windows. Even with her aural shielding on, the sound vibrated every bone in her skull, giving Slade an instant headache. Overlying it were the screams of Kirby's team as their unprotected ears took the full brunt of it.

The familiar roar of Brolin's missile launcher going off inches from her helmet was a relief in comparison. The balcony exploded in a cloud of debris, instantly silencing the awful noise.

As the echoes of the explosion died, she shut off the command channel and looked to Kirby and his team writhing on the ground, clawing ineffectually at their helmets. Her team's tell-tales were green, but Kirby's all glowed red.

"Everyone okay?" she asked on their channel, switching her attention to the lobby around them.

"Affirmative," came Tyler's response.

"Blue One, report in!" Raines broke in on their private channel. "Telemetry shows multiple injured Greens."

"Blue One, Green Team triggered a sonic device. Immediate evac needed." She gestured Hutton toward them. "Sending my medic. Current status of rebel heat sources?"

There was a delay as their handler obviously conferred with someone else.

"Cancel your last order, Captain Slade. An evac unit has been deployed for Green Team. Continue to the basement parking lot. Heat source movements are unreliable. Either their numbers are growing, or they're creating extra sources of heat to throw us off."

"I can't just leave Green Team unprotected," she objected.

"It's imperative you stop any escape by the rebels. We need the basement covered now. Armored government vehicles are parked there," said Raines.

"I want the layout of that parking lot, Raines," said Slade as Hutton headed back to her side at a run. "And isolate Green Team from our battle channel."

"Acknowledged, Blue Team. Isolating Green Team. Will feed the layout for the parking lot."

"You all heard our orders," she said. "Move out. Jones, up front with me and Tyler. Keep scanning for traps. Does that gizmo of yours show movement as well as heat sources?"

"Sure, Captain. It can track them on noise too."

"Track 'em any way that works," she said before flicking on the now quiet battle channel. "Raines, send the basement feed to Jones' HUD, as well as mine and Tyler's."

"That's a highly unusual request, Captain Slade . . ."

"Do it. Blue One out." She flicked the channel off.

Columbia City Museum

Slade shifted her position for the fifth time as she and Jones crouched in what was ostensibly Hope City Hall parking lot, waiting for the narrator to brief their audience of school children on the next phase of their mission. She hated this tour of duty, and all it stood for. It was rehab for her and Jones, and was supposed to be a public relations exercise for the military, to take the civilians, especially school children, behind the scenes and show them that an active military was necessary, that peace was a precious commodity that had to be defended, no matter the cost. But it was failing.

Through the glass that separated them from the public, she could see the large infoscreen that existed in every public area in all the domed cities on Mars. The competition. Everything was being televised these days, broadcast to the people in an unending stream of exposés and larger-than-life interactive episodes. This had become just one more episode in that daily diet.

She punched the helmet controls with her chin, opening a private channel to Jones. "Is he stringing this out longer than usual?"

"I don't think so," said Jones. "It just seems like it."

"That's for sure."

"I heard they're disbanding another regiment. Only two left."

"I heard. Channing and the United Worlds are pushing this antiwar movement." Specialist teams like theirs were safe, for now. There was always the odd hot spot of unrest that refused to accept the U.W. rulings, be it on Earth or Mars.

"You can't blame the president, considering what happened," said Jones. "Not that I'm blaming you," he added. "You know I don't."

"Channing does, and Sandler and his cronies. Sandler knew the truth but still covered it up! We perpetuate it every day with this bloody stupid reenactment!"

"Try to see it as just another day."

She nodded. It was easier than telling him the obvious.

"We're having a get together tonight in the mess bar. First anniversary. Join us, Captain. Everyone wants you to come."

A year? Where had the time gone? She was spared the need to answer as the tech gave them their cue to begin the final segment.

Hope City Hall

The small lot was L-shaped, the longer leg only 150 feet long, with the standard guarded barrier to allow access. Wide concrete pillars were set close to the walls every forty feet. Between the pair nearest the elevator were three vehicles, with a fourth opposite, and one more at the far end of the shorter leg, by the exit. Except for directly in front of the elevator, a low metal railing between the pillars separated a five-foot wide walkway from the parking area.

"Fan out," she ordered as they emerged from the staircase at the far end. "Tyler, Lydecker, check the guard post and the single vehicle. Brolin, Hutton, check those ahead. Jones, stay with me. Keep scanning."

She and Jones ran the few feet to the nearest pillar.

"Nothing showing on the scans, Captain," said Jones quietly.

"Can you set it to pick up the elevator if it starts moving?"

"Should do."

"Do it." She turned her attention to her team's tell-tales.

"Vehicles clear," said Hutton.

"Cover the elevator," she said.

Moments later, Tyler called in. "Guard post and vehicle clear. Want us to cover the exit?"

"Affirmative. Jones and I are moving position to cover the staircase." She gestured Jones to follow her.

As they settled down to wait, she monitored the traffic on the other battle channels.

After ten minutes, sporadic chat broke out among her team.

"Tell me why we're doing this, Tyler. It's a civilian police job," muttered Lydecker.

"You know why."

"Yeah, but I didn't sign up to do groundside crap like this . . . Why do we keep getting the back-up missions?"

"This time the long straw, next time the short one," Tyler replied.

"Well, it stinks."

"They didn't shoot at you enough? C'mon round here and I'll give you some dodging practice!" said Brolin.

She ignored them, concentrating on the conversation between Raines and Amber Team. They needed to let off steam—no one liked getting hyped up on a mission then left waiting on the sidelines. When push came to shove, they'd drop the bickering and be professionals again.

"There's no one here, Raines," Rice was saying. "Damned rebels lit half a dozen thermal stoves, left them on to register as heat sources!"

"Say again, Amber One."

"I said they're gone, dammit!"

"Looks like we could have visitors, guys," she said on Blue's channel. "Stay alert."

"Copy that, Captain," said Tyler.

"Remember we want them alive."

"I'm picking up something in the direction of the elevator now, Captain," interrupted Jones.

"Blue One, the rebels and hostage are not showing on *Opportunity*'s scanners. You may have incoming to your area."

"Their arrival is imminent, Base. Blue One out. Let them

clear the elevator if you can," she ordered her team. "Give them a chance to surrender. Use gas grenades, Brolin, if they don't. Try to avoid shooting if at all possible."

"Aye, Captain."

The elevator door slid open, revealing five partially armored men surrounding the familiar figure of Kirsten Channing, daughter of Mars Colony's president. Looking cautiously around them, the first two emerged, pulse rifles ready.

Slade's uneasy gut feeling returned. She hesitated just long enough to see Kirsten begin to push the two men aside.

"Halt!" Tyler called out. "Lay down your weapons. You are surrounded by marines from the USS *Opportunity*."

Turning in the direction of the voice, the leading two men began spraying the area ahead with bursts of energy.

She spared a glance at Tyler as he dove for the ground. A bolt clipped the back of his armor, the impact sending him skidding into the open. He grunted, but his light still showed green on her HUD.

She raised her rifle as one of the men grabbed the girl and, using her as a shield, ran for the open.

"Stop!" she yelled, letting off a warning shot.

They skidded, changed direction, but kept running for the single vehicle.

Hutton and Lydecker exchanged fire with the rebels in the elevator while Brolin laid down cover for Tyler as he tried to roll to safety. The girl's posture hadn't been that of a hostage. Had she really seen her elbow the men aside? It made no difference right now; it was down to her and Jones.

"Right behind you, ma'am," said Jones as she began to run toward the next pillar. "I'll cover you."

The rebels had armor, but it wasn't powered. Like all the Mars domes, gravity was Earth normal. They had the advantage.

She cleared the forty feet to the next pillar in seconds, skirted round it, dodging shots that landed within inches of her. As she leaped onto the trunk of the limo, she felt the shock of an impact hitting Jones. On her HUD, his tell-tale began to blink.

"Amber Team on its way, Blue One," said Raines' voice in her helmet. "Contain the situation for a few more minutes."

"Still got your rear, Captain." Jones' voice was shaky, but strong. "Brolin's let the gas loose. Should be over in a few."

"Slade! You got no backup!" roared a voice that nearly had her losing her footing as, without pause, she jumped off the limo. The shock over, at least she could breathe more easily knowing he and Jones were okay.

She couldn't wait for him. If she was right, then Kirsten Channing was in this right up to her ears. If she were wrong, then she was saving the hostage.

Rounding the last pillar, she stopped dead at the corner. "Halt! Drop your weapons! You're under arrest," she yelled, rifle trained on them.

"Help!" Kirsten yelled, trying to wrench herself away from the man holding her. "Help me!"

Slade froze, confused, letting the end of her gun drop down. This wasn't the way she remembered it happening.

"Help me," repeated the girl, a look of surprise briefly crossing her pleasant features as she continued to struggle with the man trying to drag her into the vehicle.

"Captain!" Jones' voice was harsh in her ears. "Remember what you have to do!"

Yes, she knew what she had to do, as she saw Kirsten and the rebel leader running for the vehicle.

"Halt, or I will shoot!" she yelled, leaving her cover.

Kirsten and he put on a burst of speed. She fired at the limo, disintegrating a tire. "I said halt!"

They slid to a stop by the hood, turning to face her.

"Shoot her, Chris," said Kirsten Channing, her face contorted in anger.

Without thinking, she fired first.

Columbia City Museum

"Nice job, Captain Slade," said their narrator through the main battle channel. "You had me worried for a moment at the end, though."

She stood up, sick to the depths of her soul with this charade, and followed Jones listlessly toward where the glass partition between them and the school children was being lowered.

"Thank you, Captain Slade and Sergeant Jones, for such an informative display," the teacher said. "Children, thank the marines."

"Thank you," forty young voices chorused.

Behind them, the infoscreen chattered away relentlessly. She glanced at it as she unlocked and removed her helmet. A young male reporter was on the lawn outside Columbia's Oval House. Underneath him, the tickertape banner scrolled past, summarizing breaking news. The words Virtual Reality Academy caught her eye but it scrolled past before she could read it.

"A pleasure, ma'am," murmured Jones, taking the lead today. "Any questions?"

"Did you really get shot?" asked a girl.

"Course he didn't," said her neighbor. "Don't be stupid. War isn't real now, it's only make-believe."

"Yes, both Captain Slade and I really were injured," said Jones. "Wars were real then, people had to go out and actually fight."

"Where were you hurt?" asked a boy.

"Did it hurt?" another called out.

"I was lucky. I only got shot in the arm. And yes, it hurt at first, till the meds in my suit treated me."

"Can we see it?"

Jones held his helmet out to her. She took it, watching as

he went through the daily ritual of removing his glove to show his artificial hand. She began to come out of her daze as the children exclaimed over it, wanting to know if it was as good as a real one.

"I want to be a soldier but we were told only women could do that," called out one young lad.

Jones looked at the teacher, unsure what to say.

"Yes, men can become soldiers, no matter what they tell you," Slade said. "We'll always need good men, and women, to defend our planet and Earth."

"Captain," interrupted the teacher, a warning note in her voice. "You know that they only accept women into the military since the United Worlds declared it illegal to fight in real time."

Slade pointed to the infoscreen where the scene had changed to the new Virtual Reality Military Center.

"That's not real, no matter what they tell you. War can't be fought in VR. All those women are is game jackers, wired up to an elaborate game. They call it war. But war isn't glamorous or fashionable, it isn't clean and nice like they show you! What do you do when someone comes along who refuses to play by U.W. rules? Freedom can't always be negotiated, sometimes you have to fight, and then people get hurt, and die!"

Her voice broke as the sound was turned up, drowning out anything else she might say.

As one, the children and the teacher turned to watch the screen.

"Here, outside the VR Military Academy, we're waiting for the latest Mars combatant to emerge after her bloodless victory on Phobos!" the enthusiastic young female reporter said. *"Our new-style virtual soldiers are mainly women, chosen because of their ability to process mental data more quickly and efficiently than men. Thanks to the U.W. ruling, the days of male-dominated warfare are gone forever, as are the inhumane consequences of it. This latest battle secured mining rights on the moon for Columbian corporations for*

*the next twenty years against stiff virtual opposition from
Earth's leading mining company, Harrison and Dewart."*

The scene shifted suddenly to the front door opening.

*"She's coming out now, the latest Virtual Warrior, our
own General Lucy Foster!"*

The children rushed over to the screen, leaving Jones and
Slade facing the teacher.

"What were you thinking, Captain Slade?" she said
stiffly. "I shall be complaining to the museum. You know the
United Worlds have agreed there will be no more fighting.
Your battle brought about that ruling! I would think after the
injuries and loss your team suffered, you would agree."

Slade stared past her at the screen where a young woman,
fair hair flowing over the shoulders of her form-fitted blue
one piece, stood at the top of the steps of the VR Academy,
waving to the crowd.

"Complain all you like. They're only playing games, they
just don't realize it. Out there are people like the rebels, and
aliens, who won't think twice about attacking us physically,
no matter what insane edicts the U.W. passes! Human rights
will count for nothing when you're being slaughtered by an
enemy that doesn't recognize their existence."

"You would choose to die for your beliefs?" demanded
the teacher.

"I have died for them," she said flatly, walking away.

The handler's call sounded through her comm-set, but
she was too busy fighting for her next breath.

"She went after the hostage and the rebel leader, Raines,"
said Tyler. *"I'm following now!"*

She knew she ought to let them know she was all right,
but the pain was so intense. Overhead, the ceiling began to
darken and blur. Two sharp pricks in her neck brought her
back from the edge of unconsciousness.

Like cold fire, the stimulant and the analgesic coursed
through her system, heightening her remaining senses while
dulling the throbbing pain in her chest and leg. She tried to

orient herself, feeling the all-too-familiar sensation of the suit's interior expanding protectively around her injuries.

I've been hit. Simultaneously she registered that she'd only wounded the rebel leader, lost her rifle, and now lay only feet from him and Kirsten Channing.

Twisting her head, she looked around, seeing a pair of elegantly booted feet below the limo some thirty yards distant.

A blast of energy hit the ground beside her. Instincts cut in and she tried to fling herself over onto her front—but nothing happened. Fear made a tight fist in the pit of her stomach as she scrabbled for the external controls on her right forearm, trying to find the flap to release her energy pistol.

"You bitch!" Kirsten ran toward her, rifle raised. "You shot Chris!"

The floor a foot from her face vaporized, surrounding her with a blast of noxious gasses. She could hear the suit's filters working overtime, then her internal air supply cut in.

"Get back here, Kirsten!" her companion yelled. "We can still make it if you help me!"

Frantically Slade pushed herself again, this time to the other side, managing at last to roll over onto her front. Arms shaking with effort, she lifted her torso off the ground, looking to the limo.

Kirsten turned back to Chris as he pulled himself into a standing position and aimed his weapon at her.

Slade's blood ran cold. It was one of the heavy rotation rifles that Brolin and Tyler used.

She heard Tyler round the corner. Kirsten fired at him as his missile hit the rebel leader.

Tyler grunted in pain as he fell. He landed beside her, his rifle falling from his hands. She grabbed it, forced herself up onto her good knee, and relying only on her tac grid, pulled the trigger, holding it down for several heartbeats. An arc of energy leaped toward the girl, felling her instantly. Beyond her, the limo, detonated by Tyler's missile, exploded, surrounding both her and Tyler in a blast of heat and poisonous fumes.

She turned to him. His tell-tale still showed green on her HUD. Fear lent her the strength to pull his unconscious form closer.

"Tyler!" she yelled, pushing him onto his back and shaking him. "Tyler, wake up!"

A secondary explosion shook the ground as the ammunition from the rebels' rifles exploded.

His eyes flickered open. "John," he said, enunciating the word carefully as he tried to focus on her face. "It's John, Emma."

"John, stay with me," she shook him again as his eyes closed and he began to cough. "Medic! Hutton! He's choking to death!" she screamed. Slowly, painfully, she began to inch them away from the inferno.

"Let me have him, Captain," said Hutton, dropping onto one knee beside her. "Lydecker, give me a hand! Brolin, help the captain."

"He's choking on the fumes," she said, barely noticing that Tyler was now lying limp and still as she surrendered him.

Lydecker lifted Tyler up, carrying him toward the exit. As Brolin picked her up, she craned her head to watch Lydecker remove Tyler's helmet.

Brolin set her down beside them then hovered.

Remembering her duties, she asked, "What about the rebels?"

"Lost one, rest are sleeping the gas off," said Brolin as Hutton reached for the small oxygen flask he carried.

"You won't be needing that," said Lydecker quietly. "He's gone."

"Use the oxygen," Brolin said forcefully as Hutton bent over to examine Tyler.

Hutton sat back and shook his head. "Too late."

Leaning forward, she snatched the oxygen from the medic. "I'll use it if you won't," she said, fumbling with the flask, looking for the way to turn the gas flow on. Something precious inside her was dying with Tyler. The pain in her chest was returning and her vision was getting blurry again.

"There's no point, Captain," he said, trying gently to take it back from her. "There's already been too much tissue damage to his lungs."

"See to the captain, Hutton," she heard Lydecker say. "Look at the hole in her chest armor. She's hurt bad."

She let the flask go, giving in to her own pain and grief as she passed out.

"Captain," said Jones, catching up to her in the corridor. "Captain—Emma, wait!"

She stopped, shocked at his use of her name.

Jones gave a small smile. "Yeah, Tyler told me your name. He made it his business to find it out. There was nothing you could have done. He chose to bypass the warning light on his suit."

"I should have insisted on checking . . ."

"He needed to be on the mission for you, Emma," Jones interrupted. "Tyler died trying to save you. You have to allow his death to count for that. Way you're behaving, you're taking his sacrifice away from him, making it worthless."

She nodded, finally listening to him. "He saved me twice that day."

"He did. You just got to hang in there. There's only a month of this duty left. I spoke to the teacher, explained about it being a year since he died. She's not going to make a complaint."

"But it matters, Jones. War isn't a game. They killed all the rebels to cover up Channing's daughter's involvement."

He held his artificial hand out to her. "Hell, I know it isn't a game! One day, so will they, and we'll be here, as always. Why don't you join us tonight? We keep asking you. Tyler would have liked it."

She and Tyler had lost what little they could have had because of the barriers between their ranks. Maybe now was the time for her to admit that even if she was a woman, she was entitled to close ties with her men.

Taking a deep breath, she took hold of his hand. "I'll come."

FIRE FROM THE SUN

by Jane Lindskold

Lindskold is well-known for her Firekeeper saga, which began with Through Wolf's Eyes *and has continued through four novels. Her most recent novel is* The Buried Pyramid, *in which she takes a break from feral women and wolves to write an archaeological adventure fantasy set in 1870s Egypt. Lindskold has published fourteen novels and over fifty short stories. She lives in New Mexico with her archaeologist husband, Jim Moore. See her Web site at www.janelindskold.com for more.*

ANDRASTA gripped her knees tightly into Flame's sides, leaving her hands free to wield sword and shield. Her spear was long since broken, the time for archery long past. What had started out as a routine patrol had turned into a pitched battle, and she had no doubt that her side was losing.

Two men erupted seemingly out of nowhere on her left side. She bashed one soundly across the face with her shield and he crumpled. His fellow dodged, grabbing for the shield's rim, seeking to unhorse her with his weight.

Andrasta cut awkwardly across. The man's fingers and a

chunk of her shield went flying. He fell back, screaming in rage and shock, but though he would never know it, his purpose had been served. Andrasta was unbalanced. When Flame danced to sidestep some hazard on her near side, Andrasta lost her seat and pitched from the saddle.

Her head hit the ground. All she knew was a flash of white light that felt like pain, then darkness.

The darkness was full of voices calling to each other in almost singsong tones.

"Dead."

"Dead here, too."

"Dead."

"All dead."

"Wait! This one's breathing. What a lot of blood."

"Let me look. Yes. She's breathing."

"Shall we?"

"Help me move her. Better see how bad it is before . . ."

The darkness took on a ruddy hue that didn't make anything clear. There was a sensation of something being manipulated. Her. Her limbs. They felt very odd and heavy, distant from her, but a thin scream beneath the heaviness made Andrasta think that the sensation would not last.

The voices went on talking as if she wasn't there.

"Bloodied nose, maybe broken. Bad cut over one eye. She's been shaken up badly. Get that arm out from under her. Is it broken?"

"No. I don't think . . . Mother, look!"

"Blessed Springtime preserve us! The griffin marks! I didn't know her for all the blood. It's our little hazelnut."

"We can't leave her, then. Mother, we can't!"

"No. We can't. We'll be taking a terrible risk, but we'd better take her back with us."

"Can't we just give her to her people?"

"There are none here. None alive."

*   *   *

When she came up again from darkness, Andrasta knew
herself, but she had no idea where she was. She was lying
on her back in a smoky, rather strong-smelling tent. The
heaviness was gone, and every part of her hurt.

"She's awake, I think," said a voice.

"Don't let her sit up, Dmaalyn," came a second voice.
"I'll be there in a moment."

After a moment of laborious thought, Andrasta placed the
voice as one of the two she had heard speaking earlier.
Through the fog that still padded portions of her mind, she
felt vaguely triumphant. The small effort of memory exhausted her, and the warrior felt no desire to sit up or even
turn her head, contenting herself with staring up at the roof
of the tent and wondering vaguely where she was.

An increase in the amount of light and a face peering into
her own roused Andrasta. The face belonged to a woman
with a lined, weathered face. Her black hair was slightly
silver-shot. Her dark eyes were thoughtful and assessing as
she gazed down at Andrasta.

"Why?" Andrasta managed to whisper.

The older woman smiled, showing worn and missing
teeth. "Hear that, Dmaalyn? Not who, not where, but 'why'?"

The older woman then turned her attention to Andrasta.

"I am Narjin, clan mother here. Time for questions and
answers later, Mistress Andrasta. First we must make sure
you are strong enough to take what we must tell you."

Mistress? And how do you know my name? Andrasta was
too fogged to shape the words. Narjin spoke as slave to free.
That would fit the squalor of the surroundings, but what was
going on? Why was she here? Why was she still alive? It
had been slaves who had risen up, slaves who had attacked
and killed Andrasta's patrol, who had tried to kill Andrasta
herself.

"Why?" she tried to ask again, but the fog had wrapped
her tongue and again her mind was flooded by darkness.

*   *   *

When she awoke the second time, Andrasta found her head blessedly clear. Narjin sat beside her, and the older woman smiled when she saw Andrasta assessing her.

"Your mind is your own again, I take it? Good. Your helmet probably saved you a broken skull, though the rim gave you a nasty cut above one eye. We've stitched the cut, but you'll likely have a new scar to go with the others."

Andrasta raised her hand, forcing it not to shake. She touched the wound, felt the rough tug of the stitches there. Her nose was very tender, and she looked at Narjin inquiringly as she fingered the swelling.

"Not broken, or if so just a hairline crack. The swelling should go down in a few days, and you won't sound so stuffed when you talk. I'm the healer here."

"What . . ." Andrasta began and stopped. It did sound like she had a bad cold.

She smiled weakly, and Narjin smiled back.

"'What?' this time, not 'why'? I'll answer both your questions, mistress, but first you must do something very unusual. You must give me your promise not to raise a fuss. We're taking a great risk hiding you here. Only the fact that I'm clan-mother has let me get away with it. Do you understand?"

"Slaves," Andrasta said, her voice still sounding stuffy. "Uprising."

"Yes. It was a slave uprising that killed your patrol, but even that's not completely true. My daughter and I went out to the battlefield after, not expecting to find any alive—and we found you."

"And saved me."

"And you want to know why."

"Yes."

Andrasta's head was beginning to ache again. Narjin must indeed be a healer, because she saw the signs.

"I'll brew you a cup of swamp-tree tea, and we'll prop you against pillows so you can drink it—unless you'd rather sleep again."

"No."

"I thought not. I knew your mother, you see, and she was a tough one, too."

With these astonishing words, the slave woman moved purposefully about the tent, setting water to boil, spilling leaves for tea from a folded bit of cloth into a squat pot. Then Andrasta let Narjin assist her into something more like an upright position.

As Andrasta sipped tea from the fat pottery cup Narjin now handed her, making a face against the bitterness, she didn't ask any questions. Had she thought Narjin was taunting her with the delay, she would have had no patience, but she saw nothing cruel in the slave woman's manner, only an understandable tension.

"Your patrol is all dead," Narjin began, "at least as far as we could tell, and we went out and examined the bodies. That's how we found you. The slaves who did the killing aren't here—now—but they may come back. That's why you have to lie low. We buried the bodies. I'm sorry, but we didn't have the fuel to fire a warrior pyre."

"My horse, a blood bay mare, ten years old."

Gharebi prized their horses above all else, and Narjin did not seem surprised at the question.

"A bay mare was near you and followed us back to camp. She has been cared for. I myself treated her cuts. Most of the other horses fled. The ones that were killed—well—fresh meat is not to be wasted."

"Yes. Good. Thank you. Now, tell on."

"I told you that what happened was a slave uprising and not, and that's true. None of my clan took part, though I won't hide that some were tempted to do so. What stopped them was no great nobility of spirit or desire to remain slaves, but the same thing I still fear. When retribution comes, we're going to be held to blame."

"Is that why you saved me?" Andrasta asked. "So I can testify to your goodness?"

"Yes.

"I can, at least in how you have treated me. I don't know if that will matter."

Andrasta's head was beginning to swim again, but she struggled to listen to Narjin's reply.

"Your words will make great Cescu listen, at least, maybe pause long enough to look at the evidence. It may save us."

"Cescu? You know . . ."

"That you are warlord Cescu's granddaughter? Yes. You are Andrasta, the Dawn Rider. We knew you by the griffin marks on your arm."

"They're just tattoos," Andrasta said, hearing her voice thick and distant, "made to look like blood and claw marks."

"We know the story. We knew you by those marks, and seeing that you of all people were the lone survivor gave us hope."

"Hope?"

Andrasta passed into darkness before she could hear the reply.

When Andrasta awoke again, the woman seated beside her was a stranger, older than herself, but not as old as Narjin. There was a similarity to Narjin in the woman's features, and Andrasta thought this must be Dmaalyn, the daughter of whom Narjin had spoken. This proved correct.

Dmaalyn looked to be in her thirties. She was less worn than her mother, but showed the same evidence of the hardness of a slave's life. While the Gharebi, Andrasta's people, wandered with their herds, their conquered peoples attended to the less dignified aspects of existence.

Some slaves worked as servants, traveling with the Gharebi. Others labored in agriculture, doing the undignified labor to which no Gharebi—quite literally—would stoop. Narjin's clan looked to be Ootoi. The Ootoi had been among the more difficult Gharebi conquests, but they had been broken just the same. For generations they had grown crops, forbidden on pain of death to mount the horses that were the Gharebi's pride.

Still, apparently, at least some Ootoi had managed to maintain a few warrior traditions. Andrasta felt her jaw lock as she thought of how the patrol of which she had been a member had been slaughtered. Narjin hoped Andrasta would preserve Narjin's clan, but right now Andrasta would be glad to see every drop of Ootoi blood spilled to feed the grass.

Narjin came in response to Dmaalyn's summons. With a respectful inclination of her head, she squatted by Andrasta's pallet to check her patient over.

"Stronger again still," the slave woman said, satisfied. "Good. We're running low on time, and there is much you should know."

"Time?"

"Your patrol will be missed. It would be best if you heard what I must tell you before then—so you can make some decisions."

Andrasta found she could sit up on her own this time, but she accepted the cup of bitter tea Narjin offered her.

"You said something about hope," Andrasta prompted.

"You remember that? Ah. I got a little carried away. First you must know about the slave uprising. It wasn't us, you see—or not wholly us. In a sense, it's you."

"Speak sense, woman," Andrasta said sternly. Then she recalled the kindnesses she had been shown and decided good manners would not be out of line. "Please. My head is better, but my ribs ache, my right arm is very sore, and I am heartsick over the deaths of my companions."

Narjin nodded. "You probably have some cracked ribs. Your shoulder was dislocated. I put it back, but no wonder it hurts. I apologize for my circumlocutious manner of speech. Perhaps Dmaalyn would explain this next part. She is the one who first learned of it."

Dmaalyn moved closer, lowering her voice. "Now, to understand this you must first know that our clan is large, and these last ten years has been largely settled in one place. My husband, Beru, is a physically powerful man. Our son—who is a few years younger than you—is already as strong as a grown man. Like many big men, they are often taken as slow-witted, and so when some strangers came looking to stir up trouble, Beru and Utberu were sounded out. Beru would have nothing of it, but he cautioned Utberu to remain silent, feeling it was best that we have an ear near the hornet's nest."

Andrasta frowned. "Some strangers came?"

Dmaalyn nodded. "As I said, these last ten years our clan has been largely settled. As trade with the road builders has increased, there has been greater demand for grain and other agricultural products."

"I had heard that," Andrasta said. "My grandfather Cescu is opposed to this increased trade, saying it makes us weak and dependent on foreign luxuries. He says fermented mare's milk is a man's drink, not wine or beer. Also," she made her voice deeper, "'What does a warrior need gold and silver ornaments for when skin can declare his deeds?'"

Andrasta smiled a touch ruefully and tapped her own tattooed arm, "Thus I earned this, though Grandfather can reward freely with gold or silver when he chooses."

"As I said," Narjin said with a gentle smile, "we knew you by those marks, knew both you and the story of how you earned them seeking a cure for your desperately ill younger brother, though you were but nine years old. There is some value in marking the skin, rather than rewarding with gold and silver."

"Only nine, though," Dmaalyn marveled aloud. "You were so young, and yet went into great danger out of love of your brother."

Andrasta nodded. "Nine, but not so greatly in love with young Cu. My little brother had all the father's and grandfather's love that I had been denied. Still, I realized I didn't want Cu to die—if for no other reason than his death would break my mother's heart, and she had been given enough grief."

"However," Andrasta continued, "this diversion into my pitiful history interrupts your much more important report. I beg your apology. Tell on."

Dmaalyn looked surprised at such courtesy from free to slave. Honestly, Andrasta was a little surprised, as well. She found she was having trouble thinking of these Ootoi as slaves. They seemed too much like people. Then, too, she was remembering her own history and when she remembered what role slaves had played in that she knew not whether to feel gratitude or bitterness.

"Tell on," Andrasta repeated. "You were speaking of being settled."

Dmaalyn nodded. "Yes. Our clan had long been trusted with early plantings and such, and when the wisdom of settled farm communities began to be seen, Mother Narjin saw that we were honored with one such."

Andrasta heard herself interrupting again. "You consider a settled life an *honor?*"

Dmaalyn gave her a curious look. "When one lacks horses and wagons to ease the road, yes, the settled life is preferable."

Andrasta nodded, then willed herself to listening silence.

"Even though we are a large clan," Dmaalyn went on, "there are times when our community has not enough hands to work our fields. Planting is one such time, as is immediately after when the seedlings are young and tender. Harvest—like now—is another, for we must get the grain in before the autumn rains. When extra help is needed, gangs of laborers, mostly men, go from farm to farm. It was one of these gangs that raised the question of rebellion."

Convenient that there be outsiders to blame, Andrasta thought.

"Beru may be big," Dmaalyn went on, her voice ringing with pride in her husband, "but he is *not* stupid. He realized something quickly. Some of these who said they were Ootoi were not Ootoi. They showed too much familiarity with horses. A few let slip from things that they said that they knew how to ride—little things, nothing obvious. One man stripped to bathe and Beru saw a small tattoo. Others managed to bathe only in each other's company. For most of the workers this behavior roused only ribald jests, but Beru wondered if these men, too, had marks to hide. Moreover, there were two he overheard speaking to each other in a language he had heard before—and that when as a boy his family had been attached as servants to a family that lived near some road builders."

It was all making impossible sense. Andrasta had wondered how her patrol, armed, lightly armored, and mounted could have been overwhelmed by mere slave farmers, no matter how enraged, but this . . . If warriors had been slipped in to foment rebellion. Yes. It would explain much.

"Why?" she said.

"You yourself have said it," Narjin said gently. "Warlord Cescu does not like these recent changes. He would have the old ways stay. He is no longer a young man, true, but he is far from elderly. He could continue to lead his allied Gharebi for many years. The road builders are impatient people, and the only ones more impatient than road builders are younger sons."

"My father, Feneki," Andrasta said stiffly, "is among Cescu's younger sons."

"I know," Narjin said. "I have met him—him and his elder brother, Louks."

"When?" It was more a demand than a question.

"Sixteen winters past, as winter was turning into spring. You have already mentioned the circumstances, mistress. I met Louks, Feneki, and Telari all on the night you were born, for you were born in this very tent."

Andrasta had known the truth, suspected it, at least, from the moment Narjin had let drop that she knew Andrasta's mother. The recollection of the ostracism that had followed her inauspicious birth awoke in Andrasta a moment of unexpected, indeed, unwanted sympathy for the Ootoi. What had they done to deserve their state other than being born in a slave tent? The Ootoi and the Gharebi looked enough alike—the same straight, jet-black hair; the same deep brown, almond-shaped eyes; the same ivory skin that darkened to golden brown in the sun—that Gharebi warriors could conceal themselves among Ootoi slaves and only be given away by marks acquired in the years following birth.

Even their languages and religious traditions were much alike, so that Rangest, Andrasta's favorite among the gods, became Rangen, in the Ootoi tongue. She wondered if the Ootoi also told the story about how Rangest had stolen fire from the sun and if in their version of the story he had given it to the Ootoi.

But when at last Andrasta spoke, she did not mention gods or cultural similarities. She spoke from another part of her heart.

"That birth night has been a blight on my life," Andrasta said bitterly. "Yet I am not so poor spirited as to blame you. Indeed, I owe you thanks. My mother's health has been fragile from that time forward. I think without your care she would have died and I with her."

It was an ungracious thanks, and Andrasta knew it, but Narjin only nodded with deep understanding.

"Yes. I have kept an ear open for news of the child I midwifed that night. I heard how, though Telari could be the least blamed for being abroad that night, she and her daughter bore the brunt of Cescu's wrath. It is odd how blind a father may be to rottenness in his sons. Cescu chose to overlook the signs then. In time, Louks redeemed his father's opinion of him through deeds of war, Feneki through abject obedience to Cescu's every whim. Yet Cescu might have been wiser to judge his sons based on their earlier ventures, rather than their later actions."

Dmaalyn asked hesitantly, "Begging your pardon, Dawn Rider, but why did your grandfather resent you and your mother when the transgression committed at the time of your birth was instigated entirely by your father and his brother? You were a babe unborn, your mother a heavily pregnant woman, surely unable to resist her husband's will."

"As my father," Andrasta said sadly, "could not resist that of his brother. Their plan was simple—to play upon my grandfather's pride of family by having me born among my grandfather's herds at the season when the mares were foaling. Uncle Louks encouraged my father to believe that I—and therefore in reality my father—would be given every foal dropped that same night. You know the Gharebi's pride in horses. In one night my father would have been transformed from a lesser son to a man of wealth—and with that wealth would come influence that otherwise he might not earn for a dozen or more years."

"And Louks thought to share in this newly gained fortune and influence," Narjin said, her understanding of the intrigues of her betters uncomfortably acute. "Younger sons, as Louks and Feneki both are, must often find odd ways to gain power."

"But I don't understand," Dmaalyn repeated, "why were you and your mother blamed?"

Andrasta sighed. "I think even if Cescu was fully aware he was being manipulated, he would have rewarded Feneki and Louks for their boldness. What forced Cescu to acknowledge his sons' attempt to effectively steal a fortune from him was the failure of their plan. What caused that plan to fail was my being born that stormy night. It was not so much that I was born among slaves that caused my shame, but that had my mother and I held on a little longer Cescu would have had a reason to brag about his younger sons and those younger sons would have gained a fortune."

"It doesn't seem right," Dmaalyn said fiercely. Then her gaze dropped in fear. "I am sorry, mistress. I have spoken out of turn."

"You have only spoken what I have often thought," Andrasta said. "Narjin, something you said troubles me. You mentioned having met Louks—surely you did not say this merely to brag that you midwifed at my birth. I have not known you long, but already I know you are not the type of woman who grovels for a few coins. Does this tie into your daughter's tale?"

"Truly the Dawn Rider is perceptive," Narjin said, sounding for a moment the very type of the groveling slave. "I am certain she would not be surprised to know that some of my clan's younger members hid and watched the apparent slave uprising from a distance. When it had ended, they came home and reported what they had seen.

"Just as I have kept a listening ear for tales of your growing years, so I have kept alert for stories of your father and uncle. It seemed to me that the ambitions that led them to bring a heavily pregnant woman abroad on a stormy night would not have died for being thwarted, only taken other shapes."

"And . . ." Andrasta said when Narjin paused.

"It is only hearsay," Narjin said, "but my grandchildren said that they were not the only ones who watched the battle. They said a man with one ear mounted astride a chestnut horse with white stockings observed the fighting from a copse where he could not be seen by those who fought."

"My uncle Louks!" Andrasta gasped.

"The description sounds very much like him," Narjin said with deceptive placidity. "But you need not take my grandchildren's word. You could confirm Louks' involvement for yourself."

"How?"

"We can tell you in which direction the work gang went. You could track them, spy upon them, confirm the tale Dmaalyn has told you. "

"I could track them," Andrasta said, "but unlike Beru I am not going to be able to blend with the members of the gang. I am not likely to see tattoos or overhear foreign speech."

"But you would know the mannerisms of warriors," Narjin pressed.

"True," Andrasta agreed, "and if my father and uncle are as deeply involved as you think, I may even recognize some friend of theirs. It is worth trying—but only after two things are done."

"Two?"

"I am not yet strong enough to ride, much less to creep about."

"And?"

"And I have promised you my testimony as a shield against my grandfather's wrath—or that of his generals. That testimony I must stay to give."

Narjin looked relieved. "Utberu said that this evening as the sun was setting he saw a rising of dust in the direction where Warlord Cescu last followed his herds. If Utberu is correct, then a second patrol has come to find what happened to the first. They will probably arrive here to question us as to what we might have seen soon after dawn."

Andrasta nodded. "And me? When would you say I will be well enough to ride?"

"Tomorrow or the next day."

Andrasta pressed her lips together as she considered her multifaceted problem. She could not testify for these Ootoi's innocence without gathering evidence for herself that what Narjin said was true. That must be confirmed first. The rest could come after.

Thus far Andrasta had risen with assistance and walked only as far as the pot in a curtained corner of tent. Now she forced herself to stand unassisted. Though her head swam, soon it steadied.

"It is night now, Narjin?"

"Full dark."

"And your clan?"

"In their tents."

"Good. I will go among them."

Narjin hesitated, and Dmaalyn made as if to leave the tent.

"No!" Andrasta commanded, and the two slaves froze in

place. "Do not leave, Dmaalyn. Do not give warning. I go now, without warning. If what Narjin has said is true, I will see nothing that I should not, and I will not expect perfect polish and readiness."

Dmaalyn bent her head in acknowledgment. Andrasta was pleased to see the other woman did not look unduly nervous. Narjin brought Andrasta clothing suitable for outside wear and a heavy cloak to cover the whole.

"Harvest-time nights can be chilly," Narjin explained, "and you are not yet strong."

Andrasta did not protest, nor, though her legs were sound, did she refuse the long staff Narjin gave her to lean upon. Moving stiffly, the staff thumping like a third leg, she ducked out of the tent and into the night. The clean air, untainted by enclosed smoke, tasted very good in her mouth, and she breathed deeply several times while assessing the layout of the community by the light of lanterns Narjin and Dmaalyn carried.

Although it was, as Dmaalyn had explained, a settled camp, the majority of the structures remained the domed tents used by Gharebi and Ootoi alike. Wood was not plentiful out on the plains, for big trees were only found near the mountains. Even so there was one timber building amid the tents. When Andrasta's gaze rested upon it, Narjin explained without being asked.

"A storage building, for grain and such. It is quite full now. By spring it will be empty of all but dust and chaff."

Andrasta nodded then made her stiff way to the nearest tent. It was separated from Narjin's by several horse-lengths, and the area in between used for storage or small gardens. A few of the big dogs the Ootoi used for hauling, since they were not permitted to own horses, rose. One growled. Narjin hushed it with a word.

Neither Dmaalyn nor Narjin tried to stop Andrasta from going where she would, nor did either leave her side. Encouraged, Andrasta chose a tent at random, then ducked inside without announcing herself. The interior was dark but for a candle lantern burning in a holder on the center pole, the residents having gone to bed with the coming of full dark.

Andrasta motioned in her lantern bearers. After ordering silence, she inspected the inhabitants closely. It was a family group: man, woman, a few small children, an elderly man. None bore signs of having been in battle—no bandaged wounds, no healing bruises. They seemed completely surprised to see Andrasta, and from this Andrasta took confirmation that Narjin had kept her presence secret.

All the other tents were inspected in this fashion, and though by the last the camp was wakeful and surprise could no longer be maintained, still Andrasta was fairly certain no one had slipped away. She found no evidence of battle injuries, nor saw any greater fear or apprehension than would be normal. Once the last tent had been inspected, Andrasta thumped outside and turned to Narjin and Dmaalyn.

"Good. Now I can speak for you with some confidence. One more thing, then rest. I must inspect the storage building and assure myself no one hides in there."

Narjin nodded. "We bar the building from the outside each night, and fasten the bar with an iron lock."

She produced the key, a heavy thing as long as Andrasta's hand. "Here."

The storage shed was packed nearly to the roof beams with sacked and baled goods: grain, dried fruit and meat, even some hay. Andrasta took the lantern from Narjin and held it high as she turned one way, then the other. She thought about how much the Gharebi had come to depend on caches such as this, not only for trade, but for survival. No matter what Grandfather Cescu said, the days in which the Gharebi had survived on horse milk and meat had not been better—especially not in the winter.

"Where did the seasonal laborers stay?"

Narjin replied, "They had their own tents pitched near the fields. They took them down that morning."

Andrasta nodded, aware that her head had begun to hurt

again, and that her side throbbed. She left the storage building without further comment, and waited while Narjin
clamped closed the lock. Then she made her way back to her
pallet by the fire. In the smoky darkness, she thought for a
long while before falling asleep. Then, her plans laid, she
slept well and long, waking only when the sound of dogs
barking and ringing of metal announced the arrival of the
Gharebi patrol.

It was led by Andrasta's uncle, Louks, her father's older
brother, and, if Andrasta's mother, Telari, was to be believed, the source of much misery in Andrasta's life.

Louks was not Cescu's eldest son, nor his favorite, but all
agreed he was the bravest—or at least the most foolhardy.
Now a man in his late thirties, Louks was seamed and
scarred, both by weather and by weapons. He was missing
an ear, though the helmet he now wore hid this. He rode a
dark chestnut with white stockings. Many times those stock-
ing had been stained red with blood, for Trampler shared his
master's fierceness in battle.

Narjin hastened into the tent as Andrasta was finishing
dressing herself.

"My apologies, mistress," the clan mother said. "I would
have been here sooner, but a child had fallen ill and . . ."

"No matter," Andrasta said. "It may be better that I come
before Louks without evident warning."

Andrasta almost eschewed the support of the staff this
morning, but remembering her plans grabbed it as she
headed out. Indeed, she leaned on it rather more heavily
than she had the night before.

An armed patrol milled in the open center of the encir-
cling tents. Louks, still mounted on Trampler, was shouting
at the old man Andrasta had seen the night before, demanding explanations.

"That old slave is not clan leader," Andrasta said loudly.
"This woman is. She came to get me, knowing you would
not wish to question Ootoi if Gharebi could be found."

Louks' seamed face could be almost impossible to read,

but Andrasta thought that pleasure was the latest expression to cross it when he saw his niece limping forward.

"Andrasta," Louks said flatly. "Alive? Horses fled into Cescu's camp last night. They were recognized as being the mounts of the patrol with which you had ridden. We mourned you."

"I am alive," Andrasta said, keeping her voice weak and gasping just a little, "though wounded. I am ready to report on what happened."

She pulled herself straight with apparent effort and gave her report, speaking the slightly edited version of the truth that she had planned the night before. She did not dare change much, for she knew Louks had been watching, but she could make it seem as if her wounds had been more grievous than indeed they were.

Louks and his patrol listened intently, but Andrasta had the feeling that Louks, at least, was listening more for what he did not hear, than to what she said. When Andrasta finished, Louks grunted and frowned.

"So you say this particular clan of Ootoi were not among those who attacked your patrol—that the damage was done by a harvest gang who then fled?"

"I would swear it on my honor and before my grandfather Cescu." Andrasta turned slightly as she spoke, making sure the famous griffin tattoo was visible to all.

The reminder that Andrasta was not just any young warrior went straight as an arrow from a bow. There were satisfied murmurs from most of the patrol. If Louks and a few others continued to look suspicious, Andrasta wondered if it was because they had reason to wish for an excuse to wipe out Narjin's clan.

Andrasta leaned there upon her staff, a seemingly frail shield between the two groups, aware she did possess the power of reputation and influence.

Even if he trusted every man in his patrol—and Andrasta was certain that every member could not be part of Louks' conspiracy—Louks must know that news of her survival could yet reach Cescu. Killing her was no longer an option—but as she realized this, Andrasta realized for the first time that it had not been chance that her patrol had been attacked. Her presence on the patrol had made it a target. If Louks wished to work against great Cescu, he must eliminate those who could rally the clans to the old warlord's side. Andrasta might be young, but already legend followed her. A wise tactician would eliminate her as a matter of course—and Louks was renowned as a schemer as well as a fighter.

Silently, Andrasta thanked Rangest and all the other gods for preserving her, even as she fought against displaying any sign of the fury that filled her when she considered how many brave men and women had died for no other crime than for being her companions.

"We shall ride after the rebels," Louks said at last. "Niece, do you ride with us?"

He failed to sound welcoming, and Andrasta was glad. Her plans would have failed had Louks insisted she come.

"I am still spitting blood," she said apologetically. "Best if I wait for my ribs to heal a day or so more."

Louks did not push her. Injuries to lungs—as to the gut—were almost impossible to recover from. Andrasta wondered if her uncle had been cheered by her lie.

The patrol was eager to ride out, though Andrasta was willing to bet not all were eager for the same reason. Some would want vengeance, but Louks and a few of his cronies . . . What did they want? She resolved to learn for herself.

Andrasta waited several hours, cleaning her weapons, making sure she had arrows and sound strings for her bow. There was no replacing her spear, but spear work was not what she was about. She also attended to Flame, and found the mare had been well kept, and was restless to move on.

When Andrasta was sure Louks had sufficient lead on her, she saddled Flame and prepared to leave. Narjin checked the bindings on her wounds, and supplied her with water and food.

"What will you do if you are seen?" the clan mother asked.

"I will present myself as a young fool, determined to prove myself before my uncle," Andrasta said. "It will be readily believed."

Narjin's smile agreed, though she was too aware of her place to say so.

"Thank you," Andrasta said, raising her voice to include all who clustered around. "For the second time I owe my life to Narjin's clan. I will not forget."

There were pleased murmurs at these words. Dmaalyn stepped forward and held up a carved token strung on a leather thong: a roughly shaped circle in which a griffin, a horse, and a pair of human figures were intertwined. Dabs of paint made the horse a bay, gave the griffin yellow feathers, and made the human figures male and female warriors.

"My son Utberu made this for you. Carry it with our blessing and our wish for luck."

Andrasta accepted it and her gaze found the awkward figure of the husky boy in the crowd.

"It will bring me luck," she said. Without further words, Andrasta pressed her heels into Flame's sides and they were away.

Outside the farm area, Andrasta easily picked up the patrol's trail. Later, she found where the group split into smaller units. Trampler's hoof marks were easily isolated from the rest.

"'We must separate,'" Andrasta said to Flame. "I'd bet my bow that's what Uncle Louks said. 'We must separate and scout.' Then Louks and at least one other whom he trusted went where Louks knew in advance the killers would be. I would have enough evidence here, I think, were this any but Grandfather Cescu's son."

She rode on, following Louks' trail, but not so intently that she forgot to watch for signs that would warn her she was coming upon a human gathering. She found these in the line drawn by a nearly smokeless fire and the tang of dreamweed in the breeze.

Dropping from Flame's saddle, Andrasta left the mare to graze behind a hillock and crept closer on foot. The long ride had jolted her ribs and sore shoulder, but her head was clear and at that moment this mattered most. She knew she needed proof that the "uprising" slaves were in league with the road builders, and hoped to find it here.

In time she came to an encampment nestled in a hollow where, in early spring, water would collect into a small lake and where water could still be found, even in summer. The place was nearly invisible to any approaching, but that concealment worked both ways. Andrasta was able to get close enough to both see clearly and to overhear some of what was said below.

Nearly thirty men were gathered in a loose circle around three others, abandoning the gaming and drinking they had been about before the meeting had been called, to judge from the items scattered around a small fire. Three horses stood drop-tied at the edge of the group. One of these was Trampler, and the man who held the attention of all the others was Louks.

Almost all the men were seated, so Andrasta guessed this meeting had been underway for a time. A few of the men on the outer edge of the circle were even drowsing. Many of the men showed signs of having been in battle: slings and crutches, bandages wrapped around heads and limbs. A few seemed sorely wounded. Andrasta felt a surge of pride for her late patrol. They had been outnumbered at least three to one, but had acquitted themselves well.

All of this was gathered without thought, part of the training she had been given by her mother since she was small. Andrasta's conscious attention was riveted on the group below, seeking something, anything that would give her an edge. She found it in a man addressed by the others as Geyz.

This Geyz was somewhat smaller than the others, who were all fairly large and husky, as one would expect farm laborers to be. This alone would not have been enough to make him stand out, but in watching the interplay between the men, Andrasta became aware of something interesting. Louks did not precisely defer to this Geyz, but he did address him with an attitude like deference.

As if Geyz is a specialist, she thought, *as a healer or mage might be addressed by a warlord when specific knowledge is needed. I would bet my spare bowstring this one is neither healer nor mage.*

Andrasta watched and listened, and as she did so, she recalled what Beru the Ootoi had said.

He heard at least two speak the language of the road builders. I think this Geyz is one. Now that I look closely, his hair shows the flatness of dye, and his eyes are not shaped quite right. Half-breed, perhaps? Or of another people entirely?

Andrasta was handicapped here by Cescu's traditionalism. She had never seen one of the road builders herself. Indeed, when Cescu must send a representative to trade gatherings, he had usually sent his despised son Feneki.

And so another piece of the puzzle falls into place, just as Narjin said it would, Andrasta thought sadly. *I wonder what she had already heard, and if she thought accusing my father to my face would be too much. She is probably right. I have no love for Feneki, but I would have felt honorbound to defend him.*

Fleetingly, Andrasta wondered if a similar sense of honor toward his sons had been why Cescu had been so merciful to them.

Andrasta watched through the daylight hours. In late afternoon, Louks and his cronies rode away, doubtless to meet with the rest of their patrol and report failure. The "rebel slaves" returned to their games and drinking. When evening came, Andrasta noted where Geyz put his bedroll and was pleased to see he selected a place somewhat away from all but one of his fellows.

As Beru said. Two foreigners. Well, all I need is one.

She had checked on Flame periodically during her vigil, found the mare well-content with the late autumn grazing. With the fall of darkness, Andrasta brought Flame close, cautioning her to silence. The mare obeyed, and under her watchfulness, Andrasta permitted herself to drowse. What she intended could not be attempted until very late.

When enough of the night had passed that even the staunchest gamers had abandoned the glow of the fire, and all had been asleep for hours, Andrasta crept into the hollow.

She was very good at escaping detection, for despised as she had been, hiding had often been the best way to escape the scornful taunts of the other children. The grass bent beneath her, but did not break, and the moon's light was ample for her to see by. The rebels had set no guards, for they had nothing to watch against. Their ally had led away the patrol, and no wild creature would attack so many humans.

When she reached where Geyz slept, Andrasta pulled her knife and put it to the bare skin of his throat. He woke with a slight gurgle of surprise, and she put her lips to his ear.

"Come with me. Be silent now. You are wanted."

Perhaps Geyz feared the knife, perhaps he thought Louks had chosen some odd way to summon him—such would not have been completely out of character for the warlord. Geyz rose like a sleepwalker, and let Andrasta take him from camp. Only when they arrived where she had left Flame did he begin to resist. Andrasta had been taught how to disable someone quite a bit larger than herself, and had only been awaiting need—after all, it was easier to have Geyz move himself than to drag him.

Afterward, she slung the now-bound road builder across Flame's withers and mounted up behind. The mare responded to the lightest touch of her rider's heels, and they were away. Before Ande, the Dawn, had given way to full day, Andrasta had ridden into Cescu's camp. Without an-swering any of the many questions shouted to her from all sides, she turned Flame's head toward Cescu's tent.

The old warlord was waiting outside, alerted by rumor, that messenger who moves faster than any horse. Telari, An-drasta's mother, stood at his side. The relief on her face when she saw her daughter alive was Andrasta's reward.

"I bring you news, warlord," Andrasta said, "and one who I think will confirm my tale."

Hours later the tale was told and Geyz had confirmed all and more.

"You are lost, old man," the road builder spat in defiant conclusion, "you and your filthy shepherd people. Even now our armies have reached the plains; our spies have infiltrated your conquered cities. These 'slave uprisings' were meant to distract and weaken you while we secured our position. Well, in this one place the Gharebi have warning, but else-where our forces will separate your clans so that you cannot ride to each other's aid. Our agents—your sons among them—have counseled us well on the Gharebi's weaker points."

After this, Geyz was taken away. Andrasta knew he would not be killed, for there might be other questions for him, but he would certainly not to be comforted.

The first thing Cescu did upon hearing Louks and Feneki's treachery confirmed was to declare his sons out-laws and place a price of two hundred horses on each of their heads. However, though many warriors rode out on their fastest horses, eager as much for the honor of the cap-ture as for the prize, the traitor brothers were well away.

Then Cescu called his war council to him. Hardened war-riors, seasoned in many battles, listened with fierce despair to Andrasta's report. She knew all too well the source of that despair. The Gharebi were less a nation than allied war bands. When peace abided, they fought and stole from each other. When a greater threat came, they could be convinced

to work together, but usually this cooperation took both considerable negotiations and a strong leader to hold the bands
together.

If the road builders had not only physically divided the
various war bands, but also had intrigued to alienate them
from within, the situation was indeed grim. The Gharebi
could be quickly defeated by a road builder army, while posturing over old rivalries and new kept the clans at odds.

Andrasta, given a place in the councils by Cescu's command, listened with increasing frustration. She hungered for
revenge upon Louks—and upon her father as well—but for
now they were out of her reach, safe in the camps of their
road builder allies. None of the tactics of defense and desperation Andrasta heard being debated would bring her
close to her goal. What was needed was attack, but Cescu's
band, large and powerful as it was, was not numerous
enough to defeat a trained road builder force.

Frustrated, Andrasta excused herself from great Cescu's
side, and when she had cleared the center of the camp she
whistled for Flame. The blood bay mare cantered to the call,
slowing, then kneeling so Andrasta might mount. Andrasta
flung herself astride, riding bareback, the only means she
needed to guide Flame the pressure of her knees and her
hands twined in the mare's long, black mane.

"Out of this noise," Andrasta said. "I can hardly think for
all the chatter."

As she rode, Andrasta found herself speaking aloud. "If
Geyz is to be believed, our clan is outflanked and outnumbered. The situation is only going to get worse as we take
losses. The road builders are not warriors. They are soldiers,
which is worse. Individually, we are more fierce, but they
work together like fingers on a hand. Geyz is right. They
will crush us like a closing fist crushes a clot of dirt. In time
we could learn to fight as they do, but how to win that
time?"

"It seems to me," said a strong, male voice from her right
side, "that you need more warriors."

Andrasta knew that voice and her heart leaped within her. She turned her head and saw the divine hero Rangest, mounted on a blood bay stallion twin to her own Flame, riding at her side. Andrasta had first seen Rangest when at nine she had ridden forth on her attempt to save Cu. The divine hero had appeared to her a few times since. Never had he assisted her, but often he had led her to a new way of thought.

"More warriors, my lord?" Andrasta said, struggling to keep her voice steady. "But Geyz the road builder says we are cut off from the other Gharebi clans. Great Cescu has sent out scouts. They have not returned, but when they do I believe they will confirm Geyz's account."

"They will," Rangest said calmly. "Think on this, my hero, the road builders have shown the Gharebi the Gharebi's own weakness, but they have also shown you a hidden strength. Find it. Turn it to your use. Only if you do so can you avoid being crushed. Only if you do so will you live long enough to win through to another clan and combine your strengths. Only if you do so will you gain your revenge on Louks and Feneki."

"But . . ." Andrasta began, but bit back the words, hating the whining note she heard in her voice.

Rangest granted her one of his winning smiles. "It may seems impossible, but can you steal fire from the sun?"

He faded away then, the hoofbeats of his horse growing fainter, then vanishing completely. Andrasta steeled herself to courage, willed herself to understand the riddle. Several lines of smoke on the horizon gave her the beginning of understanding, and she urged Flame in their direction, her mind spinning at the audacity of what she intended to do.

Andrasta recognized a few faces as she rode into the settled camp of Narjin's clan. There was the old man Louks had taken for the clan leader. There was a young woman Andrasta's nighttime inspection had surprised in the arms of a lover. There was the boy who had given her the carved emblem she now wore openly from a thong about her neck. Andrasta addressed the boy.

"You," she said, then remembered his name, "Utberu, son of Dmaalyn and Beru. If your grandmother Narjin is here, lead me to her."

The boy looked up at her, his frightened expression melting into one of pride and pleasure as he saw that Andrasta wore his gift.

"This way, mistress," he said. "A man was injured in the threshing. She tends to him."

Threshing, Andrasta thought bitterly. *How appropriate. If the road builders have their way, they will thrash us as our slaves do the grain, but only chaff will survive—if even that.*

"Lean your head back," Narjin was saying to a young man. "If you persist in wriggling, I'll have your father hold your head steady."

The young man whimpered, but did his best to comply. To Andrasta, trained for as long as she could remember to follow a warrior's path, the boy's open fear was shameful. It also made her doubt the wisdom the plan Rangest's words had awakened in her.

I thought I had figured out what the Fire Thief was hinting at, Andrasta thought, *but what if I'm wrong? I'd not only be dooming my people, but Narjin's as well.*

Utberu, full of his own new importance, would have interrupted Narjin, but Andrasta leaned down from Flame's back and laid a hand on his shoulder.

"My business can wait," she said as she dismounted. "Healers are to be respected, and never interrupted without need."

Utberu frowned. "But you are a warrior—and a Gharebi."

"Above all things," Andrasta said with a dry laugh, "a warrior learns to respect healers. We need them far too often."

Utberu looked thoughtful, but obeyed Andrasta without question. Andrasta wondered if this was how the soldiers of the road builders behaved—she had heard this was so. If true, it was a chilling thought. Gharebi warriors sometimes fell to fighting their own allies if there was a fine prize to be won. How would they do against a hand given orders by a head that was far away and safe from attack?

Poorly, I fear, Andrasta thought, *but then that is why I am here.*

Eventually, Narjin finished removing a piece of chaff that had curved against the young man's eye, pulling it free before it could cut the sensitive membranes and ruin the youth's sight. Only after Narjin had washed her hands and sprinkled scented powders in the winds as a thanks to the gods did Andrasta raise her hand from Utberu's shoulder and let him run over to his grandmother.

They conferred. Then Narjin rose and crossed the threshing ground to Andrasta's side. Although many long glances followed the clan leader, work resumed immediately. Andrasta noted the rise and fall of flails, the bending of bare muscular backs to the labor, and for a moment was strongly aware of her own vulnerability. The intangible force of Gharebi retaliation, not her own strong sword arm or battlefield prowess, was what made her safe.

And that safety, too, will vanish if the road builders have their way, Andrasta thought. *I wonder if those warlords gathered in my grandfather's tent realize how great is our danger?*

"May I speak with you, clan leader," Andrasta said to Narjin, "somewhere private?"

"My tent would be private," Narjin answered, "but the afternoon is warm and pleasant. Perhaps we can seat ourselves on that hillock." She indicated one a short distance away dominated by a tree large enough to create a patch of shade, but far too small to hide any spy.

Andrasta nodded. "That will do nicely."

Narjin turned to young Utberu. "Grandson, go fetch cool water for the mistress and her horse. Tell your mother to provide appropriate refreshment, and to bring it here."

Utberu nodded, made his bow to Andrasta, then took off at an excited run. Carrying messages—even hauling buckets of water—certainly was preferable to whatever routine tasks Andrasta's arrival had drawn him from.

Andrasta and Narjin made their way onto the hillock. Flame trailed obediently after, stopping here and there to crop a mouthful of grass. On the hillock, Narjin lowered herself to the ground, while Andrasta leaned her back against the tree truck, unconsciously scanning the surrounding area as she would on watch.

"Narjin, have you heard what I discovered after leaving your camp?"

Narjin did not pretend ignorance. "Your discoveries stirred up a hornet's nest, mistress. The hum has reached even here."

"Your people are safe," Andrasta said, "at least from being accused of complicity in the attack on my patrol. My father and uncle have fled, but far from matters being resolved, they have only grown worse."

"Worse?" Narjin asked.

"The road builders are coming," Andrasta said. "Their armies are already prepared against us."

Narjin shook her head, daring to disagree. "Matters are no worse, mistress. These things were already in motion before your discovery. The only thing that has changed is your knowledge of them. Is it worse to know of a storm before it comes?"

Andrasta smiled faintly. "Sometimes, especially when you are far from shelter or on a flat plain where the lightning can seek you out unless you lie flat in the mud. Against the storm that is coming I fear there is no shelter, and Gharebi on horseback tend to draw the lightning."

"Even the mud," Narjin said, "can be poor protection. Lightning spreads through wetness as well as striking those who ride high."

"What we need," Andrasta said, "if we are to survive this

storm intact, is to be the wind that drives back the storm clouds."

The two women, old and young, slave and free, Ootoi and Gharebi, warrior and healer, looked at each other for a space as still as the moment between claps of thunder. Then Narjin spoke.

"We Ootoi are not warriors. Once, we were a warrior people. The spirit is still there, but we lack the skills."

Andrasta indicated the threshers with a toss of her head. "Those flails lack edges, but that doesn't mean they couldn't break bones or bruise. Your farmers use scythes, your smiths hammers. Initially, those could be adapted as weapons. Later, there would be time for more sophisticated training. Swords may be difficult to acquire except as prizes of battle—especially if the road builders cut off our trade—but spears are easily enough made, and devastating against mounted opponents."

"You seem to have thought this through," Narjin said.

"You forget," Andrasta said, "someone else already did much of the thinking along these lines. That 'slave band' that slaughtered my patrol mostly used weapons such as I have named. There were a few swords among them, but not too many else the deceit could not have been maintained. The question is not whether your people could be armed, it is whether they would fight."

"Rather," Narjin countered, "it is whether they would be permitted to fight."

"Convincing Cescu that the Gharebi should permit the Ootoi to fight would be my job," Andrasta said with more conviction than she felt. "I think I have several arguments that might do so."

Narjin nodded. "Need and fear are both strong prods. Many times I have convinced patients to agree to a course of treatment that otherwise would be anathema to them on the grounds that otherwise they would die."

Andrasta smiled. "Such as drinking some noxious potion?"

"I was thinking more of amputation," Narjin replied

without humor. "That is what you must convince great Cescu to agree to—an amputation of sorts. Only one incentive will make my people rise and fight on behalf of those who have kept us enslaved for generations. Otherwise, we might as well wait and see who our next masters would be. That would be the safer course, for as slaves we have some value."

"Only one incentive, you say," Andrasta said. "Would that be a promise that no repercussions will follow your taking up arms?"

Andrasta had already thought of this. One of the often debated points of the Gharebi code regarding the treatment of slaves was what should be done about a slave who took up arms in a good cause—in defense of self, or of a master, a child, or some vulnerable animal.

The conservative argued that this was still a punishable offense, for slaves must never bear arms. The more liberal argued that self-defense, and by extension defense of those incapable of self-defense, was a natural law, one that superseded later codes. Great Cescu's views fell in between these two groups. With an enemy pressing, Andrasta thought she could get Cescu to accept the more liberal interpretation.

"I think I can convince my grandfather that any slaves who took up arms against the road builders would be free from punishment," Andrasta said aloud.

Narjin slowly shook her head. "That is not the incentive I meant, Andrasta, though such concessions would be automatically contained within it. No. What must be given to us is our freedom—pure and absolute, with no conditions attached."

"Freedom for those Ootoi who fight?" Andrasta asked woodenly, knowing this was not what Narjin meant.

Again Narjin shook her head. "Freedom for all of us, every single Ootoi: men, women, children, and aged grandlings. Each and every one. What use would freedom be to us if a husband was freed while his wife was still a slave? How would a married couple feel if they were free but their children and parents were still slaves?"

"They would feel they had traded one form of bondage for another," Andrasta said, answering as she might some instructor.

"Exactly," Narjin replied. "Freedom must be extended to each and every Ootoi—that is the only promise that will bring us to fight willingly and with strength at your side. Otherwise we will stand aside to live or die as the invaders will. Consider this, too, without the promise of freedom some slaves might indeed rise up and fight against the Gharebi or take this opportunity to flee."

"Other Ootoi might not feel as you do," Andrasta said, a trace angrily. She had thought her offer to have Cescu defer punishment quite generous, and didn't like realizing how callow, even cruel it had been.

"True," Narjin said equably. "You might win a handful here and there to fight for you on other terms, but tell me, young warrior, would you want a woman fighting beside you who would leave her kin enslaved? I wouldn't."

"I wouldn't either," Andrasta said slowly. "You're right. How will I ever convince Grandfather Cescu to understand this?"

Narjin looked at her, her expression wry. "Tell him about the coming storm. Tell him about lightning. Tell him his clan, perhaps his entire people, face extermination."

"I'd rather," Andrasta said, thinking of Rangest's words, "steal fire from the sun."

Utberu was approaching now, a waterskin over his shoulder, a pair of buckets slung from a yoke about his neck. Andrasta accepted the waterskin with a polite nod, drank, then offered it to Narjin. She took the buckets from Utberu and went to water Flame. Even as she took care that the horse did not drink too deeply or too fast, Andrasta's mind was racing, confronting the impossibility of the task before her.

Her thoughts were broken by Utberu's voice raised in alarm.

"Riders!" he cried. "Gharebi warriors."

Andrasta wheeled. Her trained eye added to Utberu's words. Gharebi warriors, yes, but among them, mounted on a strong buckskin stallion, was her grandfather Cescu. In front, mounted on a blue roan, rode a young warrior Andrasta knew from their shared training. Ignoring the Ootoi, this outrider pulled up alongside Andrasta and spoke without pause.

"Andrasta, you left the council suddenly, and when you did not return, your grandfather grew concerned. Nothing would suit him but to come immediately in search of you."

Andrasta saw the hand of the gods in great Cescu coming to her at this time in this place. She tapped Flame upon her shoulder and the mare knelt.

"I will come immediately," Andrasta said, vaulting onto Flame's back. Then she turned and faced Narjin. "Time to steal fire from the sun."

Narjin's face lit like that very sun, but it was the surety that just for a moment Andrasta saw Rangest standing alongside Narjin that gave the young warrior confidence that she could triumph. Then Andrasta the Dawn Rider wheeled her bay mare Flame and rode forth once again to do battle.

SWEETER FAR THAN FLOWING HONEY

by Stephen Leigh

Stephen Leigh is the author of sixteen science fiction and fantasy novels, including the award-winning Dark Water's Embrace *and its sequel* Speaking Stones. *Stephen has also published novels under two pseudonyms. Along with the novel-length work, he has several short fiction credits and was a frequent contributor to the* Wild Cards *shared world series, edited by George R. R. Martin. Stephen lives in Cincinnati with his wife Denise and two children; in addition to his own writing, he teaches creative writing at a local university.*

"We don't see things as they are, we see them as we are."

—Anaïs Nin

"No one rejoices more in revenge than woman."

—Juvenal

MAMA, how many Ghastlies have you killed?"
Delia forced a smile to her face. There was a picture on the nightstand alongside the bed, and Delia glanced at it,

seeing the echo of her child's soft, bright red curls frothing around her earnest, round face. "That's not important, darling," she said. "Go to sleep now."

"But I want to know, Mama. How many?"

"I don't know," Delia admitted. "I'm afraid I really don't know. It's not really possible for me to know. Now, it's time to go to sleep and let your Mama rest for tomorrow. Do you hear me?"

"Yes, Mama," Cailin answered sweetly. "I hear you. Would you sing me a song, then, before we go to sleep?"

Delia sighed. "Honey, I'm so tired . . ."

Cailin giggled at that. "Then I'll sing, Mama. Can I, Mama?"

Delia smiled. "Yes, that would be lovely. A nice, soft lullaby."

"Good dreams, 'kay?"

"I'll try, love. Good dreams."

Cailin began singing then, in a quiet, half-whisper. Listening to her daughter's voice, Delia closed her eyes.

Padding silently across the tiled floor, she placed the cold edge of the dagger against his throat as he sat in the chair, reading from one of the several scrolls on his desk in the golden candlelight. She shook her head as he started to turn. "Be still and quiet," she said, "or I will kill you here and now." He went still. "Good," she told him. "Now, put your hands underneath you and keep them there. If I see you so much as twitch, you'll die in the next instant." He complied, and she slowly moved around the high-backed chair, keeping the point of her long dagger always at his throat. She stopped just to one side, so that her shadow didn't stop the candlelight from reaching his handsome face; the face she hated.

"How did you get in here?" he grunted. He was trying to hold his bearded chin away from the point of her blade, glaring at her.

"That doesn't matter, does it? I'm here. I wonder if you can guess why."

"You're an assassin."

She smiled a bit at that. "Aye," she told him. "I am." She took a step away from him then and laid a dagger, the twin to the one she held, on the desk. The *clack* as the hilt hit lacquered wood made him flinch, and she saw his gaze go to the weapon as she took another step back.

"What are you doing?" he asked.

"Giving you the chance you never gave my family," she told him. "I think that if you're willing to kill someone, you should also be willing to look them in the face as you do it. Don't you?" She smiled at him. He still hadn't moved. "Oh, that's right. You don't. You send your people to do those things for you, don't you? You hate to sully those pretty little hands. Well, your people aren't with you now. I am. I'll even give you the chance you never gave my family and my people." She nodded to the dagger. "Take it," she said, the smile collapsing. "Now."

His eyes widened. She saw his throat pulse as he swallowed. He lurched forward, his fingers stretching toward the knife's hilt. She waited until he had it in his hand, until— grimacing, his eyes bulging and frantic—he started to slash wildly in her direction, half-rising from the chair. Then she moved, a quick and graceful turn and slide that evaded his attack and left her dagger buried in his heart. His weapon clattered to the floor as he gasped; his free hand grasped her arm, fingers clutching at the bunched white cotton sleeves. She felt his grip relax, saw his stare go distant and fixed. A thin rivulet of blood trickled from the corner of his mouth and down his chin. He fell back into the chair.

She pulled the dagger from his chest and wiped it on the fine linen cloth of his shirt before returning it to the sheath on her belt. She picked up the other blade and placed it in her boot sheath. She could smell the blood and the urine that stained the front of his trousers and pooled on the leather seat. She touched the blood on his chin, smearing it, marveling at its heat.

Bringing her stained finger to her lips, she tasted it.

She thought it would taste sweet. It did not.

Ajit Sulamin came up behind her as she queued at the security gate on Level 14: Ops Level. "What's the matter, Delia? You look tired."

Delia yawned involuntarily as she shrugged and let the line of blue light from the scanner run over her body. She felt the usual slight tingle as the gate activated the identity chip implanted under the hairline at the back of her skull. "Are you implying I look like hell, Doc?"

Ajit grinned. "What, just because you could stuff your whole wardrobe in the bags under your eyes?"

"Ouch." The light on the gate turned green and she went through. "That's pretty cruel for someone shaped like a giant walking pear."

Ajit pursed his lips and raised his hands in mock surrender as he stepped into the scanner gate. His waist grazed the gate's bars on either side. "Touché. You win. You look fine, really; you just seem . . . I don't know, a little less than your usual chipper self. Cailin been keeping you up?"

Delia grimaced at that. "You really are trying too hard, Doc, and you're not particularly funny." She shook her head. "I just didn't sleep well, that's all," she told him.

Ajit blinked as the scanner light played over him, then stepped through. Thick fingers rubbed his neck. He tilted his head as he peered at her, the way he did when she had her regular biweekly appointment with him: appraisingly, with a careful empathy in his chocolate eyes. She wondered if he was that way with all the pilots; he would be, she decided. It was his doctor-face, the one he gave everyone. "I'm fine," she told him. "You'll need to wait until our next appointment to change my psych profile."

"So . . ." Lips pursed. He rubbed his nose. "Will I need to change it?"

"No, Doc," she told him. She forced a smile to her lips. "No, you won't."

In the Ops room, Delia slid into her seat. Most of the other pilots were already under their visors; she nodded to those who were, like her, just getting into their seats. None of them talked; they never did. She reached up to pull down the helmet, then slid her hands into the gloves built into the arms of the seat. Voices whispered into her ear; the room darkened beyond the visor, vanishing. "Your coordinates for today are listed to your right. Toggle the vid for your photos from Recon. Questions?"

"No, sir," Delia said, and heard the echo of her response from under the helmet: the other dozen or so pilots in the room.

"Right. Good flights, all. Debrief is at 1300. See you then." The commander's voice clicked off. Delia blinked as the arrays settled in front of her. She was no longer seeing Ops, but the blue and white curve of a planet hovering in space. A triad of purple numbers pulsed to the right of her vision; underneath the planet was an array of virtual controls. She moved her left index finger to the right. The coordinates pulsed and a small window opened above them: a white, five-story building with a blue-roofed tower on one side, the windows just slits of smoked glass like black lines painted on snowy walls. A Ghastly building like any other. She wondered what it was: weapons manufacturing facility, a planning headquarters, research laboratory? Something of military importance, certainly. Hopefully. Though she would never, could never know. She felt the gloves tighten around her fingers and the spectral display at the bottom of her vision brightened as the image of the planet shuddered slightly and slid to her right. "B5, confirm," she heard a voice whisper.

"B5 is away," she confirmed. "Burn commencing."

She did nothing, but two lights flickered off on the floating console and number began flickering above the display:

altitude and speed. The AI controlled the craft; Delia was
there as backup if the AI failed. Redundancy. Someone for
Control to talk to and blame if things didn't go right.

The planet seemed to fall toward her. She glanced back
over her shoulder once; the headset display gave her an
image of *Revenge* in orbit, the huge cruiser now just a
thumbnail-sized collection of spires and tubes, glinting in
the reddish sun of the Ghastlies. Turning back to the planet,
she saw flailing ribbons of yellow and orange flame tear
away from the center of her vision as she hit the outer
edges of the atmosphere, brightening until she could see
little else through the glare. She moved a finger: the display shifted from visible light to ultraviolet and vision returned. The first streaks of Ghastly counterfire came at her
and the others; even before she could move her thumbs to
trigger the decoys, the AI had already done so. An explosion overloaded the screen to her right, then another,
though she felt and heard nothing. The world swayed as
the AI extended the craft's atmospheric wings and Delia
toggled back to visible light as the craft slowed to super-
sonic speeds.

For the next hour and a half, there was nothing but the
routine defenses of the Ghastlies and the AI's counters.
Once, she saw a huge fireball below and to the left of her
and heard one of the flight crew in Ops curse and slam his
helmet back against the seat rest: shot down. A quick sunset
burned the horizon behind her and she switched her view to
infrared night vision. Control chattered in her ear; she answered back and listened to the others on the flight channel.
The world slowly resolved itself into landscape, and now
she was hurtling over low hills and past villages that were
little but green-white blurs—all the Ghastly buildings used
the same exterior plaster, made, according to the intelligence
she'd heard, of crushed seashells. Her craft bobbed and
weaved through the landscape, always a bare hundred feet
or so above the dusty ground.

The coordinates pulsed violet, then green. A city appeared on the horizon. "Control," Delia said. "We have target acquisition."

"Understood, B5. You are go."

The city raced toward her, and she began to see individual buildings. She was paralleling a road filled with strange tri-wheeled vehicles; she could see Ghastlies looking up as she streaked past, some just staring, others running for the ditches alongside the roadway. Delia looked for a dark-capped tower: she could see it now, directly ahead, one of the tallest buildings in the city. The windows were lighted in the night: she could see figures moving behind the glass. There was a brief burst of anti-rocket fire, but it was already too late: neither the AI nor Delia bothered to respond. There was a click as either she or the AI armed the explosives; she didn't know which. The building plunged toward her, growing larger as she inhaled.

The display flared and went white. Static roared in her ear.

She exhaled. "Control, this is B5," she said. "We have successful contact with our target."

"Ye never worry that you're not going to come back, do you now?"

She shrugged the sheepskin belt of the sword's sheath around her shoulders, feeling the comforting weight of the blade settle across her back. She cinched it tight, grimacing as the belt tightened around bruised ribs and old scars, the leather vest she wore creaking underneath. She shook her head. "Aye," she told Padraic. "Ye know I don't. If you're worrying about coming back, you're not thinking of the fight. If you're not thinking of the fight, then you're not coming back."

She let the smile slowly lift the corners of her mouth, until Padraic too started to grin. He was a huge man, with a waist easily twice the span of her, so big that sometimes she wondered how he managed to carry his weight. Yet he was a tremendous fighter and a good companion, someone she wanted by her side in battle. He rubbed at the scar that interrupted the ruddy beard along his left cheek: his nervous habit. She remembered when he'd received the scar, three years ago at the battle of Belach Mughna. One of Cormac mac Cuilennáin's own gardai had inflicted the wound, when they broke the shield wall around the king and took him down. She'd half-hoped that with mac Cuilennáin's fall the wars would cease, but there were many kingdoms and many rivalries and there never seemed to be an end.

If it kept her people safe, back in the achingly green pastures near Lough Sheelin, that was all that mattered. That's what she told herself. If one day she didn't come back, then that would have been worth it. She remembered best that awful day that the nasty Uigingeach had come raiding out of Dubhlinn and swept over the land around Lough Sheelin. They'd laid waste to the village and burned the cottages, and her family . . . Her immediate family had all died: her parents, her husband, her daughter. But not her. Somehow, they'd left her alive. She had taken up the sword then, knowing it was the only way she could pay them back for what they'd stolen from her.

She had been taking that payment now for five years, and it never, never seemed to be enough.

She still carried a lock of her daughter's hair with her, wherever she went. It nestled on her breast under the protective leather, under the cloth of her shirt: a packet of red curls sewn into a soft, sheepskin pouch. She touched it now, remembering.

"It's time," she said to Padraic. Already they could hear the sounds of the advancing army just beyond the drumlins ahead of them.

His large hand touched her face once, and she held it there for a moment. "We'll both come back," Padraic told her. She was no longer sure of that: if not this time, then soon she would face someone and she would be slower or tired or outnumbered, and he would kill her. She'd see his face as he tore the life from her; his features would be the last she'd see. She wondered what he'd look like, whether

he would smile as he slew her, or if there would simply be
relief on his face that it was not he who fell. Until that happened, though, until she met that nameless soldier, she
would continue exacting her red-hued payment.

"We'll come back," Padraic said again.

"Aye," she told him, hoping he couldn't hear the lack of
belief in her voice, or her weariness. "Aye."

"A successful mission, Delia?"

Ajit was leaning on the wall across from Debrief, smiling
at her. She forced down her irritation as the rest of the pilots
shuffled past her, heading toward Ops. "We'll know more
when we get the next set of recon photos, but yes, it appears
so. Eighteen of twenty made it through."

"You were decimated."

"Huh?" she said, puzzled, then lifted her chin. "Ah, the
old meaning. I guess we were. I doubt the Ghastlies think of
it as a victory, though."

"No, I'm sure they don't. Do you?"

"Look, Dr. Sulamin—"

"Ajit."

"Dr. Sulamin," Delia continued. "I don't have any problem with my job. If you think I'm all of a sudden having second thoughts about killing Ghastlies, I'm not. They brought
this on themselves when they attacked us. I don't know why
you're following me around like I'm an ambulatory lab
specimen, but I really don't appreciate it, and . . ."

"I've spoken to Cailin."

She couldn't keep the anger from her voice then. "What
right do you have—?" He pushed himself heavily away
from the wall, groaning as he lifted his hand and placed a
thick finger to thicker lips.

"This isn't something we should discuss here," he said.
"If you'd like to go to my office . . ."

"Are you ordering me there, Doctor? Do you have the
clearance from Commander Esposito?"

"No." He stared. There was too much empathy in his eyes.

"Then this conversation is over. My next appointment with you is in, what, ten days? I don't expect to see you again until then." Delia glared at him a last time and stalked off. The soft soles of her boots made disappointingly little sound on the deck plates.

"I've made supper for you, Mama," Cailin said. "It's on the table."

Delia sighed. She kicked off her boots and placed them by the door before going to the tiny kitchenette. It was small; everything on *Revenge* was small. On the table a plate steamed. Delia sat and sniffed as Cailin sang to herself in the other room. "Smells good," she said.

The voice stopped in mid-verse. "Thank you, Mama. I borrowed some spices from Stores." She began singing again: a nursery rhyme. *There were two cats of Kilkenny . . .* Delia took a forkful of her dinner, savoring the unexpected bite: almost like curry, she thought. But it couldn't be. She hadn't had curry in four years now.

"Dr. Sulamin told me he spoke with you."

A pause. "Uh-huh," Cailin said, then took up the song once more. *So they fought and they fit / And they scratched and they bit . . .*

"What did you tell him, Cailin?"

"Mama . . ."

Delia sighed. She set the fork down on the table, grimacing at the percussive *clack* of the plastic. "Cailin, I know. You just want to help. But . . ." Another sigh. She pushed the plate away from her. "If he tries to talk with you again, you tell me first. Do you understand, Cailin? Tell me first."

"I will, Mama. I will . . ."

She was a warrior, but she could never see "war." War was too big a term, too large a concept. There was only the endless sequence of battles and—most important—the person you faced who wore the enemy's colors. That was all she needed to know, all she needed to concentrate on. Winning the war didn't matter, winning the battle was of no consequence: all that mattered was survival. And to survive, you had to kill those who would otherwise kill you.

War, by that definition, was simple enough. It didn't even give her time to remember why she was here.

She could see his face: spattered with gray mud and brown flecks of blood, a stubbled growth of hair on his cheeks and chin, blue eyes narrowed and teeth gritted with the effort of swinging the iron weight of his water-tempered blade. In the instant before she raised her own blade to parry the blow—the shock of the impact traveling all the way down her arms as she grunted—she could see him in terrible clarity. He was young, maybe two years younger than herself, and the boiled, studded leather of the armor he wore fit him badly, as if it had once belonged to someone else.

The steel of their blades rang, the sound harsh in her ears, though she could still hear her breathing and the clash of the individual skirmishes all around her, the screaming of the wounded, the shouts of the officers, the blare of the signal trumpets. The boy shouted, an exhalation of white in the cold air; she could smell the rot in his teeth and feel the warmth of his breath. He pulled his blade back to strike again. Too far back: *Stupid*, she thought: as she thrust her sword two-handed and hard into the opening he'd created, feeling the point penetrate leather, skin, and tissue; ripping it out again with a cry and a sideways twist that shed streams of red gore as the blade tore from his abdomen.

His mouth opened; his sky-colored eyes widened in surprise and shock, his sword still swinging forward reflexively but already falling from suddenly nerveless hands, mumbling words in a language she didn't understand, dead already but not yet realizing it. She wondered who he called to—mother, wife, friend—but there was no time for wonder, only time to react to the soldier who rushed at her from her left side even as the boy went to his knees on the ground, hands cradling the ruins of his stomach.

She didn't see the lance the new attacker held until it impaled her just under the rib cage, skewering her like a piece of meat, the daggered head burrowing up through lung and heart . . .

The missile-craft—she was B9 this time—arrowed away from *Revenge* toward the Ghastly homeworld.

The Ghastlies had beefed up their defenses following the initial rounds of attacks. The orbital cruisers themselves came under fire from Ghastly fighter-craft, attacks that had sent sister ship *Fukushuu* spiraling down to a fiery death in the atmosphere and left *Bijesan* adrift under emergency power. *Revenge, Zhànzhêng*, and *Représaill* had suffered only minimal damage. It hadn't been much of a battle: a wave of drones, either under automatic control or perhaps remotely piloted like the ones that they were using themselves—there was no way to know, and it made no difference in any case. There'd been little warning, little time to defend: the drones were destroyed or hit, and it was over—from first sighting to final explosion—in less than three minutes. Done.

The missions today were all targeted to installations Control felt were capable of directing such attacks. Delia's own target was a small building in the center of a Ghastly town on the southeastern shore of the largest continent. She kept its image up on her display as the numbers rolled down and the last vestiges of the fiery entry into the atmosphere faded. The anti-missile fire was brutal; her vision swayed dizzily as the AI (or perhaps her own movements through the gloves—it was impossible to tell) directed the craft through evasive maneuvers, fired off decoys, and sent jamming transmissions. Delia was sweating, every muscle in her body tensed, her breath coming short and fast. Adrenaline buzzed in her ears. She grunted, leaning as she tried to send the craft left, then right as it hugged the ground. Fire erupted to her left;

instinctively, she ducked. Around her, she could hear cursing as craft died.

A yellow flower bloomed directly in front of her, with petals of smoke. She yanked the craft left; another silent flower flashed into existence there in eerie silence, and her display went tumbling nauseatingly—sky/land/sky/land—before snapping off into furious white that left blobs of purple afterimages in her eyes as the display vanished entirely. Static snarled in her ears. The gloves loosened around her wrists and she slumped back.

Dead. You should be dead.

She sobbed once, her throat convulsing as she inhaled, as she took a breath that shouldn't have been hers. "Control," she said. "B9 is down."

"Understood," a voice whispered back. "Rough ride, eh?"

"Yeah," Delia answered. "A rough ride."

"Mama, what's the matter?"

"I'm tired, Cailin. That's all."

"You're sure?"

She waited a long time to answer, standing near the door with her boots still on. Finally, she reached down and took them off, listening to the soft *plops* they made as they hit the carpet over the decking. "Yes. I'm sure."

"Good," Cailin said. "Your supper's on the table. Just cold stuff tonight, I'm afraid. The Ghastlies hit the main galley."

Delia glanced toward the kitchenette, where on the tiny table a plate lay. She could see a sandwich on it, and some fruit. Delia ignored it; she walked through the main room—four strides—past to the small bedroom, filled mostly by the single bed. She sat, reaching across to pluck Cailin's picture from her nightstand. She stared at the child's face, her finger stroking the red curls on the paper under the protective plastic. She tried to remember what that hair had felt like and couldn't.

"How many Ghastlies did you kill today, Mama?" Cailin asked.

"None," Delia said. "They killed me."

There was a silence where she imagined she could hear Cailin breathing, then her voice came again. "Oh, Mama, you're making a joke." A pause. "Mama, are you okay?"

She was crying, silently, the tears hot on her cheeks. She sniffed. "Cailin," she said to the empty room. "Call Ajit and tell him I'd like to see him."

"Sure, Mama," the room answered. "I'm doing it now. Would you like me to sing a song to you?"

"Yes, Cailin," Delia said. "I'd like that very much."

The room sang quietly to her, and Delia cradled the picture to her chest as she listened.

TOKEN

by Anna Oster

*This is Anna Oster's second published story; her first
appeared in* Assassin Fantastic. *A former student of
journalism, she abandoned the truth in favor of fiction
some years ago. After studying abroad, she returned
to Sweden, where she lives in a tiny apartment with a
large number of hedgehogs.*

JUN-LI was sleepy, and her feet ached in the new sandals.
Her cousins were pushing and giggling at each other like
all the other girls in Four Petal Square, their thin faces bright
with excitement. Jun-li wore her new star-patterned wrap
that left her left breast bare. She wished she'd brought a
shawl.

Sus-qa and Annele pulled each other's hair, getting more
angry than playful, but then the gong sounded out midnight
across the square. Everyone quieted down, lining up with
their bowls as the priests of the temple of Holy Defender
brought out the huge kettles of sweetgrass porridge.

"I hope I get a rabbit," Annele whispered. "Rabbit brings
luck."

"Luck in love." Sus-qa snorted. "You won't need that
until the war's over and the men come back. And the

weaver's daughter got a rabbit last year and chipped her
tooth on it."

Annele giggled again. "And Myri got a maggot and
thought it was real and threw it away. Then she fell and
broke her foot. Jun, what do you think you'll get?"

Jun-li stifled a yawn. The square was dark; the new moon
gave little light. All around, girls whispered, and the silver
bangles on their arms chimed softly. She'd never seen any
difference between getting a rabbit token and getting a fish
or a rat or a rollerbug. There was only one token that changed
anything.

"I just want the porridge. I'm hungry." She rubbed her
fingers across the grain of her wooden bowl, feeling her
stomach growl.

"Mm. Grandmother says in her day the priests sometimes
put dried meat in the porridge."

Jun-li shook her head. She hadn't seen dried meat since
before the star festival. "I don't think they do that anymore."

"Grandmother says in her day, none of the girls were ever
chosen."

Annele shuddered, and Jun-li rubbed the back of her
neck. "That was before the Rasika came across the mountains. There was no war."

"Well, no one was chosen last year. Grandmother says—"
Annele broke off as Sus-qa elbowed her. All the girls grew
quiet as they came closer to the priests.

Jun-li held her bowl out when it was her turn, and got a
glob of porridge, already half congealed in the cool night air.
She bowed her thanks without looking at the priest and
turned away, joining her cousins on the blanket they'd
spread under one of the shofu trees. Annele was digging
through the porridge with her spoon, frowning. "I don't
think I got anything."

"Everyone gets something." Sus-qa went through her
porridge slowly and carefully. "Just eat it and mind your
teeth, or you'll look like a Rasika beast."

Annele smacked her sister's arm. "I do not have green skin!" she said. "Or a nose like a dog, or—"

"You have a voice like a monkey. Chatter, chatter, chatter."

"Oh, shut up." Annele crushed shofu needles in her hand and threw them at Sus-qa. The sharp smell tickled Jun-li's nose.

The last girl got her porridge, scraped from the bottom of the largest kettle, and the priests drew together in a watchful group as acolytes came to drag the kettles back into the temple. Jun-li ate her porridge. It was as tasty as salt could make it, but it could have used some butter. Probably not even the priests had butter any more.

"I got a rabbit! Look, Sus!"

"That's not a rabbit, that's a dog with big ears. Mine's a rabbit, look."

"Mine is too a rabbit! It's the best kind of luck. Jun, what did you get?"

Jun-li put the last spoonful in her mouth and shook her head. Then she felt something hard against her palate. She spat it out in her palm. It was an ax blade, small as the first joint of her thumb, made of smooth grayish-green stone, and wickedly sharp.

Sus-qa gasped. "You—you got—"

Jun-li stared. The blade looked so small. In the paintings of Holy Defender on the temple walls, it was always big, bigger than a real ax even. Though of course a real ax blade would not have fit in her porridge bowl.

"Jun," Annele said, clutching her arm. "Jun, I don't want it to be you, I don't want anyone to be chosen this year, hide it, throw it away!"

"She can't do that." Sus-qa smacked her sister's hand, pulling her away. "The priests would know."

"But I don't want it to be her! Maybe they can't tell."

"Holy Defender can tell."

Jun-li closed her hand about the blade, feeling the edge bite into her palm. She looked at Sus-qa. "Tell my mother," she said, and then she couldn't think of any more words.

She got up, and the bowl fell from her lap onto the blanket. Across the square she could see the priests, dark-faced and silent, watching the girls and waiting. Jun stepped off the blanket and onto the smooth earth, walked to the temple steps, and held her hand out. The blade had blooded her palm.

Jun-li expected the priests to say something to her, words of greeting and explanation, but they didn't. They grabbed her arms and twisted her around to face the square again. "One is chosen!" the oldest priest shouted, and all the girls hushed. "One is chosen!" An acolyte beat the great iron bell by the temple door, and it rang out so low Jun-li could feel it in the soles of her feet.

She thought she could see Annele crying under the shofu tree.

"You have the weapon," the youngest priest said, pointing at the blade in her hand.

"You have been chosen," the oldest priest said, gesturing at the temple behind them.

"You will go before our warriors in the sacred places."

"You will take defeat from them and give them victory."

"The Rasika beasts will fall before you."

"You are our Holy Defender."

"You walk with the spirits from this moment."

They turned her again and walked her up the temple steps before she could even draw breath to speak. The youngest priest held out a small cup to her. "Drink."

Jun-li drank. It tasted bitter, and for a moment she felt dizzy.

The oldest priest put his hand on the door and whispered low, and the door opened a crack. A cold wind blew from the darkness inside. "You walk with the spirits. Go."

Jun-li breathed in, smelling porridge and dusty earth and people, and the dry air of the spirit world. The oldest priest put his hands on her shoulders and pushed, and she stumbled inside.

The door closed behind her, and Jun-li stood alone in the

dark. The cold wind licked at her calves. She knew what the temple looked like inside. It was a long narrow building with painted walls, and at one end the altar with the stone figure of a woman with an ax, Holy Defender ready to protect her people. Jun-li took a step backward to press her shoulders against the door and get her bearings, but the door wasn't there, and she nearly fell. The cold wind grew stronger, fluttering the edges of her wrap against her legs.

Jun-li crouched down and touched the floor. That was the same, at least, worn blocks of stone joined so tightly her fingertips could barely feel the cracks. The wind blew toward her, into her face, and it smelled strange and wrong. Jun-li stood up and walked into it.

The stone blade was a tiny sharp weight in her right hand. She knew that other girls had walked here before her, holding a blade like this one, or perhaps this very one.

She knew they had never come back.

Her heartbeat pounded in her ears, louder than the wind. After a hundred steps, twice as long as the length of the temple in the world of people, Jun-li saw a light. She slowed down, but the light grew brighter. It showed her the stone floor, but no walls, no ceiling. Jun-li stopped.

A woman stepped into the light. She was tall and heavy, with strong arms, and her hair curled without moving as though carved from stone. In her right hand, she carried an ax. Jun-li felt her legs quiver. She locked her knees and straightened her back.

"So," the woman said, and her voice was like stone, also, dusty and hard. "They have sent another child."

Jun-li breathed dust and tried not to sneeze. "I'm sorry."

"So am I." The woman's eyes were grayish-green, the color of the ax blade. "You are chosen. You have the token. You know the weapon."

Jun-li looked at the ax blade in her palm. "It is very small," she said. It didn't seem enough to protect everyone.

The stone woman looked at her. "You cannot pass me without the weapon."

Jun-li frowned. She took a step forward, and the stone woman hefted her ax, raising it a little. "But you have the weapon."

"You cannot pass me without the weapon." The light had brought shadows, and Jun-li thought she saw them move at the sound of the stone woman's voice. They rose up around Jun-li, and there was no way but forward, where the woman stood.

Jun-li held her hand out as she had done to eldest priest, the stone blade cutting across the lines in her palm. "Here," she said. "Here is the token."

"That is my blade," the stone woman said and nodded. "You have given it to me. And this is yours." The stone woman took the token and put the ax into Jun-li's hands. "It is a fair exchange."

The ax was heavy, but at the same time, it weighed nothing at all. Jun-li bowed. "Thank you."

The stone woman shook her head. She looked sad. "It's yours now. You must use it."

"Oh." Jun-li gripped the ax handle harder.

"You must go before the warriors. This is what you were chosen for. To walk with the spirits and meet the enemy."

Jun-li looked at the stone woman, who was tall and strong and clothed for battle. "I'm afraid."

"Yes." The stone woman stepped closer and kissed Jun-li's forehead, and her lips were hard and cold. "Go now, my warrior."

"Holy Defender," Jun-li whispered, and then she was alone in the darkness. She held the ax in both hands and walked forward.

The stones were smooth and even under her bare feet, but she still went slowly, wary of walking into some unseen obstacle. Dust and grit stirred at her passing. The chill wind grew stronger, blowing against her, and it brought a strange smell, like lightning and rotting meat. After a while, the darkness grew less absolute. Jun-li looked down and saw her own hands on the ax handle and a faint golden glow about them.

She walked on, and the glow grew brighter around her, limning her arms and legs, shining off the edge of the ax blade. Jun-li felt faint inside. Her bones weren't made for this. She was no Holy Defender.

A gust of wind made her eyes tear up, and she drew a deep breath of the strange smell and sneezed. Jun-li blinked her eyes clear and saw, up ahead, a green light. It wavered, it flickered, and it grew stronger. Jun-li felt cold inside. She needed to pass water. Her palms sweated against the smooth handle of the ax.

"Holy Defender, help me," she whispered under her breath. "Help me be strong."

Something was standing in the green light, and Jun-li swallowed hard. Something tall and monstrous, a beast walking on two legs, with long thin arms and green skin and sharp jagged teeth. A Rasika warrior-beast, and it wore strange clothes, and it smelled horrible, and Jun-li's throat was too dry for her to scream. She lifted the ax, and the beast saw her and cried out in a terrible voice.

The air grew thick about her. Jun-li felt her bones quake within her flesh. The Rasika beast thrust its spear at her, and she jumped aside, slowly, but the beast was slower still. The point of the spear glowed green and poisonous. Jun-li drew back, and the muscles in her arms moved in new ways. She swung the ax and hit the Rasika beast in the shoulder, and it cried out like thunder and stabbed with the spear.

The stone floor was even and smooth under her feet, and all the same it felt to Jun-li as though she stood on a plain where the grass was trampled down into mud. There was no sound but her own breathing and the Rasika beast's cruel wail, and yet she heard warriors shouting in anger and pain. There was nothing but darkness beyond the green and golden light, but she felt herself stand at the head of an army under a sky high with stars.

A growl from the Rasika beast warned her. It thrust the spear at her again, and she danced aside, but this time it was faster and she was slower, and the point of the spear scored her hip. Jun-li clenched her teeth. Perhaps the beast had poisoned her now. Her heart beat faster.

Warriors shouted battle cries in her ears, and she squared her shoulders. When the beast came at her, she raised the ax and swung it, like chopping wood, like cutting saplings. The beast roared. Jun-li swung the ax again and again, and the army rushed forward.

The beast fell, and everything was silent.

Jun-li gasped for breath. The ax was heavy in her hands, and the blade was dull with blood. She bent forward with the weight of it and panted and shook. Her heart pounded in her throat. She had not fallen to the enemy.

At her feet, the Rasika beast glowed green, but the glow was dimming. Jun-li blinked. It was difficult to look at the beast; the air shifted around it, shadows jumped and twisted. It seemed as though the beast's limbs were moving, and Jun-li lifted her ax again. The green glow flared and disappeared.

Jun-li sucked in a sharp breath and shook her head. She had seen the beast, she had fought the beast, the beast had wounded her with its spear. Yet the beast was gone, and at her feet lay a girl with pale skin and terrible wounds, with her copper hair spread out in a pool of blood. The girl looked up at Jun-li with sorrowful dark eyes and said something in a strange language, and then blood ran from the corner of her mouth, and she died.

Jun-li shuddered. She fell to her knees, leaning on the ax. She could smell the blood now, and it made her sick. The golden glow clung to her skin, and she slapped at it, but only hurt herself. The beast had fallen into the mud, but Jun-li knelt next to the dead girl on the hard stone floor.

"Rasika," she whispered, stretching her hand out and touching the tips of her fingers to the girl's undamaged cheek, naming her. "Rasika."

The cut on Jun-li's hip was painful, and she had to struggle to get to her feet again. Jun-li turned around and went back into the darkness, one slow limping step at a time. The ax seemed to grow heavier and heavier, but she would not let go of it. There was no army at her back anymore. The shadows shifted and moved, but did not rise up to stop her.

She had to stop after a while and breathe and rest. Blood trickled down from her hip along her leg. She pressed her wrap against the wound and held it there as she started to walk again.

Counting her steps, she walked on and on, only to realize that she was counting one, two, one, two. The golden glow wavered around her like a candle flame. Far ahead, she saw another light, and walked toward it.

"I thought perhaps you would be the one."

The stone woman stood with her arms crossed, tall and unmoving in her own circle of light. Around her neck, the ax blade token hung on a chain of plaited straw.

"I killed her," Jun-li said.

The stone woman nodded. "You have slain the Rasika beast. You have led the warriors to victory."

Jun-li shook her head. "I killed her." She felt her stomach turn over. "I want to go home."

"This is your home now," the stone woman said.

"No." Jun-li looked around, and there was nothing but darkness. This wasn't anyone's home. "No, I want to go back. Annele and Sus-qa will be waiting. And my mother."

"You cannot go back. There is no way open for you. The door was only opened for you to come here."

Jun-li lifted her palm from her wounded hip. The bleeding had stopped. "It was the temple door," she said. "They just opened the door. They can do it again."

The stone woman looked sad, and her voice was like sand trickling down on a rock, more gentle than Jun-li had heard it before. "It was more than that. They gave you pisara and hallowroot to drink. You walk with the spirits now. You are the Holy Defender."

Jun-li looked at her hands, limned in golden light, with blood streaked across the knuckles. "Do the spirits always walk in darkness?"

"Yes," the stone woman said, "we do." Her light began to dim. She turned away, and faded like a star at dawn.

Darkness stood all around, and Jun-li bit her lip. The wound on her hip looked deep, but there was no longer any pain. She knelt down and pressed her hand against the stone again, the grit and sand, willing herself to feel it. The stone was cold, and the cold wind stirred her hair against her neck. Her hands felt cold, too. There was no warmth in the golden light.

Jun-li got to her feet and settled the ax handle over her shoulder as though she were going out for firewood on a day like any other. She turned around and went forward again, taking her direction from the wind blowing against her face. With every step, her strides grew smoother and easier, and when she had walked five times a hundred steps, she no longer limped.

She walked on, though the darkness stretched unchanging before and behind her. She walked on, though the smooth stones underfoot looked the same with every step. She walked on, wrapped in golden light, waiting for the next battle, looking for the place where a girl lay dead and spirits crossed over, the place where the stone floor turned into a trampled field of mud and blood, and she could see the sky again.

ELITES

by Kristine Kathryn Rusch

Kristine Kathryn Rusch is an award-winning mystery, romance, science fiction, and fantasy writer. She has written many novels under various names, including Kristine Grayson for romance and Kris Nelscott for mystery. Her novels have made the bestseller lists— even in London—and have been published in four-teen countries and thirteen different languages. Her awards range from the Ellery Queen Readers Choice Award to the John W. Campbell Award. She is the only person ever to have won a Hugo Award for editing and a Hugo Award for fiction. Her short work has been reprinted in seven Year's Best *fantasy collec-tions, and also in three* World's Finest Mystery and Crime *story collections.*

THE FIGHT STARTED over cleaning the toilet.

It's an old-fashioned porcelain job, swirling water, environmentally unsound. Grandfathered in because the building's ancient, kept in place because we're poor, we're a nonprofit, and we get the government to look the other way.

A self-cleaner costs twice our monthly budget. A self-cleaner that doesn't use water costs four times that.

I don't know how often I have to explain that to the troops. Not quite every day, even though *someone* has toilet duty every day, but damn close. Every time a new recruit stumbles into the House, I find myself discussing toilets, old-fashioned plumbing, and even older stoves.

I lead this group of misfits. I'm a vet myself. Two tours each in two different wars. Sixteen medals, give or take, all lost or tossed, and at least that many wounds.

The scars remain.

I found that even though the military gives you memory blocks for the post-traumatic stress, PTSD still finds a way to rear its ugly head. Only worse than the olden days.

Now you don't know what it is you're reliving.

It's scary as hell.

The House is a remodeled Victorian monstrosity. Once upon a time, it housed a single family. A single, very wealthy family. Then it became a duplex, then a series of apartments, then college housing, then an abandoned mess. It had been condemned when I found it about fifteen years ago.

I had the bright idea that restoring the thing would restore my sanity. I managed to buy it, discovered two vets living inside it already—squatting being the more accurate term— and together we ripped and tore and demolished, learning it was easier to tear down than to build. It took us a day to remove a wall and three weeks to build one right.

By the end of the first month, we were actually friends. By the middle of the second, we started to talk about our nightmares. By the end of the third, we finally learned each other's full names.

Names are a big thing. You can be traced by name. Someone can look up your identity card, find your family, send you home.

We don't do that here. Privacy is an issue for our vets. Even when the government tried to tie that last grant to the House's records, we fought.

We went to court.

We actually won.

Which has nothing to do with the toilet battle. Zoomer gets me to stop that. She's six-one, going to fat, with a long scar that runs from her left breast to her navel, a scar she refused to fix. She goes shirtless half the time, shocks the hell out of the boys who come in for the annual code inspections—fire, insects, population. We always give those boys numbers, never give 'em names. Hell, one year, we weren't even gonna give them the names of the bugs.

Zoomer stands on the balls of her toes, leaning into my office, but never entering. My office is the former front parlor, divided in half. The front half has my desk and my book collection, the back half my bed and the e-readers I really use to consume literature. I sneak back there in the dark, turn on the screen light, and read text myself rather than have the reader do it for me. I feel like I'm on the front, in the only safe place out there, my bunker, deep within the ground.

The shrink says I gotta get past that. I plan to—someday.

"Wena," Zoomer says, "they're at it again."

Zoomer's the only one who calls me Wena. Everyone else calls me Boss. My real name is Rowena, but no one uses that unless they don't know me. It's a good double-check.

"Toilet or stove?" I ask.

"Toilet," she says. "Suzanne's using the scrubber like a stick."

"Fuck." I stand up quickly. No one considers the germs—and you'd think they would, especially the Sky Vets. The Sky Vets fought our first space war in the Moon colonies, and biological agents became a big factor. How big we'll never know because that's classified, but the Sky Vets who came all the way home have some interesting diseases.

The government says everyone allowed back to Earth was quarantined, tested, and found clean.

Yeah, right.

The toilet in question is in the back of the House, in what used to be the entry to the kitchen. I know this without asking; if there's ever a fight about cleaning, it happens in that tiny hallway or worse yet, in that mean little room that never quite loses the smell of piss.

I could've followed the sounds. The closer I get, the louder voices grow—yelling obscenities, cheering, clapping in approval.

These women love fights.

I used to let them do it too, without interference, until the repair bills got too much. Then the House shrink told me about the added toll of repeated trauma—the fights would often replicate something that happened Out There—and I realized that no matter how much steam got blown off, the fights weren't worth the expense.

Still, I wished for those old days sometimes.

Like right now, as I push my way past women bunched up three together across the hallway. The place smells of grease, sweat, and old blood. The closer I get, the more those smells get replaced with the stench of backed-up sewer.

I see the toilet scrubber before I see the fighters. It flails through the air like a tree branch in a windstorm. Women are leaning forward, urging their candidate on. The sounds slowly die as I make my way to the front.

Suzanne is bent over her victim, a new recruit—Darla, Dopa, Demmi—some dumb D name. The recruit's curled up in the fetal, her face spattered with what I hope is water. She's whimpering.

I wade in, shove Suzanne against the wall, and wrench the scrubber from her. "You want to tell me what this is about?"

Suzanne's height matches my five-five, but she has broader shoulders and a powerful mean streak. Not as powerful as mine, though. When I get me an anger on, no one in the House can take me, not even the big girls.

"Bitch shoved my face in the john," Suzanne says.

That's when I realize the front part of her hair is wet. The back part isn't. I'd blamed that on sweat initially, but the smell tells me otherwise.

"Why'd she do that?" I ask.

Suzanne shrugs. "Ask her."

I glance over my shoulder. Debbie or Danni or Diane is still whimpering on the floor. I'm not even sure she knows the fight is over.

I turn back to Suzanne. "I'm asking you."

Suzanne's lips thin. She's pressing them together hard, and I know she's not answering any of my questions any time soon.

"Suzanne's been taking her ration cards."

I can't identify the voice, but it comes from behind me. All of the women are staring at us, as if they haven't heard a thing.

"Is that true?" I ask.

Suzanne's dark eyes meet mine. "I been denied."

Ration cards buy a lot of things: medication, clothing, the occasional outside meal. Most of the troops don't use them, though, because it marks the bearer as former military, and that's not the most popular thing these days.

"So?" I say. "Someone can loan you theirs."

"Thought that's what she was doing," Suzanne says.

"But that's not the case, huh?"

Suzanne shrugs. I want to hold those shoulders down, just so that Suzanne won't have the nonchalant option.

"Ask her," she says again.

"I will," I say. "When the shrink's done with her."

Then I hand the scrubber back to Suzanne. "When you finish this john, do the second and third floor johns. You can do the showers too. Make sure you take one when you're through."

"Hey," Suzanne says. "The rules say no more than one toilet a week."

"The rules also say no violence in the House."

"She dunked me."

"And you should've reported her, not beat her." I take Suzanne by those misbehaving shoulders and push her toward that horrible half bath. "Get busy."

Suzanne scowls, but knows better than to argue. No one

fights with me. They don't raise their voices to me or their scrub brushes. They know they're here on my suffrage.

This is my House and I run it as I see fit. I've tossed women on the street before.

Other vets' houses, they try to accommodate everyone. But I treat all the troops in this place like the military they once were. If they don't measure up, they get kicked down a rank. If they still don't do the work, they get my equivalent of a dishonorable discharge—my boot in their ass, my hand in their pocket as I take their key, my voice in their ear as I tell them never to darken my doorway again.

Every once in a while, some important person gives me a citation or a key to a city or some other kind of important recognition for the "good work" that I'm doing. No one else rehabs vets like I do. No one else has as high a success rate. No one else really tries.

What shocks all the regular folk is that I'm working with the hardcore. They're called Elites in the recruitment vids, and when you get to basic, you get told only the best qualify for the Elite Squad.

They don't tell you what the best is, though. The best isn't the smartest or even the strongest. The best is the fiercest—the biggest do-or-die in the entire camp, the person who gets such a mad-on that she will slaughter fifteen of the enemy before she realizes she's even activated her weapon.

The Elites get chosen for the last bastion of war, the only part that resembles what our ancestors knew of battle—hands-on combat. Most of the battles nowadays are fought at great distances—heat-seeking weapons, smart drones, bot warriors. But for clean-up and delivery, for reconnaissance and ground-clearance, nothing beats troops on the ground.

Those troops on the ground gotta be tough. Tough, indestructible, and fucking ruthless.

Once upon a time, seems the human race used men for that. Seems too that that turned out to be a mistake.

Here's how it was explained to me:

Several generations ago, the military let women join up. Women were noncoms at first; everyone was afraid their delicate sensibilities couldn't handle the violence of war.

Then warfare tech made a lot of things equal—equal weapon strength, equal machinery—and someone assumed the women could handle some combat.

But it was the biologists who changed everything. They found a way to enhance the natural self-defense reaction so that the soldiers in the thick of things became even more violent, even more determined to survive.

That still would've kept the men in the forefront if it weren't for some dog—or so the story goes—who went all feral defending her puppies. The scientist who saw it had this theory that mother-love made women even more ferocious than men in defense mode.

The scientist raised some hormone levels, altered adrenaline responses, made a few other alterations in the soldiers who volunteered for the experiments and, the rumors go, the men didn't survive.

The women ripped them to shreds.

Literally.

I've never seen the literature, though I've looked. I've never seen the studies, even though I've been searching for them for years.

What I do know is that ever since I got my booster when they approved me for the Elites, my emotions are stronger than they ever were before. And the darker the emotion, the more it controls me.

In the early days, I couldn't have broken up a fight, not without breaking the fighters. I somehow saw them as a threat not just to me, but to everything I held dear.

Hence all the medals and all the tours. Whenever I came home, I'd react "inappropriately" to "minor stimuli."

Then I got too old to reenlist. The best thing to do, I figured, was stay on the streets, get uninvolved in life.

There're lots of Elites just like me out there. Some who actually went home and then went berserk over a "minor infraction" like the cat from next door digging in the flower bed. Most held off the reaction (the few who didn't are serving time now) and lit out for the cities, places where they wouldn't ever feel at home.

That's why there's so many of us on the streets.

But I found the House and two more Elites who lived the same way I did, and we began to realize that there was more to living than survival, and more to survival than violence.

It took us a while, but eventually we figured the way the Elites survive in the field is simple: they have structure and discipline.

No Elite goes kamikaze on her squad because she knows that she's safe. She's given a protected hole in the ground, told she'd be called on when she was needed, and pointed in the right direction when the time came.

And that was how it worked.

Took me years to figure out why.

Command was scared of us. They had created monsters, managed to hold us on a short leash, but knew if that leash ever broke, the only ones who survived would be the small, enhanced women of childbearing years.

That leash works—not just for them. But for me.

The D girl's name is Davi. I'm not sure if it's her real name, but it's the name she gave when she arrived two days ago. Her entrance interview was mostly about her service— Sky Squad, Elite (of course), tattoos to prove it—three years on the streets, hints that her family might've thrown her out, might even be dead.

Hard to tell with Elites until they're ready to tell you. Sometimes they never do. Sometimes only the shrink gets in, and then we never hear what the real deal is.

We do group sessions, mostly encounter stuff, trying to pull the PTSD memories out of the block. We've had some luck with that. It gets rid of an Elite's hairtrigger.

We've gotten some funding to reduce hormone levels, try

to undo the biological changes, but we've had almost no success with that. That's like trying to make the body forget motherhood. It don't happen. The changes are too profound.

So in addition to the blocks and the group stuff, we do a lot of self-control work, and sometimes that's enough to reintegrate a woman back into society.

The thing about Davi is I get the sense I've seen her before.

Zoomer cleaned her up. Antibacterials on her skin and clothes, a super-hot shower, and a clean robe from my stash. Zoomer left her sleeping in my office, partly because Zoomer knew Davi's my responsibility now, partly because we don't dare let her back into her room—not until we're sure Suzanne's gonna stay calm.

Davi's still asleep, still whimpering, and I sit at my desk watching her, wondering if I should call the shrink. We actually have two: a soft-hearted, soft-handed, sensitive male straight out of shrink school, and Carla.

Carla's the best. She's former Elite, and part-owner of the House. She's one of the original three. She's the one who led our discussions, and realized that the PTSD blockers just blocked the memory, not the response. Years later, she made her career on that—some series of papers in the right venues, talks all over the Earth and in Moon Base too—and now she's working on a real cure for PTSD—not blocks, not memory removal (which doesn't work anyway—the brain rebuilds the neural links, unless too much is removed and then there's no real brain left), not drug therapy.

But she still comes here, she says, because she needs the contact for her research, but mostly because she's wired as tight as the rest of us, and only here does she remember that, and manage to hold on.

She's taken our toughest cases, and brought them back to society.

She's a goddamn miracle worker, and the House wouldn't be such a success without her.

But we have a deal. She comes in twice a week, generally

Tuesdays and Wednesdays (leaving the other five days for travel and research and teaching the occasional class), and I only call her for emergencies when they merit her special skills.

That whimpering says Carla to me.

But I know Carla. She'll yell if I don't try the other shrink first.

The other shrink's name is Robbie. He's not bad. In fact, he's good for a lot of these women, especially the younger ones who got out before the anger and violence hardened them into something not quite human. Some of them see him as a son, some as a husband, others as a nebbish father figure—all in desperate need of defense.

In those women, he brings up the good emotions: love and warmth and gentleness, the emotions that supposedly need defending, the ones that get forgotten in years of Elite work.

But for the hardcore, he's just one more victim waiting to be chewed.

I can't tell you how many times I've rushed into his office, and pulled him out just as the blood starts flying.

I don't know why he comes back. I can't ask him. I'm one of the hardcore. I see him as a victim. Every time he walks into a room, I shake my head and hope that he manages to walk out alive.

Carla explained his dynamic to me. She explained why he's so damn important to the House, and why she needs him as much as the recruits do.

She can't do the soft stuff.

I get all that. I probably would've gotten it eventually on my own. I just don't know what he gets out of it, and even though both he and Carla have tried to explain it to me, it doesn't stick.

The shrink—my shrink, who isn't on the premises, who's at the VA and has been my hand-holder since before I bought the House—says it won't stick because it means something to me, something deep, something that may be buried in one of my blocks.

Sounds like babble to me.

But I don't have to understand everything here so long as it all works and our boy Robbie, he works. So I call him in for Davi, and when he gets here, about a half an hour later, I let Zoomer brief him. Zoomer likes him.

She thinks he's cute.

When the briefing's done, Robbie comes into my office. Davi's still on the couch, still whimpering, arms wrapped around a pillow, knees drawn up, body tight. Not quite fetal, but close enough.

Robbie's short, round, and flabby. He wears glasses because eye enhancements scare him, and his skin has that pasty quality of old glue. He stares at Davi for a minute, then says to me,

"I don't think we should move her."

I sigh. "You want me to vacate?"

"Sorry," he says, but he isn't. I like to think I run the place, but the House wouldn't be the House without the shrinks. We all know that, and I worry about the day that Robbie and Carla burn out.

I step out of the office and head down the hallway. The smell of burned toast comes from the kitchen, and my stomach rumbles. Forgot to eat for the second—third?—day in a row. It's part of my pathology. Food is comfort to me, and I rarely think I deserve it. So I'm rope-thin, hyped up on vitamins and nutri-supplements, and a little too shaky for my own good.

I sit at the table. Amber, the third partner, slides a bowl of chili toward me, along with some homemade cornbread. Three other women are enjoying the meal. At the end of the table, Suzanne is eating the charred toast, staring at the plate as if it holds the secrets to the universe.

"You check in Davi?" I ask Amber.

She nods.

"She come in before?"

A lot of the time women walk in, then turn around. Sometimes they get dragged in by friends and family, and they're just not ready. Sometimes the idea of healing—even a little bit—scares the piss out of them. They don't want to keep living on the streets, but it's what they know.

"She's been in three times, maybe four," Amber says. "I talked her into staying this time."

She shoots a glance at Suzanne, and the glance is filled with anger. I resist the urge to sit between them, but the air crackles with a potential fight.

"Think she's gonna regret it?" I ask.

Amber shrugs. "That's Robbie's problem."

Suzanne breaks the toast, sets the crust on her plate, then shoves the plate away. There's black crumbs around her mouth.

"I didn't mean to scare the bitch," Suzanne says. "She hit me first."

"So you say." I can't quite keep the sarcasm out of my voice. Suzanne likes picking fights. She even likes staging them. But she is making progress and I'm not quite willing to send her away.

"Look," Suzanne says, "I'm sorry about the ration card. I was just trying to teach her a lesson."

"About what?" Amber asks, sounding curious. I know she spoke up before I did. Amber's better at the subtle stuff, which is why she gets the door. She can wheedle and charm and manipulate. Me, I go right through people, and usually don't care.

"About sharing," Suzanne says. "This House is about sharing, right?"

"You hit her in home," I say, even though it's a guess.

Suzanne flushes. Hitting someone in home means that you whacked the protect button, found their weak point, and made them go all berserker on you.

"Didn't mean to," she says, but her words tell me she knows it.

"You got the bathrooms cleaned?" I ask.

She nods.

"Next time Carla's in, you talk to her," I say.

Suzanne nods again. Then she picks up her plate and disappears into the kitchen.

"That's her fifth infraction," Amber says. "You usually toss them out on three."

"I know," I say.

"You're thinking potential again, aren't you?" Amber asks.

We all got weaknesses. Potential is mine. Sometimes I can see what these women would be if we can just control their demons, if we can tame them just enough to return to society.

The problem is the smart ones are the toughest to mold. Their minds have already rebelled, and won't take much more. They're usually my lost causes.

"I didn't say potential." I sound petulant and I know it.

Amber grins. "But you're thinking it."

I nod. The other women eat in silence, their spoons clanking on the bowls. The peppery scent of the chili makes my stomach rumble, but I don't reach for the food.

That too is part of my bizarre discipline. We can learn to function again, but we never really become whole.

"One more infraction, we'll have to have a House vote," Amber says.

I grab the corn bread, rip it up like Suzanne ripped up her toast. House votes always end badly. The recruits don't get along. They're team players in combat, but outside of it, they've become such rugged individualists that they don't get along with anyone.

The votes always reflect that. My candidates always lose.

Zoomer creeps into the dining room.

"Wena," she says, "Robbie needs you."

He's not, like I expect, in my office with Davi. He's in his office, a little box of a room—probably a coat closet in the House's first incarnation—and he's behind his desk.

This is serious, then.

"We need to send for Carla," he says as soon as I close the door.

"Davi's that damaged?" I ask.

He shakes his head. "I don't think she's military."

I let out a small breath of disbelief. "She's got the tattoos, the quirks. She's tried to enter three times, failed, and had to be coaxed inside."

"This isn't PTSD," Robbie says. "I'd stake my career on it. And that girl's not violent. I'd stake my career on that too."

I don't understand. "Then what's she doing here? A wannabe?"

I'd heard of them: women who pretended to be macho, pretended to have had service just to get the benefits—benefits none of the rest of us willingly claim. Or some just do it for the glory, using the various media outlets to tell their made-up stories. Sometimes doing it to get a lover—usually male—who's attracted to a woman with a violent, but sanctioned, past.

"I don't think she's a wannabe," he says.

"What then?" I ask.

He shakes his head ever so slightly. "I'd rather have Carla answer that."

"I'm not calling her," I say. "She's really clear about her hours, and I'm not hearing anything that convinces me she's needed."

"This Davi," he says, "I did the usual blood tests, ran them through my handheld, twice as a matter of fact."

He slides the handheld toward me. I see numbers, a few graphs, nothing I can read.

"I didn't know you took blood," I say to cover my ignorance. I shove the handheld back at him.

"We always have to rule out the organic cause first," he says. "Blood, temperature, a few other things. A lot of things cause violent and/or irrational behavior, from a high fever to certain kinds of drugs."

"And what's she got?"

"Nothing," he says, frowning at me.

"I don't get it," I say.

"She's *clean*," he says.

I stare at him.

"She's a Sky Vet," he says. "If nothing else, she should have antibodies to just about every known disease. She doesn't. I think she's gonna get sick from that—plunger, was it?"

"Scrubber," I say, trying to assess what he's telling me. "You're saying she wasn't on the front lines?"

"I'm saying she hasn't been off-planet. She's not inoculated for anything remotely Moon-based."

"So she's a wannabe," I say.

"With official tattoos? A great cover?" He shakes his head.

I'm cold. "What do you think she is?"

"I think Carla should decide."

I can feel it, building, that insane desire to rip out his spleen just to get him to talk faster. I clench my fists.

"Sometimes Carla isn't the most rational person," I say.

He nods, and something in his gaze tells me he understands that I'm getting angry.

"I think she's government," he says. "I found this on her as well."

He throws a bag at me. It's filled with more bags. Each one holds small items—a toothbrush, strands of hair, a scab. DNA.

"Son of a *bitch*," I say, and fight the urge to stick my fist through the wall. "What the hell are they doing?"

"Trying to identify everyone," he says. "They requested it with the last grant."

"And we fought them," I say. "We *won*."

"Still," he says. "They're not letting Sky Vets back to Earth anymore. They're talking about rounding up street people. Haven't you been listening?"

I don't pay attention to the media. It betrayed me years ago. It got me all fired up about that first war, and it turns out that the battles I thought I was fighting weren't the ones I really fought.

"So?" I say.

"So the anonymity is what's bothering them," he says. "They want to know where all the Vets are, particularly the Elites. I thought you knew this."

"I worry about the House," I mumble. And that's partly true. The other part is that I can't deal with the government. It makes me crazy.

Still.

"You were right," I say. "Call Carla. It's time for a meeting of the principals."

"I thought you were going to—"

"Just do it!" I snap, and let myself out of the room.

I play by the rules because I ask my people to play by the rules. *If you want to return to society,* I tell them, *you have to understand that the rules exist for a reason: they exist so that we can all get along, live together in close quarters, and not kill each other.*

I actually believe that.

The rules here at the House are simple:

Names aren't necessary.

Details aren't necessary.

A willingness to work is essential.

A willingness to follow the daily rules of living—clean yourself, your room, your assigned area—also essential.

Heal at your own pace.

Learn nonviolent ways to resolve disputes.

No weapons allowed.

The rules here have no particular order because they're all important. And in some ways, none of them are important. Because the House changes depending on its makeup. Sometimes we let recruits get violent. Sometimes we let them slack off work. Sometimes we let them go weeks without bathing.

But we never ever ask names. It's safer to talk to people

who think they know you rather than people who have read an official history and assume they do.

The next thing I know, I'm back in my office, Davi's off the couch, and shoved against the wall, my hand against her throat. She's flailing, and there's fear in her eyes.

She's trembling.

I'm not.

"Boss," someone says behind me. "Put her down."

I squeeze a little tighter. Bitch has messed with my House. Bitch has invaded my territory, threatened my people, trespassed in my world.

"Boss." The voice sounds a little panicked.

Maybe it reflects Davi's eyes. They're bugging out. Her skin's turning purple.

"Wena!" Zoomer has her hands on my shoulders. She's trying to pull me away.

"Rowena, stop." And that voice, official and barking, belongs to Carla.

But dammit all, I respond to official. I respond to barking. It goes deep into the training, activates the controls, and I open my hand.

The bitch drops like a dirty blanket.

Zoomer's got her, takes her away from me, does something for the neck. Robbie helps, his soft hands trying to soothe that imposter as if she's someone important.

Carla takes me back into my bunker. Amber follows.

The principals.

Carla makes me put my head down, take deep breaths, calm, calm, calm. I've seen her use this technique before on someone who's lost it, on someone who's one step away from leaving, on someone who might not be rehabbed.

"She's a fucking invader," I finally say.

"She's probably not the first," Carla says.

"Son of a bitch." This time, my hand does connect with the wall. But I reinforced those fuckers myself. My hand bangs back toward me, bruised; the wall isn't damaged at all.

"We expected it, remember?" Amber says. "You even mentioned it."

"We said we'd keep privacy. They didn't get to know which one of us heals and which one doesn't. If it's the worst of us, then they'll use it as an excuse. They'll keep doing this, they'll keep creating Elites, and—"

"And maybe they'll have a program to get us back into society." Carla's voice is soft. "That's all they want, Wena. They want something that works. They think you have the secret and aren't willing to share."

She and Amber are staring at me.

"We've been in existence ten years," Amber says. "Do you know how many people have reintegrated? How many women we've helped return to their lives?"

"No." I clutch my throbbing hand with my other one. "We're not supposed to know, remember. Government keeps statistics. Facts, figures, we're not about that. We're about healing."

"So why not let people know the system? We can patent it or whatever so that they have to follow our rules. Let them know, so others can be helped." Amber says this as if she's just thought of it.

But I know Carla's set her up to say it. Amber used to support me. Carla's been the advocate for letting the House's systems out. Carla thinks we can save the world.

"No," I say, and turn my back to them.

They sit in silence for a long time. We're good at silence. Finally, Carla says, "This girl, she hit you in home."

I let out a small breath. "I don't have a home any more."

"We all do," Carla says. "I just thought yours was House. And I thought you had remarkable control. Every time a recruit infracts, I thought how impressive it was that you didn't kamikaze all over her. But you just did. Home to you isn't the House. It's the method. You think we're the only ones who can do this. Maybe you're the only one. Don't you?"

I reach for her before I even have a chance to think.

Amber restrains me. She's strong. Not as strong as I am, but I'm not entirely gone. I let her hold me back.

I'm shaking this time.

"I should've seen it," Carla says, more to herself than to me. "I should've realized it was the method, not the building."

"Have you ever thought that I'm right?" My voice sounds harsher than I want it to.

"About what?" Carla asks. She's using her shrink voice. I hate that voice, all reasonable and calm and mommylike.

"About the method. What if we are the only ones?"

"Then other experiments'll prove it," she says. "I think it is a mixture of personalities that makes this work. But I have to remind you, Wena. Our culture's good at personalities now. That's how they found us in the first place. Maybe we should give in. Maybe they'll use this for good."

I shake myself free of Amber. She cringes.

So does Carla.

But I'm calm again. I have finally understood what I'm protecting.

"Yeah, they're good at personalities," I say. "And for a while, government facilities'll use our methods. Then they'll find other uses. Our good work'll get twisted. We'll have created new kinds of monsters."

"We won't," Amber says.

"We need to keep something pure," I say. "Just one thing. We have to hold one thing sacred. If we don't . . ."

They're staring at me, but I can't finish. The words—those words—I said them just before I led my troop—my real troop—into the worst fight of our lives. The purity I was referring to then was our friendship, which I had thought to protect, because the training was that deep—I had to pick something, something to protect, something that elicited that deep, violent response . . .

"Shit," I whisper, and put down my head.

They're right. Carla and Amber are right. I've been hit at home, and I'm not rational.

But it feels like I am.

And that's the scary part.

We can agree on a few things: We're going to press charges against Davi and whoever's behind her. We're going to keep identities in the House private. And we're going to find someone to replace me, for a week, six months, a year.

As long as Carla can convince me to stay away.

She thinks it's not healthy for me to remain. The House has helped others, she says, but then I insist that they leave. They grow outside, and become real people.

I never have.

I'm not sure she's right, but the only way to prove her wrong is to step out into the world. And not for short ceremonies or speeches at VA Hospitals.

For some significant time. On my own.

The idea scares me and exhilarates me at the same time. And my shrink—my original shrink who approves of Carla's ideas—says those emotions are normal.

But I don't like normal. And I think Carla's wrong about a few things. I'm not protecting the method. I'm believing in our uniqueness.

I don't think anyone else can create the right environment. I don't think anyone else would know when to break the rules and when to enforce them.

I don't think anyone else can nurture like we do.

Only I don't admit that to Carla. She'd say I've got a mother complex that is part of the Elites distinctive psychology. She'd say I have to get it repaired.

I'm openminded enough to think that she might be right. But I'm wary enough to know that if she's wrong, we lose everything.

The House, our home, our community. The women we've been helping and the ones we haven't helped yet.

Fifteen years of success, based in part on my own particular pathology.

And I keep thinking the House has gone beyond potential. I'm not fighting for what might be.

I'm fighting for what is.

It's our last stand—and I seem to be the only one who knows it.

Tanya Huff

The Confederation Novels

"As a heroine, Kerr shines. She is cut from the same mold as Ellen Ripley of the *Aliens* films. Like her heroine, Huff delivers the goods." *--SF Weekly*

VALOR'S CHOICE
0-88677-896-4
When a diplomatic mission becomes a battle for survival, the price of failure will be far worse than death...

THE BETTER PART OF VALOR
0-7564-0062-7
Could Torin Kerr keep disaster from striking while escorting a scientific expedition to an enormous spacecraft of unknown origin?

To Order Call: 1-800-788-6262

Tanya Huff

The Finest in Fantasy

To Order Call: 1-800-788-6262

Tanya Huff

Smoke and Shadows

First in a New Series

Tony Foster—familiar to Tanya Huff fans from her *Blood* series—has relocated to Vancouver with Henry Fitzroy, vampire son of Henry VIII. Tony landed a job as a production assistant at CB Productions, iron-ically working on a syndicated TV series, "Darkest Night," about a vampire detective. Except for his crush on Lee, the show's handsome costar, Tony was pretty content...at least until everything started to fall apart on the set. It began with shadows—shadows that seemed to be where they didn't belong, shadows that had an existence of their own. And when he found a body, and a shadow cast its claim on Lee, Tony knew he had to find out what was going on, and that he needed Henry's help.

0-7564-0183-6

To Order Call: 1-800-788-6262

DAW 46